Emanuel Del Mar

A Complete Theoretical and Practical Grammar of the Spanish language

Emanuel Del Mar

A Complete Theoretical and Practical Grammar of the Spanish language

ISBN/EAN: 9783337400682

Printed in Europe, USA, Canada, Australia, Japan

Cover: Foto ©Andreas Hilbeck / pixelio.de

More available books at **www.hansebooks.com**

A COMPLETE

THEORETICAL AND PRACTICAL

GRAMMAR

OF THE

SPANISH LANGUAGE.

BY

EMANUEL DEL MAR.

———

Twelfth Edition.

———

LONDON:

DAVID NUTT, 270, STRAND.

1886.

PREFACE.

THE very favourable reception given to the former Editions of this GRAMMAR of the SPANISH LANGUAGE has induced the Publisher to offer to the Public this NINTH and ENLARGED EDITION. The whole arrangement of the work is the result of the unremitting labour of thirty years of the Author, and of his long experience in teaching the Spanish Language; and the best proof of the preference given to this Grammar is the fact that eight editions of it have been sold almost entirely unaided by advertisements.

In every division of this work it has been the Author's aim to endeavour, as far as practicable, to overcome every obstacle that the Spanish Language presented to the student, and to make every difficulty subordinate to rule; thus rendering the acquisition of this rich, expressive, and manly Language a pleasing task to those desirous of acquiring it. The principles of the Spanish Language will be found in this Grammar clearly expounded in a SERIES OF LECTURES, and each Rule and Observation accompanied by appropriate Examples; the greater part of those intended to elucidate the peculiar construction and genius of the Spanish Language have been selected from the works of the best Castilian writers. The Lectures are followed by suitable Exercises for the pupil to practise the Rules upon ; a KEY to which, for the convenience of those who have not the assistance of a master, may be had separately.

The latest decisions of the ROYAL ACADEMY of MADRID, especially with respect to the NEW ORTHOGRAPHY, have been adopted in this Grammar, carefully pointing out wherein the new differs from the old, in order that the learner, in reading Spanish works not printed with the new orthography, may know in what the difference consists.

In describing, by comparison with English characters, the peculiar sound and power of the letters of the Spanish Alphabet, the Author has bestowed the utmost care in giving such combinations as could best convey the nicest and most correct idea of them ; and experience has proved that he has not been unsuccessful.

The Rules given in this Grammar are not intended to be learnt *by heart ;* it is the *sense* of them that the pupil should endeavour to make himself perfectly acquainted with. The Lectures, therefore, address themselves to the understanding rather than to the memory of the learner.

When the pupil has made himself acquainted with the Elements of the Spanish Language, and should desire to attain a more intimate knowledge of its origin, extent, power, and elegance, he is recommended to consult the works of CAPMANY, ALDRETE, NEBRIJA, HUERTA, and others. As works from which to glean the beauties of Spanish Literature, he has a wide field to select from; he may, however, peruse the following Authors with advantage :—

In History, SOLÍS, MARIANA, CAPMANY, MENDOZA, LLORENTE, etc.—In Novels and other works of Fiction, CERVÁNTES, ISLA, MATEO ALEMAN, GUEVARA, QUEVEDO, ZOLÓRZANO, etc.—In Sacred, Moral, and Ecclesiastical Writings, GRANADA, LEON, CLEMENT, NIEREMBERG, CARVAJAL, etc.—In Drama, CALDERON, LOPE DE VEGA, CERVÁNTES, JOVELLANOS, CIENFUEGOS, MONTALBAN, QUINTANA, MORATIN, ZÁRATE, etc.—In Epistles, Works of Criticism, and Miscellanies, CADALSO, IRIARTE, GRACIAN, CAMPOMANES, SAAVEDRA FAJARDO, SAMA-NIEGO, etc.

In Poetry, the field is still more extensive; a list of the bare names of Spanish Poets of merit would fill a moderate sized book, The student may, however, select from the following :—CALDERON, CERVÁNTES, LOPE DE VEGA, JAUREGUÍ, ARGÉNSOLA, QUEVEDO, GARCILASO DE LA VEGA, HERRERA, ERCILLA, LUZAN, IGLESIAS, MELÉNDEZ, MENDOZA, LEON, etc.

The acquisition of the Spanish language is daily becoming of greater importance; in addition to its now being acknowledged a very essential branch of a mercantile education, it is become almost indispensable to the tourist, and its interest in a literary point of view is rapidly increasing, in proportion as the works of the more celebrated Spanish writers become more extensively known to the English public, and more justly appreciated.

CONTENTS.

APPENDIX.

SPANISH AUTHORS QUOTED IN THIS GRAMMAR, AND THE EPOCHS IN WHICH THEY WROTE.

<table>
<tr><td></td><td>CENTURY</td></tr>
<tr><td>ALEMAN, Mateo</td><td>16</td></tr>
<tr><td>CADALSO, El Coronel J. V.</td><td>18</td></tr>
<tr><td>CALDERON DE LA BARCA, Pedro</td><td>17</td></tr>
<tr><td>CAPMANY, Antonio de</td><td>18</td></tr>
<tr><td>CERVÁNTES SAAVEDRA, Miguel de</td><td>16</td></tr>
<tr><td>FEIJOO, P. Benito Gerónimo</td><td>17</td></tr>
<tr><td>FORNER</td><td>16</td></tr>
<tr><td>GRANADA, Fr. Luis de</td><td>16</td></tr>
<tr><td>GRAMÁTICA DE LA REAL ACADEMIA DE MADRID</td><td>19</td></tr>
<tr><td>GUEVARA, Fr. Ant. de</td><td>16</td></tr>
<tr><td>HITA, G. Perez de</td><td>16</td></tr>
<tr><td>IRIARTE, Tomas de</td><td>18</td></tr>
<tr><td>JOVELLANOS, Gaspar de</td><td>19</td></tr>
<tr><td>LEON, Fr. Luis de</td><td>16</td></tr>
<tr><td>MARIANA, P. Juan</td><td>16</td></tr>
<tr><td>MARINA, F. M.</td><td>19</td></tr>
<tr><td>MARQUES, Fr. J.</td><td>16</td></tr>
<tr><td>MEGÍA, Pedro</td><td>16</td></tr>
<tr><td>MORATIN, Leandro Fernández de</td><td>19</td></tr>
<tr><td>NIEREMBERG, Pedro J. E.</td><td>17</td></tr>
<tr><td>PALACIOS RUBIOS, Juan López de</td><td>15</td></tr>
<tr><td>QUEVEDO VILLEGAS, Francisco de</td><td>17</td></tr>
<tr><td>QUINTANA, Manuel José</td><td>19</td></tr>
<tr><td>SAAVEDRA FAJARDO, Diego de</td><td>16</td></tr>
<tr><td>SALAZAR, Cervántes de</td><td>16</td></tr>
<tr><td>SOLÍS, Antonio de</td><td>17</td></tr>
<tr><td>TORENO, El Conde de</td><td>19</td></tr>
<tr><td>VEGA CARPIO, Lope Felix de</td><td>16</td></tr>
<tr><td>VERGEL Y PONCE</td><td>19</td></tr>
<tr><td>VILLANUEVA, M. G. de</td><td>19</td></tr>
<tr><td>VILLEGAS, E. Manuel</td><td>17</td></tr>
</table>

A COMPLETE

THEORETICAL AND PRACTICAL GRAMMAR

OF THE

SPANISH LANGUAGE.

LECTURE I.

OF GRAMMAR IN GENERAL.

PARAGRAPH 1. Grammar is the science that teaches the just manner of expressing our ideas, in speaking or writing. It is that collection of rules drawn from the established usages of a people speaking a language with propriety and precision. This definition explains the nature of Grammar as applied to all languages in *general: particular* Grammar teaches the principles peculiar to any particular language, as the SPANISH LANGUAGE ; to obtain a correct knowledge of which we must conform to the rules established by the ROYAL ACADEMY OF MADRID, and to the usages adopted by the best Castilian writers and speakers.

Grammar is divided into four branches—namely, *Orthography, Prosody, Etymology*, and *Syntax.*

2. ORTHOGRAPHY treats of the nature and use of letters, and their various combinations as employed in the formation of syllables and words.

3. PROSODY, as a branch of Grammar, teaches the true sound and just pronunciation of letters, syllables, and words, and marks the syllable on which the accent, or stress of voice, falls. Prosody treats also of the laws of versification.

B

4. ETYMOLOGY (or Analogy) treats of the origin of words; their distribution into different classes; the relation which they bear to each other; their derivation, and the various changes which they undergo in the formation of sentences.

5. SYNTAX teaches the proper arrangement of words, that our sentences may be correct, clear, free from ambiguity or obscurity, and incapable of misconstruction.

ORTHOGRAPHY AND PROSODY.

6. The Spanish Alphabet consists of twenty-eight letters, of which *a, e, i, o, u* are vowels, and the rest are consonants; *y*, however, is generally considered a vowel when it follows another vowel, or stands by itself; and a consonant when it precedes a vowel. Every Spanish vowel has a complete and fixed sound (as pointed out in the following alphabet), which *never changes* on account of its situation in a syllable. Consonants have no distinct sounds by themselves, but in combination with vowels they form syllables and words. Each of the vowels may constitute a syllable by itself.

THE ALPHABET.

7. In the comparative sounds given in English in the following alphabet, the vowels, whether coming before or after a consonant, are to be sounded thus: *a*, like *a* in *ark*; *e*, like *e* in *ell*; *i*, like *i* in *ill*; *o*, like *o* in *ode*; *u*, like *u* in *full*.

The accent points out the syllable on which the stress of voice is to be laid.

Pronounced as		*Pronounced as*	
A	*a* in *ark*.	H	*á-tche*.
B	*be* in *bell*.	I	*i* in *ill*.
C	*the* in *theft*.	J	*hó-ta*, with a strong
CH	*che* in *chess*.		aspiration of the *h*,
D	*the* in *then*.		or a *guttural sound*.
E	*e* in *ell*.	K	*ca* in *car*.
F	*éf-e*.	L	*él-e*.
G	*he* in *hen*, with a strong	LL	*él-ye*.
	aspiration of the *h*;	M	*ém-e*.
	or, rather a *guttural*	N	*én-e*.
	sound.	Ñ	*én-ye*.

	Pronounced as		*Pronounced as*
O	*o* in *ode.*	U	*u* in full.
P	*pe* in *pen.*	V	*ve* in *vent.*
Q	*coo* in *cook.*	X	*ék-is.*
R	*ér-re.*	Y	*i grié-ga.*
S	*es-se.*	Z	*thé-ta.*
T	*te* in *ten.*		

SOUND AND POWER OF LETTERS, ACCORDING TO THE ORTHOGRAPHICAL ALTERATIONS RECENTLY MADE BY THE ROYAL ACADEMY OF MADRID.

₊ An accent is placed on the *acute* syllable of every Spanish word in the Examples, until the pupil arrives at LECTURE II., where the general rule for accentuation will be given.

A—as noticed in the alphabet, sounds like *a* in *ark:* Example, *cárta, alabár, canásta.*

B—There is a very slight distinction in Spanish between the sound of this letter and that of the *v*, from the circumstance of both being pronounced much softer than in English, though in both languages the lips are pressed together in pronouncing the *b*, and the lower lip touches the upper teeth in uttering the *v;* but the pressure employed in each letter is much less in Spanish than in English : Ex. *báta, bébe, bíen, bóca, búlto, abdicár, obtenér, váso, víveres, vóto, vúlgo.* The *b*, in Spanish, may be placed immediately before *l* and *r*, which can never take place with the *v:* Ex. *blánco, brotár.* The *b* may also terminate syllables and words; but the *v* never can : Ex. *ab-sórto, ob-tenér, Job.* The syllables *am, em, im, om, um*, require *b* after them ; and *an, en, in, on, un*, require *v ;* Ex. *ámbito, embúdo:—envídia, invocár.* Some writers omit the *b* before *s* in certain words, and others retain it; thus, *oscúro*, or *obscúro; sustáncia*, or *substáncia*, etc.

C—before *e* and *i* is pronounced like *th* in *theft, thin :* Ex. *céna, cifra;* and like *k* when it precedes *a, o, u,* or a consonant : Ex. *cáma, cóla, cúbo, cláro, crítico.* It has likewise the sound of *k* when it comes after a vowel in the same syllable : Ex. *accedér, técnico.* See Z.

CH—This double consonant now sounds like *ch* in *chese*, as noticed in the alphabet: Ex. *chalán, léche, chíco, hécho, chúpa*. Formerly, in words of Hebrew and Greek origin, it had the sound of *k*, when the vowel following it was marked with the circumflex accent : Ex. *archángel, chímica;* but this practice is obsolete, and such words are now written *arcángel, química*.

D—is very differently pronounced in Spanish from what it is in English ; and for want of a proper definition of its sound in Anglo-Spanish Grammars, few learn to pronounce it properly by them, and yet its sound is more easily conveyed to the English ear by writing than to any other, from the peculiar power of the English *th*. The difference of sound between the Spanish and the English *d* arises from the distinct manner in which the two nations employ the organs of speech in pronouncing it. For instance, it is uttered in English by striking the tongue against the upper gums; whereas Spaniards, in pronouncing the *d*, slightly touch the teeth with the tongue, as the English do in pronouncing the *th* in the words *they, though ;* but observe carefully that its sound issues from the *chest*, and is therefore never like *th* in *thin* or *bath*. This different manner of pronouncing the *d* in Spanish is striking only when it immediately follows a vowel, whether that vowel be in the same syllable or word as itself, or in the one immediately preceding it : Ex. *tódo, amádo, adjúnto, cuádra, la dáma, una dósis*. But it is pronounced more like the English *d* at the beginning of a sentence, or when found immediately preceded by a consonant (whether that consonant be in the same word as itself or not), except *d*, or *z*, on account of the lisping qualities of these two letters : Ex. *Dichos del múndo, cuérda, cálandra, los dádos, un alférez de la ciudád de Córdoba*. At the end of a word, however, it is almost mute, but preserves a little of the lisp : Ex. *bondád, ardid ;* though it is heard more distinctly in the imperative mood : Ex. *Id á cása—Venid conmigo*. Observe, also, the following examples : *Don Alejándro pasó por Madrid con dos criádos de Don Pédro. Déme ustéd médio dúro. Me diéron dos docénas y dos*.

E—This vowel, as before remarked, sounds like the English *e* in *ell:* Ex. *expelér, meréce, presénte.*

F—sounds as in English: Ex. *fáma, fóro, africáno, fláco.*

G—before *a, o, u,* or a consonant, and after a vowel, sounds as the English *g* similarly placed: Ex. *gála, góma, gústo, gráno, glándula, ignorár, agnádo.* It has the same sound before the diphthongs *ue, ui,* in which the *u* is silent: Ex. *guérra, guisár.* But should the *u* be marked with the diæresis, the *u* must be sounded: Ex. *agüéro, argüír.* It has a *guttural* sound before *e* and *i,* nearly resembling the aspiration of the English *h:* Ex. *giro, génte.* It is silent when seen before *n,* in words derived from the Greek: Ex. *gnómon, gnómico;* but the *g* in such words is now dropped; as *nómon, nómico.*

H—is now considered a silent letter by the Spanish ACADEMY, and is therefore not aspirated, except when it precedes the diphthong *ue;* but even then the aspiration is very slight: Ex. *huéso, huévo.*

I—invariably sounds like the English *i* in *ill:* Ex. *irrisíble, invadír, círco.*

J—has always a guttural sound, like that of the guttural *g* before described: Ex. *jabón, jergón, pajíta, jóven, júnta, carcáj, relój.*

K—This letter is only retained in a few foreign proper names, and sounds as in English.

L—sounds as in Engilsh: Ex. *lavár, mal, lírio, blánco.*

LL—has a liquid sound, like the *gl* in *seraglio:* Ex. *lláve, llegár, bullír, cabállo, llúvia.*

M—sounds as in English: Ex. *áma, móda, complométo, alúmno.*

N—sounds as in English: Ex. *náda, nido, nudo, pan, montón.*

Ñ—This letter, with a waving line over it, called the *tilde,* has a liquid sound, like the English *n* followed by *y;* or the *gn* in the French word *seigneur,* or in the Italian word *bagno:* Ex. *niña, tañér, compañía, señór, niño.*

O—sounds as the English *o* in *ode:* Ex. *oponér, tómo, sóplo.*

P—sounds as in English: Ex. *pálo, ápto, plan, própio.* Its employment before *h,* which combination formed in Spanish, as it still does in English, the sound of *f*, is obsolete, the *f* being now used instead : Ex. *philosophía, phalánge,*—now written *filosofía, falánge.* It is no longer used before *s* in such words as *psálmc, pséudo,* which are now written *sálmo, séudo.*

Q—before *ue* and *ui* sounds like *k :* Ex. *quéso, quitár.* Before *üe, üi,* and *ua, uo,* it is used to sound like the English *q ;* but this manner of spelling is laid aside, and such words as were written *qüestión, qüidár, quánto, quóta,* are now spelled *cuestión, cuidár, cuánto, cuóta ;* so that the *q* is, by modern writers, only retained before *ue, ui,* without the diæresis.

R—has sometimes a rough and sometimes a smooth sound. It has the rough sound at the beginning of a word : Ex. *rábia, róbo ;*—when the syllable that precedes it ends in a consonant : Ex. *hón-ra, mal-róto, ab-rogár, Israél :*—also when it is doubled : Ex. *cárro, barríl.* On all other occasions it has the smooth sound : Ex. *abrír, cárta, arádo, pérla, párdo.* Observe, however, that even the smooth sound of the Spanish *r* is more distinctly heard than that of the English *r* generally.

S—always sounds like *s* in the English words *sing, us ;* but never like *s* in *muse :* Ex. *sal, espáldas, sítio, póso, subír, gástos.* It is no longer used doubled in Spanish.

T—sounds as in English : Ex. *tása, tréinta, atlántico, tómo, túmba.*

U— sounds like *u* in *full :* Ex. *usúra, tríbu, lúgubre, urbáno.*

V—see the letter B.

X—This letter was formerly employed to express two sounds, the one like that of *ks,* the other a guttural sound, like that of the Spanish *j.* This latter sound is now abolished in the *x,* which, since the late decision of the Royal Academy, is *only* employed to express that of *ks :* Ex. *axióma, éxito, fénix, extrémo, óxido.* Thus, all those words which were formerly written with *x* to indicate the guttural sound, (which was when it followed a vowel, or preceded one without the circumflex accent,) are now written with *j* before *a, o, u,* or after a vowel, and with *g* or *j* before *e* and *i :* Ex. *jabón, géfe, jícara, cajón, jubón, carcáj, relój*—formerly written *xabón, xéfe, xícara, caxón, rubón, carcáx, relóx.* And when formerly the *x* immediately preceding a vowel had the sound of *ks*, the vowel used to be marked with the circumflex, as in *axîóma, éxîto;* but the circumflex is now no longer used, as we have seen above. The *x* when immediately followed by a consonant had likewise formerly, and still retains, the sound of *ks:* Ex. *exponér, míxto.* Some modern writers, until the above decision of the ACADEMY, exploded the *x* altogether, and used to write such words as *expérto, extrémo,* with *s,* thus, *espérto, estrémo;* but the ACADEMY has properly disapproved of the substitution : first, because it destroyed the etymology of words without any visible utility; and, secondly, because words of different meaning are confounded by it; as in *expiár,* to expiate, and *espiár,* to spy. Others, in substituting *cs* for *x* before a vowel, as in *acsióma, ecsámen,* instead of *axióma, exámen,* have introduced a still more vicious innovation, since not only are the words disfigured from their original orthography by it, but that two letters are required to represent the sound of one imperfectly.

Y—as a vowel, sounds like the Spanish *i:* Ex. *hay, ley, voy;* as a consonant it sounds rather stronger than the English *y* in *yes:* Ex. *yélo, yo, ya.*

Z—sounds like *th* in the English words *thank, bath;* but never like *th* in *that, bathe;* Ex. *zága, zórra, felíz, voz.* Where this letter was formerly used before *e* and *i,* a *c* is now generally preferred : Ex. *cenzálo, cítara;* formerly written *zenzálo, zítara.*

Ca, co, cu	In these the *c* sounds like *k:*
ce, ci	And here like *th,* in *theme.*
ac, ec, ic, oc, uc .	*C* after any vowel sounds like *k.*
da, de, di, do, du . }	*D* sounds like *th* in *they, bathe;* but
ad, ed, id, od, ud . }	never like *th* in *theory, bath.*

ga, gue, gui, go, gu. In these the *g* sounds like the Eng-
                       lish hard *g*, and the *u* is mute
                       before *e* and *i*.

gua, güe, güi, guo.   Here the *g* is hard also, but the *u*
                       is sounded.

ge, gi . . . . .   In these the *g* has the *guttural*
                       sound.

ag, eg, ig, og, ug .   *G* after a vowel sounds like the
                       English hard *g*.

ja, je, ji, jo, ju. .⎫ *J* before and after a vowel has
aj, oj . . . . . .⎭ always the *guttural* sound.

lla, lle, lli, llo, llu. These sound as *liá, lié,* etc. :

ña, ñe, ñi, ño, ñu .   And these as *niá, nié,* etc.

qua, qüe, qüi, quo.   Here the *u* is sounded :

que, qui . . . .   And here the *u* is mute.

ax, ex, ix, ox, ux .   The *x* is now only used at the end
                       of a syllable, and has the sound
                       of *ks.*

za, ze, zi, zo, zu .⎧ *Z* before and after a vowel has
                     ⎪ always the sound of *th* in *thin,*
az, ez, iz, oz, uz .⎨ *bath;* but never that of *th* in
                     ⎩ *they, bathe.*

OF INITIAL AND FINAL LETTERS.

8. Every consonant may begin a Spanish word or syllable ; but the only consonants that can terminate a word are *b, d, j, l, m, n, r, s, t, x, z;* and all, except *ch, h, ll, ñ, q, v,* may end a syllable. Either of the vowels may begin and end a word or syllable.

OF DOUBLE LETTERS.

9. Strictly speaking there are no double letters in Spanish, for even the *ll* is not considered a double letter. Two letters of the same denomination may frequently be seen together in the same word, but then each belongs to a different syllable, and therefore cannot be considered as a double letter. The only letters that may be so repeated in Spanish are the vowels *a, e, i, o,* and the consonants *c, n, r,* and when so employed each must be distinctly heard : Ex. *Sa-a-vé-dra, le-ér, pi-í-si-mo, lo-ór, ac-cé-so, en-no-ble-cér, cár-ro.*

OF THE DIVISION OF SYLLABLES.

10. A consonant between two vowels forms a syllable with the second vowel. When two consonants come between two vowels, each belongs to its nearest vowel, unless the second consonant be *l*, or *r*, in which case they both form syllable with the second vowel: Ex. *re-la-tí-vo, ar-ró-jo, ha-blár, a-pre-tár*. The *ll* always goes to the following consonant: Ex. *ca-llár, bu-llír*. From this rule are excepted all compound words, which are divided by separating the syllable added to the simple word; thus, *des-atendér, sub-altérno*; and all those having an *s* befor *l*, or *r*; thus, *is-léño, Is-raél*. When three consonants come between two vowels, the first two go to the first vowel, and the third to the second: Ex. *cóns-ta, obs-tár*. And when four consonants come together, they are divided two and two: Ex. *cons-truír, abs-traér*.

OF DIPHTHONGS AND TRIPHTHONGS.

11. A *diphthong* is the union of *two vowels*, and a *triphthong* of *three vowels* in a syllable. In English in a combination of two, or even three vowels, it frequently occurs that the sound of one only, or a sound different from that of either of the vowels in the combination, is heard; observe, however, that in pronouncing the Spanish diphthongs and triphthongs, care must be taken to give to each vowel the sound which it has in the alphabet. The following is a list of all the Spanish diphthongs and triphthongs, and to guide the student, an accent is placed on the vowel which should have the greatest stress of voice.

ái,	Ex.	tomáis.	*ió,*	Ex.	biómbo.
áu,		jáula.	*íu,*		cíudad.
áy,		háy.	*oé,*		heroé.
eá,		etereá.	*ói,*		sóis.
éi,		pléito.	*óy,*		sóy.
éo.		idonéo.	*uá,*		suáve.
éu,		déuda.	*ué,*		huésped.
éy		léy.	*uí,*		fuí.
iá,		aciágo.	*úy,*		múy.
ié,		ciélo.	*uó,*		cuóta.

idi, Ex. camb*idis.*
iéi, renunci*éis.*
uái, averig*uáis.*
uéi, evac*uéis.*
uéy, b*uéy.*

12. Observe that in diphthongs and triphthongs the accent **always** falls on the vowel which is first in the order of the alphabet, except in the combinations of *io,* and *oi,* in which it falls on the *o.*

LECTURE II.

OF THE ACCENT.

1. The *acute* accent, thus ('), is employed in Spanish with words in which the stress of the voice, as regards the syllable on which it should fall, deviates from the general rule.

Every Spanish word has one syllable in it *acute*; and, as a *general* rule, let it be observed that words ending in a *consonant* have the *last* syllable acute, and those ending in a *vowel,* the *last but one*; but, as there are exceptions in this rule, every word deviating from it is always marked with the acute accent over the syllable requiring the stress. Verbs, however, have a peculiar accentuation of their own, which will be treated on separately.—See LECT. 24, PAR. 10.

EXAMPLES.—*Leccion, macis, sagaz, altar, pedestal, corazon, redentor, encomendar, felicidad, moralidad, indemnificacion, desacobardar.*

Mente, casa, tribu, mudanza, orgullo, sufrible, desarmado, continente, indicativo, inconsiderado, desalumbradamente.

Dócil, ámbar, cáliz, café, música, épico, lírico, químico, incómodo, espíritu, alegórico, escolástico.

2. The above rule applies also to words ending in two vowels, whether they form diphthongs or not: Ex. Diph-

thongs—*serio, agua, concordia, puntapié*; observing, however, that those ending in *ea, eo, oe*, must be marked with the accent on the syllable on which the stress falls : Ex. *etérea, virgíneo, héroe.* Not diphthongs—*cria, rio, empleo, albacea, sarao, canoa.* Those of more than two syllables, nevertheless, ending in *ia* or *io*, are marked with the accent : Ex. *filosofía, navío.*

3. Words ending in *y* have the stress on the las syllable, and receive no accent : Ex. *convoy, virey.*

4. Surnames ending in *ez*, being acute on the penult, receive no accent : Ex. *Fernandez, Martinez.*

5. Words in the plural number retain the stress on the same syllable which they would in the singular, except *carácter*, the plural of which is *caractéres.*

6. Adverbs ending in *mente*, formed from adjectives that deviate from the general rule of accentuation, preserve the accent on the same syllable as the adjectives do from which they are derived ; as, *bárbaramente*, from *bárbaro; intrépidamente*, from *intrépido ;* but in those formed from adjectives that follow the general rule, the stress falls on the first syllable of the termination *mente ;* as, *grandemente*, from *grande; singularmente*, from *singular*, and require no accent. All superlatives ending in *ísimo* receive the accent on the first syllable of this termination ; as, *bellísimo, fertilísimo.*

7. When monosyllables have more than one signification, the accent is employed to distinguish them, thus—

tú, thou	*tu*, thy.
él, he	*el*, the.
mí, me	*mi*, my.
sí, oneself, yes	*si*, if.
sé (from *ser*), be thou	*se*, oneself.
di (from *dar*), I gave	*di* (from *decir*), say thou.
dé „ let him give, *or* he may give	*de*, of *or* from.
ó, or	*O*, interjection *Oh.*
qué, what, used interrogatively or in exclamation.	*que*, the relative, and conjunction *that.*
vé (from *ir*), go thou	*ve* (from *ver*), he sees.

The preposition *á* (to), and the conjunctions *é* (and), *ó*, or *ú* (or), are always accented.

Qué, what; *quién*, who; *cuál*, which; *cuándo*, when;
cuánto, how much; *cómo*, how; and *dónde*, where, are
also accented when used interrogatively, or with admiration, but not otherwise.

THE DIÆRESIS.

8. The diæresis, as established by the ROYAL
ACADEMY, is now only employed over the *u* of *ue* and *ui*,
when both vowels are sounded after *g*; as in *agüero,
argüir*. However, in poetry it is allowed to be used over
the first vowel of a diphthong, to add, for the sake of the
metre, another syllable to a word.

PUNCTUATION.

9. The note of interrogation is employed in Spanish
both at the beginning and at the end of an interrogative
word or sentence.   The one at the beginning is inverted
thus (¿), and its use is to warn the reader that what
follows is a question.   The same occurs with the note of
admiration, which in the like manner is used inverted
thus (¡), to warn the reader; as, *¿Y sabeis su casa, Sancho ?
. . . . . ¿Y habeisla visto algun dia por ventura?* (CER-
VÁNTES—*Don Quijote.*)   And do you know her house,
Sancho? . . . . And have you ever seen her by chance?
   ¡Interés, único móvil del corazon humano ! (CADALSO—
Noches lúgubres.)   Interest, sole prompter of the human
heart!
   If, however, the sentence begins with a word which,
of itself, denotes its interrogative or exclamatory meaning, the word so used is written with an accent (as noticed before), and the inverted note is dispensed with;
as, *Cuándo vendrá ?* when will he come?   *Quién es ?* who
is it ?   *Qué ruido !* what a noise!   *Qué lástima !* what a
pity !
   The other points in punctuation are employed alike
in both languages.

LECTURE III.

ETYMOLOGY.

1. The definition of this branch of Grammar has been given in Lect. 1, Par. 4 : we have now to observe that words are either primitive or derivative. Primitive words are those which are not derived from any other word in the same language : thus, *naturaleza, cielo* — nature, heaven, are primitive words ; but derivative words are those that are derived from words in the same language ; thus, *natural, celeste*—natural, heavenly.

2. The words of a language are comprehended under different classes, called parts of speech—namely, *articles, nouns, adjectives, pronouns, verbs, participles, adverbs, prepositions, conjunctions,* and *interjections ;* therefore, every word in a language must belong to one or the other of these classes.

GENERAL DEFINITIONS OF THE PARTS OF SPEECH.

3. ARTICLES are words which by themselves have no meaning, but are put before nouns to point them out. They are either definite or indefinite. A *definite* article refers to some particular noun or nouns in a sentence ; as, The *letters that are in* the *desk :* but an *indefinite* article refers to an undefined thing of the kind indicated by the noun ; as, A *man brought me* a *letter.*

4. NOUNS OR SUBSTANTIVES express the name of any-thing in existence, whether animate or inanimate, ma-terial or ideal : anything that can be *felt, heard,* or *conceived in the mind,* is a noun ; as, *John, house, city, London, horse, music, wind, wisdom, love, hatred, pleasure, grief, memory, time, virtue,* etc.

NOUNS are of two kinds—namely, *common* and *proper.* A noun *common* embraces within its signification every object of the same species as itself; as, *man, book, star, province, river,* etc. :—there are many men, stars, pro-vinces, rivers, etc., but these names are applied to them in common ; but nouns *proper* refer only to particular

persons and places, and to individual objects, as *William,
Ellen, Paradise, Madrid, the Thames, the Atlantic*, etc.

5. ADJECTIVES are words that express some *character,
quality, property, dimension,* or *appearance,* of a noun ; as,
*a good man, fine cloth, the hard iron, a large house, the dark
clouds.* Here the adjective *good* expresses the *character*
of the noun *man; fine,* the *quality* of the *cloth; hard,* the
property of the *iron; large,* the *dimension* of the *house;*
and *dark,* the *appearance* of the *clouds.*

6. PRONOUNS are words used in the place of nouns,
to avoid their frequent repetition. Without this part
of speech discourse would be rendered tedious, from
the necessity of repeating every noun, the place of
which these pronouns supply. For instance, in the
sentence, *Henry gave the letter to Mary, but* she *returned* it
to him, *and* he *put* it *into* his *pocket,* were it not for the
pronouns *she, it, him, he, it, his,* we should be obliged to
repeat every noun, the place of which the pronouns
supply. There are several kinds of pronouns, the
nature and use of which will be explained in their etymology and syntax.

7. VERBS are words that denote existence and action.
They describe the various states of being of things,
animate and inanimate, material and ideal, and all the
different actions attributable to these. The verbs *to be,
to sit, to sleep, to stand,* etc., describe various states in
which objects may be found to exist ; *to write, to break,
to strike,* etc., denote actions of the body ; and *to think,
to love, to grieve,* etc., are operations of the mind. A verb
is very properly considered the essential word in a sentence, since no phrase, however short, can be formed
without a verb expressed or understood. The different
species of verbs that exist in language will be treated
on in their etymology and syntax.

8. PARTICIPLES are words so called from their par-
taking of the nature of *verbs, nouns,* and *adjectives.* There
are two participles, the one called *present,* or *active;* the
other *past,* or *passive.* In its capacity of a verb the
participle *present* denotes *action* and *being;* as, *He is
writing, She was standing.* And the participle *past,*
when joined to any part of the auxiliary verb *to have,*
forms the *compound tenses* of the verb it represents; as,

I have walked; and joined to any part of the verb *to be,* they together form the *passive voice;* as, *She is esteemed:* all which and also the employment of participles as nouns and adjectives will be fully explained in their etymology and syntax.

9. ADVERBS are words employed with verbs, adjectives, and sometimes with adverbs themselves, to modify their meaning. When employed with reference to *verbs,* they describe the *manner* of their being or acting, or some circumstance attending these; as, *He is ill;* in which the adverb *ill* expresses a circumstance attending on the state of existence denoted on the verb *is:* and in *She writes well,* the adverb *well* specifies the *manner* or quality of the writing. When employed with reference to *adjectives,* they express the *degree* of their quality; as, *An extremely good man;* in which example the adverb *extremely* specifies the *degree* of quality denoted by the adjective *good.* When joined to other adverbs they point out the extent of their signification; as, *He speaks very correctly;* in .which the adverb *very* specifies to what extent the meaning of the adverb *correctly* may be taken.

10. PREPOSITIONS are chiefly employed before nouns, pronouns, and verbs, to show the relation which they bear to some other noun, pronoun, or verb in a sentence ; as, *The beauty* of *the poem.   She is* in *the garden.   He was taken* by *the enemy.   John bought the book* for *William.   I gave the money* to *Henry.* Prepositions govern the different *cases* of nouns and pronouns. The manner of employing them differs materially in Spanish and English ; and when the student has made himself acquainted with the use of the cases (LECTURE 8) he will better comprehend the utility of prepositions.

11. CONJUNCTIONS serve to connect the words and parts of a sentence together; as, *He* and *she will go,* though *I may stay.* Here the conjunction *and* unites the pronouns *he* and *she,* while the other conjunction, *though,* connects the two members of the sentence.

12. INTERJECTIONS are a kind of ejaculations employed to denote some emotion of the mind, and which, properly speaking, are not words, nor should they be considered as forming any part of speech, since they have no agreement with any. They are mere sounds, expressive of

some affection of the mind at the time of speaking; or certain exclamations used for the purpose of calling the attention; as, *Alas! Oh! Ah sad! Hollo!*

13. The foregoing general definitions of the several parts of speech are here given preparatory to the treatment of them respectively in their etymology and syntax. Of the ten parts of speech, the *article*, the *noun*, the *adjective*, the *pronoun*, the *verb* and the *participle*, undergo frequent changes in both languages; sometimes by a slight addition to, or alteration in their orthography, and sometimes by very material alterations, and even a total difference in spelling. These variations are called *accidence*, and the parts of speech that are subject to them are called *declinable*, and the rest *indeclinable*. The manner in which the declinable parts vary will be pointed out in their etymology and syntax respectively.

SYNTAX

14. SYNTAX teaches the method of constructing sentences according to the rules of grammar. By syntax we are taught how to arrange words in their proper places, that our sentences may be correct, clear, and incapable of being misconstrued.

In the formation of sentences two things are to be considered—namely, *concord* and *government*.

15. CONCORD shows how words are made to agree with one another in *person, number, gender*, and *case*. There are five species of concord existing between the declinable parts of speech in Spanish.

First, between the *article* and *noun*, which agree in *number, gender*, and *case;* Ex.

El amor *de la* gloria.	The love of glory.
Las reglas se dieron *á los* discípulos *por el* maestro.	The rules were given to the pupils by the master.

Second, between the *adjective* and *noun*, which agree in *number* and *gender:* Ex.

La *historia general* de la *especie humana* y sus *acontecimientos extraordinarios, y trasformaciones políticas.*	The general history of the human species, and its extraordinary events, and political transformations.

Third, between the *noun* and *pronoun*, which agree sometimes in *gender*, and always in *number* and *case :* Ex.

Tú, hermano, y *tú, hermana,* podeis quedaros acá.	Thou, brother, and thou, sister, may remain here.
Juan y *María* salieron juntos; pero *él* illegó ántes que *ella.*	John and Maria went out together; but he arrived before she did.
Ellos son *amigos; los* conozco bien.	They are friends; I know them well.

Fourth, between the relative and the antecedent, which sometimes agree in *gender, number*, and *case :* Ex.

El *hombre que* lo tiene, y para *quien,* or para *el cual* se hizo.	The man who has it, and for whom it was made.
Las *mugeres que* vímos, y á las *cuales* hablámos.	The women whom we saw, and to whom we spoke.

Fifth, between the *verb* and its *nominative*, which agree in *number* and *person :* Ex.

Yo hablo, ellos escriben, nosotros tocámos, las *muchachas cantaron.*	I speak, they write, we played, and the girls sang.
Los *hombres* y las *mugeres vinieron.*	The men and women came.

16. GOVERNMENT is the power that one part of speech has over another in directing what *case, mood,* or *tense* the regimen, or word governed, is required to be in. The parts of speech in Spanish that have the power of governing are : the *noun,* the *pronoun,* the *verb,* the *preposition,* and the *conjunction.*

First, Nouns govern nouns : Ex.

La *casa* de *Pedro.*	Peter's house.
Las *leyes* del *estado.*	The laws of the state.

Second, Nouns and pronouns govern verbs : Ex.

Los *perros ladran.* Los *árboles crecen.*	The dogs bark. The trees grow.
Yo leeré miéntras *ellos* vuelvan.	I will read whilst they return.

Third, Verbs and prepositions govern nouns, pronouns, verbs and adverbs : Ex.

Tomó un *palo* y *le* **pegó.**	He took a stick and beat him.
Prometió ir mañana.	He promised to go to-morrow.
Di dinero al hombre para comprar comida para ellos.	I gave money to the man to buy victuals for them.

Fourth, Conjunctions govern verbs: Ex.

Pues que ha venido le dotendré, aménos que prometa volver pronto.	Since he is come I will detain him, unless he promise to return soon.

17. Syntax is of two kinds, *natural* and *figurative*. The natural order of syntax is when the rules of grammar are strictly adhered to, as regards the placing of words in a sentence. Its principal object being clearness, it does not admit of any diminution or superfluity of words, nor change in their natural arrangement. Figurative syntax is that in which certain licences are taken in the construction of sentences for the sake of elegance, harmony, or to add energy to the expression. From these licences there results a great variety of construction, in which the beauty of the Spanish idiom displays itself. And the language, being reduced by the rules of grammar to a comparatively few principles, yields wonderfully to those who know how to avail themselves of the variety of changes which its construction admits.

LECTURE IV.

ETYMOLOGY AND SYNTAX.

1. In Spanish we have to consider the *definite*, the *indefinite*, and the *neuter* articles; the first, of

THE DEFINITE ARTICLE.

AGREEMENT.

2. The *definite* article is *el*, and it is made to agree in

gender, *number*, and *case* with the noun to which it is prefixed: Ex.

	Singular.	*Plural.*
Mas.	*El hombre*, the man.	*Los hombres*, the man.
	Del hombre, of the man.	*De los hombres*, of the men.
Fem.	*La muger*, the woman.	*Las mugeres*, the women.
	A la muger, to the woman.	*A las mugeres*, to the women.

3. The article *el* drops the *e* when it is preceded by the preposition *de* (*of*, or *from*), and *á* (*to*, or *at*); thus instead of *de el* and *á el*, we must say *del* and *al*: Ex.

Del rey, of the king.	*Del libro*, of the book.
Al rey, to the king.	*Al libro*, to the book.

4. A noun *singular* of the *feminine* gender beginning with *a* or *ha*, and having the stress of voice on the *first* syllable, requires the *masculine* instead of the *feminine* article; thus, instead of *la alma* (the soul), *la habla* (the speech), we must say *el alma*, and *el habla*, although these nouns are of the *feminine* gender. This infringement on the laws of grammar is allowed in order to avoid the unpleasant broad sound which the concurrence of the two same vowels would produce, when the accent is on the first syllable of the noun; for which reason the rule does not apply to feminine nouns beginning with *a* or *ha* having the accent on any syllable but the first; therefore we say *la alcoba* (the alcove), *la alcaparra* (the caper); *la hacienda* (the estate), *la habilidad* (the ability); nor does it apply to feminine nouns in the *plural* number, since in them the intervening *s* prevents the clashing of the two vowels: as, *las almas* (the souls), *las hablas* (the speeches).

EXERCISE ON THE AGREEMENT OF THE DEFINITE ARTICLE.

[It is intended that the pupil should write out the Spanish part only of this and all the succeeding Exercises, supplying the words that are left out. Previously to which, however, he will observe that the words enclosed in brackets correspond with the translation above or beneath them, and consequently require no alteration, that *m.* stands for *masculine*, *f.* for *feminine*, and *p.* for *plural.* Words having an asterisk (*) under them are to be omitted in the translation. A horizontal line (—) denotes a similarity of spelling to the word above it, observing, however, that the letters *s* and *t* are never doubled in Spanish, and that *t* before *i* in English words ending in *tion* is changed into *c* in Spanish. The numeral figures indicate the order in which the Spanish words are to be arranged.]

The boy,　　　the girl　　the hatter,　　and the
muchacho, *m.*　muchacha, *f.*　sombrerero, *m.*　y.

seamstress. The sun, the moon, the stars, and the
costuerra, *f.*　　sol, *m.*　luna, *f.*　estrellas *f. p.*

planets. The knife, the fork, the beef, the salt,
planetas, *m.p.* cuchillo, *m.* tenedor, *m.* carne, *f.* sal, *f.*

the plates,　and the wine-glasses.
platos, *m.p.*　　　copillas, *f. p.*

The atrocity of the crime, The violence of the
　atrocidad, *f.*　　crímen, *m.*　violencia, *f.*

wind. From the house to the garden. From the garden
viento, *m.*　　casa, *f.*　　jardin, *m.*

to the house.　[They arrived] at the inn.
　　　　　llegaron　　　meson, *m.*

The bird　sang. Those are the birds. The water
　　ave, *f.* cantó. aquellas son　aves *f. p.*　agua, *f.*

is cold. The waters of the rivers. The eagle　soars
está fria.　aguas, *f. p.*　rios, *m.p.*　águila, *f.* vuela

very high in the air. The cunningness of the deed.
muy alto en　aire, *m.*　　astucia, *f.*　　hazaña.

EMPLOYMENT.

WHEN EMPLOYED ALIKE IN BOTH LANGUAGES.

5. The definite article is employed in both languages before nouns taken in a *particular* or *definite* sense : Ex.

El hombre elocuente huye　　*The* eloquent man flies
　de *la* arridez *del* estilo di-　　from *the* aridity of *the*
　dáctico. — (Capmany —　　didactic style.
　Filosofia de la Elocuencia).

La divinidad de sus inge-nios, y *la* alteza de sus conceptos.–(CERVÁNTES.)	*The* divinity of their ge-niuses, and *the* loftiness of their ideas.

6. Before adjectives substantively used in a general sense, that is, when they express the whole of the kind denoted by their meaning : Ex.

Los avaros y *los codiciosos* nunca estan satisfechos.	*The avaricious* and *the cove-tous* are never satisfied.

7. Before nouns and adjectives that express a whole nation, a whole sect, etc. : Ex.

Los Alemanes son muy in-dustriosos.	*The Germans* are very in-dustrious.
Hablo de *los Protestantes;* no de *los Católicos.*	I speak of *the Protestants;* not of *the Catholics.*

8. It is employed before a noun singular that ex-presses a whole species or kind: Ex.

El caballo es animal noble.	*The horse* is a noble animal.
La uva crece con abundan-cia en España.	*The grape* grows abun-dantly in Spain.

9. Also before nouns that are singular in their kind : Ex.

La luna es satélite de *la* tierra.	*The moon* is a satellite of *the earth.*

10. Before the names of seas, rivers, and mountains : Ex.

El Atlántico, *el* Tajo, y *los* Alpes.	*The* Atlantic, *the* Tagus, and *the* Alps.

11. Before the proper names of particular individuals; before surnames employed in the plural number, and when used figuratively : Ex.

La Vénus de Ticiano.	*The* Venus of Titian.
Está relacionado con *los* Olivares.	He is related to *the* Oli-vares.
Calderon puede llamarse *el* Shakspere de España.	Calderon may be styled *the* Shakspere of Spain.

Note.—It is omitted in both languages before nouns employed in the aggregate : Ex.

España, Francia, Inglaterra, Italia, y Alemania (todas), se hicieron casi á un mismo tiempo reinos independientes bajo un nuevo sistema político.— (MARINA—*Ensayo Hist. Crít.*)	Spain, France, England, Italy, and Germany, were (all) made, almost at the same period, independent kingdoms, under a new political system.

WHEN USED IN SPANISH AND NOT IN ENGLISH.

12. The definite article is used in Spanish before all nouns taken in a *general* and *unlimited* sense : that is, nouns in which the whole of the kind or species denoted by them is included : Ex.

Las acciones buenas se desprecian si nacen *del* arte, y no de *la* virtud.— (SAAVEDRA FAJARDO.)	Good actions are despised if they spring from art, and not from virtue.
La industria y *la* diligencia son hijas de *la* esperanza. —(MARIANA.)	Industry and diligence are the offspring of hope.

13. Before the names of the four quarters of the globe; before the names of empires, kingdoms, provinces, and countries; and before the four seasons of the year : Ex.

La America tiene mas variedad de clima que *la* Europa.	America has greater variety of climate than Europe.
La Austria es un imperio muy poblado.	Austria is a very populous empire.
La España produce todo lo necessario para la vida: *la* Andalucía es una de sus provincias fértiles.	Spain produces all the necessaries of life : Andalusia is one of her fertile provinces.
Algunos llaman á *la* Australia la quinta division del globo.	Some call Australia the fifth division of the globe.
La primavera es mas agradable que *el* invierno.	Spring is more agreeable than winter.

Exception 1st.—It is generally omitted in Spanish

before the name of a country, a kingdom, a province, etc.,
when a part of it only is comprehended in the name: Ex.

Fuí á Inglaterra.	I went to England.
Viene de Francia.	He comes from France.
Viven en Estremadura.	They live in Estremadura.

Exception 2nd.—It is also frequently omitted before
the names of kingdoms, provinces, etc., when they are preceded by a preposition; unless they are personified: Ex.

En España no hay tanto crepúsculo como *en* Inglaterra.	In Spain there is not so much twilight as in England.
Los actos *de la* Rusia con respecto *á la* Polonia.	The proceedings of Russia with respect to Poland.

. *Exception 3rd.*—As the article is omitted in both languages before *proper* names of individuals and places, so
it is omitted before the names of kingdoms, provinces, etc.,
bearing the same names as their capital cities : Ex.

Venecia y *Génova* eran antiguamente estados independientes.	Venice and Genoa were anciently independent states.

14. Nouns in the third person, denoting the title,
dignity, profession, etc., of an individual, require the
definite article : Ex.

La Reina Victoria.	Queen Victoria.
El General N., y *el* Capitan R.	General N., and Captain R.
El Doctor M.	Doctor M.
El Señor y *la* Señora B.	Mr. and Mrs. B.

15. When several nouns follow one another in a sentence, the article is frequently repeated before each,
particularly if they differ in gender ; and if a preposition
precede the article, it is likewise frequently repeated.
(This, however, is not to be taken as a fixed rule, since
it often yields to fancy or taste) : Ex.

(En el siglo de oro) no habia *la fraude, el engaño,* ni *la malicia* mezclándose con *la verdad* y *llaneza.*— (CERVÁNTES—*Don Quijote.*)	(In the golden age) neither did fraud, deceit, or malice mingle itself with truth and simplicity.

(La ignorancia y el error), enemigos *de la* pública tranquilidad ; *de la* prosperidad de las naciones ; *del* órden y *de la* subordinacion. — (MARINA — *Ensayo Hist. Crít.*)	(Ignorance and error), the enemies of public tranquillity; of the prosperity of nations; of order, and of subordination.

16. The days of the week are sometimes, and the hour of the day is always, preceded by the definite article in Spanish; and the preposition used in English before the days of the week is not translated. Observe also, by the following examples, how the time of day is expressed in Spanish : Ex.

Volveré á verle *el* Domingo á *la* una, ó á *las* dos.	I shall return and see you *on* Sunday, at one or two o'clock.
No vaya hasta Lúnes á *las* cuatro y media, ó Mártes á *las* siete ménos cuarto.	Do not go till Monday at half-past four, or Tuesday at a quarter to seven.
Esté Vmd. aquí Miércoles ó Juéves á *las* ocho ménos diez minutos ; ó Viérnes, ó Sábado, á *las* nueve y veinte minutos.	Be here *on* Wednesday or Thursday, at ten minutes to eight; or Friday or Saturday, at twenty minutes after nine.

17. When the noun *casa*, house, signifies *home, residence*, or *dwelling*, it is used without the article : Ex.

Me voy á casa. Estamos cerca de casa.	I am going home. We are near home.
Está en casa de su tio.	He is at his uncle's.
(See LECT. 8, PAR. 18.)	

WHEN USED IN ENGLISH AND NOT IN SPANISH.

18. The definite article is not used in Spanish before numeral adjectives following the names of sovereigns, potentates, etc. : Ex.

Isabel Segunda.	Isabelle *the* Second.
Leopoldo Primero. Pio Nono.	Leopold *the* First. Pius *the* Ninth.

19. It is omitted when we speak of the *titles* of books, chapters, etc. : Ex.

Esta obra se intitula "Historia de España."	This book is entitled "*The* History of Spain."
Capítulo cuarto, verso primero.	Chapter *the* fourth, verse *the* first.

But if we allude to the subject of the work, or any particular part of it, we employ the article : Ex.

La Historia de España trata tambien de su Literatura.	The History of Spain treats also of its Literature.
En *el* capítulo primero encontramos, etc.	In the first chapter we find, etc.

20. The article is omitted, except before the first noun, (if required there,) when several nouns are used in apposition; that is, when several nouns follow each other, all alluding to the same person or thing : Ex.

El Príncipe Alberto, consorte de la Reina Victoria.	Prince Albert, *the* consort of Queen Victoria.
Madrid, capital de España, y residencia de su corte.	Madrid, *the* capital of Spain, and residence of its court.
Entra Cide Hamete, coronista desta grande historia, con estas palabras, etc.—(CERVÁNTES.—*Don Quijote.*)	Cidi Hamet, *the* chronicler of this great history, commences with these words, etc.

21. When nouns are used in a *partitive* sense they admit no article in either language, unless we wish to refer to some particular object : Ex.

Deme Vmd.* agua.	Give me (*some*) water.
Quiére Vmd. dinero ?	Do you want (*any*) money ?
Ella posee talento y hermosura.	She possesses wit and beauty.
Deme Vmd. *del* vino de que bebí ayer.	Give me (*some*) *of the* wine of which I drank yesterday.

In these examples we see that something in the sense of *some*, or *any*, or *a little*, is understood, which in both

---

* *Vmd.* is pronounced in Spanish *Usted :* see the meaning of this abbreviation, LECT. 14, PAR. 22.

languages, may be either expressed or not, for which reason these phrases may also be construed thus:

Deme Vmd. *un poco de* agua.	Give me *some* or *a little* water.
Quiére Vmd. *algun* dinero?	Do you want *any* money?
Ella posee *algun* talento y *alguna* hermosura.	She possesses *some* wit and *some* beauty.
Deme Vmd. *un poco del* vino de que bebí ayer.	Give me *some of the* wine of which I drank yesterday.

Un poco de is equivalent to *a little*, or *a small portion*, or *quantity of*. *Algun* means *some*, or *any*: it is derived from the indefinite pronoun *alguno*, which changes its last vowel into *a* for the feminine gender, and an *s* is added to it to form the plural number; but when it precedes a noun masculine singular it drops the *o*: Ex.

¿Necesita Vmd. dinero *alguno*?	Do you require any money?
Présteme Vmd. *algun* libro, *algunos* poemas, *algunas* novelas.	Lend me *some* book, *some* poems, *some* novels.

(See *Indefinite Pronouns*, LECT. 19.)

EXERCISE ON THE EMPLOYMENT OF THE DEFINITE ARTICLE.

The beauty of the poem. The delicacy of
  hermosura, *f.*   poema, *m.*   delicadeza, *f.*
the style. The virtuous are estimable; but
  estilo, *m.*   virtuosos, *m. p.* son estimables mas
not the vicious, The Romans were a
  no viciosos, *m. p.*   Romanos, *m. p.* eran una
warlike (2) nation (1). The lion is stronger
guerrera   ——*f.*   leon, *m.* es [mas fuerte]
than the tiger. The aurora announces the approach
que tigre, *m.*   ——*f.* anuncia venida, *f.*
of the sun. The Pyrenees divide France from
    Pirinéos, *m. p.* dividen
Spain. The Tagus empties into the Atlantic.
    Tajo, *m.* desagua en   Atlántico, *m.*

The Jupiter　of　Phidias.　　He is of the family　of
　　Júpiter, _m._　　Fídias　él es　　familia, _f._
the Langfords.　Moratin is the Goldoni of Spain.
—— _m. p._　　　　　　　　—— _m._

[As soon as I received]　the　information　that　the
　luego que recibí　　　noticia, _f._　[de que]

　soldiers　　had occupied the fort　and　town,
soldados,　_m. p._ habian ocupado　fuerte, _m._　villa, _f._

my　zeal　for　the　service　[did not allow me]　to
mi　celo　por　servicio, _m._　no me permitia　　*

remain　any　longer　in the　capital.　Among the
quedarme mas　tiempo　en　　——_f._　entre

advantages that　our　arms obtained in the glorious
ventajas, _f. p._ que nuestras armas lograron　gloriosa, _f._

action, the most interesting was that of having frus-
—— _f._　　mas interesante, _f._ fué la　haber frus-

trated the　design　of the enemy..　　Care　is
trado　intento, _m,_　enemigo, _m._ cuidado, _m._ es

often　the　attendant　on greatness.　Man　is a
amenudo　compañero, _m._ de grandeza, _f._ hombre, _m._　*

slave to his passions.　Spring,　Summer,　Autumn,
esclavo de sus pasiones primavera, _f._ verano, _m._ otoño, _m._

and　Winter　are the　four　seasons　of the
　invierno, _m._ son　cuatro　estaciones, _f. p._

year. .　Cowardice and meanness are qualities of a
año, _m._ cobardía, _f._　bajeza, _f._ son cualidades　un

man　without　honour.　Impartial (2) criticism (1)
　sin　honor　imparcial　crítica, _f._

[should not offend], [on the contrary], [we ought to feel
　no debe ofender　al contrario　debiamos hon-

honoured by it]. General N.　was happily engaged　in
rarnos con ella　——_m._ [se ocupaba con feliz éxito] en

maintaining tranquillity　and repressing seditions.
　mantener tranquilidad, _f._ [en reprimir] sediciones _f. p._

The happiness of a man of　feeling　is to relieve the
　felicidad, _f._　sentimiento es * aliviar

wants   of the   poor.   The love of glory
necesidades, *f. p.*   pobres, *m. p.* amor, *m.* por gloria.*f.*
animates the   brave.   France, Spain, Italy, and
[anima á]   valerosos, *m. p.*   Italia, *f.*

Germany   have   different   forms   of government.
Germania, *f.* tienen diferentes formas   gobierno.

Russia is a vast Empire. Europa,   Asia,   Africa,
—— *f.* es un vasto Imperio Europa, *f.* —— *f.* Africa.*f.*

and America are the four   quarters of the world.
América, *f.* son   cuatro partes, *f. p.*   mundo, *m.*
Rome and   Venice were ancient (2) republics (1).   I
Roma   Venecia fueron antiguas repúblicas   *

intend to proceed from Holland to France, and from
intento * proceder   Holanda

France to England. Mr. A. lives in the   next
                               vive   próxima

street.   Mrs. B. has spoken to Mrs. C. I am a sub-
calle. *f.*   ha hablado   yo soy * subs-

stitute of Doctor Sangrado. Gil Blas, said Captain
tituto   ——— *m.* ————   —— —— dijo capitan, *m.*
Rolando.   Innocence, virtue, and   merit   should
———— inocencia, *f.* virtud, *f.*   mérito *m.* debian

be appreciated.   Never be a slave to   avarice
ser apreciados   jamás seas * esclavo de avaricia, *f.*
nor vice. Jews, Christians, and Mahometans, all
ni vicio. *m.* judíos cristianos   mahometanos todos

are offspring of the same   parent. [We shall leave
son hijos   mismo padre, *m.*   saldrémos de

London] on Wednesday at half-past four, and arrive
Lóndres   Miércoles, *m.*   llegarémos

at our destination on Friday, at one or two [o'clock].
nuestro destino   Viérnes, *m,*   ó   *
Victoria the First was proclaimed Queen of Great
————— primera fué proclamada Reina   Gran
Britain in the year 1837. Leo the Ninth was
Bretaña, *f.*   año, *m.*   Leon   nono fué

the first Pope that maintained an   army   in his
    primer Papa, *m*. que mantuvo un egército   sus
dominions.   Here is a book   entitled "The Civil (2)
    dominios   aquí está un libro intitulado   civiles
Wars (1) of Granada."   The second paragraph says
guerras   ————   segundo párrafo, *m*. dice
thus.   Hercules the son of Jupiter. Here is a paper
  así   Hércules   hijo   papel, *m*.
which I have bought.   This is the key   of the
  que * he   comprado   esta   es   llave, *f*.
garden.   Leopold Grand Duke of Tuscany.   Nicholas
      Leopoldo Gran Duque   Toscano   Nicolas
Emperor of Russia.   Quarrels   frequently
Emperador   disputas, *f. p*. [muchas veces]
produce fatal (2) consequences (I).   It is some of the
  traen fatales   consecuencias   * es
  wine that [I sent you].   They are some of the
vino, *m*. que   le mandé   *   son
    apples   from my orchard.   I have received some
manzanas, *f. p*.   mi huerto * he   recibido
  letters.   I want some paper and some   pens.
cartas, *f. p*. * necesito   papel, *m*.   plumas, *f. p*.
I have some   documents to   answer.   Have they
* tengo   documentos, *m. p*. que contestar   han *
received any wine? Yes, they have received some.
recibido   sí   *   han
    Riches   often   gain us   credit, power.
riquezas, *f. p*. amenudo [nos grangean] crédito poder
friends, and respect.
amigos   respeto

LECTURE V.

THE INDEFINITE ARTICLE.

1. The English indefinite article *a* or *an*, is rendered *un* in Spanish before a noun masculine, or its adjective, and *una* before a noun feminino : Ex.

Un libro, *un* buen caballo, *un* agente, *una* casa, *una* bella muger.	*A* book, *a* good horse, *an* agent, *a* house, *a* fine woman.

Observe that some writers and speakers employ *un*, instead of *una*, before those feminine nouns which take the masculine article, noticed in PAR. 4 of the preceding LECTURE ; as *un alma, un habla.*

2. The English *indefinite* article employed before nouns of weight, measure, number, or distance, in speaking of their value or rate, is translated by the *definite* article : Ex.

Dos duros *la* vara.	Two dollars *a* yard.
Seis peniques *la* libra.	Six pence *a* pound.
Tres chelines *el* ciento.	Three shillings *a* hundred.
A razon de diez reales *la* legua.	At the rate of ten reals *a* league.

3. Sometimes *por* is used instead of *el*, in similar cases : Ex.

A razon de seis duros *por* vara.	At the rate of six dollars *per* yard.
A diez duros *por* ciento.	At ten dollars *per* cent.
Quince reales *por* legua.	Fifteen reals *per* league.

4. When *a* or *an* is employed in English as a numeral adjective, and means particularly *one*, it is translated into Spanish also by the numeral adjective : Ex.

Aquí hay *una* onza de oro y *una* libra de plata.	Here is *an* ounce of gold and *a* pound of silver.

WHEN USED IN ENGLISH AND NOT IN SPANISH.

5. The *indefinite article* is omitted in Spanish before

nouns expressive of the *rank, profession, religion, country,* etc., of an individual, when these nouns are proceded by a verb : Ex.

El *es* embajador.	He *is an* ambassador.
Yo *soy* Inglés y ella es Francesa.	I *am an* Englishman, and she *is a* Frenchwoman.
Su padre *es* protestante.	His father *is a* Protestant.
Llegó aquí capitan, y pronto lo *hicieron* coronel.	He *arrived* here *a* captain, and was soon *made a* colonel.

But when any such nouns refer to an individual we wish to particularize, the article should be employed in Spanish : Ex.

El es *un* oficial que se distinguió en la batalla de Talavera.	He is *an* officer that distinguished himself in the battle of Talavera.

6. It is omitted in Spanish when employed in English before a noun denoting the different inclinations of the mind, and motives of action : Ex.

Tenia inclinacion de decirle.	I had *a* mind to tell him.
Estaba de mal humor.	He was in *a* bad humour.
Tengo motivo para negarlo.	I have *a* motive for denying it.

7. It is likewise omitted before nouns in apposition, and before a word or member of a sentence that specifies the nature of the antecedent noun, or that distinguishes in any particular manner the person or thing represented by it : Ex.

Cádiz, ciudad de Andalucía.	Cadiz, *a* town of Andalusia.
La gratitud, cualidad noble del alma.	Gratitude, *a* noble quality of the mind.
Lope de Vega, poeta insigne español.	Lope de Vega, *a* distinguished Spanish poet.

Thus, also, it is omitted before a phrase inserted in another by way of parenthesis : Ex.

Esto cantaba Elicio, pastor en las riberas del Tajo, etc. — (CERVÁNTES—*La Galatea.*)	Thus sung Elicio, *a* shepherd on the borders of the Tagus, etc.

8. Also when employed in English before a noun pre ceded by a word denoting comparison : Ex.

Tan bella muger, *or,* muger tan bella.	So beautiful *a* woman.
Hombre tan elocuente como Ciceron.	As eloquent *a* man as Cicero.
Tal persona ; tal gusto.	Such *a* person; such *a* pleasure.

9. It is also omitted after the word *que,* what, used in exclamation or surprise before a noun : Ex.

Qué ruido ! Qué bella vista !	What *a* noise ! What *a* fine view !

10. It is omitted before the adjective *cierto,* certain, when used in an indefinite manner ; but when *cierto* means *sure,* it may be employed with or without the indefinite article. *Cierto* changes the final *o* into *a,* when it refers to a noun feminine : Ex.

Cierto hombre y cierta muger me digeron que . . .	*A* certain man and *a* certain woman told me that...
Es (*una*) cosa cierta.	It is *a* certain thing.

11. It is dispensed with in the title of a book : Ex.

Diccionario Español.	*A* Spanish Dictionary.
Gramática Inglesa.	*An* English Grammar.
Ensayo sobre la Educacion.	*An* Essay on Education.

12. It is omitted before the fractional parts of an integer : Ex.

Dos y medio.	Two and *a* half.
Libra y cuarto.	One pound and *a* quarter.
Cuatro varas y tercio.	Four yards and *a* third.

Also before an integer preceded or followed by a fractional part : Ex.

Media onza.	Half *an* ounce.
Dos tercios de vara.	Two-thirds of *a* yard.
Docena y cuarto.	*A* dozen and *a* quarter.
Legua y dos tercios.	*A* league and two-thirds.

Likewise before a *hundred* and *a thousand :* it is retained, however, before a *million,* but not before *half* a million, nor a *million and a half*: Ex.

Cien libras : mil pesos.	*A* hundred pounds : *a* thousand dollars.
Un millon de reales.	*A* million of reals.
Medio millon de libras.	Half *a* million of pounds.
Millon y medio de duros.	*A* million **and** *a* half of dollars.

EXERCISE ON THE INDEFINITE ARTICLE.

Fortune is a capricious (2) deity (1).　A guilty (2)
fortuna, *f.* es caprichosa deidad, *f.*　　criminal

conscience (1) is a perpetual (2) torment (1). I bought
conciencia, *f.*　　perpétuo tormento, *m.*　* compré

a book, an ink-stand, and a dozen of pens. How
libro, *m.*　tintero, *m.*　docena, *f.* plumas　á

much a yard? Two dollars a pound. Six dollars a
como　vara, *f.* dos　libra, *f.* seis

hundred. We travelled at the rate of ten leagues a day.
ciento, *m.*　* caminámos　* razon diez leguas dia, *m.*

The ship sails six miles an hour. Give me a dozen
buque, *m.* anda seis millas　hora, *f.* deme Vmd.

at two guineas a dozen. I will let you have nine
[de á]　————　[Le daré á Vmd.] nueve

pounds at a shilling a pound. He is a bookbinder and his
á chelin, *m.*　él es encuadernador su

brother a bookseller. He is a German, and she an
hermano librero　Aleman ella

Irishwoman. He acted like a traitor. Parnassus, a
Irlandesa　* obró como traidor Parnaso, *m.*

mountain of Phocis, is famous for being the residence of
monte Focida, *f.* famoso por ser residencia, *f.*

the Muses. Captain M., an officer in the French (2)
musas, *f. p.* capitan, *m.*　oficial francés

service (1), fought a duel with Count F., an
servicio, *m.* tuvo desafío, *m.* con conde, *m.*

Italian (2) Colonel (1). Cornelius Tacitus, a famous
italiano coronel Cornelio Tácito famoso

Latin (2) historian (1), was born in the reign
latino　historiador　　*　nació en　　reinado, *m.*

of Nero, a cruel (2) and detestable (3) Prince (1).
　Neron　——　　　　——　　　príncipe

He obtained so complete a victory. She has such a
　*　logró　completa　victoria .　* tiene tan

fine house, and so beautiful a garden! What an excellent
bella　　　　hermoso　　　　　bellísima

idea! What a fine horse! A certain friend of mine
——　　　hermoso caballo　　amigo, *m.* * mio

[spoke to me about] a certain person. It is a certain (2)
me habló acerca de　　persona, *f.* * es

　evidence (1) of the fact.　[It is worth] a thousand
evidencia, *f.*　　hecho, *m.*　vale

pounds. [I lent him] a hundred dollars. This palace cost
　　lo presté　　　　　este palacio costó

a million of dollars, and that, a million and a half. Give
　　　　　　aquel　　　　　　　dé

me two dollars and a half.　Here is an ounce and a half
me　　　　　　　aquí hay

of gold, and half an ounce of silver.　A Treatise on
　oro　　　　　　　, plata　tratado

Philosophy.　A History of the World.
filosofía　historia　　mundo, *m.*

———

LECTURE VI.

THE NEUTER ARTICLE.

1. The neuter article *lo* is employed, first, before
adjectives in the *singular* number used as substantives,
expressing some abstract quality; and observe, that all
Spanish adjectives may be so converted into substantives, by simply prefixing the article *lo* to them: Ex.

Es menester ejercitarse en ver como en sentir, y en juzgar de *lo hermoso* por los ojos, y de *lo bueno* por el sentimiento moral. (CAPMANY—*Filosofía de la Elocuencia.*)	It is necessary to exercise oneself in seeing as in feeling, and to judge of *the beautiful* (or *that which is beautiful*) by the sight, and of *the good* (or *that which is good*) by the moral feeling.

Here we see that *lo* stands in the place of *that which is*, or of *what is*. We may likewise employ in Spanish, though, perhaps, with less elegance, those words, the place of which is supplied by the neuter article *lo;* thus, *juzgar de* aquello que es *hermoso*, etc., and *de* aquello que es *bueno*, etc.—or, *de lo* que es *hermoso*, etc., and *de lo* que es *bueno*, etc. : in either way they mean *that which is beautiful, or what is beautiful;* and *that which is good*, or *what is good*. In such instances neither the masculine nor the feminine article could be employed, since there is no noun with which it could agree : the *lo*, therefore, stands in the place of *lo que es; that which is*, or *what is*.

Secondly, the neuter article *lo* is frequently employed with the words *que* and *cual*, before verbs; *lo que* meaning *what*, or *that which*, and *lo cual*, *which*, or *the which :* Ex.

Estos trabajos, moderadamente tomados, se acostumbran los hombres á sufrir y hacer *lo que* deben; *lo cual* no podrian hacer ni sufrir si, etc.—(J. L. DE PALACIOS RUBIOS.)	These labours, exercised with moderation, accustom men to bear and to do *what* they ought : *which* they would never be able to do nor to bear, if, etc.

And here, also, the neuter article is brought in to refer to some act, or occurrence, which, not being expressed by a noun, no gender can be attributed to it ; hence neither the masculine nor the feminine article could be employed.

EXERCISE ON THE NEUTER ARTICLE.

The work treats on the sublime and beautiful. [Let us obra, *f.* trata sobre ———	prefi-

prefer] that which is solid and useful. [Let him abide] by
ramos   sólido   útil   que se limite á
what is just. Of greater value is the little that the
    justo [es de mayor estimacion] poco que
 wise man knows, than the much that the rich man
sabio, m. * sabe que mucho   rico *
possesses. What is most desirable is (2) not (1) always the
 tiene   mas apetecible   no siempre
most easy to obtain. The beautiful acquires under his
  fácil de conseguir   toma bajo de su
 pen new beauty; the tender, new softness; tho
pluma nueva hermosura   tierno suavidad
energetic, new vigour; the awful, new sublimity. I
 onérgico nuevo vigor   terrible sublimidad *
listened to all what (or, that which) he said, by which I
escuché * todo   * dijo por   *.
learnt that, etc. What I know is not what you think.
 supe   yo sé   Vmd. piensa
All that glitters is not gold. I did what he desired me
todo reluce   oro * hice *[me encargó]
 to do, which (or, the which) was the following.
que hiciese   fué   siguiente

LECTURE VII.

ETYMOLOGY AND SYNTAX OF NOUNS.

NUMBER.

1. Nouns have two numbers, the singular and the
plural. When the Spanish noun ends in a vowel on which
the stress of voice does *not* fall, its plural is formed by
adding *s* to the noun in the singular number; as, *estrella*,
star; *estrellas*, stars :—*ave*, bird ; *aves*, birds :—*catálogo*,
catalogue; *catálogos*, catalogues.

2. When the noun ends in *a*, or *i*, accented, or in *y*, the plural is formed by the addition of *es*.　The same takes place with nouns ending in a consonant, except *z*, in which latter the plural is formed by changing the *z* into *ces*; as *bajá*, bashaw; *bajáes*, bashaws; *jabalí*, wild boar; *jabalíes*, wild boars; *ley*, law; *leyes*, laws; *barril*, barrel; *barriles*, barrels; *luz*, light; *luces*, lights.

From the above rule are excepted *mamá*, mamma, *papá*, papa; and *sofá*, sofa; which take only an *s* in the plural.

The very few Spanish nouns that end in *e*, *o*, and *u*, accented, take *s* alone in the plural; as *corsé*, corset; *corsés*, corsets; *rondó*, rondo; *rondós*, rondos; *ambigú*, medley; *ambigús*, medleys.

3. Nouns ending in *s*, accented on the penult or antepenult, are written alike in both numbers; as: *éxtasis*, ecstasy *or* ecstasies; *crisis*, crisis *or* crises.

4. There are some nouns which in their nature have always a plural signification, and consequently require that the article employed with them be in the plural number: such are *albricias*, a reward; *alicates*, pincers; *andas*, bier; *angarillas*, hand-barrow; *antiparras*, spectacles; *bofes*, lungs; *bragas*, breeches; *calendas*, calends; *calzoncillos*, drawers; *carnestolendas*, last three carnival days; *cosquillas*, tickling; *despabiladeras*, snuffers; *efemérides*, f., ephemeris; *enaguas*, under-petticoat; *exequias*, exequies; *fauces*, f., gullet; *llares*, f., pot-hanger; *maitines*, matins; *modales*, manners; *nupcias*, wedding; *parillas*, grid-iron; *preces*, prayers; *semejas*, similitude; *tenazas*, tongs; *tercianas*, ague; *tinieblas*, darkness; *trébedes*, trevet; *vísperas*, vespers; *víveres*, provisions; and a few others not much used.

5. There are others which, notwithstanding their plural termination, have not a plural signification, and therefore require the article in the singular number; such are *azotacalles*, lounger, ; *besamanos*, court-day; *brindis*, saluting toast; *sacacorchos*, corkscrew; *sacatrapos*, gun-worm; *guardapies*, over-petticoat; *sacabotas*, boot-jack; *sacamuelas*, tooth-drawer; *cortaplumas*, pen-knife; and a few more, little used.

EXERCISE ON THE FORMATION OF THE PLURAL NOUNS.

[Observe, that in all the future exercises, every Spanish noun will be put in the singular number, whatever may be that of the corresponding nouns in English. The student will therefore have to consider the number of the English noun previous to translating it, and be guided by the rules for the formation of the plural of Spanish nouns, when required.]

The beauty of the birds, and the melody of their voices.
　　hermosura, *f.*　　　　　　　　melodía, *f.* sus voz
The woods in those countries are very extensive. The
　bosque, *m.* en aquellos pais　son muy extensos
　flocks in the meadows. The niceties of the languages.
rebaño, *m.*　　prado, *m.*　delicadeza, *f.*　　lengua, *f.*
The gilly-flowers and roses grow in abundance. Until
　　alelí, *m.*　　　rosa, *f.* crecian abundancia [hasta que]
prisons be converted into houses of industry and schools of
cárcel, *f.* se conviertan en　　　　industria　　　escuela
　reform [we shall never draw any benefit] from the
reforma　　nunca sacarémos　　　provecho
sentences of the judges. Men and women should be
sentencia, *f.*　　juez, *m.* hombre, *m.* muger, *f.* deben ser
faithful [to each other]. Those ministers framed good
　fieles unos con otros aquellos ministro formaron buenas
laws for their countries. The scholars received the books
ley para sus　pueblo　discípulo, *m.* recibieron libro, *m.*
and pens from their masters. There is the penknife.
　pluma, *f.*　　sus maestro　　allí está cortaplumas, *m.*
Those garrets are verry roomy. The flowers of those
　　zaquizamí son　　espaciosos　　　flor, *f.*
gardens are beautiful. [There would be] few contentions,
　　hermosas　　habria　　　pocas contienda
frauds, and perjuries, if men [would set] bounds to their
fraude　　perjurio si　　pusiesen límite　　sus
desires. The bashaws were seated on rich sofas.
　deseo　　　　estaban sentados en ricos
The different theses which they advocated. He has
　diferentes tésis, *f.* que　*　apoyaban　*　ha

written several rondos. The manners of that gentleman
escrito varios   modales, *m. p.* ese   caballero
are very polished.
son muy finos.

6. Some nouns are called *collective,* which are divided
into *definite* and *indefinite.*   Under the head of *collective
definite* are classed all those nouns that represent an organized body of objects ; as *un egército,* an army; *una nacion,*
a nation, etc. ; and under *collective indefinite* are classed
those that do not comprehend unity in their meaning ;
as *una multitud,* a multitude; *un enjambre,* a swarm, etc.
See Agreement of the Verb with its Nominative.   Lect.
27, Par. 2.

OF AUGMENTATIVE AND DIMINUTIVE NOUNS.

7. These derivatives denote larger or smaller objects
of their kind, than those which their primitives express.
They are formed in Spanish by the addition of various
terminations to the noun in its primitive state, dropping
the final vowel, should it have one.

8. Nouns *augmentative,* of the masculine gender, ending in a consonant, are formed by the addition of the
letters *on, ote,* or *azo ;* those of the feminine gender *ona,
ota,* or *aza.*   These terminations are equivalent in their
meanings to the English words *big, large, stout, tall,* and
such like : Ex.

Primitives.	*Derivatives.*
Hombre, a man.	*Hombron, hombrazo,* a tall, or large man.
Muger, a woman.	*Mugerona,* a masculine woman.
Sombrero, a hat.	*Sombrerote,* a large, or big hat.

Hombron also signifies a man distinguished for talent,
or valour.

9. The terminations *azo* and *iza* are sometimes used
also to express the injury that a weapon is capable of
inflicting, and the gender of the noun so employed follows
the rule of the termination of these additionals (see
Par. 13): Ex.

La mató de un pistoletazo.	He killed her with a pistol shot.
Me tiró en tierra de un garrotazo.	He knocked me down with the blow of a bludgeon.
Le dí una buena paliza.	I gave him a good beating with a stick.

10. By a double termination some augmentatives ending in *on* and *ona* acquire a greater force; as from *picaron, picaronazo*; from *mugerona, mugeronaza*.

11. Nouns *diminutive* are formed by the addition of the terminations *in, illo, ito, ete, uelo,* or *uejo,* to the masculine: the feminine are formed by adding *a* to the termination *in,* and by changing the final vowel of the others into *a* (dropping the final vowel of the primitive nouns of either gender ending in one); observing, however, that diminutives ending in *ito* and *ico* denote not only *smallness,* but a kind of endearing expression; and those that end in *illo, uelo,* or *uejo,* generally denote *contempt* or *disgust:* Ex.

Primitives.	*Derivatives.*
Muchacho, a boy.	*Muchachito,* a little boy.
	Muchachillo, a pitiful little fellow.
Casa, a house.	*Casita,* a nice little house.
	Casilla, a mean little house.

12. Many of the diminutive terminations may acquire a still further diminutive signification, by adding other terminations to them; thus, *chico,* small; *chiquito,* or *chiquitillo,* very small; *chiquiritito,* a tiny little thing.

These rules, however, are not always strictly uniform; practice alone can make the pupil familiar with the peculiar meanings of these terminations, of which, besides those already mentioned, many others may be formed at fancy.

GENDER.

13. Gender is that property in nouns which marks the distinction of sex; thus in English there are the *masculine,* the *feminine,* and what is called the *neuter* gender; the *masculine* being applied to living creatures of the *male* kind, the *feminine* to those of the *female* kind, and the

neuter generally to inanimate objects, with some exceptions.   In Spanish, however, there are but *two* genders
in nouns, the *masculine* and the *feminine ;* and the gender
of Spanish nouns is distinguished—First, by their signification, as all animate objects are of the gender of their
respective sex ; and the rank, professions, employments,
kindred, and so forth, of persons, are of the gender of
the individuals to which they belong. Secondly—by
their termination—namely, nouns ending in *a*, *d*, or *ion*,
are generally of the *feminine* gender : those that end in
any other letter are mostly *masculine :* Ex.

FEM. *Inocencia*, innocence.   MASC. *honor*, honour.
    virtud, virtue.   *sombrero*, hat.
    relacion, relation.   *valle*, valley.

Though this rule has exceptions, it is an easy one to
be guided by.   A list of the exceptions will here follow :
observe, first, however, that there are two other distinc-
tions in the gender of nouns to be considered, that one
called *common*, from its being equally · applied to male
and female ; for instance, *el tigre*, the tiger ; *la tigre*, the
tigress ; *un albacéa*, an executor; *una albacéa*, an exe-
cutrix ; in which the article in Spanish marks the distinction of sex.   The other is called *epicene*, which is
applied to those nouns that express both genders by the
same word ; as *el pato*, the duck, or the drake; *la hiena*,
the he or she hyena ; but the article prefixed to them
does not vary to mark their gender ; to point out which,
it is necessary to add some word to them descriptive of
their sex : as, *el pato* macho, *el pato* hembra ; *la hiena*
macho, *la hiena* hembra ; *macho* signifying male, and
hembra female.

14. The gender of nouns that are used in the *plural*
number only, such as *la tenazas*, the tongs ; *el sacacorchos*
the corkscrew, are distinguished by their terminations,
supposing they could be used in the singular number ;
except *efemérides*, diary ; *faúces*, gullet ; *fases*, phases ;
llares, pot-hanger; *preces*, prayers ; *trébedes*, trevet, which
are feminine.

GENDER OF NOUNS THAT REFER TO KINDRED, RANK, PROFESSIONS, ETC.

15. The greater part of those that refer to males end in *o*, and some in *e*; the feminine termination is formed by changing those final vowels into *a*; thus, *hermano, hermana*, brother, sister; *tio, tia*, uncle, aunt; *criado, criada*, male-servant, female-servant; *monje, monja*, monk, nun. Those ending in *r*, add an *a* for the feminine; as *autor, autora*, male author, female author; *pescador, pescadora*, fisherman, fisherwoman.

The gender of the following nouns of kindred is denoted by different words : viz., *padre, madre*, father, mother; *marido, muger*, husband, wife; *padrastro, madrastra*, step-father, step-mother; *yerno, nuera*, son-in-law, daughter-in-law; *padrino, madrina*, god-father, god-mother; *hombre, muger*, man, woman; *soltero, doncella*, bachelor, maid.

The following are distinguished by various terminations : viz. *emperador, emperatriz*, emperor, empress; *rey, reina*, king, queen; *príncipe, princesa*, prince, princess; *duque, duquesa*, duke, duchess; *marqués, marquesa*, marquis, marchioness; *conde, condesa*, earl, countess; *baron, baronesa*, baron, baroness; *abad, abadesa*, abbot, abbess; *actor, actriz*, actor, actress; *cantor, cantatriz*, male and female singer, *comadron, comadre*, man-midwife, midwife.

LIST OF EXCEPTIONS IN THE GENDER OF NOUNS.

Masculine nouns ending in a.

Adema,	prop.	axioma,	axiom.
albacéa,	executor.	carisma,	divine gift.
alcabala,	excise duty.	clima,	climate.
alméa,	storax.	cometa,	comet.
anagrama,	anagram.	crisma,	chrism.
aneurisma,	aneurism.	dia,	day.
antípoda,	antipode.	diafragma,	diaphragm, midriff.
apotegma,	apothegm.		

diagrama,	diagram.	mapa.	map.
digama,	digamma.	metaplasma,	metaplasm.
dilema,	dilemma.	minimista,	student.
diploma,	diploma.	paradigma,	paradigm.
dogma,	dogma.	paradoja,	paradox.
drama,*	drama,*	paragua,	umbrella.
edema,	œdema.	pentagrama,	musical stave.
enigma,	enigma.	planeta,	planet.
entimema,	entymeme.	poema,	poem.
epigrama,	epigram.	prisma,	prism.
esperma,	sperm.	problema,	problem.
Etna,	Ætna.	progimnasma,	essay.
guardacosta,	custom-house boat.	síntoma,	symptom.
		sistema,	system.
guardavela,	topsail tackle.	sofá,	sofa.
guardaropa,	wardrobe.	sofisma,	sophism.
idioma,	idiom.	tapaboca,	slap on the mouth.
jesuita,†	jesuit.		
largomira,	telescope.	tema,	theme.
lema,	lemma.	teorema,	theorem.
maná,	manna.	viva,	huzza.

Masculine nouns ending in d.

Adalid,	a chief, leader.	césped,	turf.
alamud,	door bar.	huésped,	guest.
almud,	a measure.	laud,	lute.
archilaud,	species of lute.	sud,	south.
ardid,	stratagem.	talmud,	talmud.
ataud,	coffin.		

Masculine nouns ending in ion.

Embrion,	embryo.	morrion,	murrain.
gorrion,	sparrow.	sarampion,	measles.

---

* And all its compounds, as *melodrama,* etc.

† And all those which from their meaning denote males, as *Papa, anabaptista,* etc.; *Pope, anabaptist,* etc.

Feminine nouns ending in e.

Anade,	duck.	fase,	phasis.
alache,	shad.	fé,	faith.
alsine,	chickweed.	fiebre,	fever.
anagálide,	pimpernel.	frente,	front, fore-
ave,	fowl, bird.		head.
azumbre,	a measure.	fuelle,	bellows.
barbarie,	barbarity.	fuente,	fountain.
base,	basis.	gente,	people.
calvicie,	baldness.	hambre,	hunger.
calle,	street.	hélice,	helix.
capelardente,	funeral pile.	helgine,	pellitory.
cariátide,	caryatides.	hemionite,	hemionite.
carne,	flesh.	herrumbre,	rust of iron.
catástrofe,	catastrophe.	hipérbole,	hyperbole.
certidumbre,	certainty.	hipocístide,	hypocistas.
chinche,	bug.	hojaldre,	kind of pan-
churre,	grease.		cake.
clase,	class.	incertidum-	uncertainty.
clave,	key.	bre,	
clemátide,	climber.	índole,	temper.
cohorte,	cohort.	inglo,	groin.
compage,	joint.	intemperie,	intemperate-
corambre,	hides.		ness.
corriente,	stream.	jeride,	xirys.
corte,	court.	lande,	kind of acorn.
costumbre,	custom.	landre,	glandular
crasicie,	fatness.		swelling.
creciente,	flood-tide.	laringe,	larynx.
crencho,	the parting of	laude,	praise, an epi-
	the hair.		taph.
cumbre,	summit.	leche,	milk.
dulcedumbre,	sweetness.	legumbre,	pulse.
elatine,	waterwort.	lente,	lens.
epipáctide,	bastard helle-	liebre,	hare.
	bore.	liendre,	nit.
esferóide,	spheroid.	lite,	litigation.
especie,	species.	llave,	key.
epígrafe,	epigraph.	lumbre,	fire.
estirpe,	race, or origin.	mansedum-	meekness.
etiópide,	clary, an herb.	bre,	
falange,	phalanx.	menguante.	ebb-tide.

mente,	the mind.	salve,	salve regina.
mole,	mass.	sangre,	blood.
molicie,	effeminacy.	sede,	a see.
muchedum-	multitude.	serie,	series.
bre,		servidumbre,	servitude.
muerte,	death.	serpiente,	serpent.
mugre,	dirt.	sirte,	quicksand.
nave,	ship.	suerte,	chance.
nieve,	snow.	superficie,	superficies.
noche,	night.	tarde,	afternoon.
nube,	cloud.	teame,	kind of stone.
paralage,	parallax.	techumbre,	roof.
paraselene,	mock-moon.	temperie,	temperature.
parte,	a part.	tilde,	a tittle: a line
patente,	patent.		placed some-
péplide,	wild purslain.		times over
pesadumbre,	grief.		the Spanish
peste,	the plague.		n, thus ñ.
pirámide,	pyramid.	torre,	tower.
pixide,	pix.	trabe,	a beam.
planicie,	plain.	trípode,	tripod.
plebe,	rabble.	troge,	granary.
podre,	pus.	ubre,	udder.
podredumbre,	rottenness.	urdiembre,	warp.
progenie,	progeny.	varicie,	varix.
prole,	issue.	velambre,	nuptial rites.
quiete,	repose.	vislumbre,	glimmering.
salumbre,	oxide of salt.		

Feminine nouns ending in i *or* y.

Diócesi,	diocese.	ley,	law.
graciadei,	gratiola, an herb.	metrópoli,	metropolis.
		palmacristi,	palmachristi.
grei, or grey,	flock.	paráfrasi,	paraphrase.

Feminine nouns ending in l.

Aguamiel,	hydromel.	hiel,	gall.
cal,	lime.	miel,	honey.
capital,	capital.	piel,	skin.
cárcel,	prison.	sal,	salt.
col,	cabbage.	señal,	signal.
decretal,	decretal.	vocal,	vowel.

Feminine nouns ending in n.

Armazon,	stowage.	razon,	reason.
barbechazon,	fallowing time	sarten,	frying-pan.
binazon,	second plough-	sazon,	season.
cargazon,	cargo. [ing.	segazon,	reaping time.
clavazon,	row of nails.	sien,	temple, (part
clin, or crin,	mane.		of the head.)
desazon,	uneasiness.	sinrazon,	injustice.
imágen,	image.	trabazon,	splicing.
plomazon,	a gilder's cushion.		

Feminine nouns ending in o.

Mano,	hand.	nao,	ship.

Feminine nouns ending in r.

Bezar,	bezoar.	segur,	axe.
flor,	flower.	zoster,	shingles (a
labor,	labour.		disease).

Feminine nouns ending in s.

Anagíris,	bean trefoil.	metamorfósis,	metamorphosis.
antiperistasis,	antiperistasis.	metempsícosis,	metempsychosis.
apoteósis,	apotheosis.	mies,	crop.
bilis,	bile.	paraláxis,	parallax.
colapíscis,	isinglass.	paralísis,	palsy.
crísis,	crisis.	parénesis,	parenesis.
diatrásis,	diathrasis.	polispástos,	engine to raise weights.
diésis,	diesis.		
enfitéusis,	emphyteusis.	raquítis,	rickets.
epífisis,	epiphysis.	res,	head of cattle.
epiglóttis,	epiglottis.	selenítes,	selenites.
etítes,	ætites.	sindéresis,	remorse.
galiópsis,	dead-nettle.	sintáxis,	syntax.
hematítes,	hœmatites.	tésis,	thesis. .
hipóstasis,	hypostasis.	tísis,	phthisis.
hipótesis,	hypothesis.	tos,	cough.
lis, .	fleur-de-lys.		
macis,	mace.		

Feminine nouns ending in u.

Tribu,   tribe.

Feminine nouns ending in x.

salsifrax,	saxifrage.	trox,	granary.
sardónix,	sardonyx.		

Feminine nouns ending in z.

Cerviz,	cervix.	nuez,	nut.
cocatriz,	cockatrice.	paz,	peace.
codorniz,	quail.	perdiz,	partridge.
coz,	kick.	pez,	pitch.
cruz,	cross.	pómez,	pumice.
faz,	visage.	raiz,	root.
haz,	bundle.	sobrehaz,	surface.
hez,	dregs.	sobrepelliz,	surplice.
hoz,	sickle, defile.	tez,	complexion.
luz,	light.	vez,	time.
matriz,	matrix.	vejez,	old age.
nariz,	nose.	voz,	voice.
niñez,	childhood.		

And almost all those nouns ending in *ez*, denoting qualities in the abstract; as *brillantez*, brilliancy; *escasez*, scarcity; and many others.

There are also a few nouns, of which the gender is not generally settled; as some authors consider them masculine, and others feminine. The following is a list of them.

Albalá,	certificate, docket.	hermafrodita,	hermaphrodite.
anatema,	anathema.	hipérbole,	hyperbole.
arte,*	art.	mar,†	sea.
azúcar,	sugar.	márgen,	margin.
calor,	heat.	nema,	letter-seal.
canal,	canal.	órden,‡	order.
cisma,	schism.	pringue,	grease.
cútis,	skin.	puente,	bridge.
dote,	dowry.	tribu,	tribe.
emblema,	emblem.		

---

* *Arte* is always feminine when used in the plural number.

† The compounds of *mar* are universally feminine; as, *bajamar*, low water; *pleamar*, high water.

‡ *Orden* is feminine when it means *order* in the sense of *command*.

EXERCISE ON THE GENDER OF NOUNS.

[The Gender of the Spanish nouns will not be pointed out in the exercises in future, as it is presumed the rules which refer to them will enable the student to distinguish them.]

Self-love and pride are the offspring of ignorance.
amor propio orgullo son   hijos ignorancia

Innocence, honour, and the love of virtue are estimable.
 inocencia   amor virtud apreciables

The summits of the mountains are very pleasant.
    cima   monte   muy agradables

Cultivation contributes to the fertility of the soil.
——————— contribuye   fertilidad   tierra

I require a footman and a maid-servant. My nephew
* necesito lacayo   criada   sobrino

and niece [are just arrived.] Who is her husband?
    acaban de llegar quién es su

Is that lady his wife? His son-in-law, and daughter-
 esa señora su   su

in-law are going in company with the Marquis and
   * van en compañia de

Marchioness. The situation of the country. The
   —————   pais

treatise appears to have been written by an historian.
tratado parece * haber sido escrito por historiador

The Duke and Duchess were walking with the Earl
      estaban paseando con

and Countess. Amplification or climax is a
   —— —— ——— [ó sea] graduacion

figure of speech that gradually heightens the
figura retórica que [va subiendo de grado en grado]

circumstances of an object. They follow the same
circunstancia   objeto * siguen mismo

system. He was decorated with the cross of honour.
  * fué condecorado con

The symptoms of the disease. It is the custom of
     enfermedad * es

the times. The brilliancy of their voices. The aridity
   tiempo   brillantez   sus   aridez
of that land. On the map are seen all the planets
  aquel terreno en   se   ven todos
and comets   recently   discovered.
        recientemente descubiertos

LECTURE VIII.

CASE.

1. CASE is that declension, or variation, to which nouns
and pronouns are subject, in their different positions
with regard to other nouns and pronouns, or to verbs and
prepositions. For instance, a noun that *governs* a verb
is in a very different position, or case, from a noun that
is governed *by* a verb. In the sentence, *The man struck
me*, it is obvious that the *man* is in a different position,
or state, from what he is in, *I struck the man*. In the
first example he is in the case of *governing* the verb
to strike; he is the *agent* of that verb; but in the second
he is governed *by* the verb, and is the *object* upon which
the action, or energy, of that verb falls. In the first
case he *acts;* in the second, he is *acted upon*.

2. Besides these two cases of acting, and being acted
upon, a noun or pronoun may be in the case of *possessing*
some person or thing; as, *Here is Edward's book;* in
which example *Edward* is the possessor of the noun *book*.
It may likewise be in the case of having something *sent*
or *directed* to it; as, *I sent the letter to Henry;* where
Henry is the *receiver* of the noun *letter*. It may also be
in the case of having something *separated*, or *taken away*
from it; as, *He took the book from the shelf;* where we
see that the noun *shelf* is in the case of having something
taken away from it. Or, it may be in the case of being
instrumental in the performing of an action; as, *The letter
was carried by John;* in which *John* is *instrumental* in

conveying the noun *letter*. Here, then, are nouns exhibited in five different positions or cases—namely, that of *acting*, that of *being acted upon*, that of *possessing*, that of *receiving*, and that of having something *separated from* it, and in being *instrumental* in the performance of an action (the latter two being included by grammarians in one case). These different cases are called, the NOMINATIVE, which denotes the *actor*; the GENITIVE, the *possessor*; the DATIVE, the *receiver*; the ACCUSATIVE, the *sufferer of an action*; and the ABLATIVE, either that which has something *separated from* it, or that which is *instrumental* in the performance of an action.

3. The names by which the cases are designated are of Latin origin; and the following is the manner in which nouns are declined in Latin, Spanish, and English :—

NOMINATIVE, .	Dominus,	*El Señor,*	The Lord.
GENITIVE, or POSSESSIVE }	Domini,	*Del Señor,*	Of the Lord.
DATIVE, ...	Domino	*Al Señor,*	To the Lord.
ACCUSATIVE, or OBJECTIVE, }	Dominum	*Al Señor,*	The Lord.
ABLATIVE, . . .	Domino,	*Por el Señor,*	By the Lord.

We here see that, in Latin, neither article nor preposition is required to designate the case of the nouns, the terminations alone of the nouns being adequate to that purpose; but, in Spanish and English, prepositions and articles are employed for this end.

Not always is the same preposition used with the same case in Spanish and English; indeed, very frequently a preposition is employed in one language, and not in the other. This is a subject of some difficulty in all languages; and, as regards the Spanish and English, it will be amply treated upon in its place.

4. In addition to the above five cases, we see in Latin grammars another case, called the VOCATIVE; as *Domine, O Señor, O Lord*. But, however, indispensable this case may be in Latin, it appears that it may be reasonably dispensed with in those languages in which nouns have not the inflections of Latin nouns, since a noun in the *vocative* case is evidently a nominative in a different

attitude; for when we say *O Lord*, we make use of an ellipsis, by leaving out the words that are wanted to make the sense complete; thus, *O* [*thou who art the*] *Lord;* and here we see that the noun *Lord* is the nominative case coming *after* the verb *art*, and *who* (the relative pronoun) is the nominative *before* the verb.

5. The cases, as before observed, are designated in Latin by the terminations of the noun; in English, one case—namely, the possessive—is frequently formed by the addition of an *s* with the apostrophe; as, *the Lord's*. In Spanish, the noun itself never undergoes any variation to denote case; but pronouns frequently do, in both Spanish and English.

6. We will now proceed to the explanation and application of the cases. Observe, first, that the nominative, being the case that governs, is itself never governed; the accusative is governed by verbs; the genitive, the dative, and the ablative are governed by prepositions.

7. A noun or pronoun is in the *nominative* case when it names a person or thing in a state of *being* or *doing* anything, at any period; as, *Charles is ill. He has written a letter. The ship will sail to-morrow*. In these examples, *Charles, he*, and the *ship* are each in the nominative case; the noun *Charles* denotes a person who is in a *state of being* ill; the pronoun *he* refers to a person who has performed some action—namely, that of *writing;* and the noun *ship* describes an inanimate object about to do something—namely, *to sail*. Therefore the person or thing that *is*, or that *acts*, is in the nominative case; and as *being* and *action* are expressed by verbs, the nominative *governs* the verb, and is the *subject* or *agent* of the verb.

The following are some examples, in Spanish and English, of nouns and pronouns in the nominative case:

José está durmiendo.	*Joseph* is asleep.
El escribe bien.	*He* writes well.
Los *árboles* crecen.	The *trees* grow.
Ellos han hablado.	*They* have spoken.

8. A noun or pronoun is in the *genitive* or *possessive* case when it describes anything as the *possessor* of any person or thing; as, *Maria's fan. His sword*. Or when it describes any person or thing to which another noun

relates; as, *The laws of the country. The Prince of Wales.* In these examples, the noun *Maria* and the pronoun *his* are in the *genitive* case; the former being the *possessor* of the noun *fan,* the latter of the noun *sword. Country* and *Wales* are likewise in the genitive case, because the noun *laws* relates to the first, and the noun *Prince* to the second. *De,* of, is the only preposition employed in the genitive case. Observe that *de* governs the ablative case when it means *from, by, out of,* etc., and is only employed in the genitive case when it means *of.* See PAR. 12.

The following are examples in the genitive case:—

El caballo *de Pedro.*	*Peter's* horse.
El reinado *de Augusto.*	The reign *of Augustus.*
Su libro. *Sus* plumas.	*His* book. *Their* pens.

9. Those persons or things to which any thing is *given, sent,* or *directed,* or for which any thing is *intended,* are in the *dative* case; as, *I gave the book to Horace. He sent James a present. Frederick bought the desk for Alfred. They wrote him a letter.* In these examples we see that the nouns *Horace, James, Alfred,* and the persons represented by the pronoun *him,* have respectively something *given, sent, directed to,* or *intended for* them; and that they are the *receivers* of the things so *given, sent,* etc. Nouns in the dative case are preceded by the prepositions *á,* or *para—to,* or *for.* Pronouns in this case are sometimes, but not always, preceded by prepositions. See the Declension of Pronouns after PAR. 13.

Observe that a noun or pronoun in the dative case is not the *direct* or *immediate* object of the verb; that is the action of the verb does not fall immediately upon it; it is the *indirect* object: the thing *given, sent,* etc., is the immediate object of the verb, and is in the *accusative* or *objective* case, as we shall presently see.

Examples in the dative case:—

Escribí *al Capitan.*	I wrote *to the Captain.*
Él lo compró *para Elena.*	He bought it *for Helen.*
Le enviarán la carta.	They will send *him* the letter.
Ella *les* ha dado la noticia.	She has given *them* the news.

Note.—The prepositions *á* and *para* govern the dative case only when the noun which they precede receives the benefit or injury of the action of the verb, as in the above examples; otherwise they govern the accusative. See PAR. 11.

10. A noun or pronoun is in the *accusative* or *objective* case when it represents the person or thing affected by some action done to it, or on which the action of the verb falls; as, *James beat Henry. Charles vexed him.* In the first example, *Henry* is the *object beaten;* the action of the verb falls on him. In the second, the person represented by the pronoun *him* is the object of the verb *to vex*, and is affected by the action of that verb. All nouns and pronouns in this case are the *immediate* or *direct objects* of the verb, as noticed before. Generally speaking, when the noun in the accusative case represents a *person*, it is preceded in Spanish by the preposition *á*. See observations on this preposition, PAR. 13.

Examples in the accusative case :—

Ignacio ama *á Carlota.*	Ignatius loves *Charlotte.*
He escrito una *carta.*	I have written a *letter.*
Teresa *le* vió.	Theresa saw *him.*
El *la* estima.	He esteems *her.*

11. Besides the preposition *á*, the following prepositions sometimes govern the accusative case—namely, *ante, contra. entre, hacia, hasta, para, segun, tras :* Ex.

Respondió *á* la carta.	He answered the letter.
Compareció *ante* el juez.	He appeared *before* the judge.
Dió *contra* la peña.	It struck *against* the rock.
Le hallé *entre* la gente.	I found him *amongst* the people.
Van *hacia* Valencia.	They are going *towards* Valencia.
Fueron *hasta* Segovia.	They went *as far as* Segovia.
Salió *para* Madrid.	He set out *for* Madrid.
Es *segun* la ley.	It is *according to* law.
Tras el Duque venia el Conde.	*After* the Duke came the Count.

The preposition *por*, through, by, also governs the

accusative when preceded by verbs denoting movement; as. *Pasó* por *mi ventana :* He passed *by* my window. But when it is preceded by verbs that do not denote movement, it governs the *ablative* case; as, *Lo hice* por *yerro :* I did it *through* mistake. *Agrada* por *su cortesía :* Ho pleases *by* his courteous behaviour.

The preposition *sobre*, above, upon, likewise governs the accusative when it denotes *moral superiority ;* as, *La caridad es* sobre *todas las virtudes :* Charity is *above* all virtues. But when it denotes *locality*, it governs tho *ablative ;* as, *Está* sobre *la mesa :* It is *upon* tho table.

12. A noun or pronoun is in the *ablative* case whcn it denotes a person or thing in the state of having something *taken away*, or *separated* from it; as, *He drew the money from his pocket. They separated the child from the mother.* Here the nouns *pocket* and *mother* are in the *ablative* case, because each has had something *taken* or *separated* from it. The person or thing that is *instrumental* in the doing of an action, or that denotes tho *means through*, or *by* which a thing is done, is likewiso in the *ablative* case; as, *He succeeded through the aid of his friends. The box was sent by the coach.*

Besides the prepositions *de, por,* and *sobre,* already mentioned, the following aro also employed in the ablative case—namely, *con,* with; *desde,* from; *en,* in; *sin,* without.

Examples in tho ablative case :—

Ho recibido una carta *de* mi *socio.*	I have received a letter *from* my *partner.*
Trage este libro *de* la *librería.*	I brought this book *from* the *library.*
Lo hizo *de,* or *por envidia.*	He did it *through envy.*
Murió *de* una *caida.*	He was killed *by* a *fall.*
La música está *sobre* el *piano.*	The music is *upon* tho *piano.*
Fueron *con él.*	They went *with him.*
Vengo *desde Granada* á caballo.	I come *from Granada* on horseback.
Van *en coche.*	They are going *in* a *coach.*
Estoy *sin dinero.*	I am *without money.*

OBSERVATIONS ON THE EMPLOYMENT OF THE PREPOSITION *á* IN THE ACCUSATIVE OR OBJECTIVE CASE.

13. Active verbs in Spanish generally govern a noun in the accusative case with the preposition *á*, if it represent a person. The use of the preposition *á* is to point out the immediate object of the verb, when it is not sufficiently denoted without its assistance; a circumstance that very frequently occurs in Spanish, from the great variety of syntactical inversion, which the language admits, as will be observed by the following sentence, which may, with the same words, be expressed in six different ways, without altering the sense in the least; and where, but for the preposition, we could not ascertain which of the two nouns was the nominative, and which the object of the verb. (See Construction of Nouns, PAR. 14): Ex.

Cain mató á Abel . . .	
Cain á Abel mató . . .	
Á Abel mató Cain . . .	Cain killed Abel.
Á Abel Cain mató . . .	
Mató Cain á Abel . . .	
Mató á Abel Cain . . .	

When the immediate object of the verb is not an animate being, the preposition *á* is seldom used; except, sometimes, when both the nominative and the accusative are of the same number; in which latter case the preposition may be of use to prevent ambiguity: Ex. *El árbol abrigó á la casa* : The tree sheltered the house.

Here the preposition points out *casa* to be the object of the verb; and if, the syntactical order of the sentence be inverted, thus, *A la casa abrigó el árbol*, still *casa* appears in the objective case; but if we dispense with the preposition *á* in the sentence as it now stands, its meaning would be quite the opposite to what it was in its original form; since it would signify, *The house sheltered the tree.*

Sentences occur in which there are two nouns of the same number, one in the *accusative*, the other in the *dative* case, and both representing *persons*; as, *We sent the* captain *to the* merchant. Now, if in translating this sentence into Spanish we employ the preposition *á* before both nouns, it would produce ambiguity, for we should not know whether the person sent was the captain or the merchant. Therefore, to avoid obscurity in instances of this nature, we should dispense with the preposition in the *accusative* case, and employ it only in the *dative;* thus, *Enviámos* el *capitan* al *negociante;* and not *Enviámos* al *capitan* al *negociante.*

Upon the whole, therefore, there seems always to have existed a tendency to the general adoption of the preposition *á* before *personal* nouns in the accusative case. And as regards nouns that do not represent persons, it would be advisable to employ the preposition in such instances only where the object of the verb is not sufficiently conspicuous without it; and, generally, where ambiguity might result from its exclusion. This method would be the safest to practise, and would harmonise with the idiom of the Spanish language.

DECLENSION OF NOUNS WITH THE ARTICLE.

Masculine nouns referring to persons.

Singular.

Nom.	El hombre,	The man.
Gen.	del hombre,	of the man.
Dat.	al hombre, *or* para el hombre,	to *or* for the man.
Acc.	al hombre,	the man.
Abl.	por, de, en, sin, con, sobre el hombre,	by, from, in, without, with, upon the man.

Plural.

Nom.	Los hombres,	The men.
Gen.	de los hombres,	of the men.
Dat.	á *or* para los hombres,	to *or* for the men.
Acc.	á los hombres,	the men.
Abl.	por, etc., los hombres,	by, etc., the men.

Feminine nouns referring to persons.
Singular.

NOM.	La muger,	The woman.
GEN.	de la muger,	of the woman.
DAT.	á *or* para la muger,	to *or* for the woman.
ACC.	á la muger,	the woman.
ABL.	por, etc., la muger,	by, etc., the woman.

Plural.

NOM.	Las mugeres,	The women.
GEN.	de las mugeres,	of the women.
DAT.	á *or* para las mugeres,	to *or* for the women.
ACC.	á las mugeres,	the women.
ABL.	por, etc., las mugeres.	by, etc., the women.

Masculine nouns referring to things.

Singular.

NOM.	El libro,	The book.
GEN.	del libro,	of the book.
DAT.	al libro *or* para el libro,	to *or* for the book.
ACC.	el libro,	the book.
ABL.	por, etc., el libro,	by, etc., the book.

Plural.

NOM.	Los libros,	The books.
GEN.	de los libros,	of the books.
DAT.	á *or* para los libros,	to *or* for the books.
ACC.	los libros,	the books.
ABL.	por, etc., los libros,	by, etc., the books.

Feminine nouns referring to things.
Singular.

NOM.	La carta,	The letter.
GEN.	de la carta,	of the letter.
DAT.	á *or* para la carta,	to *or* for the letter.
ACC.	la carta,	the letter.
ABL.	por, etc., la carta,	by, etc., the letter.

Plural.

Nom.	Las cartas.	The letters.
Gen.	de las cartas.	of the letters.
Dat.	á *or* para las cartas,	to *or* for the letters.
Acc.	las cartas,	the letters.
Abl.	por, etc., las cartas,	by, etc., the letters.

CONSTRUCTION OF NOUNS.

14. In the natural order of the construction of Spanish nouns, the nominative precedes, and the accusative follows the verb, as is the case in English; but this order, for the sake of energy, elegance, or euphony, may be inverted in Spanish at pleasure, placing the nominative after, and the accusative before the verb. The latter inversion, however, does not occur so frequently as the former. The latitude of inversion of the syntactical order which is allowed in Spanish gives to it a power, facility, and beauty, which, perhaps, no other modern language possesses to the same extent: Ex.

NOMINATIVE AFTER THE VERB.

Con la precipitada ruina del imperio de occidente *varió* del todo el *semblante* político de la Europa; y *cesando* desde entónces las *relaciones* y mútuos *intereses* de las partes principales de aquel gran cuerpo social, y *quebrantados* los *eslabones* que unian las vastas provincias del imperio con su capital, que los débiles mortales llamaban ciudad eterna, se *vieron* como de repente nacer, crecer, y levantarse sobre las ruinas y escombros del viejo imperio todas las *monarquías* modernas. —(Marina — *Ensayo Hist. Crit.*)

With the precipitate ruin of the empire of the west, the political aspect of all Europe changed entirely; and the relations and mutual interests of the principal parts of that great social body ceasing from that period, and the links being broken that united the vast provinces of the empire with the capital, which weak mortals called the eternal city, all the modern monarchies were seen to spring up suddenly, grow, and raise themselves on the ruins and fragments of the old empire.

Dió voces la castísima *Su-*
sana entónces, y *viendo*
los atrevidos *viejos*, etc.—
(LOPE DE VEGA.—*Pastores de Belen.*)

The chaste Susanna then
called aloud, and the dar-
ing old men seeing, etc.

Así, en todas las lenguas,
arde el *corazon, ciega* la
cólera, embriaga el *amor.*
(—CAPMANY.—*Filosofía de la Elocuencia.*)

Thus, in all languages,
the heart kindles, anger
blinds, love intoxicates...

ACCUSATIVE BEFORE THE VERB.

Pocas *cosas tenemos* que no
sean comunes á todos.
Tenemos muchas abili-
dades que feliz *fin* nos
prometen. — (CERVÁNTES.
La Gitanilla.)

Few things we possess that
are not common to all.
We have many abilities
that promise us a happy
end.

15. The genitive, the dative, and the ablative, always
follow the prepositions by which they are governed : Ex.

La casa es *de Juan.* The house is John's.
Enviaron la noticia *á Pedro.* They sent the news to Peter.
Irán *con* el *criado.* They will go with the ser-
vant.

The order of these sentences may be inverted, as far
as regards the position of the verb ; still, however, the
preposition must invariably precede the noun ; as, *Es de*
Juan la casa. A Pedro enviaron la noticia. Con el criado
irán.

16. When in English two nouns follow each other,
the first specifying the kind, purpose, occupation, or the
like, of the other, their order is reversed in the translation, and the second noun in Spanish is placed in the
genitive case, preceded by the preposition *de :* Ex.

Mesa de caoba. Mahogany table.
Cerradura de puerta. Door-lock.
Relojes de oro. Gold watches.
Oficial de artillería. Artillery officer.

17. The same inversion of order is likewise observed
when one or more possessive cases follow one another in
English ; and the nouns are all translated in a retro-
grading order : Ex.

Los rayos del sol.	The sun's rays.
El caballo del padre de Juan.	John's father's horse.
La hermana de la esposa de mi tio.	My uncle's wife's sister.

Sometimes the same order is used in English also; in such cases, whether the second noun be preceded by *of* or by *to*, it always requires *de* in Spanish : Ex.

Son primos *del* duque.	They are cousins *to* the duke.
El cumplimiento *de* las leyes *del* estado.	The fulfilment *of* the laws *of* the state.

If the English noun with the sign ('s) be preceded by *of*, the preposition and article are required before both nouns in Spanish. Should, however, one of the nouns be preceded by a possessive pronoun, this supplies the place of the article : Ex.

Dos de los criados del duque.	Two servants of the duke's.
Uno de los ministros de su majestad.	One of her majesty's ministers.

18. There are sentences in English in which the sign of the possessive case ('s) is employed as a substitute for the noun which it represents ; as, *He lives at the general's;* where the *'s* occupies the place of *house* or *residence ;* in such instances the order of the foregoing example is observed in the translation; translating *house,* or *residence,* by *casa* : Ex.

Vive en casa del general.	He lives at the general's.
Vengo de casa del médico.	I come from the doctor's.

EXERCISE ON THE CONSTRUCTION OF NOUNS.

The human (2) heart (1) [is not satisfied] with what
   humano   corazon   no se   harta   con

fortune or heaven [bestows on it]. The estimation of sati-
fortuna   cielo.   le concede.   ——————   satí-

rical (2) works (1) increases with their prohibition.
ricas   obra   crece   la   ——————

Valour is seldom found where modesty [is wanting].
valor [pocas veces se halla] donde   falta

In   any   species of virtue one individual (2) act (1)
en cualquiera especie   particular   acto

[does not suffice]   for   a man to be virtuous. In
    no basta   para que   * sea

war,   judgment   conquers more than arms. They
guerra entendimiento vence   mas que arma

   attacked the castle on the [weakest side]. Good
acometieron   castillo por   lado mas flaco. buenas

actions should exceed offences. This letter is for you,
 obra [han de exceder] ofensa   esta carta   para

and the newspaper for me. The dispatches will go by
       diario   mí   despacho   * irán

the post. The two adversaries fought with pistols.
 correo   dos adversario riñeron   pistola

She is [first cousin] to the ambassador of Austria's
       prima hermana   embajador   ——————

daughter. Here is your watch chain.   The bed
  hija   aquí está su   reloj cadena   cama

curtains were of India muslin. The front of the
cortina   eran   ——— muselina   frontera

 edifice was adorned with marble columns; in the
edificio estaba adornada de mármol columna;

interior were seen several bronze statues. Show me
——————— se veian varias bronce estátua [muéstreme Vmd.]

the   straw hats, buck-skin gloves, and the silk
    paja sombrero ante cuero guante   seda

ribbons. My brother's house is situated near to the
cinta   mi hermano   está situada cerca de

Governor's garden. He is at the shoemaker's. I
Gobernador   * está en   zapatero   Yo

saw (2) them (1) at the tailor's. I speak of the Duke's
ví   los   sastre * hablo   Duque

brother's conduct.   Anacreon flourished   after
       conducta   ——————— floreció [despues de]

Homer's death, and after the defeat of Croesus, the
Homero muerte, f.   derrota   Creso

King of Lydia. Darius's son, Xerxes, ascended the throne
 Rey   Lidia   Dario hijo Sérses ascendió al trono
of Persia after his father's death.
———   su

———

LECTURE IX.

ETYMOLOGY AND SYNTAX OF ADJECTIVES.

GENERAL AGREEMENT WITH THE NOUN.

1. Adjectives, and participles used as adjectives, agree
in Spanish in *number* and *gender* with the nouns to which
they refer, as, *Un hombre alto*, a tall man; *una muger alta*,
a tall woman; *hombres altos*, tall men; *mugeres altas*,
tall women.

Observe that the plural of adjectives is formed in
precisely the same manner as the plural of nouns.

AGREEMENT IN NUMBER.

2. An adjective that refers to two or more nouns *singular* is used in the *singular* number if it *precedes* the nouns,
and in the *plural* if it *follows* them : Ex.

El *merecido* aplauso y elogio	) The merited applause
El aplauso y elogio *merecidos*	) and praise.

3. When the adjective refers to nouns of *different*
numbers, it is put in the *plural* if it *follows* the nouns,
and agrees in number with the *first* if it *precedes*
them: Ex.

Su palacio y jardines *hermosos*	) His beautiful palace
Su *hermoso* palacio y jardines	) and gardens.
Sus palacios y jardin *hermosos*	) His beautiful palaces
Sus *hermosos* palacios y jardin	) and garden.

But should a verb intervene between the noun and
the adjective that precedes it, the adjective should be in
the plural number: Ex.

Inclusos van factura y cono-	Enclosed are the invoice
cimientos.	and bills of lading.

AGREEMENT IN GENDER.

4. Adjectives agree in gender with the nouns to which they refer, according to the following rules : previously, however, to the pupil's becoming acquainted with them, it is necessary that he should know how to distinguish the gender of adjectives. This will be first explained.

5. Adjectives that terminate in *an, on, or,* and *o,* are of the *masculine* gender; those ending in *an, on,* and *or,* are made feminine by the addition of an *a;* and those ending in *o,* by changing this vowel into *a:* those that end in any other letter are common to both genders : Ex.

Un hombre *haragan.*	An indolent man.
Una muger *haragana.*	An indolent woman.
Un muchacho *jugueton.*	A playful boy.
Una muchacha *juguetona.*	A playful girl.
Un hombre *emprendedor.*	An enterprising man.
Una muger *emprendedora.*	An enterprising woman.
Un guerrero *famoso.*	A famous warrior.
Una accion *famosa.*	A famous action.
El marido *feliz.*	The happy husband.
La esposa *feliz.*	The happy wife.
Un motivo *evidente.*	An evident motive.
Una prueba *evidente.*	An evident proof.

Of those ending in *or,* the following are exceptions, as they have only one termination : *inferior,* inferior; *mayor,* greater; *mejor,* better ; *menor,* less ; *peor,* worse ; *superior,* superior ; and *ulterior,* ulterior.

6. Adjectives that qualify the feminine noun *nada* are always used in the masculine termination : Ex.

Nada es mas *contagioso* que el ejemplo.	Nothing is more contagious than example.
Nada es mas *cierto.*	Nothing is more certain.

7. To adjectives derived from the names of kingdoms, countries, etc., ending in a consonant, an *a* is generally added to form their feminine termination : those that end in *o* change this vowel into *a* and those ending in *e* are common to both genders : Thus, *Inglés,* m. *inglesa,* f. English. *Español,* m. *española,* f. Spanish. *Americano,* m. *Americana,* f. American. *Arabe,* m. and f. Arabian.

8. When this kind of adjectives is employed in Eng-

lish with reference to articles of commerce, the productions of a country, and such like, the noun expressive of the name of the country that produces those articles, or in which they are manufactured, is generally used in Spanish instead of the adjective; thus, Spanish wine, *Vino de España.* French Silks, *Seda de Francia.* Literally, Wine of Spain; Silk of France.

9. The same construction is likewise generally observed, in Spanish, in referring to persons of whom we rather intend to describe the country from which they come, or in whose government they are employed, than the place of their nativity : as, *El Embajador de Austria,* The Austrian Ambassador. *El Cónsul de España,* The Spanish Consul. This, however, must not be taken as an absolute rule, for such sentences may also be translated thus, *Seda Francesa, El Cónsul Español,* etc.

10. We have now to consider the *agreement* of adjectives in *gender* with the nouns which they qualify. Adjectives that refer to two or more nouns *singular*, of *different* genders, are employed in the masculine gender if they *follow* the nouns; but agree in gender with the first noun if they *precede* the nouns : Ex.

El egército y la armada *derotados.*	The army and navy defeated.
La armada y el egército *derotados y destruidos.*	The navy and army defeated and destroyed.
Su *hermoso episodio* y novela.	His beautiful episode and novel.
Su *hermosa y entretenida novela* y episodio.	His beautiful and entertaining novel and episode.

11. When adjectives refer to *two* or *more* nouns *plural,* whether they are put before or after them, they agree in gender with the *nearest* noun : Ex.

Las *hermosas montañas* y valles.	The beautiful mountains and valleys.
Los *hermosos y amenos valles* y montañas.	The beautiful and pleasant valleys and mountains.
Los castillos y *baterías bombardeadas.*	The bombarded castles and batteries.
Las baterías y *castillos bombardeados y tomados.*	The batteries and castles bombarded and taken.

12. When the adjective refers to nouns of *different numbers* and *genders*, it is generally put in the plural number and masculine gender if it follow the nouns, and made to agree with the first when it precedes the nouns: Ex.

El (*incluso*) conocimiento y facturas (*inclusos*).	The enclosed bill of lading and invoices.
Los (*inclusos*)conocimientos y factura (*inclusos*).	The enclosed bills of lading and invoice.
La (*inclusa*) factura y conocimientos (*inclusos*).	The enclosed invoice and bills of lading
Las (*inclusas*) facturas y conocimiento (*inclusos*).	The enclosed invoices and bill of lading.

Note.—We should nevertheless endeavour to avoid qualifying two nouns that differ in gender and number, with an adjective that admits of both the masculine and feminine terminations. For instance, though we may see examples of the following nature, *Los* vinos *y la* fruta *eran* exquisitos,—The wines and fruit were exquisite; *Las* frutas *y el* vino *eran* exquisitos,—The fruits and wine were exquisite; yet there is something in them that offends the ear. In such cases it would be much better to employ an adjective of the common gender; as, *Los* vinos *y la* fruta *eran* excelentes—The wines and fruit were excellent; *Las* frutas *y el* vino *eran* admirables—The fruits and wine were admirable; or to employ a corresponding adjective with each noun; as, *Los* vinos *eran* exquisitos *y la* fruta deliciosa—The wines were excellent and the fruit delicious; *Las* frutas *eran* deliciosas *y el* vino exquisito—The fruits were delicious and the wine exquisite.—GRAMMAR OF THE ACADEMY.

13. Adjectives referring to the *titles* of individuals, agree in gender with the *persons* to whom the titles belong: Ex.

Su *Alteza* está *indispuesto*.	His Highness is indisposed.
Son muy *bondadosos* sus *Señorías*.	Their lordships are very kind.
Su *Alteza* está *indispuesta*.	Her Highness is indisposed.
Son muy *bondadosas* sus *Señorías*.	Their Ladyships are very kind.

14. With nouns that are common to both genders the

adjective varies to distinguish the gender; as, *Un jóven hermoso*, A handsome youth. *Una jóven hermosa*, A handsome lass.

15. When the adjectives *bueno, malo,* and *postrero,* precede a noun masculine singular, they drop the final *o;* as, *Un buen hombre,* A good man. *Un mal consejo,* A bad advice. *El postrer dia,* The last day.

Note.—See also the numeral adjectives *uno, primero, tercero,* and *ciento.* (LECT. 12, PAR. 1 to 4.)

16. *Santo,* saint, when employed in the singular number, before proper names of persons and places, drops the last syllable, except before *Domingo, Tomás, Tomé,* and *Toribio* ; as, *San Pablo,* Saint Paul ; *San Juan,* Saint John ; *San Petersburgo,* Saint Petersburgh ; *Santo Tomás,* St. Thomas; *Santo Domingo,* St. Dominique.

17. *Grande,* great or large, when used before a noun in the *singular* number of either gender, beginning with a consonant, generally drops the final syllable ; and also when, in referring to nouns, it rather conveys an idea of *size* or *quantity* than of *greatness* or *excellence ;* in which latter sense it generally retains the final syllable; and also when the substantive which follows it begins with a vowel or with *h.* This, however, is not to be taken as an absolute rule ; as, *Un gran castillo,* A large castle. *Una gran fiesta,* A great feast. *Un gran cuchillo,* A large knife. *Grande amor,* Great love. *Grande hazaña,* A great achievement.

EXERCISE ON THE AGREEMENT OF ADJECTIVES IN
NUMBER AND GENDER.

Disinterestedness and honour deserve to be praised.
   desinterés   ———— merecen * ser alabado

Her virtue and her beauty are universally admired·
   virtud   hermosura son universalmente admirado

Modesty, affability, and kindness are recommendable.
modestia afabilidad   bondad son recomendable

[Let us reflect] on the sad consequences that are
 reflexionemos en   triste consecuencia que son

inseparable from protracted (2) wars (1). His fears
———————— dilatado guerra   temor

were vain.   The streets and squares of the city are
fueron vano   calle   plaza   ciudad

spacious, and the public (2) buildings (1) magnificent.
espacioso   público   edificio   magnífico

It is a convincing (2) and palpable (3) proof (1).   He is
* es convincente   ————   prueba   * es

a brave (2) and faithful (3) man (1).   She is very
   bizarro   fiel   *   muy

   lazy.   They live in a fine house [on the banks]
holgazan   * viven en   bella   á orillas

of a rich (2) river (1), near a   small village.
     caudaloso   rio   [cerca de] pequeño aldea

These are consolatory (2) tidings (1).   They possess
estas son consolador   noticia   *   poseen

considerable moral (2) strength (1) and heroic virtue ;
   mucho   ————   fuerza   heróica

   ardent (2) imaginations (1) and noble (2) hearts (1).
ardiente   ————————   ————   corazon

It is a happy (2) idea (1).   He is a happy (2) man (1).
*   feliz   ————   *

A sagacious (2) boy (1).   A sagacious girl.   A
       sagaz   muchacho

French (2) frigate (1) and a Spanish (2) schooner (1)
francés   fragata   español   goleta

have arrived from the Danish (2) colonies (1).   That
han llegado   dinamarqués colonia   aquella

is a Spanish (2) cloak (1).   Those ladies are
               capa   aquellas señora son

Portuguese.   Spanish wool is considered very good.   I
portugués   lana se· considera muy   *

have purchased some French goods.   The Russian
he comprado   género

Plenipotentiary and the English Ambassador had
Plenipotenciario   tuvieron

a conference with the French Emissary.   Honour and
  conferencia   Emisario

virtue are solid.   Fame and valour are celebrated.   He
     son sólido   fama   valor   celebrado   *

has a beautiful house and garden.   His   usual
tiene   su acostumbrado

haughtiness   and   pride.   Such   discussions   and
     altivez   orgullo.   tal   ——————

  reasonings are frivolous.   I do not give ear to tales
razonamiento son   frívolo   yo * no presto oido cuento

and stories so   ill founded.   His Holiness and their
     historia tan mal fundado   su Santidad   sus

Worships   were   escorted   to   their   palaces.   His
Dignidad fueron escoltado   palacio

Lordship the Earl of B. was presented to Her Majesty
  Señoría   Conde   fué presentado   su Majestad

the Queen, who was   attended   by their Ladyships
               que estaba acompañado de   Señoría

the Marchionesses of E. The conscience of a good man
                                 conciencia   bueno

 is   ever   free, but [that of a bad man] [is a prey to
está siempre libre mas   la del malo   está en un

continual   remorse.] He preached from the epistles
contínuo remordimiento * predicaba   epístola

of St. Paul.   They   came   lately   from the islands
     Pablo   * vinieron últimamente   isla

of St. Dominic and St. Thomas.   A great project!   A
   Domingo   Tomas   proyecto

great victory. That is a great deed. [I have no] great
 .victoria   ese es   hecho   no tengo

appetite.   A large ship.
 apetito   navío.

LECTURE X.

SITUATION OF THE ADJECTIVE.

1. Adjectives in Spanish *generally follow* the nouns to which they refer : Ex.

El objeto *principal*.	The *principal* object.
El egército *inglés*.	The *English* army.
Una vida *ociosa*.	An *idle* life.

2. To the foregoing rule the following instances are exceptions, as in them the adjective *usually precedes* the noun.

1st. Adjectives employed as attributes, or that denote the natural or inherent properties of nouns, as also those used as epithets : Ex.

Los *hermosos colores* del iris.	The beautiful colours of the rainbow.
El *duro hierro*.	The hard iron.
El *paciente Job*.	The patient Job.
El *soberbio Lúcifer*.	The proud Lucifer.

2nd. Adjectives accented on the antepenult; hence, likewise, superlatives that terminate in *ísimo* : Ex.

Su *pérfida conducta*.	His perfidious conduct.
Son *hermosísimas obras*.	They are most beautiful works.
Qué *bellísimo dia!*	What a very fine day !

3rd. Numeral adjectives : Ex.

Veinte hombres.	Twenty men.
La *primera* cosa.	The first thing.

In referring to royalty and other dignities, however, the numeral adjective *follows* the noun : Ex.

Isabel *Segunda*.	Isabelle the Second.
Gregorio *Primero*.	Gregory the First.

4th. The adjectives *todo, mucho, poco, pocos, cierto,*

cada, varios, tal, dicho, mismo, (all, much, little, few,
certain, each or every, several, such, said, same,) likewise generally *precede* the noun : Ex.

Todo el mundo.	All the world.
Todas las señoras.	All the ladies.
Mucho dinero.	Much money.
Muchas veces.	Many times.
Poco mérito.	Little merit.
Pocas alabanzas.	Few praises.
Cierto sujeto.	A certain person.
Ciertas indicaciones.	Certain indications.
Cada indivíduo.	Each individual.
Varias cosas.	Various things.
Tal hombre.	Such a man.
Tales personas.	Such persons.
Dicho hombre y *dichas* mugeres.	The said man and women.
El *mismo* dia.	The same day.
Las *mismas* ideas.	The same ideas.

Cierto, nevertheless, in the sense of *sure,* generally
follows the noun : Ex.

Es cosa *cierta.*	It is a certain thing.
Son noticias *ciertas.*	They are certain news.

3. The foregoing rules on the situation of adjectives,
are not to be considered as *positive* rules; the situation
of the adjective depends much on taste ; as writers, for
the sake of energy, harmony, and variety, place the
adjective variously with respect to the noun which it
qualifies. As a general rule, it might be said that adjectives in Spanish commonly *follow* the noun, except when,
for particular emphasis or elegance, they are placed
before it. For instance, in the following example, Lope
DE VEGA adds greater emphasis to the meaning of the
adjectives, and more elegance to the construction of the
clause, by placing them before the nouns : "*Entre otras*
apacibles *partes que alegraban y ennoblecian el* ameno
sitio, era un espeso *bosque de* blancos *álamos,*" etc.—
Amongst other pleasant parts that enlivened and embel-
lished the delightful spot, was a thick forest of white
poplars, etc. Again, CADALSO, in describing the local

situation of Spain, says, "*Esta* feliz *situacion la hizo objeto de la codicia de los Fenicios y otros pueblos.*"—This happy locality made her an object of the desire of the Phœnicians and other nations. In which he no doubt placed the adjective *feliz* before the noun *situacion,* because it was his principal intention to express the *superiority* of the local situation of Spain. In the following sentence, MARINA, in his *Ensayo Histórico-Crítico,* adds more harmony, strength, and elegance to its construction by appropriately placing some of the adjectives before the nouns : "*El* grandioso y magnífico *espectáculo de la historia general de la especie humana, y su* varia *y* continuada *perspectiva de acontecimientos extraordinarios y trasformaciones políticas,*" etc.—The grand and magnificent spectacle of the general history of the human species, and its varied and continued perspective of extraordinary events and political transformations," etc.

EXERCISE ON THE SITUATION OF THE ADJECTIVE.

The sight of a fine landscape is an inexhaustible
    vista   bello paisage   inagotable
source of delightful sensations. Various parts in
manantial   delicioso ————   vario punto de
North   America discover evident signs of remote
septentrional   descubren evidente indicio remoto
epochs, and prove the existence of a great and powerful
época   manifiestan existencia   poderoso
people, whose history [is doubtless lost] for ever.
poblacion cuya historia sin duda se perdió para siempre
Immense heights, unfrequented by the modern Indians,
inmenso elevacion no frecuentado por   moderno Indio
covered with human bones, unknown arms, remains
cubierto de humano hueso desconocido arma resto
of walled cities, and numerous inscriptions in unknown
circundado ciudad numeroso ———— desconocido
languages, announce the indisputable existence of a
idioma, *m.* anuncian   ————

people, different from those which European navigators
pueblo diferente   aquellos que   européo navegante

   found   in those countries.   The fierce lion devoured
encontraron   pais   fiero leon [devoró á]

the tame sheep.   On   that   step   of   hard   marble
   manso oveja   sobre aquel escalon   duro   mármol

she rested her   weary   limbs.   The   cold   snow
   * reposó sus fatigado miembro   frio niеve, f.

withered the delicate flowers.   My dear father; where
marchitó   delicado flor, f.   querido   dónde

   are   my   dear   sisters? The wise Solomon ; the
están mis   hermana   sabio ——————

   worthy   Titus ; the ambitious Alexander.   What
benemérito Tito   ambicioso Alejandro

[a very fine] day ! The regiment consisted of twelve
  bellísimo   regimiento [se componia]   doce

companies of fifty men   each.   They captured
compañía   cincuenta   [cada una]   *   apresaron

all the ships and   sunk   all the gun   boats.
      navío   [echaron á pique]   cañonera lancha

He made many friends, but contracted many debts·
  * hizo   amigo pero   contrajo   deuda

Many are the disappointments in the life of man. Few
         son   contratiempo   vida

men are happy.   His virtues are few. A certain friend
         sus   amigo

of mine gave (2) me (1) certain instructions respecting a
 * mio dió   —   ·   ·————— [acerca de]

certain person. It is a certain thing. Every day
   persona   * es   cosa

   you come   you will examine each lesson. Such
[que Vmd. venga] *   *   repasará   leccion

orders could never have been given by such a general.
  órden   * más pudieran ser dadas

LECTURE XI.

DEGREES OF COMPARISON.

1. As adjectives express some quality or property of the noun, this quality or property, when compared with that of other nouns, may be *equal, superior,* or *inferior* to it: for instance, *Your cloth is* fine, *his is* finer, *but mine is the* finest *of the three.* Here are specified *three* different *degrees* in the quality of the cloth; these are called *degrees of comparison,* and are distinguished by the names of *positive, comparative* and *superlative.*

2. The *positive* expresses the quality without any reference or comparison, as in the foregoing example, *Your cloth is fine;* but when we say *his is finer,* there is a *comparison* drawn between the two ; and in the conclusion of the sentence, *mine is the finest of the three,* the quality of the cloth is placed in the *highest degree* of fineness as regards the three qualities.

3. In the *comparative* there are three states to be considered— namely, that of *equality,* that of *superiority,* and that of *inferiority;* as, *My house is* as *commodious as* yours; *Yours is* more *commodious than his; His is* less *commodious than theirs.*

4. The superlative expresses the quality in the *highest* or *lowest* degree : it is of two kinds, the one *relative,* the other *absolute.* The superlative *relative* expresses the quality of one thing with reference to that of others ; as, *This is the* handsomest *house in the square.* But the superlative *absolute* expresses the quality of an object without reference to any other object ; as, *This is a* very handsome, *or a* most elegant *house.*

FORMATION OF THE DEGREES OF COMPARISON IN SPANISH.

THE COMPARATIVE.

5. The comparative of *equality* is formed in Spanish by placing the word *tan* (so *or* as) before, and *como* (as) after the adjective : Ex.

El es *tan* rico *como* su her-   He is *as* rich *as* his brother.
mano.

If an *adjective* follow the comparative instead of a noun, *cuan* may be used in the place of *como*; as, Es tan rico *cuan soberbio*: or, Es tan rico *como soberbio*—He is as rich as he is proud. The latter form, however, is more frequently used.

Generally speaking, nevertheless, *cuan* (which is abbreviated from *cuanto*, like *tan* from *tanto*) is mostly used in the sense of the English comparative adverb *how*, employed in admiration; as in the following passage of FR. ANT. DE GUEVARA, in his *Reloj de Príncipes*, when he proposes Marcus Aurelius to Charles V. as a model worthy of his imitation:—*Ved, Serenísimo Príncipe, la vida de este príncipe, y vereis* cuan *claro fué en su juicio,* cuan *recto en su justicia,* cuan *recatado en su vida,* cuan *agradecido á sus amigos,* cuan *sufrido en los trabajos, etc.*— Observe, Illustrious Prince, the life of this prince, and you will see *how* clear he was in his judgment, *how* correct in his justice, *how* careful in his living, *how* grateful to his friends, *how* patient in troubles, etc.

In a negative sense, no other alteration is required in Spanish than to place the negative particle before the verb; and this applies to all the following comparisons : Ex.

No es *tan* fuerte *como* el   It is *not so* strong *as the*
otro.   other.

6. The comparative of *superiority* is formed by placing the word *mas* (more) before the adjective, and *que* (than) after it ; that of *inferiority*, by *ménos* (less) before, and *que* after: Ex.

Es *mas* rico *que* su hermano.   He is *richer than* his brother.
Es *ménos* vana *que* hermosa.   She is *less* vain *than* beautiful.

7. When both the comparative of equality and superiority are used in the same sentence, the conjunction expressed in Spanish should correspond with the last: Ex.

Mis libros son tan buenos   My books are as good as,
(como), ó *mejores que* los   or *better than* his.
suyos.

8. When in English the preposition *by* is used in comparing the dimensions of two objects, the sentence takes a different turn in Spanish: Ex.

Esta sala es seis piés mas   This hall is longer than that
  larga que aquella.   *by* six feet.

Which means literally, *This hall is six feet longer than that.*

THE SUPERLATIVE.

9. The superlative *relative* is formed in Spanish by prefixing the definite article to the adjective in the comparative degree: Ex.

Era *la mas* hermosa muger   She was the *handsomest*
  que habia en la sala.   woman in the room.

Note.—Sentences of this kind might also be expressed in Spanish without the second verb, then, either the preposition *en*, or *de*, may be employed; as, *Era la mas hermosa muger* en *or* de *la sala.*

10. The superlative *absolute* is formed by placing the word *muy* (very *or* most) before the adjective in the positive degree, or by affixing *isimo* to the adjective in this degree ending in a consonant; those which end in a vowel drop the vowel before they admit the *isimo* : Ex.

Es *muy* hermosa muger.   She is a *very* beautiful, or a
                   most beautiful woman.

Son *cortesísimos.*   They are *very* courteous.
Es *bellísima* idea.   It is a *very* fine, or a *most*
                  beautiful idea.

Of the two manners of forming the superlative, that in *isimo* adds greater strength to the meaning of the adjective.

11. Some Spanish adjectives, in order to preserve their primitive hard or soft sound, undergo a slight alteration in their orthography before they admit the termination *isimo* : thus, adjectives ending in *co* and *go* change these letters respectively into *qu* and *gu* ; as *chico, chiquísimo* ; *amargo, amarguísimo.* Those ending in *io* drop these two vowels ; as *amplio, amplísimo* ; except *frio,* which only drops the *o,* as *friísimo.* Those ending in

ble change this syllable into *bil;* as, *amable, amabilísimo.*
And those ending in *z* change this letter into *c;* as, *feliz,*
felicísimo.   Acre changes into *acérrimo; antiguo* into *an-*
tiquísimo; benéfico into *beneficentísimo; benévolo* into *bene-*
volentísimo: célebre into *celebérrimo; fiel* into *fidelísimo;*
fuerte into *fortísimo; libre* into *libérrimo; magnífico* into
magnificentísimo; mísero, into *misérrimo; munífico* into
munificentísimo; noble into *nobilísimo; sagrado* into *sacra-*
tísimo; salubre into *salubérrimo; sabio* into *sapientísimo.*

Some positives ending in *iente* drop the *i* when *ísimo*
is added to them; such are, *ardiente, ardentísimo; fer-*
viente, ferventísimo; luciente, lucentísimo, valiente, valentí-
simo.   Some adjectives having the diphthong *ie* in the
penult also drop the *i;* as, *cierto, certísimo; tierno, ter-*
nísimo.   Some few, as *bueno, grueso, nuevo, fuerte,* change
the diphthong *ue* into *o;* thus, *bonísimo, grosísimo, noví-*
simo, fortísimo.

12. The following comparatives and superlatives are
irregularly formed :

Positives.	Comparatives.	Superlatives.			
Bueno,	mejor,	óptimo.	Good,	better,	best.
Malo,	peor,	pésimo.	bad,	worse,	worst.
Grande,	mayor,	máximo.	{ great, large,	greater, larger,	greatest. largest.
Pequeño,	menor,	mínimo.	{ small, little,	smaller, less,	smallest. least.
Bajo,	inferior,	ínfimo.	low,	lower,	lowest.
Alto,	superior,	supremo.	high,	higher,	highest.
Mucho,	mas.		much,	more.	
Poco,	ménos.		little,	less.	

Of this list, the positives and comparatives may also
be formed into superlatives, by prefixing the adverb
muy to the positives, or by the addition of the termination *ísimo,* according to the directions already given ; and
by prefixing the definite article to the comparatives; as,
Muy bueno, or *bonísimo,* very good ; *muy malo,* or
malísimo, very bad ; *el mejor,* the best ; *el peor,* the
worst.

And all the positives, except *mucho,* may likewise be
formed into comparatives by prefixing the adverb *mas*

to them ; as, *Mas bueno*, better; *mas malo*, worse; *mas grande*, larger, or greater ; *mas pequeño*, smaller.

13. Comparison may also take place with relation to *nouns*, *verbs*, and *adverbs*, in the following manner.

14. The comparative of *equality* in relation to *nouns*, is formed in Spanish by placing *tanto* (as much) before, and *como* (as) after the noun :   Ex.

Posee *tanto* talento *como* ella. He has *as much* talent *as* she.

15. In relation to *verbs*, it is formed by placing *tanto cuanto*, or *tanto como* (as much as) after the verb : Ex.

Gasta *tanto cuanto,* or *tanto como* gana.	He spends *as much as* he earns.

Or thus, *Tanto gasta cuanto gana.*

16. In relation to *adverbs*, it is formed by placing *tan* (as) before, and *como* (as) after the adverb : Ex.

Escribe *tan* bien *como* habla. He writes *as* well *as* he speaks.

17. *As much*, and *as many, so much*, and *so many*, re each translated *tanto*, which agrees in gender and number with the noun to which it is prefixed : Ex.

Tengo *tantos libros* y *tanto papel* como él.	I have *as many* books and *as much* paper as he.
¿Porqué *tantas palabras ?*	Why *so many* words ?
¡ Hicieron *tanto ruido !*	They made *so much* noise !
No necesito *tanto dinero.*	I do not require *so much* money.

Quite as much, and *quite as many* are translated *cuanto*, which also agrees in number and gender with the noun : Ex.

Tengo *cuanto dinero* y *cuantos alhajas* pudiera desear.	I have *quite as much* money and *as many* jewels as I could desire.

18. *So as*, employed with an infinitive, require *tan que* in the translation, and *such as* require *tal que;* and the English infinitive is generally rendered in Spanish by a verb in the same tense as that in which the preceding verb is placed : Ex.

La noche fué *tan* oscura *que* nos *impidió* el salir.	The night *was so* dark *as to* prevent our going out.
Tal fué su conducta *que excitó* un disgusto general.	*Such was* his conduct *as to* excite a general disgust.

19. The comparative of *superiority* with relation to *nouns* and *adverbs*, is formed by placing *mas* (more) before, and *que* (than) after them: Ex.

Posee *mas* talento *que* ella.	He has *more* talent *than* she.
Lee *mas* despacio *que* él.	She reads *more* slowly *than* he.

20. In relation to *verbs*, it is formed by placing *mas que* (more than) after them: Ex.

Escribe *mas que* su hermano.	He writes *more than* his brother.

21. The comparative of *inferiority*, in relation to *nouns* and *adverbs*, is formed by placing *ménos* (less) before, and *que* (than) after them: Ex.

Posee *ménos* talento *que* ella.	He has *less* talent *than* she.
Escribe *ménos* elegantemente *que* su predecesor.	He writes *less* elegantly *than* his predecessor.
No leo *ménos* despacio *que* Vmd.	I do not read *less* slowly *than* you.

22. In relation to *verbs*, it is formed by placing *ménos que* (less than) after them: Ex.

Aprende *ménos que* su hermano.	He learns *less than* his brother.

23. *Than*, after a comparative (either of superiority or inferiority) coming before *what*, expressed or understood, is generally translated *de* in the affirmative, and *que* in the negative sense: Ex.

Mas *de* lo que él tiene.	More *than what* he has.
Ménos *de* lo que creia.	Less *than what* I thought.
No mas *que* lo que dije.	No more *than what* I said.
Nada ménos *que* lo que merece.	Nothing less *than* he deserves.

24. *Than*, after comparatives coming before numeral adjectives, is also generally translated *de* in the affirmative, and *que* in the negative: Ex.

Tengo *mas de ciento.*	I have *more than one hundred.*
No tengo *mas* que mil libras.	I have no more *than* a thousand pounds.

25. *The more, the more ; the less, the less ; the more, the less ;* and *the less, the more ;* being used in different parts of a sentence, the latter part of the expression being consequent on the former, are translated *cuanto mas, tanto mas ; cuanto ménos, tanto ménos ; cuanto mas, tanto ménos ;* and *cuanto ménos, tanto mas :* Ex.

Cuanto mas estudiamos *tanto mas* sabrémos.	The *more* we study, the *more* we shall know.
Cuanto ménos lea Vmd. *tanto ménos* sabrá.	The *less* you read, *the less* you will know.
Cuanto mas lee, *tanto ménos* aprende.	The *more* he reads, *the less* he learns.
Cuanto ménos gastaren, *tanto mas* ahorrarán.	The *less* they spend, *the more* they will save.

Sentences of this nature may also be expressed in the following manner : *Mas lee, ménos aprende ;* or *miéntras ménos lea, ménos sabrá Vmd.*

26. *Most,* or *most of,* and *the greater part of,* are translated as follows :

La mayor parte de los hombres ; or *los mas de* los hombres.	*Most* men, or *the greater part* of men.
La mayor parte del vino.	*Most of,* or *the greater part of* the wine.

27. The superlative degree, with relation to *verbs* and *adverbs,* is formed as follows : Ex.

Habla *muy poco,* or *poquísimo.*	He speaks *very little.*
Está *malísimamente* hecho, or *muy malamente* hecho.	It is *very badly* done.

28. There are some adjectives that have no comparatives and superlatives ; others that form comparatives, but not superlatives ; others that form superlatives with the adverb *muy,* and not with the termination *ísimo. Numeral* adjectives have no comparatives, nor superlatives. Many adjectives ending in *l,* as *paternal, varonil,* do not form

their superlatives in *ísimo;* nor do many of those ending
in *i, n,* or *r,* as *turquí, ruin, seeular;* but these niceties
of language can only be learnt by use, and the reading
of good books.

EXERCISE ON THE DEGREES OF COMPARISON.

His progress was as slow as certain.   My books are
  su   progreso era   lento   mis   son
as good as   his.   Some   consider   Virgil as
         [los suyos] algunos consideran á Virgilio
great a poet as Homer; and [it would be] very difficult
     poeta Homero   seria   difícil
to say which is entitled to greater praise. The poem
* decir cual es digno de   elogio   poema
of the former, called the Georgics, is the most perfect
  *   aquel intitulado Geórgicas   perfecto
of all Latin compositions. In the Iliad and the Odyssey,
    latino —————————   Iliada   Odiséa
Homer   has displayed the most consummate know-
   [ha mostrado tener]   .consumado conoci-
  ledge of human nature: he is the most ancient of all
miento humano naturaleza*   antiguo
profane writers. Nature has more charms than art.
profano escritor   tiene   encanto   arte
The climate of England is more changeable than that of
    clima, *m.*   variable
Spain: the summer days in the former are much longer,
                    * aquella son   largo
and those in winter much shorter. It is one of the finest
   los de   corto   * es   bello
novels that I have read; its descriptions are of the most
novela que * he leido sus —————
beautiful, and its lessons are very moral. The republic
hermoso   leccion   ——   república
of Athens was more illustrious than that of Lacedemon.
  Aténas era   ilustre   Lacedemonia

The second Punic war lasted six yearsless than the
        púnico guerra duró

first. This is higher than that. His style is less
    esto es alto   aquello su estilo

harmonious than that of Father Isla. He is (2) not (1)
harmonioso   el   Padre

so obliging as his brother. Xerxes was more ambitious
complaciente su   Sérses era   ambicioso

than prudent. The writings of Calderon are much
    prudente   escrito   son

valued. The Philosophy of Eloquence of Capmany is a
apreciado   filosofía   elocuencia

most profound work. Some of Cervantes' most celebrated
  profundo   célebre

productions are his Don Quixote, his very beautiful
———— son su — Quijote sus

Exemplary Novels, his Journey to Parnassus, etc. The
  egemplar novela . viage al Parnaso

literary Fables of Iriarte contain most admirable
literaria fábula   encierran   ————

lessons. She is a very prudent woman. He is a very
leccion *   prudente   *

learned man. How very good he is, and how very bad
  docto   qué   *

he appeared. It is a most easy work to translate.
* parecia *   fácil obra de traducir

Gratitude is the noblest quality of the mind. Ingratitude
 gratitud   noble cualidad   alma ingratitud

deserves the severest punishment. They read as much
  merece   severo   castigo * leen

as they write, but they do not speak as much as they
    * escriben mas * * no hablan   *

think. Such was the confusion as [to endanger]
piensan   fué   ————   puso en peligro

  our safety. He made so much noise as [to oblige
nuestra seguridad * hizo   ruido nos obligo

us] to go out. We have as much money as you.
    salir.   * tenemos   dinero   Vmd.

She plays as well as she sings. She possesses more wit
  * toca   * canta *   posee   talento

than beauty. He has as much protection and as many
  hermosura * tiene   ——————

friends as you.   She learns better than her sister.   He
 amigo   * aprende   su   *

thinks more profoundly than his contemporaries. The
piensa   profundamente   contemporáneo

more she reads the more she improves. Her sister has
     *   lee   * adelanta   tiene

less pride than she. The less you study the less
     orgullo   ella   * estudie

[you will gain.]   [It is not] more difficult to do than
 ganará Vmd.   no es   difícil de hacer

what he says.   I do not admire the style of Feijoo less
        dice   * * no aprecio   estilo

than (what) it deserves.   [It is worth] more than a
          * merece   vale

million. I remained in France and Italy more than two
      me detuve

years. They speak Spanish less fluently than you.
      * hablan   corriente

He writes worse every time. [He does not give himself]
  escribe   cada vez   no se   da

the least trouble.
      pena

LECTURE XII.

NUMERAL ADJECTIVES.

CARDINAL NUMBERS.

Uno,	one.
dos,	two.
tres,	three.
cuatro,	four.
cinco,	five.
seis,	six.
siete,	seven.
ocho,	eight.
nueve,	nine.
diez,	ten.
once,	eleven.
doce,	twelve.
trece,	thirteen.
catorce,	fourteen.
quince,	fifteen.
diez y seis,	sixteen.
diez y siete,	seventeen.
diez y ocho,	eighteen.
diez y nueve,	nineteen.
veinte,	twenty.
veinte y uno,	twenty-one.
veinte y dos,	twenty-two.
veinte y tres,	twenty-three.
veinte y cuatro,	twenty-four.
veinte y cinco,	twenty-five.
veinte y seis,	twenty-six.
veinte y siete,	twenty-seven.
veinte y ocho,	twenty-eight.
veinte y nueve,	twenty-nine.
treinta,	thirty.
treinta y uno,	thirty-one.
cuarenta,	forty.
cincuenta,	fifty.

sesenta,	sixty.
setenta,	seventy.
ochenta,	eighty.
noventa,	ninety.
ciento,	one hundred.
ciento y uno,	one hundred and one.
ciento y dos,	one hundred and two.
dos cientos,	two hundred.
tres cientos,	three hundred.
cuatro cientos,	four hundred.
cinco cientos, or quinientos,	five hundred.
seis cientos,	six hundred.
setecientos,	seven hundred.
ochocientos,	eight hundred.
novecientos,	nine hundred.
mil,	one thousand.
dos mil,	two thousand.
tres mil,	three thousand.
cuatro mil,	four thousand.
diez mil,	ten thousand.
cien mil,	one hundred thousand.
dos cientos mil,	two hundred thousand.
un millon,*	a million.

1. Observe that in compound numerals in Spanish it is necessary always to begin with the highest number, and descend gradually to the lowest, placing, the conjunction *y* before the last; as, *veinte y tres*, twenty-three ; *dos cientos treinta y uno*, two hundred and thirty-one; *mil ocho cientos cincuenta y tres*, 1853 ; consequently the following manner, sometimes adopted in English, is never followed in Spanish, namely, *three and twenty*, *eighteen hundred and fifty-three*, etc.

2. All the cardinal numbers except *uno*, and the compounds of *ciento*, are indeclinable.

Uno agrees in gender with the noun to which it refers, but drops the *o* when it immediately precedes a noun masculine singular or its adjective : Ex.

---

* *Millon*, however, belongs rather to the class of nouns, and governs the following noun with the preposition *de ;* as, *un millon de hombres.*

Uno de los documentos.	One of the documents.
Una cuestion.	A question.
Un hombre; *un* gran libro.	A man; a great book.

Ciento drops the last syllable when it immediately precedes a noun of either gender. The compounds of *ciento* agree in number and gender with the nouns to which they refer: Ex.

Cien hombres y cien mugeres.	A hundred men and a hundred women.
Ciento y veinte libras.	A hundred and twenty pounds.
Dos cientos soldados.	Two hundred soldiers.
Tres cientas escopetas.	Three hundred muskets.

ORDINAL NUMBERS.

Primero,	First.
segundo,	second.
tercero,	third.
cuarto,	fourth.
quinto,	fifth.
sexto,	sixth.
séptimo,	seventh.
octavo,	eighth.
noveno, or, nono,	ninth.
décimo, or, deceno,	tenth.
undécimo, or, onceno,	eleventh.
duodécimo, or, doceno,	twelfth.
décimo tercio, or, treceno,	thirteenth.
décimo cuarto, or, catorceno,	fourteenth.
décimo quinto, or, quinceno,	fifteenth.
décimo sexto,	sixteenth.
décimo séptimo,	seventeenth.
décimo octavo,	eighteenth.
décimo nono,	nineteenth.
vigésimo,	twentieth.
vigésimo primo,	twenty-first.
vigésimo segundo,	twenty-second.
vigésimo tercio,	twenty-third.
vigésimo cuarto,	twenty-fourth

vigésimo quinto.	twenty-fifth.
vigésimo sexto,	twenty-sixth.
vigésimo séptimo,	twenty-seventh.
vigésimo octavo,	twenty-eighth.
vigésimo nono,	twenty-ninth.
trigésimo,	thirtieth.
trigésimo primo,	thirty-first.
cuadragésimo,	fortieth.
quincuagésimo.	fiftieth.
sexagésimo,	sixtieth.
septuagésimo,	seventieth.
octagésimo,	eightieth.
nonagésimo,	ninetieth.
centésimo,	hundredth.
centésimo primo	hundred and first.
centésimo secundo,	hundred and second.
docentésimo,	two hundredth.
trecentésimo,	three hundredth.
cuadragentésimo,	four hundredth.
quingentésimo,	five hundredth.
sesentésimo,	six hundredth.
septengentésimo,	seven hundredth,
octagentésimo,	eight hundredth.
nonagentésimo,	nine hundredth.
milésimo,	a thousandth.

3. All the ordinal numbers agree with the nouns to which they refer in gender and number: *primero* drops the *o* when placed immediately before a noun masculine singular, or its adjective: Ex.

El *primer* dia.	The first day.
El *primer* buen tiempo.	The first fine weather.
El *primero* de todos.	The first of all.
Los *primeros* dias.	The first days.
Las noches *primeras.*	The first nights.
El tomo *segundo.*	The second volume.
Las órdenes *segundas.*	The second orders.

4. *Tercero* or *tercer* may be indiscriminately used: for we may either say *el* tercero *dia*, or *el* tercer *dia*.

5. Few persons now use the ordinal numbers in Spanish after the *tenth* or *twelfth*, on account of their

length; instead of which, the cardinal numbers are employed. And with reference to the date of the month, the ordinal numbers are seldom if ever used in Spanish after *primero, segundo,* and *tercero.*—See EPISTOLARY CORRESPONDENCE, in the APPENDIX.

6. Numeral adjectives referring to a noun or adjective of dimension, require the preposition *de* after them : Ex

Dos varas *de ancho.*	Two yards wide.
Tres pies *de altura,* or *de alto.*	Three feet in height, or high.

7. When the English numeral adjective that relates to a noun or adjective of dimension is preceded by some part of the verb *to be,* this verb is rendered by *tener,* to have : Ex.

La mesa *tiene tres* pies de alto, *or* de altura.	The table *is three* feet high, or in height.

8. *Six feet by four, twelve inches by eight,* and so forth, are translated literally ; as, *Seis pies por cuatro, doce pulgadas por ocho.*

9. Besides the cardinal and ordinal numbers, we must notice the *collective,* the *distributive,* and the *proportional :* but observe, that these are nouns, and not adjectives.

10. The *collective* denote a determined number of things collected into one distinct mass or body : Ex.

Un *par,*	a pair, or couple.
una *docena,*	a dozen.
media *docena,*	half a dozen.
una *venitena,*	a score.
una *centena,*	a hundred
centenares.	hundreds.
un *millar,*	a thousand.
un *millon,* or *cuento,*	a million.

11. The *distributive* denote the different parts of a whole : Ex.

La mitad,	the half.
el tercio, *or* la tercera parte,	the third.
el cuarto, *or* la cuarta parte,	the fourth.
el décimo, *or* la décima parte,	the tenth.

el dozavo, *or* la duodécima parte, the twelfth.
dos tercios,   two-thirds,
cuatro quintos,   four-fifths.
tres octavos,   three-eighths.

12. The *proportional* are such as denote the progressive increase of things: Ex.

El doble, *or* duplo,   the double.
el triple, *or* triplo,   the triple.
el cuadruplo,   the quadruple.
el quintuplo,   the five-fold.
el decuplo,   the ten-fold.
el centuplo,   the hundred-fold.

Once is translated *una vez;* twice, *dos veces;* three times, *tres veces;* and so on.

EXERCISE ON NUMERAL ADJECTIVES.

In the year sixteen hundred and eighty-seven the sea
en   año   mar

retired from the shores of Peru, returning in tremendous
se retiró   playa   Perú volviéndose   tremendo

waves that destroyed [every thing they encountered] on
ola   que destruyeron   todo lo que   encontraron   en

the coast, and amongst other places the city of Callao.
costa   entre   otro lugar   ciudad ————

In seventeen hundred and eighty-six the same phenome-
mismo fenóme-

non [occurred again], when out of four thousand souls
no   volvió á suceder cuando *   alma

that the said city contained, two hundred only were
dicho   contenia   solamente se

saved; nineteen vessels were   sunk   and four,
salvaron   buque fueron [echados á pique]

including a frigate, were deposited some distance
incluyendo   fragata   depositado alguna distancia

inland.   Our voyage lasted eight and forty
[dentro de tierra] nuestro viage   duró

days, of which six and twenty were of contrary winds. Of
                        eran   contrario viento

the thirteen hundred wounded more than the fourth part
                      heridos

died.   A street of one mile long, by eighty feet wide.
murieron   calle, *f.*

A tower two hundred feet high, by sixty in circumference.
 torre, *f.*   circunferencia

The pedestal is forty feet square, and fifty-five high. [I
    ————————   en cuadro

was speaking] of a third person.   This is a second
 hablaba   persona

warning. Three hundred and twenty-four pounds. One
 aviso

dozen and a half.   The first act.   The first two scenes.
                              escena

The third year.   Millions of men and hundreds of

women. Two scores of these, and three pairs of those.
             estos   aquellos

I went twice, if not thrice.
* fuí   si no

————

LECTURE XIII.

PREPOSITIONS EMPLOYED WITH ADJECTIVES.

1. Adjectives are frequently followed by certain prepositions that govern the word to which the meaning of
the adjective is directed.   This is a matter in which not
only do the English and Spanish languages often differ
as regards the preposition employed, but one that cannot
be reduced to any fixed rules.   The following are some
examples from the GRAMMAR OF THE ROYAL ACADEMY,
showing in their translation wherein the two languages
differ in respect to the prepositions employed in each :

Agradecido *á* los beneficios.	Grateful *for* kindnesses.
Fiel *á*, or *con* sus amigos.	Faithful *to* one's friends.
Igual *á*, or *con* otro.	Equal *to* another.
Increible *á*, or *para* muchos.	Incredible *to* many.
Ingrato *á* los beneficios.	Ungrateful *for* favours.
Próximo *á* morir.	*On* the point of death.
Visible *á*, or *para* todos.	Visible *to* all.
Ageno *de* la verdad.	Foreign *to* truth.
Agudo *de* ingenio.	Acute *in* intellect.
Alto *de* cuerpo.	Tall *in* stature.
Ancho *de* boca.	Wide *at* the mouth.
Angosto *de* mangas.	Narrow *in* the sleeves.
Bajo *de* cuerpo.	Low *in* stature.
Boto *de* punta.	Blunt *in* the point.
Bueno *de*, or *para* comer.	Good *to* eat.
Capaz *de*, or *para* el empleo.	Fit *for* the employment.
Chico *de* cuerpo.	Small *in* stature.
Dotado *de* ciencia.	Gifted *with* learning.
Escaso *de* medios.	Scanty *in* means.
Fácil *de* digerir.	Easy to digest.
Falto *de* juicio.	Deficient *in* judgment.
Impropio *de*, or *para* su edad.	Unfit *for* his age.
Inapeable *de* su opinion.	Obstinate *in* his opinion.
Infecto *de* heregía.	Tainted *with* heresy.
Inficionado *de* peste.	Infected *with* plague.
Largo *de* manos.	Liberal, openhanded.
Ligero *de* pies.	Lightfooted.
Precedido *de* otro.	Preceded *by* another.
Amable *con* todos.	Amiable *to* everybody.
Amoroso *con* los suyos.	Affectionate *to* one's relations.
Atento *con* sus mayores.	Attentive *to* one's superiors.
Parco *en* la comida.	Sparing *at* meals.
Benéfico *para* la salud.	Beneficial *to* health.

2. It would be impracticable, from the uncertainty of
their application, to attempt to lay down a set of rules to
apply to what custom has rendered so arbitrary and capricious, and what can only be attained by practice, and the
constant reading of good authors. But though no *fixed*
rules can be given for the choice of prepositions to be employed with adjectives, the following *general* observations

will, it is hoped, materially assist the learner on this head.

In many instances a corresponding preposition with the one used in English accompanies the adjective in Spanish. The following are exceptions:

1st. Adjectives that denote *proximity* are mostly accompanied by *á* before a noun, a pronoun, or an infinitive: Ex.

Junto *á* mi casa.	Adjoining my house.
Inmediato *á* el.	Close *to* him.
Próximo *á* caer.	Near falling.

2nd. Adjectives that qualify any *particular part* or portion of the noun to which they refer are followed by *de* : Ex.

Una casaca ancha *de* mangas.	A coat wide *in* the sleeves.
Un sombrero alto *de* copa.	A high-crowned hat.

3rd. The same preposition is required after adjectives coming before nouns or infinitives that denote the *cause* that produced the effect expressed by the adjective : Ex.

Se mostró *alegre de* verme.	He appeared *glad to* see me.
Está *pálida de* miedo.	She is *pale with* fear.

Note.—As participles past are sometimes so nearly allied to adjectives, it may not be deemed out of place to mention here that they also are followed by the preposition *de*, and sometimes by *por*, before nouns or infinitives that denote the cause producing the effect expressed by the participle. The following are examples of this nature from the GRAMMAR OF THE ACADEMY:

Aburrido *de* las desgracias.	Worried *by* misfortunes.
Curtido *del* sol.	Tanned *by* the sun.
Impelido *de* la necesidad.	Impelled *by* necessity.
Importunado *de*, or *por* otro.	Importuned *by* another.
Molido *de* andar.	Fatigued *with* walking.
Penetrado *de* dolor.	Pierced *with* grief.
Tocado *de* enfermedad.	Touched *with* disease.

4th. Numeral adjectives also require *de* before a noun or adjective of dimension : Ex.

Tres piés *de altura*.	Three feet *in* height.
Dos varas *de largo*.	Two yards long.

5th. Adjectives are accompanied by *en* when followed by nouns or infinitives that represent the objects or actions in which the quality of the adjective is *conspicuous :* Ex.

Diestro *en* el juego.   Expert *at* play.
Pronto *en* resolver.   Prompt *at* or *in* resolving.

6th. Adjectives that denote *fitness* or *unfitness* are accompanied by *para* before a noun, and by *de* or *para* before an infinitive : Ex.

Prejudicial *para* la salud.   Injurious *to* health.
Bueno *de*, or *para* comer.   Good *to* eat.

7th. Adjectives denoting *behaviour* towards anybody are generally followed by *con*, or *para con :* Ex.

Cortés *con* sus amigos.   Courteous *to* his friends.
Amoroso *para con* los suyos.   Kind *towards* his relations.
Ingrato *con* todos.   Ungrateful *to* everybody.

OBSERVATION.—Although, as seen in the foregoing examples, the ACADEMY has assigned certain prepositions to accompany certain adjectives, it does not necessarily follow as a rule that they must *in all* cases be accompanied by the same preposition; since the same adjective may frequently be followed by various prepositions, according to the relation which it may have with the word governed by the preposition; as, for instance, the adjective *bueno* may be accompanied by *de, con,* or *para,* as the occasion may require : Ex. *Bueno* de *comer*—Good to eat. *Bueno* para *la salud*—Conducive *to* health. *El es muy bueno* con *los suyos*—He is very kind *to* his relations. In a like manner the adjective *duro* may be accompanied by *de, en,* or *con :* Ex. *Duro* de *entendimiento* —Hard *of* understanding. *Duro* en *sus palabras*—Harsh *in* his words. *Duro* con *sus inferiores*—Severe *towards* his inferiors.   See also Employment and Government of Prepositions, LECT. 30.

LECTURE XIV.

ETYMOLOGY AND SYNTAX OF PRONOUNS.

1. Pronouns are generally classed under six different heads—namely, *personal, possessive, demonstrative, relative, interrogative,* and *indefinite.*

PERSONAL PRONOUNS.

2. *Personal* pronouns are those that are employed in reference to persons whose places they supply.   There are three persons—the *first,* or the person that *speaks;* the *second,* or the person *spoken to:* and the *third,* or the person *spoken of;* as, I *wrote the letter,* you *read it,* and he *delivered it.*

3. Personal pronouns are subject to a variation of *number, person, gender,* and *case,* as follows:

DECLENSION OF PERSONAL PRONOUNS.

First person singular number, common to both genders.

Nom.	Yo	I.
Gen.	de mí	of me.
Dat.	á mí, *or* para mí, me .	to *or* for me.
Acc.	me, *or* á mí	me.
Abl.	por mí.	by me.

First person plural number.

Mas.—	Nom.	Nosotros	We.
	Gen.	de nosotros	of us.
	Dat.	á *or* para nosotros, nos	to *or* for us.
	Acc.	nos, *or* á nosotros . .	us.
	Abl.	por nosotros	by us.
Fem.—	Nom.	Nosotras	We.
	Gen.	de nosotras	of us.
	Dat.	á *or* para nosotras, nos	to *or* for us.
	Acc.	nos, *or* á nosotras . .	us.
	Abl.	por nosotras	by us.

Second person singular number, common to both genders.

Nom.	Tú	Thou.
Gen.	de tí	of thee.
Dat.	á tí, *or* para tí, te	to *or* for thee.
Acc.	te, *or* á tí	thee.
Abl.	por tí	by thee.

Second person plural number.

Mas.—	Nom.	Vosotros	You *or* ye.
	Gen.	de vosotros	of you.
	Dat.	á, *or* para vosotros, os	to *or* for you.
	Acc.	os, *or* á vosotros	you.
	Abl.	por vosotros	by you.
Fem.—	Nom.	Vosotras	You *or* ye.
	Gen.	de vosotras	of you.
	Dat.	á *or* para vosotras, os	to *or* for you.
	Acc.	os, *or* á vosotras	you.
	Abl.	por vosotras	by you.

Third person masculine gender.

Sing.—	Nom.	Él	He.
	Gen.	de él	of him.
	Dat.	á él, *or* para él, le	to *or* for him.
	Acc.	le, *or* á él	him.
	Abl.	por él	by him.
Plur.—	Nom.	Ellos	They.
	Gen.	de ellos	of them.
	Dat.	á ellos, *or* para ellos, les	to *or* for them.
	Acc.	los, *or* á ellos	them.
	Abl.	por ellos	by them.

Third person feminine gender.

Sing.—	Nom.	Ella	She.
	Gen.	de ella	of her.
	Dat.	á ella, *or* para ella, le	to *or* for her.
	Acc.	la, *or* á ella	her.
	Abl.	por ella	by her.

Plur.—Nom. Ellas . . . . . . They.
　　　Gen. de ellas. . . . . . of them.
　　　Dat. á ellas, *or* para ellas, les to *or* for them.
　　　Acc. las, *or* á ellas. . . . them.
　　　Abl. por ellas . . . . . by them.

Third person neuter gender.

Nom. Ello . . . . It.
Gen. de ello. . . . . . . of it.
Dat. á ello, *or* para ello, lo . to *or* for it.
Acc. lo, *or* á ello . . . . . it.
Abl. por ello. . . . . . by it.

The neuter pronoun has no plural.

4. The third person is also used *reflectively*, declined without the nominative case, and is common to all genders and numbers: Ex.
　　　Gen. De sí . . . . . Of oneself, himself, herself, itself, *or* themselves.
　　　Dat. á sí, *or* para sí, se to *or* for oneself, etc.
　　　Acc. se, *or* á sí . . . oneself, etc.
　　　Abl. por sí. . . . . by oneself, etc.

5. *Nos* may sometimes be seen used in the nominative case, instead of *nosotros*, and *vos* instead of *vosotros*; but this practice is antiquated. In poetry, also, *del*, *dellos*, *dellas*, and *dello*, are sometimes used instead of *de él, de ellos, de ellas,* and *de ello.*

Note.—Care should be taken never to misapply the pronouns of the dative and accusative cases of the third person. The dative is always *le, les* in both genders, and the accusative *le, los* in the masculine, and *la, las* in the feminine. This is noticed here because they have frequently been confounded, even by writers of merit.

In order to distinguish immediately the dative from the accusative case in personal pronouns, observe the following: When the action of a verb falls *immediately* on the pronoun, it is the direct object of the verb, and is in the *accusative* case; but when the energy of the verb falls on any other word in the sentence, the pronoun will be the *indirect* object, and therefore in the *dative* case, and the

word on which the energy of the verb falls will be the
accusative case; as, *Yo* le *dí el libro*—I gave *him*, or *her*
the book. *Yo* les *dí el libro*—I gave *them* the book. In
these examples the pronouns *le* and *les* are in the *dative*
case, because the action of the verb does not fall on them;
it falls on the noun *libro;* but in the four following
examples the pronouns are in the *accusative* case, because
the action of the verb does fall on them. *Él* le *llamó*
—He called him. *Él* los *llamó*—He called them. *Él*
la *llamó*—He called her. *Él* las *llamó*—He called them.

6. The neuter pronoun *lo,* of the accusative case, is
often employed by the best of writers and speakers instead of the masculine *le.* Yet, properly speaking, *lo*
should only be employed in reference to something of
which the gender is not denoted; as, for instance, *Ya*
lo *sabia yo*—I knew *it* already. Here the *lo* refers to
some circumstance understood, connected with the verb
sabia; and in the following example it refers also to
something of which the gender is unknown to the
speaker: *Qué es eso?—Permítame Vmd.* que lo *vea*—
What is that?—Allow me to see *it.*

Before we dismiss the neuter pronoun *lo,* it must be
observed that it is sometimes employed in reference to
a whole, or part of a sentence, and then it is equivalent
to *so,* or *it:* Ex.

Dicen que habrá guerra; pero yo no *lo* creo.	They say there will be war, but I do not think *so;* or, I do not believe *it.*
Quién *lo* dice? Los papeles *lo* dicen.	Who says *so?* The papers mention *it.*

7. The pronoun *se* is frequently employed in the *third*
person singular and plural in any of the tenses, to form
the *passive* voice : Ex.

El dinero *se* recibirá.	The money will be received.
Se han recibido los libros.	The books have been re-ceived.

(See Observations on the Passive Voice, LECT. 24,
PAR. 7.)

PERSONAL PRONOUNS IN THE NOMINATIVE CASE.

8. Personal pronouns in the nominative case, in the natural construction of the language, precede the verb in Spanish; as, *Yo hablo*—I speak. *Tú has venido*—Thou hast come. *El tomará*—He will take. *Nosotros somos vistos*—We are seen. *Vosotros prometisteis*—You promised. *Ellos irán*—They will go.

9. This natural order of placing the pronoun in the nominative case before the verb, may, for the sake of elegance, or to add greater energy to the expression, be inverted. Indeed, the natural construction of the Spanish language admits of great variety of syntactical inversion, as regards several of the other parts of speech, as we have already seen with the nominative and accusative with regard to the noun and verb, and with the substantive and adjective, and as we shall further see as we arrive at the other parts of speech respectively. Custom seems to have established as a rule, that the word we would have appear the most conspicuous in a sentence should take precedence of those with which it has relation. This licence is allowed a much wider latitude in Spanish than in English; and writers that know how to avail themselves of it with judgment, are able to display the variety, elegance, and force of expression, of which the Spanish language is capable. The following are some examples of placing the nominative pronoun after the verb :—

Ántes que me deis la embajada, ilustre capitan y valerosos estrangeros, del príncipe grande que os envia, *debeis vosotros,* y *debo yo*, desestimar y poner en olvido lo que ha divulgado la fama de nuestras personas y costumbres. — (Solís—*Razonamiento de Montezuma á Cortés.*)

Before you deliver me, illustrious captain and brave strangers, the embassy from the great prince who has sent you, you should, and so should I, disregard and forget what rumour has spread respecting our persons and customs.

Quisiera yo saber si la pupila de mi docto hermano seria capaz de proceder así. . . . . que comprenda

I should like to know if my learned brother's pupil could act in this manner. . . . that he may under-

bien que *soy yo* la que se   stand well that it is I
lo dice. — (MORATIN—   who tell him so.
Escuela de los Maridos.)

10. In interrogative sentences, personal pronouns generally follow the verb in Spanish: Ex.

¿ *Habló él* con ella?   Did he speak to her?
¿ *Están ellos* acquí?   Are they here?

11. Personal pronouns in the imperative mood likewise usually follow the verb in Spanish: Ex.

Venga Vmd. conmigo.   Come with me.
Hagamos nosotros nuestro   Let us do our duty.
   deber.

12. Personal pronouns are generally omitted in Spanish in the nominative case, unless they be the emphatical words in the sentence, or when their omission would create ambiguity: Ex.

Mira, hermano, si no *qui-*   Look, brother, unless you
   eres que *riñamos* muy de   wish us to quarrel in right
   veras, no *hablémos* mas   earnest, let us talk no
   del asunto . . . .   more on the subject . . . .
¿ No *es ella* mi sobrina; no   Is she not my niece; art
   eres tú mi hermano ?—   thou not my brother ?
   (MORATIN—*La Morgigata.*)

In the first example, the termination of the verb *quieres* denotes its nominative to be of the second person singular, and those of *riñamos* and *hablémos* the first person plural, and therefore the pronouns *tú* and *nosotros* are dispensed with as unnecessary. In the second example, *ella* and *tú* are emphatically used, and are therefore expressed. In the sentence *Él escribe y ella canta* (He writes and she sings), both verbs being in the third person singular, the omission of the pronouns would create ambiguity as regards the gender of their nominatives. And in the following sentence, *Es muy hermosa* (She is very beautiful), the verb *es* denotes its nominative to be of the third person singular, while the feminine termination of the adjective *hermosa* marks its gender.

13. The nominative case of *impersonal* verbs (which is the neuter pronoun *ello*) is most generally suppressed in Spanish: Ex.

Parece que lloverá hoy. It appears that it will rain to-day.

Es preciso que vayamos. It is necessary that we go.

PERSONAL PRONOUNS IN THE DATIVE AND ACCUSATIVE CASES.

14. The pronouns *me, te, le, la, lo, nos, os, les, las, los, se,* in the dative and accusative cases, are placed *after* and *joined to* the verb in the *infinitive* and *imperative* moods and the *participle active:* Ex.

DAT.—Voyá *darle* la pluma. I am going to give him the pen.

   Enséñeme Vmd. el libro. Show me the book.

   Escribiéndonos una carta. In writing us a letter.

ACC.—Quiére Vmd. *verle?* Do you wish to see him?

   Tráiganla Vmds. aquí. Bring her here.

   Estan *maltratándolos.* They are ill-treating them.

Note 1.—When, however, the *imperative* is in the third person singular or plural, except if the nominative be *Vmd.;* the pronouns in the dative and accusative cases usually *precede* the verb with the conjunction *que:* Ex.

   Que me diga él. Let him tell me.
   Que ella *las traiga.* Let her bring them.

Note 2.—As the infinitive and participle active are governed by some other verb in the sentence, it is optional to place the governed pronoun either after the governed verb, as in the above examples, or before the governing verb, as follows: *Le voy á dar la pluma. ¿ Le quiére Vmd. ver? Los estan maltratando.*

15. The first and second persons plural of the verb in the imperative mood, drop the final letter when *nos* and *os* are affixed to them; as, *salvémonos,* let us save ourselves; *instruíos,* instruct yourselves; instead of *salvémosnos, instruidos.*

On all other occasions, the foregoing pronouns are most *generally* placed before the verb : Ex.

DAT.—Él *nos dió* la noticia. He gave us the news.
  Yo *le he escrito* la carta. I have written him the letter.
  Ellos *me enviaron* el libro. They sent me the book.
ACC.—Nosotros *le vimos.* We saw him.
  Ellos *se han lasti-mado.* They have hurt themselves.
  Él *la acompañará.* He will accompany her.

16. However, to give energy to the expression, the syntactical order of the pronouns in the dative and accusative cases may be inverted, especially when a sentence or clause begins with a verb : Ex.

Sentóse á comer con su esposa, reprimiendo el dolor en el pecho. — (QUINTANA— *Vida de Españoles Celebres.*) He sat down to dine with his wife, repressing his grief within his bosom.

Dirásme que la docilidad declina muchas veces en ligereza.— (FEIJOO— *Teatro Crítico.*) You will tell me that mildness often degenerates into levity.

The like sometimes occurs in poetry ; even though not at the beginning of a sentence : Ex.

Todos *os incubrid* los rostros, All of you cover your faces,
Que es diligencia impor-tante, etc. — (CALDERON—*La Vida es Sueño.*) For it is of great import-ance, etc.
Ten tú lástima de ti, Have thou pity on thyself,
Fernando, y *tendréla yo.*— (IDEM—*El Príncipe Constante.*) Fernando, and then will I.

But such constructions as the two latter examples would now be considered as archaisms, and could only be tolerated in poetry.

17. When an English sentence has two pronouns following each other, the first in the accusative, the second in the dative case, their order must be *reversed* in the translation ; observing, that in such instances the *third*

person *singular* or *plural*, of the *dative* case is, for the sake of euphony, translated *se:* Ex.

Él *me lo* dió.	He gave *it to me.*
Os los mostraré.	I will show *them to you.*
Ellos *nos lo* dijeron.	They told *it to us.*
Yo *te lo* daré.	I will give *it to thee.*
Ellos *me los* han enviado.	They have sent *them to me.*
Se lo escribiré.	I will write it *to him, her,* or *them.*
Se lo he dicho.	I have told it *to him, her,* or *them.*
Te la enviarémos.	We will send *her to thee.*
Voy á decír*oslo.*	I am going to tell *it to you.*
En dicíendo*melo.*	In telling *it to me.*
Vuélve*melos.*	Return *them to me.*
Enséña*selos.*	Show them to *him, her,* or *them.*

18. We have now to consider those personal pronouns of the dative and accusative cases that are preceded by a preposition—namely, *á mí, á tí, á él, á ella, á ello, á sí, á nosotros, á nosotras, á vosotros, á vosotras, á ellos, á ellas.* These pronouns are frequently employed with the other class of pronouns of the dative and accusative cases before mentioned: their use is either to place the direct or indirect object of the verb in a more conspicuous light, or to distinguish more particularly the gender of the object: Ex.

La llevaron *á ella á* su casa, y *á mí me* enviaron al despacho.	They took *her* to her house, and sent *me* to the office.
Yo *le* escribí *á él* con preferencia.	I wrote to *him* in preference.

In the first example, the additional pronouns *á ella* and *á mí* individualise more particularly the objects of the verbs ; and in the second, *á él* determines the gender of the object ; for without this explanatory pronoun, *le escribí* would be ambiguous in its meaning, and signify either *I wrote to him,* or *I wrote to her.*

19. These pronouns are frequently employed by themselves in the *dative* case ; they are also required after *comparatives:* Ex.

Dé Vmd. el libro *á él*, y la carta *á ella*.	Give the book *to him*, and the letter *to her*.
Nos han dado ménos que *á ellos*.	They have given us less than *them*.

20. There is in English what is called the *emphatic word* of a sentence, and an English phrase may have as many significations as it contains words, according as to which of the words is pronounced emphatically. This is not the case in Spanish, in which there is no emphatical *word;* and what is effected in English by emphasis, requires circumlocution in Spanish. Take for instance the following :

¿Es cierto que la vió esta mañana ?	*Did* he see her this morning?
¿La vió él esta mañana?	Did *he* see her this morning?
¿Es que la vió esta mañana?	Did he *see* her this morning?
¿La vió á ella esta mañana?	Did he see *her* this morning?
¿La vió esta misma mañana?	Did he see her *this* morning?
¿Fué esta mañana que la vió ?	Did he see her this *morning ?*

PERSONAL PRONOUNS IN THE GENITIVE AND ABLATIVE
CASES.

21. There is nothing very particular to be observed in the employment of personal pronouns in these two cases : they are always preceded by prepositions that govern them, as seen in the declensions.   Observe, however, that when *mí, tí, sí* are preceded by *con,* they are written thus—*conmigo,* with me, or with myself; *contigo,* with thee, or with thyself; *consigo,* with him, her, or them; or with himself, herself, or themselves : Ex.

Él habla *conmigo.*	He speaks *with*, or *to me.*
Lo llevaré *conmigo.*	I will take it *with me.*
Yo hablo *contigo.*	I speak *to thee.*
¿Hablas *contigo ?*	Dost thou speak *to thyself ?*
Él me lleva *consigo.*	He takes me *with him.*
Ella habla *consigo.*	She speaks *to herself.*

In each of the last two examples the nominative of the verb and the pronoun *sigo,* refer to the same person ; but should they refer to different individuals, then, instead of

consigo we must say *con él, con ella, con ellos,* or *con ellas :*
Ex.

Hablo *con él, ella, ellos,*   I speak to him, her, or
   ellas.   them.

Ella habla *con él,* etc.   She speaks to him, etc.

EXERCISE ON PERSONAL PRONOUNS.

I have a book. Thou [wilt come] to-morrow. He
  tengo   vendrás   mañana

and she [will be] here to-day. We *m.* have written.
     estarán   aquí hoy   hemos escrito

We *f.* have told the truth. You *m.* are happy.
        dicho   verdad   sois dichoso

You *f.* [will follow.] They *m.* answered. They *f.*
   seguiréis   respondieron

heard. He came, said he, but it was too late. They
oyeron   vino   dijo   pero fué muy tarde

knew (2) not (1) what to choose. Art thou there?
sabian   no   que * escoger estás   allí

Who is he? What are they? Go thou. Stay ye
quién es   qué son   vé   quedad

here. He returned within an hour. He was more
     volvió [dentro de]   hora   fué

unfortunate than guilty. *They* lost; *we* did not
desgraciado   delincuente   perdieron   *

lose. We had [set off] before they arrived.
perdimos habiamos partido [ántes que]   llegasen

He came to pay me the debt. I went to see him. He
      pagar   deuda   fuí   ver

cannot accuse us. Give us some wine. Examine
[no puede] acusar   da   examinad

yourselves well. Let us arm ourselves with patience.
      bien * armémos   de paciencia

They were persuading me. I [should like] to
  estaban persuadiendo   quisiera   *

know him.   Bring her here.   Comfort thyself and
conocer   trae   consuela

listen to me.   They are preparing him.   He was
escucha   estan preparando   estaba

beating her.   We paid them.   I have spoken to her.
pegando   pagámos   he hablado

Vice deceives us.   Prosperity gains us friends, but
      engaña   prosperidad grangea   amigo   mas

adversity   tries   them.   I accompanied
adversidad [pone á la prueba]   acompañé

her [as far as] her house.   I related to him all her
      hasta   conté   todo

history.   I brought a letter and gave it to her.   Here
historia   trage   dí

are the drawings, show them to them.   I have repre-
estan   dibujo muestre   repre-

sented it to her.   Having referred it to me.   They
sentado   habiendo referido

[would have] repeated it to us.   [Wilt thou refuse] it to
    habrian   repetido   negarás

them.   I saw *her*, but could (2) not (1) see *him*.   I
        ví   pero pude   ver

give it to thee in preference.   They cheated *us*, and
doy   preferencia   engañaron

robbed *them*.   I am going to send it to *him* that
robaron   *   voy   mandar   [para que]

he [may forward] it to *her*.   It is to *them*   that   I
    remita   es   [á quienes]

spoke.   It is better to give it to *her* than to *him*.   They
hablé   mejor   dar

[would send] it to *us* rather than return it to *him*.   Do
    enviarian   ántes   volver   *

they speak of me or of him ?   What does he say about
    hablan   ó   qué   *   dice de

it ?   He says (2) nothing (1) of himself.   Was it done
        dice   nada   fué   hecho

by him or by her? He is gone with them. He did it
               ha ido con   hizo
for me. I can go without him. They spoke
para   puedo ir   sin   hablaron
against me. [He would neither stay] with me, nor with
 contra   no quiso quedarse   ni
thee. He carried it along with him. I sang with her,
     llevó   *   canté
but not with him.
mas no

OBSERVATION ON THE SECOND PERSONAL PRONOUN.

22. The *second personal pronoun* is only employed in
Spanish in addressing those persons with whom we are
on terms of great intimacy ; also by parents to their
children, but not by children to their parents ; by uncles
and aunts to their nephews and nieces; between brothers
sisters, and cousins ; sometimes by masters to their
servants : it is also used in scripture and in poetry. In
novels and romances we frequently see the second personal pronoun *plural* used in Spanish in addressing
persons for whom a high respect is entertained.

But in polite conversation, or in addressing strangers,
instead of the second personal pronoun, *Usted* is used
with both genders in the singular number, and *Ustedes* in
the plural. *Usted* is an abbreviation of *Vuestra Merced*,
a term nearly equivalent in meaning to *your grace*, or
your honour. In writing, *Usted* is thus contracted, *Vmd.*
Some write it thus, *Vm.;* others *Vd.* or *V.* An *s* is
added to either mode of abbreviation to form the plural
number ; and observe that the verb and the possessive
pronoun are put in the *third* person singular to agree
with *Vmd.*, and in the third person plural to agree with
Vmds. : Ex.

¿ Le *ha* visto *Vmd.*, Senor?   Have *you* seen him, Sir ?
Este es *su* reloj de *Vmd.*,   This is *your* watch, Madam.
   Señora.
Cómo *estan Vmds.*, Señores?   How do *you* do, Gentlemen?
Dónde estan *sus* libros de   Where are *your* books,
   Vmds., Señoritas ?   young ladies ?

Observe also that the adjective which refers to *Vmd.* or *Vmds.* agrees in gender and number with the person or persons to whom these abbreviations allude : Ex.

¿ Está Vmd. *bueno, Cabal-*   Are you well, Sir ?
   lero?

¿ Estan Vmds. *cansadas,*   Are you tired, Ladies ?
   Señoras ?

In speaking *of* an individual, instead of a pronoun in the third person, *su merced* is sometimes employed in the singular, and *sus mercedes* in the plural ; but this usage is now mostly confined to persons in a lower station when speaking of others in a higher ; as, *Don Vicente me dió esta carta para Vmd., y me encargó* su merced que *la entregase en manos propias*—Don Vincent gave me this letter for you, and *his honour* desired me to deliver it into your own hands. *Cuando dí el recado á las Señoras, me dijeron* sus mercedes *que,* etc.—When I delivered the message to the Ladies, *their Ladyships* told me, etc.

LECTURE XV.

POSSESSIVE PRONOUNS.

1. *Possessive* pronouns are those that denote the possession of anything by the person or things to which they refer: they do not vary their form in Spanish on account of case ; but they admit the same prepositions in the several cases as personal pronouns do.   They are of two kinds—namely, *conjunctive,* or those that *precede* the noun, and *disjunctive,* or those that *follow* the noun, or that refer to some noun understood.

CONJUNCTIVE POSSESSIVE PRONOUNS.

Mi,	my.	*nuestro,*	our.
tu,	thy.	*vuestro,*	your.
su,	his, her, its.	*su,*	their.

2. These refer to things possessed in the *singular* number; an *s* is added to them to form the plural : *mi*, *tu*, *su* are applicable to both genders ; but *nuestro* and *vuestro* are of the *masculine* gender, and change their final letter into *a* to form the *feminine :* Ex.

Mi sombrero, *mis* espadas.	*My* hat, *my* swords.
Tu carta, *tus* libros.	*Thy* letter, *thy* books.
Su valor, *sus* virtudes.	*His, her,* or *its,* valour, *or* virtues.
Nuestro deber, *nuestras* leyes.	*Our* duty, *our* laws.
Vuestro juicio, *vuestros* hechos.	*Your* judgment, *your* deeds.
Su talento, *sus* esperanzas.	*Their* talent, *their* hopes.

In these examples we see that in Spanish these possessive pronouns agree in *person* with the *possessor,* and in *number* with the thing *possessed ;* and that the first and second persons *plural* agree also in *gender* with the things *possessed.*

DISJUNCTIVE POSSESSIVE PRONOUNS.

Mio,	mine.	*nuestro,*	ours.
tuyo,	thine.	*vuestro,*	yours.
suyo,	his, hers, its.	*suyo,*	theirs.

3. This class of possessive pronouns are made to agree in *person* with the *possessor,* and in *gender* and *number* with the thing *possessed.* They change the final letter into *a* to form the feminine gender, and an *s* is added to them to form the plural number : Ex.

El cuidado *mio.*	*My* care.
Las esperanzas *mias.*	*My* hopes.
El candor *suyo.*	*His, her,* or *their* candour.
Los esfuerzos *nuestros.*	*Our* efforts.
La carta *vuestra.*	*Your* letter.

4. When these pronouns are employed in reference to a noun understood, or one going before, they are preceded by the definite article, agreeing with them in gender and number ; except when used in answer to a question, and

likewise when a verb intervenes between the noun and
the pronoun; in which cases the article is not necessary,
unless we wish to identify or to particularise the thing
to which the pronoun refers : Ex.

Mi libro y *el tuyo* estan
aquí, pero *el suyo* no está.

My book and *thine* are here,
but *his, hers,* or *theirs* is
not.

De quién es este libro? *Mio.*

Whose book is this?—*Mine.*

Cuál quiere Vmd., *el nuestro ó el suyo ?—El nues-
tro.*

Which will you have, *ours,*
or his ?—*Ours.*

Esa casa era *nuestra.*

That house was *ours.*

Este sello es *el mio.*

This seal is *mine.*

5. When *disjunctive* possessive pronouns refer in a
vague manner to something possessed, they are sometimes
used with the neuter article, in the same manner as adjectives substantively employed are ; as, *Lo mio,* Mine, or
that which is mine; *lo suyo,* his, hers, its, or theirs ; or that
which is his, hers, etc. ; *lo nuestro,* ours, or what is ours.

6. *Disjunctive* possessive pronouns, preceded in English by the preposition *of,* require no preposition in
Spanish : Ex.

Un vestido *mio.*

A dress *of mine.*

Dos criados *suyos.*

Two servants *of his.*

La carta *vuestra* de la que
hablo.

The letter *of yours* of which
I speak.

But when we wish to lay a particular emphasis on
the pronoun, then both the preposition and article are
required in Spanish : Ex.

Dos criados *de los suyos,* y
uno *de los mios.*

Two servants *of his* and one
of mine.

Two of my servants, one of his friends, would be rendered, *Dos de mis criados, uno de sus amigos.*

7. The pronoun *my,* used in English in addresses, is
translated *mio,* and follows the noun : Ex.

No vayas, hijo *mio.*

Do not go, *my* son.

Créame Vmd., Señor *mio.*

Believe me, *my* dear Sir.

Acuérdate, hija *mia !*

Remember, *my* child !

8. As in the employment of possessive pronouns of the

third person, ambiguity may sometimes arise respecting the *gender* and *number* of the possessor, it would be preferable in doubtful cases to employ a *personal* pronoun in the genitive case after the noun allusive to the possessor, in addition to the possessive pronoun, or in addition to the definite article before the noun, by which means every ambiguity will be avoided : Ex.

Su casa *de él,* or *la* casa de *él.*	His house.
Su casa *de ella,* or *la* casa de *ella.*	Her house.
Mis libros y *los de Vmd.*	My books and yours.
Los libros *de ella* y los mios.	Her books and mine.
Sus, or *las* cartas *de Vmd.* y las mias.	Your letters and mine.

9. In alluding to any *part* or *member* of a person or thing affected by a verb or a preposition, or to anything worn by, or appertaining to a person or thing, instead of the *possessive pronoun* employed in English, a *personal pronoun* in the *dative* case is used in Spanish in reference to the object itself, and the *definite article* points out the particular *part* affected by the verb : Ex.

Le herí *el* brazo derecho.	I wounded *his* right arm.
Me dió en *la* cabeza.	He struck me on *my* head.
Nos quitaron *las* espadas.	They took away *our* swords.
Le cortaron *la* casaca.	They tore *his* coat.
Me han alborotado *los* sesos.	They have turned *my* brain.

In all these examples there appears a subject that acts, and an object acted upon. When, however, there is but one individual in question, or that the actor acts upon anything belonging to himself, the definite article alone is sufficient in Spanish, except when the verb is used reflectively : Ex.

Ha perdido *la* vista.	She has lost *her* sight.
Sacó *la* espada.	He drew out *his* sword.
Me duele *la* cabeza.	*My* head aches.
Se lavó *las* manos.	She washed *her* hands.

The possessive pronoun, however, should be retained whenever the use of the article might occasion ambiguity or obscurity, and also where identity or emphasis is desired : Ex.

He aquí *mi* bolsa; tómala.	Here is *my* purse ; take it.
Saqué yo *mi* espada luego que sacó él la suya.	I drew out *my* sword as soon as he drew out his.

10. The word *own*, used in English together with possessive pronouns, is translated *propio*, or *mismo :* Ex.

Hablaba de *mis propios* negocios.	I was speaking of *my own* business.
Habla de *sí mismo*.	He speaks of *his own self*.
Esas casas son *suyas propias*.	Those are *his own* houses.

11. Sometimes the possessive pronoun is employed in Spanish in a vague sense, and is then equivalent to *one's* in English : Ex.

Es preciso obrar segun *su* poder.	It is necessary to act according to *one's* strength.
Conviene gastar segun *sus* medios.	It is prudent to spend according to *one's* means.

EXERCISE ON POSSESSIVE PRONOUNS.

My father and my mother are at home. My books are
                           estan en casa

well bound. Your houses are well built, and your
bien encuadernado   edificado

gardens are adorned with beautiful flowers. Her servant
         adornado de   bello   criado

took her horses to the stable. His genius and his talent
llevó   caballo   caballeriza   genio   talento

are esteemed. Our constancy and our efforts [will surmount]
son estimado   constancia   esfuerzo   vencerán

every obstacle. Thy candour and thy virtue are well known.
todo obstáculo   candor   virtud son   conocido

Soldiers! your brave conduct has satisfied my hopes.
 soldado   bizarro conducta ha   llenado   esperanza

That is his own idea. My friends did not serve me
aquella es   ——   amigo * no obsequiaron

with the same zeal as his. All the pictures were   sold,
      mismo celo   pintura   se vendieron
except yours and mine.   Your misfortune [cannot be
ménos   desgracia   no puede
compared] with ours.   Their confidence deserves mine.
  cotejarse   confianza   merece
Whose gloves are these ?—Mine.   And that hat ?—His.
cuyos guante son estos   ese
Is this her coach ?—No, it is mine.   A friend of mine
   este   coche
has spoken to a relation of his concerning some business
  ha hablado   pariente   [acerca de]   negocio
of yours.   We sent a servant of ours to an aunt of
              enviámos   tia
hers. He has   sold   one of his horses. [What ails thee]
       ha vendido   que   tienes
my child ?   Here it is, my friend.   Ours is to go first;
              está   ha de ir
yours [will go] next;   and lastly,   theirs.   That
       irá   últimamente   aquella
house is *hers;* not *his.*   *Her* letter is better written
                      carta está   escrito
than *his.*   They hurt his leg in taking off his
              lastimaron pierna * sacando
boot.   Her teeth ache.   I put the money into my
bota   muelas duelen   metí   en
  pocket.   I took off my hat. [It is better] for a man to
faltriquera   quité *   mas vale   que   *
  lose his life than his honour. He is   putting on his
pierda   vida   está poniéndose *
  coat.   She cut her finger.   He lost his life in a duel.
casaca   se cortó   dedo   perdió   desafío

LECTURE XVI.

DEMONSTRATIVE PRONOUNS.

1. *Demonstrative* pronouns are those that point to the objects which they refer to, or which they stand in the place of. In Spanish there are *three* kinds of demonstrative pronouns : the first, *este*, refers to an object near to the speaker ; the second, *ese*, refers to an object nearer to the person or thing spoken to than to the speaker; and the third, *aquel*, refers to an object that is distant both from the speaker and from the object spoken to : Ex.

Este libro que estoy leyendo, *ese* tratado que tiene Vmd. en la mano, y *aquel* folleto que está sobre la mesa.	*This* book which I am reading, *that* treatise which you have in your hand, and *that* pamphlet which is on the table.

2. Demonstrative pronouns in Spanish, are subject to a variation of *gender* and *number;* they are never preceded by the article, and do not vary their form on account of case, but admit the same prepositions to point out their cases as personal pronouns do : Ex.

	Masculine.	*Feminine.*	*Neuter.*	
SING.—	*Este*	*esta*	*esto*	This.
	ese	*esa*	*eso*	that.
	aquel	*aquella*	*aquello*	that yonder.
PLUR.—	*Estos*	*estas*	no neuter,	These.
	esos	*esas*	no neuter,	those.
	aquellos.	*aquellas*	no neuter,	those yonder.

In novels, etc., the first and second of these classes of demonstratives are sometimes compounded with the adjective *otro*, dropping their final vowel; thus, SING.—*Estotro, estotra, estotro,* this other. *Esotro, esotra, esotro,* that other. PLUR.—*Estotros, estotras,* these others. *Esotros, esotras,* those others. The neuter has no plural.

This compounding of the two words does not take place with the third class, but they are written separately; thus, SING.—*Aquel otro, aquella otra, aquello otro,* that other yonder.   PLUR.—*Aquellos otros, aquellas otras,* those others yonder.

In poetry, *aqueste, aquesta, aqueso,* are sometimes used instead of *este, esa, eso—aquestos, aquestas,* for *estos, estas —aquese, aquesa, aqueso,* for *ese, esa, eso—*and *aquesos, aquesas,* for *esos, esas.*

3. The terms *the former* and *the latter* are translated *aquel* and *este* : Ex.

Si sobresalió en las mate-máticas Leibnitz, tambien sobresalió Alfonso ; *aquel* desde el sosiego de su gabinete, *este* desde las turbulencias de las campañas. (VERGEL Y	If Leibnitz excelled in mathematics, so did Alphonsus; the *former* in the tranquillity of his closet, the *latter* amidst the tumult of campaigns.

PONCE—*Elogio de Don Alfonso el Sabio.*)

4. When demonstrative pronouns refer to time, *este* is applied to the present, and *ese* or *aquel* to the past, according to the remoteness of the time alluded to : Ex.

Este es el siglo de la ilustracion.	*This* is the age of knowledge.
Me acuerdo bien de *ese* dia.	I recollect *that* day well.
Aquellos eran tiempos de mucha barbaridad.	*Those* were times of much barbarity.

5. Sometimes the demonstrative pronoun is used in English to refer to some determined space of time ; as, I have not seen him *this month, these ten days, these two years ;* in such cases the impersonal verb *hacer* (it is) is employed in Spanish instead.   (See Impersonal Verbs, LECT. 26) : Ex.

No han estado aquí *hace un mes ; hace tres años.*	They have not been here *this month ; these three years.*
Hace una hora; dos horas que estoy aguardando aquí.	I have been waiting here *this hour ; these two hours.*

6. Although what has been observed in PAR. 1, with regard to the application of the three kinds of demon-

strative pronouns, is conformable with the rules given by the SPANISH ACADEMY, yet there are instances in which two objects pointed to at different distances from the speaker, may have the same relative distance from the person addressed, if he be near to the speaker; in such cases it would be more recommendable to employ *ese* or *aquel*, according as the distance of the locality of the objects, or their remoteness with regard to time, could be more accurately denoted in English by an adverb: Ex.

Ese libro que está sobre la mesa, y *aquel* que esta en el estante.	*That* book *there* on the table, and *that* one *yonder* on the shelf.
Ese buque que llegó *ayer*, y *aquel* que naufragó *el año pasado*.	*That* vessel which arrived *yesterday*, and *that* one which was shipwrecked *last year*.

7. The expressions *namely*, and *that is*, or *that is to say*, are translated *esto es:* Ex.

Le encomendé que no caminase mucho; *esto es*, que solo hiciese un poco de ejercicio.	I desired him not to walk much; *that is*, that he should only take a little exercise.
Me dijo que le comprara lo siguiente; *esto es*.	He told me to purchase him the following; *namely*.

THE ARTICLE USED INSTEAD OF THE DEMONSTRATIVE AND PERSONAL PRONOUNS.

8. When in English the *demonstrative* pronoun is followed by *who*, *which*, or *that*, expressed or understood, it is sometimes rendered in Spanish by the *definite article*. This, however, is not to be understood as a general rule, as in this case the employment of the one in preference to the other, is a mere matter of taste, although the demonstrative pronoun appears to identify more particularly the object referred to: Ex.

Mis libros y *los que* (or *aquellos que*) él tiene.	My books and *those which* he has.
Los que (or *aquellos que*) lo dicen se engañan.	*Those who* say so are mistaken.

Tráigame Vmd, *el que* (or   Bring me *that which* you
    aquel que) á Vmd, le   think best.
    parezca mejor.

9. Also when the English *personal* pronoun is followed
by *who,* or *that,* expressed or understood, it may be translated either by the article, or by the demonstrative pronoun *aquel:* Ex.

Délo Vmd. *al que* (or *á*   Give it to *him who* should
    aquel que) primero venga.   first come.
El que es sabio (or *aquel*   *He that* is wise would not
    que es sabio) no lo diria.   say so.
Los que (or *aquellos que*) lo   *They who* heard it know it.
    oyeron lo saben.

EXERCISE ON DEMONSTRATIVE PRONOUNS.

They belong to this man and this girl. [Have you
        pertenecen   muchacha ha leido
read] these verses? These pens do not write well.
Vmd.   verso   *   no escriben bien
This garden is full of flowers. These apples are
            está lleno   manzana son
better than those. He is a relation of that gentleman
                    es   pariente   caballero
 whom you (2) met (1) here [some days ago]. [Are
[á quien]   encontró   hace dias
you acquainted with] those ladies there? That was a
conoce Vmd. á   fué
brilliant age with the Athenians. He arrived on that
brillante siglo con   Ateniense   llegó   *
very day. What is that?—and this? Prefer virtue to
            qué es   prefiere virtud
vice; the former [will make] thee happy; the latter
vicio   hará   feliz
miserable. Two things appear to contribute to form
——— ———   parece que concurren para formar

an orator—reason, and the heart; the former to
   orador razon   corazon
convince, the latter to move and persuade. That is
convencer   mover   persuadir   es
what he may do; that is to say, what he ought to do.
       puede hacer   debe *
Those that cultivate learning should be encouraged.
           cultivan ciencias deben ser protegido
Happy they who are virtuous. I prefer that which you
 feliz   que son virtuoso.   prefiero   que
have, to those which I bought. Those who speak ill
tiene   compré   hablan mal
of her do not know her. He that is wise speaks when
     *   conocen   que sabio habla cuando
it is necessary; but he that only [presumes to be so]
  necessario mas   solo   lo presume
speaks incessantly.
    incesantamente

LECTURE XVII.

RELATIVE PRONOUNS.

1. *Relative* pronouns are those that relate to some
person or thing in a sentence, called the *antecedent*; for
instance, *The man* who *spoke: The bird* which *I caught;
The ship* that *was lost*. In these examples *who, which,*
and *that*, are *relative* pronouns, and refer to the antecedent
nouns, *man, bird, ship*.

There are four relative pronouns in Spanish—namely,
quien, who; *cual*, which; *que*, who, which, or that; and
cuyo, whose, or of which. *Whom* is rendered *á quien;
to*, or *for* whom, etc.; *á*, or *para quien*, etc. They do
not vary their terminations on account of case, but admit
the same prepositions as personal pronouns do in the
several cases.

2. *Quien* and *cual* have a plural termination, as *quienes*, *cuales;* but they are common to both genders.   *Quien* refers to persons only, and *cual* both to persons and things. *Quien* is seldom preceded by the article, but *cual*, as a relative, generally is : Ex.

Él es *quien* lo tiene.	It is he who has it.
Las señoras *que*, or *á quienes*, or *á las cuales* vimos.	The ladies whom we saw.
Los señores con *quienes* hablé.	The gentlemen to whom I spoke.
Es una ciencia de la *cual* tengo muy poco conocimiento.	It is a science of which I have but little knowledge.

Note.—When the antecedent is understood, the relative occupies its place as the nominative of the verb; as, *Quien lo dice se engaña*—Who says so is in error.

3. We sometimes see *quien* and *cual* used in the sense of *some* and *others*, and *one* and *another :* Ex.

Quien se salvó á nado, *quien* en lanchas.	*Some* saved themselves by swimming, *others* in boats.
Cual llevaba la fatigada madre, y *cual* el pequeño hijo. — (CERVÁNTES — *Pérsiles y Sigismunda.*)	*One* bore away the wearied mother, *another* the infant child.

4. *Cuál*, in exclamatory sentences, means *how*, or *in what a state* or *condition;* as, *Cuál le hallé!*—How wretched, *or* in what a wretched state I found him!

5. *Que* is common to both numbers and genders, and is applied to persons and things : Ex.

El *hombre que* vino.	The *man who* (or *that*) came.
Las *mugeres que* acompañámos.	The *women whom* (*that* or *which*) we accompanied.
Las *cosas á que* Vmd. se refiere.	The *things* to *which* you allude.

6. The second and third examples might also be thus expressed, *Las mugeres á* quienes acompañámos. *Las cosas á* las cuales *Vmd. se refiere.* This construction is used when we wish to identify an object more particularly. In the like manner when *who* or *that* is repeated in a sentence, it may be translated either *que* or *el cual :* Ex.

El hombre *que* partió ayer, y *que,* or *el cual* fué asesinado.	The *man who* or *that* left yesterday, and *that* was murdered.

Observe, that when *who* or *that* has its antecedent expressed in English, it is seldom translated *quien*, but most generally *que*, especially if it agree in case with the antecedent. It would therefore be unidiomatical to say, *El hombre* quien *vino; Las mugeres* quienes *fueron :* they should be, *El hombre* que *vino*—The man who or *that* came; *Las mugeres* que *fueron*—The women who or *that* went. In the following example, *who* does not agree in case with its antecedent, the latter being in the accusative ; therefore *quien* should be preferred to *que : Todos aplaudieron á* Emilia, quien *se retiró llena de alegría*—They all applauded Emily, who retired full of joy.

7. If *whom* be repeated in a sentence, it may be either translated *quien* or *el cual* preceded by a preposition : Ex.

El *hombre á quien* vimos, y *de quien,* or *del cual* huimos.	The *man whom* we saw, and from *whom* we fled.

8. *What* is sometimes translated *lo que*, and *which, lo cual :* (See LECT. 6, on the Neuter Article *lo :*) Ex.

Lo que él dice no es *lo que* Vmd. piensa.	*What* he says is not *what* you think.
Lo que digo es verdad, *lo cual* estas cartas lo prueban.	*What* I say is true, *which* these letters prove.

9. *Cuyo* partakes of the nature both of a relative and a possessive pronoun : as a relative it relates to an antecedent, and as a possessive pronoun it refers to the person or thing possessed ; in which latter capacity it agrees in number and gender with the person or thing possessed, and not with the possessor : Ex.

El *hombre cuyo dinero* tengo.	The *man whose money* I have.
Los *autores cuyos libros* leo.	The *authors whose books* I read.
El *árbol cuya fruta* es madura.	The *tree of which the fruit* is ripe.
Las *mugeres cuyas desgracias* acabo de referir.	The *women whose misfortunes* I have just related.

10. The expressions *than whom*, and *than which* are rendered *que*, in the following manner : Ex.

Hablo de su hermano de Vmd., *que* á nadie aprecio mas que á él.	I speak of your brother, *tan whom* I estem noe one better.
Este jardin, *que* nada puede ser mas hermoso.	This garden, *than which* nothing can be more beautiful.

11. Relatives are always expressed in Spanish, although frequently omitted in English : Ex.

La casa *que* fuimos á ver.	. The house we went to see.
La ciudad de *que* hablo.	The city I speak of.

12. The relative in English does not invariably *follow* the preposition by which it is governed ; as, for instance, *The gentleman* whom *I wrote* to ; *The houses* which *you speak* of. In Spanish, however, it must *immediately follow* the preposition by which it is governed ; as, *El caballero* á quien *escribí; Las casas* de que *Vmd. habla.*

EXERCISE ON RELATIVE PRONOUNS.

It is he who has sent us here. The gentlemen from
    ha enviado

whom I have received so much kindness. The men whom
   he recibido   bondad

we   met,   and whom we questioned. Where is
 encontrámos   preguntámos donde está

the man of whom you speak ? The lady with whom you
     habla

danced. The ladies to whom you sent the drawings.
 bailó   envió dibujo.

The man who wrote it. The house that you see there.
   escribió   vé

These are the works that you should read in preference
    obra   debia leer con preferencia

to those which you have selected. The general who
     eligido

conducted the battle, and that [was killed] in it. A man
  dirigió   batalla   murió   en

that spends his life in idleness dies miserable. Give
     pasa   vida   ociosidad muere   dé

it to whom you please. Cervantes, whose works we
                guste

admire. It is an evil, the cause of which is unknown.
admiramos   mal   causa   desconocida

The estate, the owner of which I am. They fought,
   hacienda   dueño   soy   peleaban

some with knives, others with swords; all was confusion
                    espada todo era ——

one [called for] assistance, another [sued for] mercy.
    pedia   socorro   • misericordia

Lope de Vega, whose ardent spirit knew (2) no (1)
           ardiente espíritu conocia

bounds. Idleness is a vice we ought to shun. The
  límite   debemos evitar

men we saw this morning. The lad I [was speaking]
   vimos   mañana   jóven   hablaba

of. The idea you referred to.
        [se referia]

——

LECTURE XVIII.

INTERROGATIVE PRONOUNS.

1. *Interrogative* pronouns are so called from their
being employed in asking questions: they are relative
pronouns used interrogatively: Ex.

Quién es aquel sugeto?	*Who* is that person?
Cuál es de Vmd.?	*Which* is yours?
Qué es aquello?	*What* is that?
Cúya es esta casa?	*Whose* house is this?

2. *Cuyo*, in interrogative sentences, is frequently substituted by *de quién;* therefore we may with equal propriety say, *De quién es esta casa?* or, *Cúya es esta casa?*

3. The same preposition employed in the interrogation is required in the answer; and it must be expressed in Spanish, although sometimes omitted in English : Ex.

Con quién vino?—*Con* migo. Whom did he come *with?* —Me.

En qué viajaban?—*En* coche. What did they travel *in?* —*In* a coach.

Note.—Should the question be asked with *cúyo*, the preposition *de* is required with the answer, in the same manner as if the question were put with *de quién;* as, *Cúyo* es este reloj?—*De* mi padre.—Whose watch is this?—My father's.

EXERCISE ON INTERROGATIVE PRONOUNS.

Who are those ladies?   Who is that gentleman?
son

Whom [did you give it] to?   Which of those carriages
lo ha dado Vmd.   carroza

[do you like best]?   Which are your works?   What
le gusta à Vmd. mas.

say you to that? What [shall I take] with me? Who is
dice   llevaré

he?   What [shall we buy]?   What [shall we do]?
comprarémos   harémos

Whose is this seal?   Whose jewels are those?   What
sello   alhaja

hour is it?   [What did you do it for]?—To save her.
hora   para qué lo hizo Vmd.   salvar

[What was it painted on]?—On paper. Whom [did he go]
en qué fué dibujado   papel   fué

for?—Me. [Whom do they fight against]?—The Turks.
por   contra   quién pelean   Turco

Whose was the decision?—The judge's.
fué   juez.

LECTURE XIX.

INDEFINITE PRONOUNS.

1. These are so called because they are employed in an indefinite manner with regard to the objects to which they refer. The following is a list of words employed as indefinite pronouns; most of them, when used with nouns, are more properly adjectives. They do not vary their terminations on account of case, but admit the same prepositions as all other pronouns do in the several cases :—

Alguno, álguien,	some, somebody, anybody.
algo, alguna cosa,	something.
uno,	one, a person.
unos,	some, some persons.
uno á otro,	one another, each other.
uno ú otro,	either, one or the other.
uno y otro,	one, and the other.
cada,	each, every.
cada uno, cada cual,	each, every one.
otro,	another, other.
ámbos,	both.
todo,	all, everything.
todos,	every one, everybody.
poco,	little.
pocos,	few.
unos pocos, } unos cuantos, }	a few.
mucho,	much.
muchos,	many.
varios,	several.
cualquiera,	whichsoever, any.
cualquiera cosa,	whatever.
quienquiera,	whosoever.
tal,	such.
fulano,	such a person.

fulano y zutano,	such and such a person.
cuanto,	how much.
cuantos,	how many.
ninguno, nadie,	none, no one, nobody.
nada,	nothing.
ni uno ni otro,	neither.

2. These indefinites are subject to a variation of number and gender, except *álguien, algo, cada, nadie,* and *nada,* which are always used in the *singular* number, and are common to *both* genders : *tal,* and its plural *tales,* are common to both genders : *ámbos, entrámbos,* and *varios,* are always employed in the *plural* number, and are made to agree in *gender* with the nouns to which they refer. *Cualquiera* forms its plural by *cualesquiera,* and is common to both genders. *Quienquiera* is seldom used in the plural number, which is *quienesquiera,* but it is common to both genders. *Cualquiera, cualquiera cosa,* and *quienquiera,* require *que* after them, when followed by a verb in the *subjunctive. Álguien, quienquiera, fulano, zutano,* and *nadie,* refer to persons only ; *algo* and *nada* to things only, and all the rest to both. The following are examples of the use of each of the *indefinite* pronouns.

ALGUNO, ÁLGUIEN.

Alguno está ahí.	*Somebody,* or *some one* is there.
Algunos lo dicen.	*Some* say so.
¿ Lo ha visto *álguien,* or *alguno?*	Has *any one,* or *anybody* seen it?
Necesito *algun* dinero y *algunas* letras de cambio.	I want *some* money and *some* bills of exchange.

Note 1.—When *some one* or *any one* is followed by *of,* we must use *alguno* in the translation, and not *álguien;* as, *Si alguno de ellos viniere*—If any one of them should come. *Alguno de ellos lo opuso*—Some one of them opposed it.

Note 2.—*Any one* or *anybody,* not used interrogatively, is translated *cualquiera;* as, *Cualquiera lo creeria*—Any one, *or* anybody would believe it.

ALGO, ALGUNA COSA.

Tengo *algo,* or *alguna cosa* que decirle.	I have *something* to tell you.
¿ Tiene *algo* para mí ?	Has he *anything* for me ?
Sí, *algo* tiene.	Yes, he has *something.*

Note 1.—Anything, not used interrogatively, is translated *cualquiera cosa;* as, *Cualquiera cosa que se ofrezca*—Anything that may offer.

Note 2.—When *algo* is employed as a noun, and followed by an adjective, the latter is preceded by the preposition *de;* and if followed by an infinitive, *que* is required instead of *de;* as ¿ *Trae algo de bueno ?*—Does he bring anything good? *Hay algo que temer en eso*—There is something to fear in that.—See also NADA.

UNO, UNOS.

Qué puede hacer *uno* en tal caso ?	What can *one* (or a person) do in such a case ?
Unos dicen que sí ; *unos* dicen que no.	Some say yes; some say no.
Deme Vmd. *unas* almendras; *unas* pasas.	Give me *a few* almonds; *a few* raisins.

Note.—One or ones, employed in English in place of a noun after an adjective, is not translated into Spanish : Ex. There is a dollar; see if it is a good one—*Allí está un peso; vea Vmd. si es bueno.* Have you any kid gloves ? Yes, sir, very excellent ones —¿ *Tiene Vmd. guantes de ante? Sí, Señor, muy excelentes.*

UNO Á OTRO, UNO Ú OTRO, UNO Y OTRO.

Se aman *uno á otro.*	They love *one another,* or *each other.*
Que venga *uno ú otro.*	Let *one* or *the other* come.
Que *uno y otro* decidan.	Let *one and the other* decide.
Unos y otros han de sufrir.	The *ones* and the *others* must suffer.

CADA, CADA UNO, CADA CUAL.

When *each* or *every* is immediately followed by a noun,
cada must be used in the translation : Ex.

Cada pais tiene sus costumbres.	*Every country* has its customs.
Dí un duro por *cada tomo*.	I gave a dollar for *each volume*.

When *each* or *every* is not followed by a noun, it is
translated *cada uno*, or *cada cual :* Ex.

Cada uno me costó una libra.	*Each* cost me a pound.
Cada cual sabe lo que le duele.	*Every one* knows what troubles him.

OTRO, OTROS.

Deme Vmd. *otro*.	Give me *another*.
Otros han hecho lo mismo.	*Others* have done the same.
Tengo *otras* cosas que hacer.	I have *other* things to do.

Note.—Another's, and *other people's*, used in a vague
sense are sometimes translated *ageno ;* as, *No codicies el
bien ageno*—Do not covet another's wealth. *Debemos
respetar lo ageno*—We must respect what belongs to
other people, *or* what is other people's.

ÁMBOS, *or sometimes* ENTRÁMBOS.

Ámbos se encapricharon de ella.	*Both* took a fancy to her.
Ambas murieron.	They *both* died.
Los ví á *entrámbos*.	I saw them *both*.

Note.—Both, employed in English before two nouns,
pronouns, or adjectives, is not translated: Ex. She is
both rich and handsome—*Ella es rica y hermosa*. I
begged both him and her to remain. *Rogué á él y á ella
que se quedasen.*

TODO, TODOS.

Todo tiene su fin.	*Everything* has its end.
Todos lo saben.	*All* know it, or *everybody* knows it.
Toda la ciudad salió a recibirle.	*All* the town went out to receive him.

POCO, POCOS.

Poco bastará.	A *little* will suffice.
A *pocos* les pesa.	*Few* regret it.
Tomaré *unos pocos*, or *unos, cuantos*.	I will take a *few*.

Note.—But *little*, and *but few* are translated *pocuísimo*, and *pocuísimos ;* as, I have but little to do—*Tengo pocuísimo que hacer.* They have but few left—*Les queda pocuísimos.*

MUCHO, MUCHOS.

No me dé Vmd. *mucho.*	Do not give me *much.*
Muchos lo toleran.	*Many* tolerate it.

Note.—*A great many* is translated *muchísimos*, and a *great deal, muchísimo ;* as, I have a great many complaints to make to you.—*Tengo muchísimas quejas que hacerle.* You have given me a great deal—*Me ha dado Vmd. muchísimo.*

VARIOS.

Varios se acordaron de él.	*Several* remembered him.
Lo he visto *varias* veces.	I have seen it *several* times.

CUALQUIERA, CUALESQUIERA.

Cualquiera que Vmd. guste.	*Whichever,* or *whichsoever* you please.
Cualesquiera, or *cualquiera* personas que se atreviesen.	*Whatever* persons should venture.
Cualquiera de ellos servirá.	*Either,* or *any* of them will do.

CUALQUIERA COSA.

Cualquiera cosa que digan.	*Whatever* they may say.
Cualesquiera cosas que compren.	*Whatever* things they may buy.
Cualquiera cosa le basta.	*Anything* will do for him.

Note 1.— *Whatever*, meaning *all what*, or *all that which,* is translated *todo lo que ;* as, *Haré todo le que Vmd. me mande*—I will do whatever you desire me.

Note 2.—Some writers drop the final vowel of *cual-quiera* before a noun masculine; as, *cualquier hombre;* but the retention or omission of it is a mere matter of taste.

QUIENQUIERA.

Quienquiera que sea.	*Whoever* or *whosoever* he may be.
De *quienquiera* que Vmd. hable.	Of *whomsoever* you may speak.

TAL, TALES.

Tal hombre; *tal* muger.	*Such* a man; *such* a woman.
Tales cosas; *tales* papeles.	*Such* things; *such* papers.

FULANO, FULANO Y ZUTANO.

Quién es el Señor *fulano?*	Who is Mr. *Such-a-one?*
Vmd. dijo que *fulano* y *zu-tano* ya la sabian.	You said that *such* and *such-a-one* already knew it.

CUANTO, CUANTOS.

Cuánto quiere Vmd.?	*How much* do you want?
No sé *cuantos.*	I don't know *how many.*

NINGUNO, NADIE.

Ninguna persona, *ninguno,* or *nadie* lo sabe.	*No* person, *nobody,* or *no one* knows it.
Ningunos esfuerzos suyos.	*No* efforts of his.
No se lo dé Vmd. á *nadie,* or á *ninguno.*	Do *not* give it to *anybody.*
Nadie, or *ninguno* volvió.	*None,* or *no one* returned.

Note 1.—*Ninguno* relates to persons and things; but *nadie* to persons only.

Note 2.—When *none* or *no one* is followed by *of*, we must employ *ninguno* in the translation, and not *nadie;* as, *Ninguno de esos soldados*—None of those soldiers. *Ninguno de los que Vmd. conoce*—No one of those you know.

NADA.

No trajo *nada,* or *nada* trajo consigo.	He did *not* bring *anything,* or he brought *nothing* with him.
No vale *nada.*	It is worth *nothing.*

Note.—When *nada* is employed as a noun and followed by an adjective, the latter is preceded by the preposition *de;* and if followed by an infinitive, *que* is required instead of *de* (as we have seen is the case with ALGO); as, *No traen nada de nuevo*—They bring nothing new. *No falta nada que hacer*—There is nothing wanting to be done.

NI UNO NI OTRO.

Ni uno ni otro me gusta.	I do *not* like *either;* or I like *neither.*
Ni unos ni otros me acomodan.	*Neither* the *ones* nor *the others* suit me.
Ni las unas ni las otras saben lo que hacen.	*Neither* do *the ones* nor *the others* know what they are about.

EXERCISE ON INDEFINITE PRONOUNS.

Let some one follow him. I am waiting for somebody.
  que   siga   estoy esperando á

Some [will go] to-day, and some to-morrow. If anybody
    irán   si

should consent. Can any one [be ignorant of it]?
  * consintiese puede   ignorarlo

Have (1) you (3) bought (2) anything for me? One
  ha   Vmd.   comprado   para

[is not certain] of living till to-morrow. Some will,
no está cierto   vivir hasta   quieren

some will (2) not (1). Take a few walnuts. They com-
         no   tome   nuez   co-

municate their ideas to one another. One or the other
munican

must go. Both listened. We revised each paragraph.
debe ir   escucharon   revisámos   párrafo.

Each came with her own complaint.   Another (person)
    venia con   *   queja

would have acted differently.   Other people do
hubiera   obrado diferentemente   hacen

the same.   All was sold.   Every one applauded him.
  mismo   se vendió   aplaudieron

Give me a little.   Few are happy.   I eat a few of those
 dé   son   comí

raisins.   We do not require   much to be happy.
 pasa   no necesitamos   para ser

Many disappeared.   Many [have been exalted] many
   desaparecieron   se   han   alzado

times with the name of great, by the false opinions of
 vez con   nombre   por   falso ——

the vulgar.   [There were] several of his opinion.   Give
 vulgo   habia   parecer

me whichever you please.   Either of them [will do].
    guste   servirá

Whatever situation he may hold. Whatever [might hap-
   colocacion   que tenga   suceda

pen]. Whoever he [may be].   I never saw such a thing.
    sea   jamas ví

Such actions are unworthy of him.   Such-a-one knew
   —— son indigno   supo

it.   Such and such-a-one witnessed it.   How much
    presenciaron

[shall I bring]?   How many would rejoice at it!
  traeré   se alegrarian de

[There is not] any of them there.   No promises could
  no hay   allí   promesa pudieron

tempt him. No one knows him. Nothing should hinder
tentar   conoce   debia impedir

us from doing our duty.   Neither has finished his task.
  hacer   deber   ha concluido   tarea

Neither of these comedies has much merit.
    comedia tiene   mérito

LECTURE XX.

ETYMOLOGY AND SYNTAX OF VERBS.

1. There are four kind of verbs to be considered— namely, *auxiliary*, *active*, *passive*, and *neuter*.

2. The *auxiliary* verbs in Spanish are *haber*, to have, and *ser* and *estar*, to be. They are called auxiliary from their peculiar office in assisting to form the compound tenses of all other verbs in general.

3. A verb is called *active* when its action passes from one person or thing to another; for which reason it is also called *transitive;* thus, *to strike, to hate, to write, to see,* etc., are *active* verbs, because the action described by them may pass over to a person or thing acted upon, called the *object* of the verb : for instance, *William struck Henry ; They hate vice ;* in which examples the noun *William,* and the pronoun *they,* are the agents or nominatives of the verbs *to strike* and *to hate,* respectively; and the nouns *Henry* and *vice,* being the person and thing *acted upon,* or affected by the verbs, are the *objects* of these verbs.

4. *Active* verbs become *reflective* when their agent and object are but one person or thing ; that is, when the agent acts upon himself. In the examples, *I see myself; He loves himself;* it is observed that the action described by each verb does not affect any other object besides its agent. When there is a *reciprocity* of action between two or more persons or things, the verb denoting the action is called a *reciprocal* verb : for instance, *We see each other ; They love one another.*

5. A verb is called *passive* when it describes the state of a person or thing suffering from, or *enduring* an action done by another person or thing. All active verbs, and a few neuter verbs, become passive when employed with the auxiliary *to be ;* thus, *Henry was beaten by William ; Vice is abhorred by the virtuous.* Here we see that the verbs *to be beaten* and *to be abhorred* express a *suffering,* or a *passiveness,* on which account they are called *passive* verbs. In the first example, although *Henry* is the

sufferer, he is not the *accusative* case of the verb *to be beaten*; because, wherever there is the verb *to be*, it can have reference only to a *nominative* case, and *Henry* is described to be in a *state of suffering* from an action. *William* is not the nominative of the verb, because he is governed by the preposition *by*, which denotes *instrumentality*; *William* is therefore in the *ablative* case. The same observations apply to the second example.

6. A *neuter* verb is neither active nor passive. By a neuter verb something is represented as *existing* or *being*, denoting only the state of the agent of the verb; the action of the verb does not pass over to any other person or thing; for which reason neuter verbs have also been called intransitive. *To live, to sit, to sleep, to stand*, are *neuter* verbs, because they merely denote the various states of being of their agents: for the same reason *to be*, besides being an auxiliary, is likewise a neuter verb. To distinguish a neuter from an active verb, we have only to put a noun after it, and if it makes sense with the noun, it is active; if it does not, it is neuter.

Although neuter verbs are not called active, still there are some that denote a visible action, such as, *to go, to come, to run*, and many others; but the actions denoted by them are not *transitive*, since they remain with their agents; as, *the man walks, the horse runs, the boy swims*, etc. Verbs of this kind are called *active intransitive*.

7. There are some verbs which, according to the manner they are employed, are sometimes *active*, and at others *neuter*; thus, *to run* is *active*, when we say, *To run a race*, because the action of the verb passes on to the object *race*; but it is neuter in, *He runs fast*, because the action of the verb remains with its agent *He*, and admits of no objective case after it.

8. Verbs are again subdivided into *regular, irregular, impersonal*, and *defective*.

9. *Regular* verbs are all those that are conjugated throughout every mood and tense according to certain models which are considered standards for all regular verbs. In the conjugations of regular verbs in this grammar (LECT. 24), *hablar*, to speak; *temer*, to fear; and *sufrir*, to suffer, are given as models for conjugating all the regular verbs in the Spanish language.

10. *Irregular* verbs are those that deviate in some instances from the general standard. In LECT. 25 are given lists of all the irregular verbs in the Spanish language, exhibiting the irregularities of each.

11. *Impersonal* verbs are those that are employed in the *third* person only of every tense ; thus, *to rain, to thunder, to dawn*, and many others, are *impersonal* verbs. They are so called because in their employment there appears no apparent person or thing acting as their agent; for when we say *it rains, it thunders*, etc., we do not express *who* or *what* it is that *rains* or *thunders*. See the Conjugation of *Impersonal* Verbs, LECT. 26.

12. *Defective* verbs are such as are only used in certain tenses, and with certain persons, because their peculiar meaning does not admit them to be employed with every tense and person. See the Conjugations of *Defective* Verbs, LECT. 26.

13. We have now four more things connected with verbs to be considered—namely, the *conjugations*, the *moods*, the *tenses*, and the *person* and *number*.

THE CONJUGATIONS.

14. The conjugation of a verb is the exhibiting under one view all the various changes which it undergoes in the several moods, tenses, persons, and numbers. These variations are much more numerous in verbs in the Spanish and other foreign languages than they are in English verbs, and therefore become a matter of moment to attend to.

THE MOODS.

15. *Mood*, or *mode*, which signifies *manner*, expresses the intention of the mind concerning the manner in which we use the verb. There are four moods—namely, the *infinitive*, the *indicative*, the *subjunctive*, and the *imperative*.

16. The *infinitive*, which is the root of the verb, represents the action, or the state of being, in a general and unlimited manner, without any reference to time, number or person ; thus, the verbs *hablar, temer,* and *sufrir*, to speak, to fear, and to suffer, in the manner here expressed,

do not denote when, nor in what manner, the actions represented by them take place, nor who act as their agents; to determine all which, a verb in the infinitive mood must have an antecedent verb, or, as it is sometimes called, a governing verb; as, Voy *á hablar*—I am going to speak. *No* pude *venir*—I could not come. *Nos* harán *sufrir*—They will make us suffer. In these examples it is also seen that the infinitive in both languages is sometimes preceded by a preposition, and sometimes not: this is a subject that will be treated on in the Government of Verbs, LECT. 28.

17. The Spanish infinitive frequently partakes of the nature of a noun, and becomes a nominative or an objective case. The greater part of infinitives may be thus employed by prefixing the definite article to them : Ex.

El mucho *estudiar á* veces prejudica á la salud.	Too much study sometimes injures the health.
Al salir de casa encontré á mi amigo.	On going out of the house I met my friend.

Sometimes, chiefly at the beginning of a sentence, the infinitive is employed as a subordinate verb, and is equivalent to a verb in the subjunctive mood preceded by the conjunction *si*, if: Ex.

Á saber yo que hubiera venido, no habria salido.	If I had known that he would have come, I would not have gone out.

Which is equivalent to *si yo hubiera sabido que*, etc.

18. The *indicative* mood is so called because it simply *indicates* or points out the action or state of being in a positive and unconditional manner, depending on no other verb to determine its signification : Ex.

Yo confio; vosotros procedeis; ellos prohiben.	I trust; you proceed; they prohibit.

19. It does not always occur that the same mood and tense are employed in both languages; it frequently happens that when one particular mood or tense is employed in English, a different one is required in Spanish; this matter will be fully explained in LECT. 28.

20. The *subjunctive* mood makes no complete sense of itself, as the indicative does; but it represents the

action, or state of being, under some *doubt, condition,* or *uncertainty,* being dependent for its signification on, or subordinate to some other verb (expressed or understood), to which it is subjoined by means of a conjunction. A verb in the subjunctive mood, therefore, depends on some circumstance denoted by the antecedent verb to render its signification complete : Ex.

Leeria *si tuviera* tiempo.	I would read *if I had* time.
Temo *que riñan.*	I fear *that they may quarrel.*
Deseaba *que hubiese* triunfado.	I wished *that* he *had* triumphed.
Lo haré *con tal que con-sienta.*	I will do it *provided he consent.*

21. The conjunction *que* (that), which governs the verb in the subjunctive mood, may, by way of ellipsis, be suppressed in both languages, but less often in Spanish than in English ; as, *Ojalá* (que) *haga buen tiempo mañana*—I hope (*that*) it may be fine to-morrow. *Deseaba* (que) *volviese Vmd. pronto*—I wished (*that*) you might soon return.

22. It is not every conjunction that governs the subjunctive mood; for instance, some govern the infinitive, which are those that are followed by the preposition *de;* such as, *á fin de,* in order to; *por miedo de,* for fear of, etc. The following may govern the indicative when they do not express doubt or uncertainty—namely, *como,* as ; *porque,* because ; *pues que,* since ; *miéntras,* whilst ; *aunque,* though, etc. But all those govern the subjunctive that denote *doubt, wish, supposition,* or *uncertainty;* as, *aménos que,* unless ; *á fin que,* in order that; *bien que, aunque,* although ; *sea que,* whether ; *no obstante que,* notwithstanding ; *sí,* if, whether ; *en caso que,* in case that ; *ántes que,* before ; *hasta que,* until ; *cuando,* when ; *cuando quiera que,* whenever ; *á condicion que,* on condition that, providing ; *para que,* in order that ; *sin que,* without, unless ; *por miedo que,* for fear that ; *dado que,* granted ; *supuesto que,* provided, etc. The following examples will show how the same conjunction governs the verb, sometimes in the indicative, and sometimes in the subjunctive, according to the sense in which it is used :

Aunque le *conozco* no le hablo.	*Although* I *know* him, I do not speak to him.
No le hablaria *aunque* le *conociera*.	I would not speak to him, *though* I *knew* him.
Creo *que viene* cada dia.	I believe *that* he *comes* every day.
Creo *que venga* esta noche.	I think *that* he *may come* to-night.
Si engaña, no es mi culpa.	*If* he *deceives*, it is not my fault.
Si le *engañare*, Vmd. tendrá la culpa.	*If* he *should deceive* you, it will be your fault.

By these examples it will be seen that when we speak *positively*, the indicative is employed; but whenever there exists the least indication of *doubt* in our expressions, the subjunctive must be used.

23. In the natural construction of language that member of the sentence containing the antecedent verb precedes the one with the subordinate verb, but they may exchange situations for the sake of variety or energy; as, *Con tal que Vmd. consienta, lo haré*—Provided you consent, I will do it. For the manner of employing the subjunctive mood, see LECT. 21, PAR. 22 to 28; and LECT. 28, PAR. 8, from Observation 5th to 9th.

24. The *imperative* mood is used for *commanding*, or for *entreatiug* : Ex.

Acuérdate de tu deber.	*Remember* thy duty.
Elija Vmd. el que guste.	*Choose* which you like.
Suplico á Vmd. me lo explique.	I beseech you to explain it to me.

When the imperative is employed in English in a *negative* sense, the present tense of the subjunctive mood preceded by a negative particle, is used in Spanish instead : Ex.

No le *compadezcas*.	Do not (thou) pity him.
No me *ofendais*.	Do not (you) offend me.
Jamas *lisonjees* á nadie.	Never do (thou) flatter any one.

This deviation is only striking in the second person singular and plural, since in the other persons the verb is spelled alike in the imperative and the present of the subjunctive; as, *exija*, that he may exact, or, let him exact; *imploremos*, that we may implore, or, let us implore; *cometan*, that they may commit, or, let them commit.

THE TENSES.

25. Tense signifies *time*, and as all actions and states of existence must necessarily be limited to time, they are said to be either in the *present*, the *past*, or the *future* tense. These are the three grand divisions of time. The present tense denotes that the action or the state of being represented by the verb is taking place, or existing at the time of expressing it; as, *I write, you explain, he sleeps*. In the *past* tense the action or state of being is represented as having taken place, or to have already commenced; as, *I wrote, you explained, he slept*. And in the future tense the action or state of being is represented as a circumstance to take place at a time which is yet to come; as, *I shall write, you will explain, they will sleep*.

26. Each of these three grand divisions of time has, by philologers, been subdivided, in order to denote the time of being, or of action, with greater minuteness and precision. These subdivisions of time are what are called the *compound tenses*. They are so called because, to express them, more than one word is required in the English and Spanish languages; for instance, *I have written*, is the *compound* of the *present* tense of the verb *to write; you had explained*, is the *compound* of the *past* tense of the verb *to explain;* and *he will have slept*, is the *compound* of the *future* tense of the verb *to sleep*. We here see that each of these tenses is formed by compounding the auxiliary *to have*, with the *past participle* of the verb denoting the action or the state of being. Latin verbs admit of such great variety of inflections, that each of their tenses is formed by a single word, and to each is given a different name. Many of the writers of modern grammars have adopted Latin names in a variety of forms to designate the several tenses by; but the foregoing disposition of them has been considered more simple and comprehensive. The following are the names of tenses of Latin origin that are most generally

adopted :—*Present*, I write. *Preterimperfect*, or *perfect indefinite*, I wrote. *Preterperfect*, or *perfect definite*, I have written. *Preterpluperfect*, I had written. *Future imperfect*, I shall write. *Future perfect*, I shall have written.

PERSON AND NUMBER.

27. Every verb has at least one noun or pronoun for its agent or nominative. Sometimes, however, the nominative may not be expressed, but then it is always understood, and this suppression of the nominative occurs with much more frequency in Spanish than in English, especially as regards pronouns, as we have seen in LECT. 14, PAR. 12.

28. There are three persons and two numbers. *I read, thou singest, the man walks*, are the first, second, and third persons singular number; and *we read, you sing*, and *the men walk*, are the first, second, and third persons plural number.

LECTURE XXI.

USE AND EMPLOYMENT OF THE TENSES.

PRESENT TENSE OF THE INDICATIVE MOOD.

1. This tense expresses the existing state of things; what is being done, or taking place at the present time; and what exists permanently. All present customs, habits, and professions of individuals and nations, are also expressed by this tense: Ex.

El gobierno de los Estados Unidos *es* democrático.	The government of the United States *is* democratic.
Yo *escribo* y ella *dibuja*.	I *write* and she *draws*.
La luna *acompaña* á la tierra.	The moon *accompanies* the earth.
Los Européos *cultivan* las sciencias.	The Europeans *cultivate* the sciences.
Ella se *levanta* tarde.	She *rises* late.
El *es* coronel.	He *is* a colonel.

2. This tense is sometimes formed in both languages with the verb *estar*, to be, and the present participle of the verb denoting the action, and, in a more forcible manner, describes it as occurring at the time of expressing it: Ex.

| Estoy escribiendo. | I am writing. |
| Estan leyendo. | They are reading. |

The same construction is likewise made use of to describe any action in a present progressive state, though, perhaps, not actually in operation at the precise moment of naming it: Ex.

| Mi amigo *está viajando*. | My friend *is travelling*. |
| *Estoy componiendo* una obra. | *I am getting* up a work. |

3. In English there are three ways of forming the present tense; for instance, *I think, I am thinking, I do think;* the first and second forms are likewise used in Spanish, as we have just seen; but the third, with the auxiliary *do*, the employment of which adds greater energy to the affirmative, does not admit of a literal translation into Spanish; instead of which, the verb is sometimes modified by an adverb: Ex.

| Canta muy bien, *devéras*. | She *does* sing very well. |
| *Sí*, lo creo. | I *do* believe it. |

4. When the auxiliary *do* is employed in English as a substitute for the verb which it represents, if the verb and auxiliary are in the same number and person, the affirmative particle *sí*, or the negative *no*, is used instead in Spanish; but if the English verb and auxiliary are in different persons and numbers, the verb in Spanish is repeated, each verb agreeing in number and person with its own agent: Ex.

Él no se *queja*, pero ella *sí*.	He does not *complain*, but she *does*.
Ella *necesita* dinero, pero él no.	She *wants* money, but he *does* not.
Vmd. no le *conoce*, pero nosotros le *conocemos*.	You do not *know* him, but we *do*.
Yo le *perdono*, y ellos tambien le *perdonan*.	I *pardon* him, and so *do* they.

The like is observed with *can, shall, will,* and all other verbs employed in English as auxiliaries.—See PAR. 18 and 30 of this LECTURE.

Observe, that when *to do* is employed as a principal verb, and not as an auxiliary, it is translated by the verb *hacer;* as, Haré *lo que Vmd. me manda* hacer—I will *do* what you desire me to *do.*

For the auxiliary *do,* employed as the sign of negative and interrogative sentences, see LECT. 24, PAR. 8 and 9.

5. There is what is called the *historical present tense,* by which historians, in order to give more animation to their descriptions, represent past events in the present form of the verb; as, *Apénas dada la órden,* se avanza *la caballería,* ataca *al enemigo, que presto* queda *completamente derrotado*—The order was scarcely given, when the cavalry *advances, attacks* the enemy, who soon *remains* completely routed.

6. The present tense is sometimes used to express a future movement, to the performance of which the mind has already been made up; as, *Nosotros nos* vamos *mañana, y ellos* salen *el dia despues*—We *go* to-morrow, and they *leave* the following day.

PAST TENSE OF THE INDICATIVE MOOD.

7. This tense in Spanish is divided into the past *imperfect* and the past *perfect,* and as in English, both are frequently expressed by the same inflection of the verb, learners of the Spanish language are often at a loss to know which of the two forms of the verb to employ, since, in translating from English, they must, in most cases, be guided by the meaning of the sentence, in order to determine whether the verb be in the past *imperfect* or the past *perfect* tense.

Those who are acquainted with the Latin, Italian, or French language will immediately perceive the distinction between these two tenses, since their employment in Spanish is almost precisely the same as in those three languages, as will be seen by the following exposition.

Past Imperf.	ENGLISH . .	I *went* to the theatre very frequently.
	SPANISH . .	*Iba* muy amenudo al teatro.
	ITALIAN . .	*Andava* spessissimo al teatro.
	FRENCH . .	*J'allois* très souvent au théâtre.
	LATIN . . .	Theatrum sœpissime *adibam*.
Past Perfect.	ENGLISH . .	I *went* to the theatre last night.
	SPANISH . .	*Fuí* al teatro anoche.
	ITALIAN . .	*Andai* jersera al teatro.
	FRENCH . .	*J'allai* au théâtre hier au soir.
	LATIN . . .	Superiori nocte theatrum *adivi*.
Past Imperf.	ENGLISH . .	The Romans *were* great warriors.
	SPANISH . .	Los Romanos *eran* grandes guerreros.
	ITALIAN . .	I Romani *erano* grandi guerrieri.
	FRENCH . .	Les Romains *etaient* de grands guerriers.
	LATIN . . .	Romani bello fortes *erant*.
Past Perfect.	ENGLISH . .	The Romans *conquered* Britain.
	SPANISH . .	Los Romanos *conquistaron* á la Bretaña.
	ITALIAN . .	I Romani *conquistarono* la Britannia.
	FRENCH . .	Les Romains *conquirent* la Bretagne.
	LATIN . . .	Romani Britanniam *domuerunt*.

8. The principal and most general characteristics of these two tenses are, that the past *imperfect* denotes, first, the action of existence *to be* in a *continuative* or *progressive* state; or, secondly, that it has some connexion with the *present* time; or, thirdly, its occurring at a time whilst another action was taking place, and therefore *co-existing* with it; whereas the past *perfect* tense denotes the action or state of being to have *completely* or *perfectly passed*, at some particular or defined period, having no connexion with the present time; for which reason it is sometimes called the past *definite* tense, as the *imperfect* is sometimes called the past *indefinite*. For instance, if I say, *James loved Ellen*, my hearer is in doubt whether that love con-

tinues to exist, or has ceased, or whether it existed at a period when another circumstance, having reference to the time of its existence, was taking place. This doubt will be removed by continuing the sentence; as *James* loved *Ellen, and still loves her.* Now we see that the act of loving is described to be in a *continuative* or *progressive* state, and it is also connected with the *present* time; the verb is therefore in the past *imperfect* tense. In the following example, *James* loved *Ellen long before he married her*, although the act of loving may have no reference to the present time, nevertheless it is represented to be in a *continuative* state; therefore *loved* is here likewise in the past *imperfect* tense. Again, in *James* loved *Ellen when he married her*, the act of loving is represented to have existed at the time that the marriage took place; that is, it expresses an action *present* with respect to a time *past;* therefore that action is also in the past *imperfect* tense. But in the sentence, *I* wrote to *John last Monday*, the act of writing is represented as having taken place at a particular or definite period, which is entirely *gone by;* it is not in a *progressive* state, nor has it any reference to another action; it is therefore in the past *perfect* tense.

9. It is of essential importance to the student to know how to distinguish these two tenses at once; and, therefore, for the better illustration of them, some examples are here given in both languages: for instance, Past Imperfect—*Iba* á la librería. Past Perfect—*Fuí* á la librería. Both these examples are translated, *I* went *to the library;* but the meaning of the first is, *I used to go;* or, *I was in the habit of going;* or, *was accustomed to go to the library;* as, *Cuando estaba en Madrid* iba *todos los dias á la librería*—When I was in Madrid I *went,* or, I *used to go* to the library every day. In which the act of *going* is described as a *reiterated* action, or one that the actor was *accustomed* to do, or in the *habit* of doing; but in the second instance the verb alludes to some *particular* or *stated* period; as, Fuí *á la librería* ayer—I *went* to the library *yesterday.* And here we see that the particular period in which the act of *going* took place, is referred to; it is *perfectly* passed at a definite period, and has no connection with the present time.

10. With the past *imperfect* tense are also described

all former customs, habits, professions, etc., of individuals and nations no longer existing, as well as those which belonged formerly to persons still existing : Ex.

Los Israelitas *hacian* sacrificios á Dios.	The Israelites *made* sacrifices to God : i.e. *were in the habit of making.*
Los Egipcios *cultivaban* las sciencias.	The Egyptians *cultivated* the sciences.
Ciceron *era* grande orador.	Cicero *was* a great orator.
Yo *viajaba* mucho cuando *era* mas jóven.	I *used to travel* much when I *was* younger.

11. The past *perfect* tense describes a former, but not a progressive act, or state of being. It represents the occurrence as *entirely passed* at some particular period, as before stated. To authorise the use of this tense, the time in which the circumstance represented by it occurred must have no relation whatever with the present period ; that is, it cannot be employed in reference to anything that has taken place in the century, year, month, week, or day, of which the period in which we are speaking forms a portion : Ex.

Fui á verle *ayer.*	I *went* to see him *yesterday.*
Llegué á Lóndres *en el año* de 1838.	I *arrived* in London *in the year* 1838.
Murió hace dos meses.	He *died* two months ago.
Cervántes *nació* á mediados del siglo diez y seis, y *murió* á principios del diez y siete.	Cervantes *was* born about the middle of the 16th century, and *died* towards the beginning of the 17th.

12. In the *historical* style the past *perfect* tense is generally used, for which reason it has been called the *historical past* tense : (See PAR. 5) : Ex.

No se *atrevieron* los enemigos á subir la cuesta, ni *dieron* indicio de intentar el asalto, pero se *acercaron* á tiro de piedra.—(SOLIS—*Hist. de la Conquista de México.*)	The enemy *did* not venture to ascend the hill, nor *did* he give any indication of attempting an assault, but he *approached* within a stone's throw.

Ya entónces se *mostraron* por toda la línea victorio-sos los aliados. *Recogié-ronse* los Franceses á su antigua posicion	Then the allies *proved* victorious throughout the whole line. The French *retired* to their former position.

(EL CONDE DE TORENO—*Hist. de la Revol. de España.*)

13. The observations made in the *present* tense, on the manner of forming it with the help of auxiliaries, are equally applicable to the *past* tense, by employing these auxiliaries in their *past* form; and in the translation the verb is put in the *past* tense accordingly: Ex.

Estaba escuchando.	*I was* listening.
Estuvimos paseando.	*We were* walking.
Vmds. no le *vieron*, pero yo le *ví*.	You did not *see* him, but I *did*.
Yo le *conocia*, mas ellos no le *conocian*.	I *knew* him, but they *did* not know him.
Él la *encontró*; *¿ no es ver-dad ?*	He *met* her; *did* he not ?

FUTURE TENSE OF THE INDICATIVE.

14. This tense indicates that something will exist or take place at a time which is not yet arrived: Ex.

Él *será* eligido.	He *will be* elected.
Lo *considerarémos*.	We *will consider* it.
Enviaré la carta mañana.	I *shall send* the letter to-morrow.

15. The *future* tense is sometimes used in Spanish instead of the *present*, when something is affirmed, respecting the certainty of which some doubt is entertained; as, Vendrá, *quizá, para amenazarme*—He *comes*, perhaps, to threaten me :—instead of *Viene quizá*, etc.

16. It is likewise used in Spanish instead of the *present* or *past* tense in *interrogative* sentences, when the interrogator is almost persuaded that a contradictory reply could not be given to his interrogation : Ex.

¿ Habrá desgracia mayor que la mia ?	*Can* there be a greater misfortune than mine ?
¿ Se habrá visto cosa mas primorosa ?	*Was* there ever seen any thing more exquisite ?

17. When *shall* and *will* are not employed as signs of
the English future tense, but as principal verbs denoting
a *voluntary act, will*, or *threat*, they must be translated
by verbs equivalent in meaning : Ex.

¿ *Quiére* Vmd. prestarme su cortaplumas ?	*Will* you lend me your penknife ?
Quiere ir, *or*, se obstina en que *ah* de ir, aunque le dige que no fuera.	He *will* go, although I desired him not to go.
¿ *He* de aguantar tal impertinencia ?	*Shall* I suffer such impertinence ?
Me he empeñado en que *ha* de ser como digo.	I insist that it *shall* be as I say.

18. When *shall* and *will* are employed as substitutes
for the verbs which they represent, the same rule is to
be observed as with the auxiliary *do* when so employed :
See PAR. 4 of this LECTURE : Ex.

Yo no *procederé*, pero él *procederá*.	I shall not proceed, but he *will*.
Ella *esperará*, mas yo no *esperaré*.	She will wait, but I *shall* not.
Vmds. lo *evitarán*, yo no lo *evitaré*.	You will avoid it, I *will* not.
Quiere aventurarse ; ¿ *no es verdad ?*	He will venture ; *will* he ?

COMPOUND OF THE PRESENT OF THE INDICATIVE MOOD.

19. This tense denotes a past action or state of being,
but at a period of which the present time forms a part ;
as, *Le* he escrito *tres veces esta semana—I have written* to
him three times this week.

In this sentence we see that the act of writing is
passed, but the period in which it has been performed,
namely, the *week*, still exists. This tense, therefore,
denotes an occurrence that has taken place during the
present day, week, month, year, century, or during any
period which is not entirely elapsed : Ex.

No le *he visto* hoy, ni en todo este mes.	I *have* not *seen* him to-day, nor during the whole of this month.

Muchas obras de mérito *han sido escritas* durante el presente siglo.	Many works of merit *have been written* during the present century.

In a like manner it denotes an action, or a state of being continued to the time of affirming it; as, *Hasta hoy no* he sentido *dolor alguno*—I *have felt* no pain whatever until to-day.

COMPOUND OF THE PAST TENSE OF THE INDICATIVE.

20. This tense, like the simple past, is divided into the *imperfect* and the *perfect*, and the difference between them is, that with the former the action is described to have taken place at some *unlimited* period prior to the occurrence of another action; but with the latter, an action is denoted to have occurred *immediately* before the taking place of another, and is therefore always preceded by some adverb of time, expressive of that effect; such as, *despues que*, after; *luego que*, or *así que*, as soon as; *no bien*, scarcely: Ex.

Habia acabado de almorzar ántes que él viniese.	I *had finished* breakfast before he came.
Ya *habia oido* la noticia.	I *had* already *heard* the news.
Llegaron *así que hubimos acabado* de comer.	They arrived *as soon as* we *had finished* dinner.
No bien hube acabado de escribir cuando entró ella.	I *had scarcely finished writing* when she entered.

The compound perfect is sometimes emphatically expressed in the following manner: *Acabado que hube de escribir entró ella.*

COMPOUND OF THE FUTURE OF THE INDICATIVE.

21. This tense denotes that an action or an event will have occurred at or before the taking place of another future action or event: Ex.

Mañana á esta hora ya lo *habrémos sabido*.	We *shall have known* it by to-morrow at this hour.
Habrán esparcido la noticia ántes que se acabe el dia.	They *will have spread* the news before the day is out.

TENSES OF THE SUBJUNCTIVE MOOD.

22. In this mood are given three tenses according to the GRAMMAR of the SPANISH ACADEMY—namely, the *present*, the *imperfect*, and the *future*, with their compounds. A verb in any tense of this mood denotes, as in English, a subordination to some event expressed by some other verb in the sentence. But as the English subjunctive is not so striking as the Spanish, care should be taken by the student to analyse every doubtful sentence before he attempts to translate it.

23. In Spanish a verb in the *simple present* of the subjunctive, or the *imperfect* of the same mood with the termination *ra*, or *se*, may have reference to a *present* or *future* subordinate action or state of being; but the termination *ria*, of the imperfect subjunctive, denotes a *future conditional* action, or state : Ex.

Temo que lo *sepa ahora,* ó mañana. — I fear he *may know* it *now, or to-morrow.*

Aunque yo le *amara ahora,* ó *despues.* — Although I *might love* him now, or *afterwards.*

Me *pesaria* mucho si no viniere. — I *would be* very sorry if he should not come.

24. In the *compound present* the verb may have reference to a *past* or *future* occurrence : Ex.

Aunque me lo *haya dicho el otro dia,* no me acuerdo ya de ello. — Although he *may have told* it me *the other day,* I no longer remember it.

No volveré hasta que me *hayan entregado* el dinero. — I shall not return until they *have delivered* me the money.

25. But in the *compound of the imperfect* the verb can only have reference to a *past* occurrence : Ex.

Le *hubiera ido* á ver ayer si *hubiese sabido* que estaba enfermo. — I *would have gone* to see him yesterday *had I known* he was ill.

Me *habria pagado* si *hubiera tenido* dinero en casa. — He *would have paid* me if he *had had* money at home.

26. The *future simple* can only refer to a *future subordinate* action or state of being: Ex.

Le traeré á Vmd. lo que me *dieren.*	I will bring you whatever they *may give* me.
Si *permaneciere* aquí algun tiempo se lo avisaré.	If I *should,* or *should I remain* here any time, I will let you know.

The *present* of the subjunctive may be substituted for this tense, except when the verb is preceded by the conditional *si;* as, *Todo lo que me* den—All that they may give me. *Cuando vengan*—When they (should) come.

27. The *future compound* refers to a past occurrence subordinate to a future event: Ex.

Si él *hubiere dejado* Granada ántes que le *alcance* mi carta.	If he *should have left* Granada before my letter (*should*) *reach* him.
Aun cuando le *hubiere escrito* ántes que llegase.	If even he *should have written* him before he (might) arrive.

The *compound present* of the subjunctive may be substituted for this tense, except when the verb is preceded by the conditional *si;* as, *Cuando* haya acabado, or *luego que* haya acabado *mi tarea,* etc.—When I shall have finished, or as soon as I should have finished my task, etc. See Government of Verbs as relates to Moods and Tenses, LECT. 28, PAR. 8.

EMPLOYMENT OF THE TERMINATIONS *ra, se,* AND *ria,* OF THE IMPERFECT TENSE OF THE SUBJUNCTIVE.

28. A verb in the imperfect tense of the subjunctive mood in Spanish has three terminations—namely, *ra, se,* and *ria;* as, *hablara, hablase, hablaria;* and the employment of the one or the other of these terminations is by no means a matter of indifference. It happens the same in English with the signs *should, might,* and *would,* of the subjunctive mood,* the use of which so often embarrasses foreigners, and not unfrequently even Englishmen. A Spaniard seldom errs in the application of the terminations *ra, se,* and *ria,* although it would, perhaps, be impracticable to give *fixed* rules for their employment to

---

* See the Author's English Grammar for the use of Spaniards, on this subject.

apply in *all* cases. Nevertheless the pupil is here presented with rules which, in *most* cases, will guide him through what has been considered, by many, as one of the intricate labyrinths in the Spanish language.

In the conjugations of verbs, the signs *should, might,* and *would,* are given as equivalents to the terminations *ra, se* and *ria;* yet they do not always correspond with them in the order as they there appear. The most general rule that can be given for the employment of these terminations is, that *ra* or *se* correspond with the signs *might* or *should;* and *ria* corresponds with *would.* This rule, however, will be subject to some exceptions; nevertheless the learner will find it very useful. A still better rule, indeed, almost a general one, for those who are acquainted with the French or Italian language, is, that the termination *ria* corresponds with the conditional of those two languages, and *ra* and *se,* indiscriminately, with the *imperfect of the subjunctive.** To those who are unacquainted with these languages, the following observations (many of which are extracted from the GRAMMAR OF THE ACADEMY) will afford a comprehensive view of the peculiar import of these inflections.

1st. When the verb in the imperfect of the subjunctive *is* preceded by a *conditional* conjunction, such as *si, con tal que, cuando,* etc., if, provided, when, etc., or by an interjection expressive of desire, either the termination *ra* or *se* may be employed: Ex.

---

* The plan set forth by the ROYAL ACADEMY OF MADRID, and adopted by almost every Spanish philologer, has, for the sake of uniformity, been followed in this Grammar, with regard to the placing of the three terminations, *ra, se,* and *ria,* of Spanish verbs in the *imperfect* tense of the *subjunctive* mood. But, in reality, the termination *ria* indicates the verb to be in a *conditional* mood, and not *subjunctive.* And if we analyse these terminations, we shall find that *amára,* and *amáse,* are derived from the Latin subjunctive *amarem,* and *amavissem;* and that the termination *ria —amaria—* and the future of the indicative—*amaré*—are derived from the Spanish infinitive *amar* and the auxiliary *haber;* thus, *amaré,* from *amar-he; amards,* from *amar-has,* etc.; and *amaria,* from *amar-habia,* or *amar-hia,* etc. Thus it is that *amára* and *amáse* coincide with the French and Italian subjunctive, *j'aimasse,* and *io amassi;* and *amaria,* with the conditional of those languages, *j'aimerais,* and *io amerei.* (See also LECT. 24, PAR. 4, on the ancient manner of forming the tenses of Spanish verbs.)

Si tuviera, or *tuviese* dinero compraria libros.	*If I had* money I would buy books.
Aun cuando tratara, or *tratase* de remediar el mal.	*Even when* he *should*, or *though* he *might* endeavour to remedy the evil.
Ojalá fuera, or *fuese* cierto.	*Would to God* it *were* true.

2nd. When the verb in the imperfect of the subjunctive *is not* preceded by a conditional conjunction, the termination *ra* or *ria* may be used : Ex.

Bueno *fuera*, or *seria* que le desterrasen.	It *would be* well that they banished him.
De buena gana *saliera*, or *saldria*.	I *would* willingly *go* out.

It results from the foregoing examples that the termination *ra* accommodates itself sometimes to serve in the place of *ria* or *se;* but that the latter two always differ in signification : also that *ra* and *se* may be preceded by a *conditional* conjunction, but *ria* cannot.

3rd. *Se* is generally employed if the imperfect subjunctive be preceded by a *relative*, or by the words *cuanto* or *cuantos*, as much or as many : Ex.

Premiaré á todos los *que hubiesen* hecho su deber.	I will reward all those *who may have* done their duty.
Compre Vmd. *cuanto*, or *cuantos quisiese*.	Buy *as much*, or *as many* as you *wish*.

4th. *Ria* is employed to denote a supposition that something may have occurred at any past period : Ex.

Le *pareceria* que yendo temprano la alcanzaria.	It perhaps *appeared* to him that by going early he would overtake her.

5th. When a verb in the imperfect of the subjunctive, governed by a conjunction, is preceded by a verb in any of the past tenses of the indicative or the subjunctive, either of the terminations *ra* or *se* may be employed with the governed verb, when it expresses a *power* or a *duty;* but if it denote a *will* or an *inclination*, *ria* is required : Ex.

Le llamé para que *saliera*, or *saliese* conmigo.	I called him that he *might* go out with me.

Si hubiera dicho que *viniera* or *viniese* Vmd.	If he had said that you *should* come, or *were* to come. . . . .
No creiamos que le *recompensaria.*	We did not think that he *would* reward him.
En ese caso hubiera pensado que lo *arreglaria.*	In that case I should have thought that he *would* arrange it.

6th. If the governing verb denote a *promise*, we should only employ the termination *ria* with the verb governed: Ex.

Prometió que me *prestaria* el dinero.	He *promised* that he *would* lend me the money.
Me *aseguró* que no me *expondria.*	He *assured* me that he *would* not expose me.

7th. When the conjunction *if* is employed in the sense of *whether*, the termination *ria* is required in the translation: Ex.

No sé si me lo *concederia ó no.*	I do not know *if*, or *whether* he would grant it to me.

8th. When the expression *had I*, or *had he*, etc., is used instead of *if I had*, etc., the termination *ra* or *se* may be employed in the translation: Ex.

Si *tuviera*, or *tuviese* buenos libros leeria.	*Had I*, or *if I had* good books I would read.

9th. When *were* is employed in the sense of *would be*, the termination *ria* is required in the translation: Ex.

Seria locura ir con este tiempo.	It *were* folly to go in this weather.

MANNER OF TRANSLATING *may*, *might*, *should*, AND *would*, AS PRINCIPAL VERBS.

29. When these words are *not* employed in English as *signs* of the subjunctive or conditional moods, but are used as principal verbs, they are translated into Spanish by verbs corresponding with them in signification; thus, *may* and *might* denote *power* or *liberty*; *should* denotes *duty* or *obligation*; and *would* expresses an *inclination* of

the mind. *May* and *might* are translated by *poder;* *should* by *deber;* and *would* by *querer :* Ex.

Puedo concluir cuando quiero.	I *may* finish it when I like.
Podia haberlo destruido.	I *might* have destroyed it.
No *debian* molestarle.	They *should* not molest him.
No *quiso* admitirlo.	He *would* not accept it.

Note.—It may not be improper to notice here that *can* and *could* are also translated by *poder,* as they likewise denote *power;* though it is a power different from that expressed by *may* and *might,* inasmuch as the latter two denote a *moral* power or a *permission;* whereas the former two denote a *physical* or *absolute* power; as, I *can* write now, but I *could* not before—Puedo *escribir ahora, pero ántes* no podia.

30. When *may, might, can, should,* and *would* are employed as substitutes for the verbs which they represent, the same rule is observed as with the auxiliaries *do, shall,* and *will,* noticed in PAR. 4 and 18 of this LECTURE : Ex.

Vmd. *puede* oir, pero yo no *puedo.*	You *can* hear, but I *cannot.*
Yo *pudiera* haber hablado, y él *tambien.*	I *might* have spoken, and so *might* he.
Debiera haberlo dicho; ¿no es verdad?	He *should* have said so; *should* he not?

LECTURE XXII.

ETYMOLOGY AND SYNTAX OF PARTICIPLES.

1. There are two participles to be considered, the one *active* or *present,* the other *passive* or *past.* Participles active derived from verbs of the first conjugation end in *ando;* as, *hablando,* speaking; those of the second and third conjugations end in *iendo;* as, *temiendo,* fearing; *sufriendo,* suffering. Participles past derived from verbs

of the first conjugation end in *ado;* as *hablado,* spoken; those of the second and third conjugations end in *ido;* as, *temido,* feared; *sufrido,* suffered. We will first see how participles are employed as forming part of the verb.

2. The *participle active,* as part of a verb, denotes action or state of being, and is preceded by some verb to denote the *time* of action or being : Ex.

Está, estaba, ha estado, *or* estará *escribiendo.*	He is, was, has been, *or* will be *writing.*

3. The participle active is sometimes used without the governing verb, in an absolute manner, either with or without reference to any particular time : Ex.

En fin se va, *creyendo* que le desprecia su amada.— (Moratin—*El Viejo y la Niña.*)	In fine, he is going, *believing* that his beloved despises him.
Y dime, *hablando* de otra materia que nos interesa mas. (Idem—*El Baron.*)	And tell me, *speaking* of another matter that interests us more.
En *viéndole :* en *oyendo.*	In *seeing* him: in *hearing.*
Hablando la verdad no sé.	*Speaking* the truth, I don't know.

Note.—Sometimes the participle active is silent before a noun; as in the following passage from Ginez Perez de Hita's *Guerras Civiles de Granada :*

El marques (*siendo*) *sabedor,* de que Abenhumeya estaba tan pujante y apercibido para la batalla ...	The marquis (*being*) *aware* that Abenhumeya was so powerful and well prepared for the battle ...

4. When in English the participle active has reference to a noun or pronoun that is *not* the nominative case, the participle is frequently rendered in Spanish by a verb in some tense of the indicative or subjunctive mood. But should the English participle active refer to a noun or pronoun that *is* the nominative case, it is translated into Spanish by a participle active also : Ex.

Se lo dí al *dependiente* que *hacia* de apoderado.	I gave it to the *clerk acting* as agent.
Haciendo yo de apoderado, le escribí sobre el asunto.	*I, acting* as agent, wrote to him on the subject.

5. When the participle active of the verbs *to go* and *to come* is preceded by any tense of the verb *to be*, denoting an action about to take place, the participle is translated by an equivalent verb in the same mood and tense as those in which the verb *to be* is placed : Ex.

Nos *vamos* á embarcar hoy. We *are going to* embark to-day.

Si Vmd. *pasare* por aquí. If you *should be coming* this way.

Viene hoy. He *is coming* to-day.
Iban á salir. They *were going* out.

6. Sometimes, particularly after verbs that denote *intention*, and after the verbs to *see*, to *hear*, and to *feel*, the participle active, or the infinitive may be used indifferently in English; but in such cases the *infinitive* is required in Spanish : Ex.

La casa que intento *comprar*. The house I intend *purchasing*, or *to purchase*.

Hago idea de *volver* en una semana. I purpose *returning*, or *to return* in a week.

Los veo *venir*. I see them *coming*.

La oigo *llorar*. I hear her *cry*, or *crying*.

Sentí *helárseme* la sangre. I felt my blood *freezing*.

7. Whenever the employment of the participle active is likely to produce ambiguity, it is preferable to resolve it into some tense of the verb from which it is derived: for instance, in the example *Los vimos* yendo *á pasear esta mañana*—We saw them *going* to walk this morning, the sense is ambiguous in both languages; for it is not clearly demonstrated by the participle active whether *we* or *they* were going to walk; it would therefore be preferable to say,

Los vimos cuando *iban* á pasear esta mañana, *or* We saw them when *they were going* to walk this morning, *or*

Los vimos cuando *ibamos* á pasear esta mañana. We saw them when *we were going* to walk this morning.

8. When the past participle is used with any part of the verb *haber*, it is *indeclinable*; but when used with the

verbs *ser*, or *estar*, it agrees in gender and number with the nominative of these verbs; see also PAR. 14: Ex.

He dado; habiamos visto.	I have given; we had seen.
Soy amado, *or* amada; serán vendidos, *or* vendidas.	I am loved; they will be sold.
Estan cansados, *or* cansadas.	They are tired.

9. The participle past is frequently used in Spanish in an absolute manner; in which case one of the participles active, *habiendo*, *siendo*, or *estando*, is understood. The participle past so used must agree in number and gender with the noun forming the subject of discourse: Ex.

Entrado pues Don Pedro en la tienda de Don Beltran, díjole que era tiempo que se fuesen.— (MARIANA—*Hist. Gen. de España.*	Don Pedro then *having entered* Don Beltran's tent, said to him that it was time they should depart.
Logradas estas ventajas, se facilita la sabiduría.— (GRAMMAR OF THE ACADEMY.)	These advantages *being gained*, knowledge is facilitated.

10. We have now to consider how participles are employed in their capacity as *nouns* and *adjectives;* and first of the *participle active.*

When in English the *participle active* is preceded by an article, a possessive or a demonstrative pronoun, a preposition, or by any word that makes it assume the character of a noun, or when used by itself in that capacity, it is generally rendered in Spanish by a *noun* or an *infinitive*, and sometimes by a *past participle:* Ex.

El *silbido* del viento.	The *whistling* of the wind.
Su *venida* me sorprendió.	*His coming* surprised me.
Aquel *balar* de las ovejas.	*That bleating* of the sheep.
Se dedica al *dibujo.*	She devotes herself *to drawing.*
El *andar* contribuye á la salud.	*Walking* is conducive to health.
Sin *haberlo* observado.	*Without having* observed it.
Me gusta el *leer.*	I am fond of *reading.*
Es *obrar* con prudencia.	It is *acting* with prudence.

From this rule may be generally excepted those active participles that are preceded by the prepositions *in* and *by*, in which cases the participle active is used in Spanish without the preposition : Ex.

Trabajando se conserva la salud.

By working we preserve health.

Considerando el asunto, etc.

In considering the subject, etc.

Frequently, however, when the English participle active is preceded by the preposition *by*, it may be translated by the infinitive preceded by *con*; as, Horses become strengthened by *exercising* them—*Los caballos se fortalecen* con ejercitarlos, *or* ejercitándolos.

11. Instead of a compound participle, a simple participle active is sometimes used in English in an absolute manner; in such cases the compound infinitive is required in the translation ; as, Their *coming* late was the cause of his not seeing them: (*i.e.* their *having come* late, etc.) *El* haber *ellos* venido *tarde fué casua que él no los viese.*

12. There is a kind of participle active in Spanish employed in the capacity of verbal adjectives. Those derived from verbs of the first conjugation end in *ante*, as *amante*; those of the second and third conjugations end in *iente*, as *obediente, viviente*: they agree in number with the noun to which they refer, and are common to both genders. They sometimes also stand in the place of nouns ; as, *Un marido amante*—A loving husband. *La hija obediente*—The obedient daughter. *Los autores vivientes*—Living authors. *Los creyentes*—The believers. *Los oyentes*—The hearers.

Observe, that participles active, ending in *ndo*, as *amando, obedeciendo, viviendo*, are never used as adjectives.

13. There remains now to consider the *participle past* in the capacity of an adjective. It is so used when it does not denote action, but a state of being referring to, or characterizing some noun, and agrees with it in Spanish in number and gender; as, *El soldado vencido*—The conquered soldier. *Los soldados vencidos*—The conquered soldiers. *Una muger casada*—A married woman. *Mugeres casadas*—Married women.

14. When the *participle past* is employed with any part of the verb *ser* or *estar*, to be, it likewise assumes the character of an adjective, and agrees in number and gender with the person or thing to which it alludes: Ex.

El *hijo* es *parecido* al padre, y la *hija* es *parecida* á la madre.	The son is *like* the father, and the daughter is *like* the mother.
Son *palacios* bien *construidos* y *casas* bien *acabadas*.	They are well *constructed* palaces and well *finished* houses.
Él está *nombrado*.	He is *appointed*.
Nosotros estamos *perdidos*.	We are *lost*.
Los *platos* estan *quebrados*.	The plates are *broken*.
Las *casas* estan *vendidas*.	The houses are *sold*.

LECTURE XXIII.

CONJUGATION OF VERBS.

1. Previous to the conjugations of regular verbs, those of the auxiliary verbs *haber* and *ser*, to have, and to be, are here given, as it is necessary that they should be first learnt, from their peculiar office in assisting in the conjugation of other verbs. The verb *tener* has also been conjugated next to *haber*, as they are both expressed by the same verb in English ; and *estar* has been conjugated next to *ser*, for the same reason. Their significations and manner of employment are explained after their conjugations.

*** In the following conjugations of verbs an accent is placed over the syllable on which the stress of voice should fall, in order to assist the learner, until he arrives at the rules for the Accentuation of Verbs, in LECT. 24, PAR. 10.

AUXILIARY VERB, *HABER*, TO HAVE.

INFINITIVE MOOD.

Haber, To have.

INDICATIVE MOOD.

Present Tense.

	Singular.			Plural.	
Yo	he,	I have.	Nosótros	hémos,*	We have.
tú	has,	thou hast.	vosótros	habéis,	you have.
él	ha,	he has.	ellos	han,	they have.

Past Imperfect Tense.

Yo	había,	I had.	Nosótros	habíamos,	We had.
tú	habías,	thou hadst.	vosótros	habíais,	you had.
él	había,	he had.	ellos	habían,	they had.

Past Perfect Tense.

Yo	húbe,	I had.	Nosótros	hubímos,	We had.
tú	hubíste,	thou hadst.	vosótros	hubísteis,	you had.
él	húbo,	he had.	ellos	hubiéron,	they had.

Future Tense.

Yo	habré,	I shall *or* will have.	Nosótros	habrémos,	We shall have
tú	habrás,	thou shalt, etc., have.	vosótros	habréis,	you shall have
él	habrá,	he shall, etc., have.	ellos	habrán	they shall, etc.

SUBJUNCTIVE MOOD.

Present Tense.

Yo	háya,	I may have.	Nosótros	hayámos,	We may have.
tú	háyas,	thou mayest have.	vosótros	hayáis,	you may have.
él	háya,	he may have.	ellos	háyan,	they may, etc.

Imperfect Tense.

	Singular.			[*or* would have.
Yo	hubiéra,	hubiése,	habría,	I should, might,
tú	hubiéras,	hubiéses,	habrías,	thou shouldst, etc.
él	hubiéra,	hubiése,	habría,	he should, etc.

	Plural.			
Nosótros	hubiéramos,	hubiésemos,	habríamos,	We should, etc.
vosótros	hubiérais,	hubiéseis,	habríais,	you should, etc.
ellos	hubiéran,	hubiésen,	habrían,	they should, etc.

---

* Or *habémos,* now, however, little used.

Future Tense.

Singular.

Si yo hubiére,	If I should have.
si tú hubiéres,	if thou shouldst have.
si él hubiére,	if he should have

Plural.

Si nosótros hubiéremos,	If we should have.
si vosótros hubiéreis,	if you should have.
si ellos hubiéren,	if they should have.

Participle Active . . . Habiéndo, Having.

Note 1.—As this verb is now only employed as an *auxiliary*, the compound tenses are omitted. Formerly it was used as an equivalent to *tener*, and was conjugated throughout the compound tenses, having *habido* for its participle past. *Haber* is also used as an *impersonal* verb: (See LECT. 26.)

Note 2.—In the conjugations of all the following verbs, the personal pronouns in Spanish are omitted, as in most cases they are not required: (See LECT. 14, PAR. 12.)

ACTIVE VERB, *TENER*, TO HAVE.

INFINITIVE MOOD.

Simple.		*Compound.*
Tenér	To have.	Habér tenído, To have had.

INDICATIVE MOOD.

Present Tense.		*Compound of the Present.*	
Téngo,	I have.	He tenído,	I have had.
tiénes,	thou hast.	has tenído,	thou hast had.
tiéne,	he has.	ha tenído,	he has had.
tenémos,	we have.	hémos tenído,	we have had.
tenéis,	you have.	habéis tenído,	you have had.
tiénen,	they have.	han tenído,	they have had.

Past Imperfect Tense.		*Compound of the Past Imperfect.*	
Tenía,	I had.	Había tenído,	I had had.
tenías,	thou hadst.	habías tenído,	thou hadst had.
tenía,	he had.	había tenído,	he had had.
teníamos,	we had.	habíamos tenído,	we had had.
teníais,	you had.	habíais tenído,	you had had.
tenían,	they had.	habían tenído,	they had had.

Past Perfect Tense.		*Compound of the Past Perfect.*	
Túve,	I had.	Húbe tenído,	I had had.
tuvíste,	thou hadst.	hubíste tenído,	thou hadst had.
túvo,	he had.	húbo tenído,	he had had.
tuvímos,	we had.	hubímos tenído,	we had had.
tuvísteis,	you had.	hubísteis tenído,	you had had.
tuviéron,	they had.	hubiéron tenído,	they had had.

Future Tense.		*Compound of the Future.*	
Tendré,	I shall *or* will have.	Habré tenído,	I shall have had.
tendrás,	thou shalt, etc., have.	habrás tenído,	thou shalt, etc.
tendrá,	he shall, etc., have.	habrá tenído,	he shall, etc.
tendrémos,	we shall, etc., have.	habrémos tenído,	we shall, etc.
tendréis,	you shall, etc., have.	habréis tenído,	you shall, etc.
tendrán,	they shall, etc., have.	habrán tenído,	they shall, etc.

SUBJUNCTIVE MOOD.

Present Tense.		*Compound of the Present.*	
Ténga,	I may have.	Háya tenído,	I may have had.
téngas,	thou mayest have.	háyas tenído,	thou mayest, etc.
ténga,	he may have.	háya tenído,	he may, etc.
tengámos,	we may have.	hayámos tenído,	we may, etc.
tengáis,	you may have.	hayáis tenído,	you may, etc.
téngan,	they may have.	háyan tenído,	they may, etc.

Imperfect Tense.

Tuviéra,	tuviése,	tendría,	I should, might, *or* would have.
tuviéras,	tuviéses,	tendrías,	thou shouldst, mightest, etc.
tuviéra,	tuviése,	tendría,	he should, might, etc.
tuviéramos,	tuviésemos,	tendríamos,	we should, might, etc.
tuviérais,	tuviéseis,	tendríais,	you should, might, etc.
tuviéran,	tuviésen,	tendrían,	they should, might, etc.

Compound of the Imperfect Tense.

Hubiéra,	hubiése,	habría,	tenído, I should, etc., have had.
hubiéras,	hubiéses,	habrías,	tenído, thou shouldst, etc.
hubiéra,	hubiése,	habría,	tenído, he should, might, etc.
hubiéramos,	hubiésemos,	habríamos,	tenído, we should, might, etc.
hubiérais,	hubiéseis,	habríais,	tenído, you should, might, etc.
hubiéran,	hubiésen,	habrían,	tenído, they should, might, etc.

Future Tense.

Si tuviére,	If I should have.
si tuviéres,	if thou shouldst have.
si tuviére,	if he should have.
si tuviéremos,	if we should have.
si tuviéreis,	if you should have.
si tuviéren,	if they should have.

Compound of the Future.

Si hubiére tenído,	If I should have had.
si hubiéres tenído,	if thou shouldst have had.
si hubiére tenído,	if he should have had.
si hubiéremos tenído,	if we should have had.
si hubiéreis tenído,	if you should have had.
si hubiéren tenído,	if they should have had.

IMPERATIVE MOOD.

Ten tú,	Have thou.
ténga él,	let him have.
tengámos nosótros,	let us have.
tenéd vosótros,	have you.
téngan ellos,	let them have.

Participle Active . . .	Teniéndo,	Having.
Compound ditto . . .	Habiéndo tenído,	Having had.
Participle Past. . . .	Tenído,	Had.

OBSERVATION.

2. When the verb *to have* is used in English in the capacity of an *auxiliary*, it is translated *haber*; but when employed as an *active* verb, denoting *possession*, it must be translated *tener*. We therefore say, *He comprado un libro*, for, *I have bought a book*; but we must say, *Tengo un libro*, for, *I have a book*. In the first instance, *to have* is used as an *auxiliary* to the verb *to buy*; but in the second, it is employed as an *active* verb, denoting the *possession* of the book. Nevertheless, in familiar discourse, we sometimes, though not frequently, notice *tener* governing a participle, in which case the participle is indeclinable; as, *Tengo* ido *dos veces*—I have been twice. *Tenemos* hablado *con él*—We have spoken to him. But if there be a noun or pronoun in the sentence governed by *tener*, the participle is made to agree with it; as, *Tengo ya* comprados *mis libros*—I have my books already bought. *Tengo* leidas *todas esas novelas*—I have read all those novels.

CONJUGATION OF THE VERB *SER*, TO BE.

INFINITIVE MOOD.

Simple.		*Compound.*	
Ser,	To be.	Habér sído,	To have been.

INDICATIVE MOOD.

Present Tense.

Sóy,	I am.	Sómos,	We are.
eres,	thou art.	sóis,	you are.
es,	he is.	son,	they are.

Past Imperfect Tense.

Éra,	I was.	Éramos,	We were.
éras,	thou wast.	érais,	you were.
éra,	he was.	éran,	they were.

Past Perfect Tense.

Fui,	I was.	Fuímos,	We were.
fuíste,	thou wast.	fuísteis,	you were.
fué,	he was.	fuéron,	they were.

Future Tense.

Seré,	I shall *or* will be.	Serémos,	We shall *or* will be.
serás,	thou shalt, etc., be.	seréis,	you shall, etc., be.
será,	he shall, etc., be.	serán,	they shall, etc., be.

COMPOUND TENSES OF THE INDICATIVE MOOD.

Compound of the Present.

He sído, etc.   I have been, etc.

Compound of the Past Imperfect.

Había sído, etc.   I had been, etc.

Compound of the Past Perfect.

Húbe sído, etc.   I had been, etc.

Compound of the Future.

Habré sído, etc.   I shall have been, etc.

SUBJUNCTIVE MOOD.

Present Tense.

Séa,	I may be,	Seámos,	We may be.
séas,	thou mayest be.	seáis,	you may be.
séa,	he may be.	séan,	they may be.

Imperfect Tense.

Fuéra,	fuése,	sería,	I should, might, *or* would be.
fuéras,	fuéses,	serías,	thou shouldst, mightest, etc., be.
fuéra,	fuése,	sería,	he should, might, *or* would be.
fuéramos,	fuésemos,	seríamos,	we should, might, *or* would be.
fuérais,	fuéseis,	seríais,	you should, might, *or* would be.
fuéran,	fuésen,	serían,	they should, might, *or* would be.

Future Tense.

Si fuére,	If I should be.	Si fuéremos,	If we should be.
si fuéres,	if thou shouldst be.	si fuéreis,	if you should be.
si fuére,	if he should be.	si fuéren,	if they should be.

COMPOUND TENSES OF THE SUBJUNCTIVE MOOD.

Compound of the Present.

Háya sído, etc.	I may have been, etc.

Compound of the Imperfect.

Hubiéra sído, etc. ⎫
Hubiése sído, etc. ⎬ I should, might, *or* would have been, etc.
Habría sído, etc. ⎭

Compound of the Future.

Hubiére sído, etc.	If I should have been.

IMPERATIVE MOOD.

Sé tú,	Be thou.
séa él,	let him be.
seámos nosótros,	let us be.
sed vosótros,	be you.
séan ellos,	let them be.

Participle Active . .	Siéndo,	Being.
Compound ditto . .	Habiéndo sído,	Having been.
Participle Past . .	Sído,	Been.

CONJUGATION OF THE VERB *ESTAR*, TO BE.

INFINITIVE MOOD.

Simple.		*Compound.*	
Estár,	To Be.	Habér estádo,	To have been.

INDICATIVE MOOD.

Present Tense.

Estóy,	I am.	Estámos,	We are.
estás,	thou art.	estáis,	you are.
está,	he is.	están,	they are.

Past Imperfect Tense.

Estába,	I was.	Estábamos,	We were.
estábas,	thou wast.	estábais,	you were.
estába,	he was.	estában,	they were.

Past Perfect Tense.

Estúve,	I was.	Estuvímos,	We were.
estuvíste,	thou wast.	Estuvísteis,	you were.
estúvo,	he was.	estuviéron,	they were.

Future Tense.

Estaré,	I shall *or* will be.	Estarémos,	We shall *or* will be.
estarás,	thou shalt, etc., be.	estaréis,	you shall, etc., be.
estará,	he shall, etc., be.	estarán,	they shall, etc., be.

COMPOUND TENSES OF THE INDICATIVE MOOD.

Compound of the Present.

He estádo, etc.	I have been, etc.

Compound of the Imperfect.

Había estádo, etc.	I had been, etc.

Compound of the Perfect.

Húbe estádo, etc.	I had been, etc.

Compound of the Future.

Habré estádo, etc.	I shall have been, etc.

SUBJUNCTIVE MOOD.

Present Tense.

Esté,	I may be.	Estémos,	We may be.
estés,	thou mayest be.	estéis,	you may be.
esté,	he may be.	estén,	they may be.

Imperfect Tense.

Estuviéra,	estuviése,	estaría,	I should, might, etc., be.
estuviéras,	estuviéses,	estarías,	thou shouldst, etc., be.
estuviéra,	estuviése,	estaría,	he should, might, etc., be.
estuviéramos,	estuviésemos,	estaríamos,	we should, might, etc., be.
estuviérais,	estuviéseis,	estaríais,	you should, might, etc., be.
estuviéran,	estuviésen,	estarían,	they should, might, etc., be.

Future Tense.

Si estuviére,	If I should be.	Si estuviéremos,	If we should be.
si estuviéres,	if thou shouldst be.	si estuviéreis,	if you should be.
si estuviére,	if he should be.	si estuviéren,	if they should be.

COMPOUND TENSES OF THE SUBJUNCTIVE MOOD.

Compound of the Present.

Háya estádo, etc.	I may have been, etc.

Compound of the Imperfect.

Hubiéra estádo, etc.)
Hubiése estádo, etc. } I should, might, *or* would have been, etc.
Habría estádo, etc.)

Compound of the Future.

Sí hubiére estádo, etc.　　　If I should have been, etc.

IMPERATIVE MOOD.

Está tú,	Be thou.
esté él,	let him be.
estémos nosótros,	let us be.
estád vosótros,	be you.
estén ellos,	let them be.

Participle Active . .	Estándo,	Being.
Compound ditto . .	Habiéndo estádo,	Having been.
Participle Past . .	Estádo,	Been.

3. When the auxiliary *to have* precedes an infinitive, it is rendered *tener que:* Ex.

Tengo que hacer ahora.	*I have to do* at present.
Tuve que decirle.	*I had to tell* him.
Tendrémos que ir mañana.	We shall *have to go* to-morrow.

4. But should a noun expressive of any sentiment, feeling, or duty, intervene between the two verbs, then *de* is used instead of *que:* Ex.

Tengo el *gusto de* anunciarle.	I have the pleasure to inform you.
Tuve la *satisfaccion de* verla.	I had the satisfaction to see her.

5. And when *to be* precedes an infinitive, it is translated *haber de,* or *deber,* or *deber de:* Ex.

Ella *ha de cantar,* or, *debe cantar,* or *debe de cantar* esta noche.	She *is to sing* this evening.
Nosotros *hemos de ser,* or *debemos de ser* los testigos.	We *are to be* the witnesses.

6. The past perfect tense of *haber* is sometimes used governing an infinitive with the preposition *de* in the sense of *to be within an ace of;* and *to be compelled to:* Ex.

Este hecho *hubo de compro-meter* el éxito de la expedicion.	This act *was very near compromising* the success of the expedition.
Tal fué su conducta que *hube de despedirlo.*	Such was his conduct that I *was forced to dismiss* him.

7. When *haber* is employed as an impersonal verb (see LECT. 26), it also requires *que* before an infinitive : Ex.

¿ *Hay* algo *que hacer ?*	Is there anything to do ?
No *hay que temer.*	There is nothing to fear.

8. In English the compound tenses of the verb *to go, to come,* and *to arrive,* are sometimes formed with the verb *to be ;* in Spanish, however, the compound tenses of every verb, except passive verbs, must be formed with *haber ;* as, *Se han ido*—They are gone. *Hemos venido*—We are come. *Ha llegado*—She is come.

9. When in English the verb *to be* precedes adjectives expressive of the state of one's feelings, physical or moral, such as *hungry, thirsty, warm, cold, sleepy, afraid, ashamed,* etc., it is translated *tener,* and the adjective is rendered by a corresponding noun in Spanish ; as, *Tengo hambre y sed*—I am hungry and thirsty. *Tienen calor y no frio*—They are warm, and not cold. *Teniamos miedo*—We were afraid. *Tengo sueño*—I am sleepy. *Tiene vergüenza*—He is ashamed.

The same construction is also observed when we allude to a person's age ; as, *Qué edad tiene ?*—How old is he ? *Tiene cincuenta años de edad*—He is fifty years old.

OBSERVATIONS ON SER AND ESTAR.

10. In the foregoing conjugations of these two verbs, both are translated by the same verb in English—namely, *to be ;* yet by no means can they be indiscriminately used in Spanish, since they differ materially from each other in signification.   It is therefore essentially necessary that the learner be acquainted with their peculiar meaning and use ; a matter that frequently embarrasses students of the Spanish language, and which has justly been con-

sidered one of its greatest difficulties to surmount, but which it is hoped the following observations will remove.

When we wish to express the absolute, natural, or inherent quality of any thing, the qualities of the mind, the natural beauties and defects of the body, and all general truths, we must employ *ser :* Ex.

El oro *es* pesado.	Gold *is* heavy.
La piedra *es* dura.	Stone *is* hard.
La nieve *es* blanca.	Snow *is* white.
Ellos *son* humildes.	They *are* humble.
Él *es* docto.	He *is* learned.
Ella *es* hermosa.	She *is* handsome.
Él *es* ciego.	He *is* blind.
La costumbre *es* otra naturaleza.	Custom *is* second nature.
La necesidad *es* madre de la invencion.	Necessity *is* the mother of invention.

But to denote any accidental circumstance, chemical and mechanical changes, locality, the emotions of the mind, or when we speak of the state of one's health, we must use *estar :* Ex.

Estoy pronto.	I *am* ready.
Está durmiendo.	He *is* asleep.
Esta agua *está* caliente.	This water *is* warm.
El vino ya *está* agrio.	The wine *is* already sour.
Estan en Madrid.	They *are* in Madrid.
Estaré aquí mañana.	I shall *be* here to-morrow.
Está triste. *Estoy* contento.	She *is* sad. I *am* contented.
Estoy bueno. *Estan* malos.	I *am* well. They *are* ill.

In the following example, the learner will observe the striking difference in the meaning of these two verbs : *Este* es *el niño que* está *enfermo*—This *is* the child that *is* ill. Here we see that the *absolute being* of the child is expressed by *ser*, but the *accidental circumstance* of its being *ill* is denoted by *estar*.

In speaking of a fruit, the peculiar nature of which is *sour*, we must say, *Esta fruta* es *agria*—This fruit *is* sour : but if we change the verb *ser* into *estar*, we denote that the fruit became sour by some accidental circumstance, or that, from its being gathered too early, it had not reached the necessary degree of maturity, and not that it belonged to any species of fruit of a *naturally sour* kind. Again: if we allude to two men, one with a wooden leg, and the other walking with both legs, assisted by crutches, we should express the lameness of the former by the verb *ser*, because it is evident that it is *permanent*; thus, *Aquel hombre* es *cojo*—That man is lame; but the lameness of the latter may be translated either *es cojo*, or *está cojo*, according as we considered it permanent or temporary.

We must employ *ser* to express *possession*, and also to denote what a thing is *intended for* : Ex.

La hacienda *es* de ella, pero el dinero *es* mio.	The property *is* hers, but the money *is* mine.
Los libros *son* para estudiar.	Books *are* to study from.
Esta carta *es* para Vmd.	This letter *is* for you.

Likewise to signify the materials of which things are formed: Ex.

Este reloj *es* de oro.	This *is* a gold watch.
Ese paño *es* de lana de Sajonia.	That cloth *is* of Saxony wool.

Estar is always employed with the *participle active*; as, *Estoy leyendo*—I am reading. *Estaban escribiendo*—They were writing.

Ser cannot be employed before a *participle active*, nor *estar* before a *noun :* both may be used with the other parts of speech respectively, according as the one or the other is required.

Ser is required to form the *passive voice*; as, *Son amados*—They are loved. *Fuímos elegidos*—We were elected.

There are some instances in which either *ser* or *estar* may be used, according to the meaning we wish to give to the construction. For instance, *I am of the same opinion*, may be translated, Soy *or* Estoy *del mismo parecer*; but with *ser*, an unalterable state of opinion is meant, whereas with *estar*, only casual opinion is expressed. Again, *Eso* es *muy alto*, and *Eso* está *muy alto*—That is very high. The first expression refers to something that is *lofty in stature*, etc. ; but the second, to something *placed* or *located very high*.

Some adjectives also vary their meaning, according as they are employed with *ser* or *estar*: Ex.

Ser bueno.   *Estar* bueno.   To *be* good.   To *be* well.
Ser vivo   *Estar* vivo.   To *be* lively. To *be* alive.
Ser despierto. *Estar* despierto. To *be* vigilant. To *be* awake.
Ser malo.   *Estar* malo.   To *be* wicked. To *be* ill.

EXERCISE ON THE VERBS *SER* AND *ESTAR*.

Arion was the first inventor of tragic verse.   The
———.   ———   trágico verso
Athenians were the first who built a permanent theatre.
Ateniense   fabricar   estable   teatro
The theatre at Athens was under the care of the
            de Aténas   á   cuidado
principal magistrates.   Iron is hard.   How soft this
———— magistrado hierro duro   blando
iron is already.   These cherries are not ripe.   The
        ya   cereza   maduro
orange is a very wholesome fruit.   These grapes are
naranja   sano   uva
  yet sour. He is a very kind man; but how angry
todavía agrio   benigno   enojado
he was! Although [it is some time] that he is ill,
        aunque   hace tiempo
nevertheless he is not an infirm man.   Deceit is
sinembargo   enfermizo   engaño
odious. Flattery should be despised. He has been
odioso   lisonja   despreciado
blind these three months. She is very pale. They were
ciego hace   pálido
frightened.   He is a poor cripple.   If they should be
espantado   pobre estropeado
there, tell them that I shall be at home the whole day.
 allí diga   en casa
He was much agitated; but he is more quiet now.
            agitado   sosegado ahora

He is very tractable, and is satisfied with his situation.
   dócil   satisfecho   colocacion.

The house is mine, but the furniture is his.   Is this hat
          muebles

yours?—No; it is my brother's.   The message was for
            recado

him.   This is a silver cup.   The coat is of superfine
       taza   casaca   superior

cloth.   What is he doing?   He is sleeping.   Quarrels
    haciendo   durmiendo quimera

are detestable, and envy is despicable.   She is beloved
—————   envidia   despreciable   amada

by everybody. He is a very dull man.   We were
           triste

dull the whole day.   How tiresome he is!   We are very
           cansado

 tired.
cansado.

LECTURE XXIV.

CONJUGATION OF REGULAR VERBS.

1. The infinitives of all Spanish verbs end in one or
other of the following terminations—namely, *ar, er, ir;*
as, *hablar,* to speak; *temer,* to fear; *sufrir,* to suffer: those
ending in *ar* are of the first conjugation; those in *er* of
the second; and those in *ir* of the third.   All regular
verbs of the *first* conjugation vary their endings so as to
correspond with those exhibited in the following conjugation of the verb *hablar;* all those of the *second* conjugation correspond with the terminations of *temer;* and
all those of the *third* correspond with those of *sufrir.*

FIRST CONJUGATON, *HABLAR*, TO SPEAK.

INFINITIVE MOOD.

Simple.		*Compound.*
Hablár,	To speak.	Habér habládo, To have spoken.

I

INDICATIVE MOOD.

Present Tense.

Háblo,	I speak.	Hablámos,	We speak.
háblas,	thou speakest.	habláis,	you speak.
hábla,	he speaks.	háblan,	they speak.

Past Imperfect Tense.

Hablába,	I spoke.	Hablábamos,	We spoke.
hablábas,	thou spokest.	hablábais,	you spoke.
hablába,	he spoke.	hablában,	they spoke.

Past Perfect Tense.

Hablé,	I spoke.	Hablámos,	We spoke.
habláste,	thou spokest.	hablásteis,	you spoke.
habló,	he spoke.	habláron,	they spoke.

Future Tense.

Hablaré,	I shall *or* will speak.	Hablarémos,	We shall *or* will speak
hablarás,	thou shalt speak.	hablaréis,	you shall speak.
hablará,	he shall speak.	hablarán,	they shall speak.

COMPOUND TENSES OF THE INDICATIVE MOOD.

Compound of the Present.

He habládo, etc.   I have spoken, etc.

Compound of the Imperfect.

Había habládo, etc.   I had spoken, etc.

Compound of the Perfect.

Húbe habládo, etc.   I had spoken, etc.

Compound of the Future.

Habré habládo, etc.   I shall *or* will have spoken, etc.

SUBJUNCTIVE MOOD.

Present Tense.

Háble,	I may speak.	Hablémos,	We may speak.
hábles,	thou mayest speak.	habléis,	you may speak.
hable,	he may speak.	háblen,	they may speak.

Imperfect Tense.

Hablára,	habláse,	hablaría,	I should, might, *or* would speak.
habláras,	hablások,	hablarías,	thou shouldst, mightst, etc.
hablára,	habláse,	hablaría,	he should, might, etc.
habláramos,	hablásemos,	hablaríamos,	we should, might, etc.
hablárais,	habláseis,	hablaríais,	you should, might, etc.
habláran,	hablásen,	hablarían,	they should, might, etc.

Future Tense.

Si habláre, If I should speak.	Si habláremos, If we should speak.
si habláres, if thou shouldst, etc.	si habláreis, if you should, etc.
si habláre, if he should speak.	si habláren, if they should, etc.

COMPOUND TENSES OF THE SUBJUNCTIVE MOOD.

Compound of the Present.

Háya habládo, etc.   I may have spoken, etc.

Compound of the Imperfect.

Hubiéra habládo, etc.
Hubiése habládo, etc. } I should, might, *or* would have spoken, etc.
Habría habládo, etc.

Compound of the Future.

Si hubiére habládo, etc.   If I should have spoken, etc.

IMPERATIVE MOOD.

Hábla tú,	Speak thou.
háble él,	let him speak.
hablémos nosótros,	let us speak.
hablád vosótros,	speak you.
háblen ellos,	let them speak.

Participle Active . .	Hablándo,	Speaking.
Compound ditto . . .	Hahiéndo habládo,	Having spoken.
Participle Past . . .	Habládo,	Spoken.

SECÓND CONJUGATION, *TEMER*, TO FEAR.

INFINITIVE MOOD.

Simple.		*Compound.*
Temér,	To fear.	Habér temído, To have feared.

INDICATIVE MOOD.

Present Tense.

Témo,	I fear.	Temémos,	We fear.
témes,	thou fearest.	teméis,	you fear.
téme,	he fears.	témen,	they fear.

Past Imperfect Tense.

Temía,	I feared.	Temíamos,	We feared.
temias,	thou fearedst.	temíais,	you feared.
temía,	he feared.	temian,	they feared.

Past Perfect Tense.

Temí,	I feared.	Temímos,	We feared.
temisto,	thou fearedst.	temisteis,	you feared.
temió,	he feared.	temiéron,	they feared.

Future Tense.

Temeré,	I shall *or* will fear.	Temerémos,	We shall, etc., fear.
temerás,	thou shalt fear.	temeréis,	you shall fear.
temerá,	he shall fear.	temerán,	they shall fear.

COMPOUND TENSES OF THE INDICATIVE MOOD.

Compound of the Present.

He temído, etc.   I have feared, etc.

Compound of the Past Imperfect.

Había temído, etc.   I had feared, etc.

Compound of the Past Perfect.

Húbe temído, etc.   I had feared, etc.

Compound of the Future.

Habré temído, etc.   I shall have feared, etc.

SUBJUNCTIVE MOOD.

Present Tense.

Téma,	I may fear.	Temámos,	We may fear.
témas	thou mayst fear.	temáis,	you may fear.
téma	he may fear.	téman,	they may fear.

Imperfect Tense.

Temiéra,	temiése,	temería,	I should, might, etc., fear.
temiéras,	temiéses,	temerías,	thou shouldst, etc., fear.
temiéra,	temiése,	temería,	he should, might, etc., fear.
temiéramos,	temiésemos,	temeríamos,	we should, might, etc., fear.
temiérais,	temiéseis,	temeríais,	you should, might, etc., fear.
temiéran,	temiésen,	temerían,	they should, might, etc., fear.

Future Tense.

Si temiére,	If I should fear.	Si temiéremos,	If we should fear.
si temiéres,	if thou shouldst fear.	si temiéreis,	if you should fear.
si temiére,	if he should fear.	si temiéren,	if they should fear.

COMPOUND TENSES OF THE SUBJUNCTIVE MOOD.

Compound of the Present.

Háya temído, etc.   I may have feared, etc.

Compound of the Imperfect.

Hubiéra temído, etc. }
Hubiése temído, etc. } I should, might, *or* would have feared, etc.
Habría temído, etc. }

Compound of the Future.

Si hubiére temído, etc.   If I should have feared, etc.

IMPERATIVE MOOD.

Téme tú,	Fear thou.
téma él,	let him fear.
temámos nosótros,	let us fear.
teméd vosótros,	fear you.
téman ellos,	let them fear.

Participle Active . .	Temiéndo,	Fearing.
Compound ditto . . .	Habiéndo temído,	Having feared.
Participle Past . . .	Temído,	Feared.

THIRD CONJUGATION, *SUFRIR*, TO SUFFER.

INFINITIVE MOOD.

Simple.		*Compound.*	
Sufrír,	To suffer.	Habér sufrído,	To have suffered

INDICATIVE MOOD.

Present Tense.

Súfro,	I suffer.	Sufrímos,	We suffer.
súfres,	thou sufferest,	sufrís,	you suffer.
súfre,	he suffers.	súfren,	they suffer.

Past Imperfect Tense.

Sufría,	I suffered.	Sufríamos,	We suffered.
sufrías,	thou sufferedst,	sufríais,	you suffered.
sufría,	he suffered.	sufrían,	they suffered.

Past Perfect Tense.

Sufrí,	I suffered.	Sufrimos,	We suffered.
sufriste,	thou sufferedst.	sufristeis,	you suffered.
sufrió,	he suffered.	sufriéron,	they suffered.

Future Tense.

Sufriré,	I shall *or* will suffer.	Sufrirémos,	We shall, etc., suffer,
sufrirás,	thou shalt suffer.	sufriréis,	you shall suffer.
sufrirá,	he shall suffer.	sufrirán,	they shall suffer.

COMPOUND TENSES OF THE INDICATIVE MOOD.

Compound of the Present.

He sufrido, etc.   I have suffered, etc.

Compound of the Imperfect.

Había sufrido, etc.   I had suffered, etc.

Compound of the Perfect.

Húbe sufrido, etc.   I had suffered, etc.

Compound of the Future.

Habré sufrido, etc.   I shall have suffered, etc.

SUBJUNCTIVE MOOD.

Present Tense.

Súfra,	I may suffer.	Sufrámos,	We may suffer.
súfras,	thou mayest suffer.	sufráis,	you may suffer.
súfra,	he may suffer.	súfran,	they may suffer.

Imperfect Tense.

Sufriéra,	sufriése,	sufriría,	I should, might, etc., suffer.
sufriéras,	sufriéses,	sufrirías,	thou shouldst, mightst, etc.
sufriéra,	sufriése,	sufriría,	he should, might, etc.
sufriéramos,	sufriésemos,	sufriríamos,	we should, might, etc.
sufriérais,	sufriéseis,	sufriríais,	you should, might, etc.
sufriéran,	sufriésen,	sufrirían,	they should, might, etc.

Future Tense.

Si sufriére,	If I should suffer.	Si sufriéremos,	If we should suffer.
si sufriéres,	if thou shouldst suffer.	si sufriéreis,	if you should suffer.
si sufriére,	if he should suffer.	si sufriéren,	if they should suffer.

COMPOUND TENSES OF THE SUBJUNCTIVE MOOD.

Compound of the Present.

Háya sufrído, etc.   I may have suffered, eto.

Compound of the Imperfect.

Hubiéra sufrído, etc. }
Hubiése sufrído, etc. } I should, might, *or* would have suffered, etc.
Habría sufrído, etc. }

Compound of the Future.

Si hubiére sufrído, etc.   If I should have suffered, eto.

IMPERATIVE MOOD.

Súfre tú,	Suffer thou.
súfra él,	let him suffer.
suframos nosótros,	let us suffer.
sufríd vosótros,	suffer you.
súfran ellos,	let them suffer.

Participle Active . .	Sufriéndo,	Suffering.
Compound ditto . . .	Habiéndo sufrído,	Having suffered.
Participle Past . . .	Sufrído,	Suffered.

Note.—The following observations will assist the learner in conjugating regular verbs:

1st. The future indicative and the future subjunctive of the three conjugations, and the first and third terminations of the imperfect subjunctive of the first conjugation, take in the whole of the infinitive.

2nd. The vowel with which the *termination* of the first person of any tense of the subjunctive begins is continued throughout every person in the tense, in all the three conjugations.

3rd. The present of the subjunctive is accented like the present of the indicative in the three conjugations.

4th. The first and second terminations of the imperfect subjunctive, and the future of this mood, are accented like the imperfect of the indicative in the three conjugations.

2. The annexed synopsis exhibits at one view all the inflections in the regular verbs. The infinitives of Spanish verbs are divided into the *root* and the *termina-*

tion; as, *habl-ar, tem-er, sufr-ir*: in which the roots are *habl, tem, sufr*, and the terminations *ar, er, ir*. The roots of regular verbs remain unalterable throughout the whole conjugation; except a few, which, in order to retain the primitive sound of certain consonants, undergo some slight alterations, as will be presently noticed; but such verbs are not on that account considered irregular, the alterations being merely orthoepical. See PAR. 3.

The student, by way of exercise, may apply the roots of some of the adjoining verbs, which are all regular, to the respective terminations in the following synopsis; by which means he may very soon become familiar with the conjugation of regular verbs.

Acabar, to finish; *alabar*, to praise; *cortar*, to cut; *ganar*, to gain; *librar*, to free; *molestar*, to molest. *Acometer*, to attack; *beber*, to drink; *comer*, to eat; *ofender*, to offend; *prometer*, to promise; *vender*, to sell. *Aturdir*, to stun; *combatir*, to combat; *omitir*, to omit; *partir*, to depart; *permitir*, to permit; *suprimir*, to suppress.

A COMPARATIVE VIEW OF THE TERMINATIONS IN REGULAR VERBS.

[Observe, that where the inflection is not marked with the accent, the syllable immediately preceding it is the acute one.]

INFINITIVE MOOD.

1st Conjugation	. . . .	Habl-	ár.
2nd	ditto	. . . .	Tem-	ér.
3rd	ditto	. . . .	Sufr-	ír.

INDICATIVE MOOD.

Present Tense.

1st Conj.	Habl-	o	as	a	ámos	áis	an.
2nd ...	Tem-	o	es	e	émos	éis	en.
3rd ...	Sufr-	o	es	e	ímos	ís	en.

Past Imperfect Tense.

1. ...	Habl-	ába	ábas	ába	ábamos	ábais	ában.
2. ...	Tem-	ía	ías	ía	íamos	íais	ían.
3. ...	Sufr-	ía	ías	ía	íamos	íais	ían.

Past Perfect Tense.

1st Conj.	Habl-	ó	áste	ó	ámos	ásteis	áron.
2nd ...	Tem-	í	íste	íó	ímos	ísteis	iéron.
3rd ...	Sufr-	í	íste	íó	ímos	ísteis	iéron.

Future Tense.

1. ...	Habl-	aré	arás	ará	arémos	aréis	arán.
2. ...	Tem-	eré	erás	erá	erémos	eréis	erán.
3. ...	Sufr-	iré	irás	irá	irémos	iréis	irán.

SUBJUNCTIVE MOOD.

Present Tense.

1. ...	Habl-	e	es	e	émos	éis	en.
2. ...	Tem-	a	as	a	ámos	áis	an.
3. ...	Sufr-	a	as	a	ámos	áis	an.

Imperfect Tense.

1. ...	Habl-	ára	áras	ára	áramos	árais	áran.
		áse	áses	áse	ásemos	áseis	ásen.
		aría	arías	aría	aríamos	arías	arían.
2. ...	Tem-	iéra	iéras	iéra	iéramos	iérais	iéran.
		iése	iéses	iése	iésemos	iéseis	iésen.
		ería	erías	ería	eríamos	eríais	erían.
3. ...	Sufr-	iéra	iéras	iéra	iéramos	iérais	iérar.
		iése	iéses	iése	iésemos	iéseis	iésen.
		iría	irías	iría	iríamos	iríais	irían.

Future Tense.

1. ...	Habl-	áre	áres	áre	áremos	áreis	áren.
2. ...	Tem-	iére	iéres	iére	iéremos	iéreis	iéren.
3. ...	Sufr-	iére	iéres	iére	iéremos	iéreis	iéren

IMPERATIVE MOOD.

1. ...	Habl-	a	e		émos	ád	en
2. ...	Tem-	e	a		ámos	éd	an.
3. ...	Sufr-	e	a		ámos	íd	an.

Participle Active.	Participle Past.
1. Habl-ándo.	Habl-ádo.
2. Tem-iéndo.	Tem-ído.
3. Sufr-iéndo.	Sufr-ído.

3. It has just been noticed in PAR. 2, that there are a
few regular verbs that undergo some slight orthoepical
alterations, which are made in order to preserve,

throughout the whole of their conjugations, the hard or soft sound which certain consonants have in the infinitive, and are liable to change their primitive sound when followed by certain vowels. The alterations that take place are the following:

C before *e* changes into *qu*, when in the infinitive it has the sound of *k*; as, *arrancár*, to pluck, *arranquémos*, *arránquen*, etc. It changes into *z*, when in the infinitive it has the soft sound; as, *vencér*, to conquer, *vénzo*, *venzámos*, etc.

G, having in the infinitive the hard sound, requires *u* between it and the *e* following it; as *vengár*, to revenge, *venguémos*, *vénguen*, etc.

G before *o* or *a* changes into *j*, when in the infinitive it has the guttural sound; as *cogér*, to catch, *cójo*, *cójan*, etc.

Gu drop the *u* whenever *o* or *a* immediately follows; as *distíngo*, *distínga*, etc.

Qu change into *c* when the sound of the hard *c* is required to be preserved; as *delinquír*, to transgress, *delínco*, *delíncan*, etc.

Note.—Verbs of the second and third conjugations, having their roots terminating in a vowel, would, in some tenses, according to the regular conjugation of verbs, change the *e* of their termination into *i*; thus, *leér*, to read, would change into *leió*, *leiéra*, etc.; but in such cases a *y* should be substituted for the *i*; thus, *leyó*, *leyéra*, etc. (This, however, does not happen when the stress falls on the *i*, and therefore the rule does not apply to the imperfect of the indicative, as *leía*, *leías*, etc.) This rule extends even to the regular tenses of irregular verbs.

Observe, also, that verbs of the second or third conjugation, having either of the liquid letters *ll* or *ñ* in their root, as *bullir*, to boil, *tañer*, to play on a musical instrument, drop the *i* of the termination in the third person singular and plural of the perfect indicative; throughout the terminations *ra* and *se* of the imperfect subjunctive, and future of the same mood; and in the participle active; as, perfect indicative *tañó*, *tañéron*; *bulló*, *bulléron*:—imperfect subjunctive, *tañéra*, etc., *tañése*, etc.; *bulléra*, etc., *bullése*, etc. :—future subjunctive, *tañére*, etc.; *bullére*, etc. :—participle active, *tañéndo*, *bulléndo*.

EXERCISE ON THE MOODS AND TENSES OF VERBS.

The boys run.   She sings.   The ladies are walking
     correr   cantar   pasear

He is eating it.   They are selling them.   The English
   comer   vender

send their ships to all parts of the world.   He writes
enviar   buque   escribir

much.   He plays on the flute.   I do think so.   He does
          tocar *   flauta   creer

not dine   early, but she does.   You do not observe
  comer temprano pero   observar

it, but I do.   The pagans sacrificed victims to their
              pagano sacrificar victima

gods.   Solon was one of the seven sages of Greece, and
 dios ————   sabio   Grecia

learnt at Athens.   Plato   studied   under   Socrates,
aprender   Platon   estudiar   bajo de Sócrates

after whose death he began his travels through Greece:
        muerte empezar   viage   por

he afterwards went to Egypt, where, at that period,
   despues   pasar   Egipto donde en   período

flourished Theodorus.   I was breakfasting when you
 florecer   Teodoro   almorzar

arrived.   She   consulted him, and   so did I.   He
llegar   consultar   tambien

did not relieve them, but she did.   I shall speak to
   socorrer   pero

him to-morrow.   He shall remain here if he likes.   I
            quedar aquí   le gusta

will surmount every difficulty.   I will surprise them.
  vencer   dificultad   sorprender

Will he sacrifice his interests in this manner ? Shall we
                  en   manera

study our lesson ? He *will* remain, and [there is no]
estudiar   no hay

remedy.   You *shall* not take it.   We *shall* free them,
remedio   tomar   librar

and nothing shall prevent us.   He *will* not listen, but
      nada   impedir   escuchar

she will.   We shall succeed; shall we not?   They have
                          lograr

paid me.   They had not reflected.   I have not
pagar   reflexionar

considered it.   He had concluded his discourse when
considerar   concluir   discurso cuando

we entered.   I had scarcely finished when he began.
      entrar   apénas acabar   empezar

I imagine he may have the same views.   Perhaps
    imaginar   mismo mira [puede que]

he may reward her.   I fear he may not answer
        recompensar   responder

me.   Even though he should believe it.   Although he
              aun cuando   creer   aunque

might read much, he would learn but little. If he
      leer   aprender *

should pass [by this way] I would call him.   You may
                  por aquí

omit what you please.   I can work now, but I could
omitir   gustar   trabajar

not then.   He would watch the whole night.   They
      entónces   velar   noche

should [take care of] her.   You should promise, and so
            cuidar   prometer

should she.   He might permit me; might he not?   I
                            permitir

expect to depart to-morrow. I resolved not to mention
            partir   resolver   mencionar

it. Speak thou to him. Let them promise me. Suppress
                                                          suprimir

your tears. Let him not sell them. Do ye not offend
      lágrima   ofender

ANCIENT MANNER OF FORMING SOME OF THE TENSES
OF SPANISH REGULAR VERBS.

4. As in reading the works of ancient authors the student will find some parts of the verb written differently from what they are now, it has been deemed proper to point out what these variations consist in. They are as follow.

The future indicative was anciently formed of two words—namely, the infinitive of the verb denoting the action, followed by some inflection of the auxiliary *haber*. This form of the verb occurred especially when it was followed by a governed pronoun: Ex:

Miéntras que yo pueda, *facerlo he* así.—(Crónica General.)	Whilst I can, *I will do so.*
Lo que oistes en poridad *predicarlo hédes* (or *habédes*) sobre los tejados.—(Leyes de las Partidas.)	What you heard in private *you will proclaim* on the roofs.

In these examples *facerlo he*, and *predicarlo hédes*, are equivalent to *lo haré*, and *lo predicaréis.*

In a like manner the imperfect subjunctive in the termination *ria*, was used anciently as a compound verb, especially when it was followed by a governed pronoun. Thus, in the Crónicas Generales are frequently seen the expressions *tornarse hía*, or *tornarseía*, *pecharme hía*, or *pecharmeía*, for *se tornaría*, he would turn ; and *me pecharía*, he would pay me.

The verb in the imperfect subjunctive, with the termination *ra*, was also employed anciently (and is sometimes now, in poetry), instead of the compound of the past imperfect of the indicative: Ex.

El caballero á quien el rey *diera* el caballo.	The gentleman to whom the king *had given* the horse.
El rey mandó entónces que sopieran cuantos hombres *morieran*.—(Crónica General.)	The king then ordered that they should know how many men *had died.*

In which examples *diera*, and *morieran*, are equivalent to *habia dado.*

Besides which, the second person plural in every tense of the indicative and subjunctive moods was formerly written with *de*, where *i* is now used, as seen in the following list :—

First Conjugation.

		Modern.	Ancient.
INDIC.	*Pres.*	Amáis.	Amádes.
	Imperf.	amábais.	amábades.
	Perf.	amásteis.	amástedes.
	Future.	amaréis.	amarédes.
SUBJ.	*Pres.*	améis.	amédes.
		amárais.	amárades.
	Imperf.	amáscis.	amásedes.
		amaraíais.	amaríades.
	Future.	amáreis.	amáredes.

Second Conjugation.

INDIC.	*Pres.*	Bebéis.	bebédes.
	Imperf.	bebíais.	bedíades.
	Perf.	bebísteis.	bebístedes.
	Future.	beberéis.	beberédes.
SUBJ.	*Pres.*	bebáis.	bebádes.
		bebiérais.	bebiérades.
	Imperf.	bebiéscis.	bebiésedes.
		beberíais.	beberíades.
	Future.	bebiéreis.	bebiéredes.

Third Conjugation.

INDIC.	*Pres.*	Partís.	Partídes.
	Imperf.	partíais.	partíades.
	Perf.	partísteis.	partístedes.
	Future.	partiréis.	partirédes.
SUBJ.	*Pres.*	partáis.	partádes.
		partiérais.	partiérades.
	Imperf.	partiéseis.	partiésedes.
		partiríais.	partiríades.
	Future.	partiéreis.	partiéredes.

The *d* used also to be omitted in the second person plural of the imperative; thus, *mirá, bebé, subí,* instead of *mirád, bebéd, subíd.* And when the pronouns, *le, la, lo,* were affixed to the second person plural of the imperative, the *l* used to be put before the *d*; thus, *mirálde, bebélda, subíldo,* instead of *mirádle, bebédla, subídlo.* The *i* was frequently omitted in the second person plural of the perfect indicative; thus, *amástes, vendístes, partístes,*

instead of *amásteis, vendísteis, partísteis.* And the final
r of the infinitive was often changed into *l,* when followed
by the pronouns *le, la, lo;* thus, *tomálle, comélla, partíllo,*
instead of *tomárle, comérla, partírlo.*

(For the difference in spelling in ancient irregular
verbs, see LECT. 25, PAR. 3.)

FORMATION OF REFLECTIVE VERBS.

5. These are formed in Spanish by prefixing the
personal pronouns of the objective case to each corresponding person of the verb, in every tense of the
indicative and subjunctive moods, in the following
manner :—

Indicative Present.

Me ámo,	I love myself.	Nos amámos,	We love ourselves.
te ámas,	thou lovest thyself.	os amáis,	you love yourselves.
se áma,	he loves himself.	se áman,	they love themselves.

And so on in all the other tenses. In the Infinitive, the
participle active, and the imperative, the pronouns are
subjoined to the verb ; and observe that the final letter
of the first and second persons plural of the imperative is
dropped when *nos* and *os* are affixed to them respectively:
Ex.

Infinitive.	Amárse,	To love oneself.
Part. Active.	amándose,	loving oneself.
	ámate tú,	love thou thyself.
	ámese él,	let him love himself.
Imperative.	amémonos nosotros,	let us love ourselves.
	amáos vosotros,	love you yourselves, etc.
	ámense ellos,	let them love themselves, etc.

It is optional, for the sake of energy, etc., to place
the reflective pronoun *after* the verb in the first and
third persons singular, and third plural of the tenses of
the indicative.

Note.—When the verb denotes a *reciprocity* of action
between two or more individuals, it is formed in Spanish
in the same manner as the plural of *reflective* verbs ; as,
Nos amamos—We love one another. *Os engañasteis*—
You deceived each other. *Se perderán*—They will lose
one another.

FORMATION OF PASSIVE VERBS.

6. Passive verbs are formed in Spanish by adding the past participle of the verb to be used passively to the verb *ser*, throughout every mood and tense; and observe that the participle passive must agree in *number* and *gender* with the nominative of the verb : Ex.

Infinitive.	Ser amádo,	To be loved.
Part. Active.	siéndo amádo,	being loved.

Participle Passive.	*Sing. Mas.* amádo.		
	Plur. Mas. amádos.	Loved.	
	Sing. Fem. amáda.		
	Plur. Fem. amádas.		

Indicative Present.

Sóy amádo,	I am loved.	Sómos amádos,	We are loved.
éres amádo,	thou art loved.	sóis amádos,	you are loved.
es amádo,	he is loved.	son amádos,	they are loved.

And so on throughout the verb.

OBSERVATION ON THE PASSIVE VOICE. .

7. A *reflective* verb in the *third* person singular or plural in any of the moods and tenses, is often employed in Spanish when the meaning intended to be conveyed by it is *passive* : for instance, *Ten men were employed,* is frequently translated, *Se emplearon diez hombres,* instead of, *Diez hombres fueron empleados* : and, *The necessary precautions have been taken,* might be translated, *Se han tomado las precauciones necesarias,* as well as, *Las precauciones necesarias han sido tomadas.* Nevertheless, the learner should be very cautious how he employs this manner of expressing the *passive* voice, for fear of rendering his sentences ambiguous. We see that the first example, *Se emplearon diez hombres,* might be either taken for *Ten men were employed,* or *Ten men employed themselves.* In the second example, however, no ambiguity can arise from employing the verb in either manner, since, as it is impossible for the precautions *to take themselves,* we must understand that the sense intended to be conveyed is, that the precautions *were taken.*

However, as this manner of forming the passive voice with the pronoun *se* is so frequently made use of in Spanish, the pupil is recommended to make himself as familiar as possible with this peculiarity, by directing his attention to it while reading. Observe the following examples :—

Mañana *se venderá* la casa.	The house *will be sold* to-morrow.
Los muchachos *se esperan* esta noche.	The boys *are expected* to-night.
Qué *se ha de hacer ?*	What *is to be done ?*
No *se puede remediar.*	It *cannot be helped.*
En su glorioso reinado *se ejercitaron* todas las artes de la paz y de la guerra, y *se vieron* los accidentes de ámbas fortunas, próspera y adversa. — (SAAVEDRA FAJARDO —*Empresas Políticas.*)	In his glorious reign (Ferdinand V.'s) all the arts of peace and war *were practised*, and the chances of both adverse and prosperous fortune *were witnessed*.
Debió mucho á este Príncipe la lengua Castellana ; pues ademas de haberla ilustrado con la pluma, mandó *se usase* en todos los decretos y privilegios reales, y en las escrituras públicas, que ántes *se escribian* en Latin. —(T. IRIARTE—*Hist. de España.*)	The Castilian language owed much to this Prince (Alphonsus X.) ; for besides having enriched it with his pen, he commanded that it *should be used* in all the royal orders and immunities, and in all public documents, which *were formerly written* in Latin.

In translating a complete passive sentence, such as *Wisdom is praised by all*, if it be done with the verb *ser*, the ablative *todos* (all) may be governed by the preposition *de* or *por ;* but if it be construed with the pronoun *se*, then the ablative can only be governed by *por* : Ex. *La sabiduría es alabada de*, or *por todos : La sabiduría se alaba por todos.*—GRAMMAR OF THE ACADEMY.

Note.—The pronoun *se*, with the third person singular of the *active* voice, is employed in Spanish in all vague and general reports : Ex.

Se dice que, etc.	They say, *or* it is said that, etc.
Se cree que la noticia es verdadera.	It is believed that the news is true.
Se habla de guerra.	War is spoken of.
Se dice que es grande orador.	He is said to be a great orator.

The active voice alone, without the pronoun *se*, may also be employed with the like expressions, in the following manner:

Dicen que, etc.	They say that, etc.
Creen que la noticia es verdadera.	They believe that the news is true.
Hablan de guerra.	They speak of war.
Dicen que es grande orador.	They say he is a great orator.

The pronoun *se*, with a verb in the third person, is also sometimes used as an equivalent for *one*: Ex. Se *necesita descanso despues del trabajo—One* réquires rest after labour.

The same pronoun is sometimes also used as occupying the place of some third person before a pronoun in the dative or accusative case; as, *Se me pregunta si*, etc.— I am asked if, etc. *Se le busca á Vmd.*—You are enquired for. *Se me ha pasado de la memoria*—It has escaped my memory.

EXERCISE ON REFLECTIVE AND PASSIVE VERBS.

He gives himself up to melancholy. They accuse
    abandonarse   melancolía   acusarse

themselves of the crime. You will hurt yourself.
        delito   lastimarse

Do not trouble yourself. He freed himself from the
   molestarse   librarse

enemy. They had wounded one another. They have
enemigo   herirse

always praised each other. If they should offend
siempre alabarse   ofenderse

one another. Let us seat ourselves down here.
     sentarse   *

Comfort yourselves, my children. She is esteemed by
consolarse   estimar de

her acquaintances. He was protected by them. They
  conocido.   proteger

were attacked by the enemy. That they may be declared
  atacar   declarar

innocent. That I might be elected by the committee.
inocente   elegir   comitiva

Let us be convinced of the truth. To be accused
  convencer   acusar

[it is sufficient] to be suspected. They were employed.
  basta   sospechar   emplear

The street has been paved. Having been captured.
  calle   empedrar   apresar

The houses were thrown down. A new comedy will be
    derribar *   comedia

performed to-morrow. Some treaty of commerce has
representar   tratado comercio

been spoken of. It is believed to be true. He is said
            verdad

to be a great musician.
  músico.

VERBS USED NEGATIVELY.

8. In Spanish the negative *no* invariably precedes the
verb, or its auxiliary ; and should there be a pronoun of
the dative or accusative case before the verb, the negative
precedes both. (Observe that the auxiliary *do*, of negative and interrogative sentences, is not translated): Ex.

 No puedo venir.   I cannot come.
 No la veo.   I do not see her.
 No le ha hablado. He has not spoken to him.

If the nominative is expressed, it may be placed either
before the negative particle, or after the verb ; thus : *Yo
no puedo venir;* or, *no puedo yo venir;* or, *no puedo venir
yo ;* but never *no yo puedo venir.*

Two negatives do not destroy each other in Spanish as they do in English; on the contrary, they add strength to one another: Ex.

No tengo *nada* que dar á   I have *nothing* to give you.
  Vmd.
No lo sabe *nadie*.   *Nobody* knows it.
No lo he visto *jamas*.   I have *never* seen it.

These phrases, nevertheless, may, with equal propriety, though, perhaps, with less energy, be expressed thus: *Nada tengo que dar á Vmd.; Nadie lo sabe; Jamas lo he visto.* The *no* can never be used when any other negative precedes the verb.

There are some instances, however, in which one negative naturally destroys the other in Spanish as well as in English; thus, *No deseo verla nunca*, means, I never wish to see her; but *No deseo nunca verla*, means, I do not desire never to see her; signifying, by the latter expression, a wish to see her *sometimes*. And *No pretendo sinó que me pague*, denotes, I only pretend that he should pay me.

The following sentence of JOVELLANOS, in his *Memoria á sus Compatriotas*, "No *podian* no *ser complices en la usurpacion de la autoridad*," means, They *could not do less* than connive at the usurpation of the authority.

In many instances the negative *no* is seen used in Spanish by way of pleonasm when nothing of a negative sense exists; thus, *El es mas rico que* no *ella*—He is richer than she. *Temia* no *entrara y me hallaria durmiendo*—I feared he might come in and find me asleep. *Por poco* no *me caigo*—I was near falling. But in these and the like phrases, the *no* had better be omitted.

And, on the contrary, in phrases where any portion of time is qualified by the word *todo*, the negative is frequently omitted, when the sense required it to be expressed, as, *En* toda la noche *he podido dormir*—I have *not* been able to sleep the whole night.

VERBS USED INTERROGATIVELY.

9. With regard to the order of construction preserved in interrogative sentences, no precise rule can be given; it is the modulation of the voice that mostly determines,

in speaking, when the verb is used interrogatively; and
in writing, the note of interrogation. However, in the
natural order, the nominative, in interrogative sentences,
when expressed, is generally placed after the verb (though
not always immediately after it, unless it be a pronoun);
but this order may, for energy or elegance, be inverted.
If the interrogative sentence has a negative also, the
negative is still always put before the verb : Ex.

¿ *Sabe él* que estoy aquí ? — *Does he know* that I am
here ?

Dónde se *fueron* vuestras *alegrías* antiguas . . . ? — Whither *are* all your former *joys gone* . . . . ?

¿ *Este es* el rostro que yo ví traspasado. . . . ? (Fr. Luis de Granada.) — *Is this* the countenance that I saw afflicted . . . . ?

¿ No te *lastiman* mas los *lamentos* de todos esos infelices ?—(Feijoo.) — *Do not* the *cries* of those unhappy creatures any longer move thee to pity?

EXERCISE ON NEGATIVE AND INTERROGATIVE VERBS.

They are not the same. I have not heard it. She
        mismo   oir

was not there. They had no arms. I do not aspire to
            arma   aspirar

so much. They could not defend him. We should not
              defender

desire what is not ours. They should not believe it. I am
desear

not engaged. They were not condemned. You shall
  comprometer   condenar

not be insulted. That they may not be received. I do not
    insultar

flatter myself. They do not trouble themselves. I never
lisongear   incomodar   jamas

knew it. I will never believe it. They have no patience.
saber   paciencia

He knew nobody. Do not sell him anything. Do I
  conocer   vender

answer well?   Shall we arrive to-day?   Would he lend
responder   prestar
it to me? Were they increased? Have they confirmed it?
                  aumentar   confirmar
Has he been rewarded? Would they spare themselves that
            premiar   ahorrar
trouble?   Have they procured nothing?   Will they not
                  procurar
 pretend it?   Would they not have reported him?
protender   reportar
Will they not be published?
                  publicar

OBSERVATIONS ON THE ACCENTUATION OF VERBS.

10. In all the foregoing conjugations of verbs an
accent has been placed over the syllable requiring the
stress of voice, in order to assist the learner. But verbs
are not always found written with the accent for this
purpose. The following rules, which are applicable to all
regular verbs, will point out where the stress is required
in them. Many of the irregular verbs also are accented
in the same manner; but as no general rule can be given
for the accentuation of these, the student will be guided
by the accent laid on the syllable requiring the stress, in
their respective conjugations.

INDIC.—*Present.*—In this tense the stress is laid on
the last syllable but one, in every person except the
second plural, which is acute on the last.

Imperfect.—Here the acute syllable is the last but
one in every person except the first plural, which has
the stress on the last syllable but two.

Perfect.—The first and third persons singular are
acute in this tense on the last syllable, and all the rest
on the last but one.

Future.—The last syllable of this tense is acute in
every person except the first plural, which has the stress
upon the last but one.

SUB.—*Present.*—The same syllables are acute in this
tense as in the present indicative.

Imperfect and future. — These two tenses have the same syllables acute as those in the imperfect indicative.

IMPERAT.—Here the second person plural is acute on the last syllable, and the rest are so on the last but one.

The INFINITIVE is always acute on the last syllable, and the PARTICIPLES on the last but one.

REMARK.—Should the accent fall upon a syllable having the diphthong *ie*, or *io*, the latter of the two vowels has the stress; as, *vendiéndo, unió.*

If the accented syllable contains a combination of the vowels *ia* or *iai*, the stress falls on the first vowel; as, *vendía, temíais.*

When the syllable contains the diphthong *ei*, the stress falls on the *e*; as, *compraréis, venderéis.*

The foregoing observations point out what particular syllable of the verb requires the *stress* of voice; but it is not every syllable on which the stress falls that is written with the *accent.* The accent is required only when the verb is spelled alike in more than one tense : and its use then is to distinguish the one from the other, as follows:

INDIC.—*Perfect.*—Here the accent is employed on the first and third persons singular, and first person plural; as, *hablé, habló, hablámos,* to distinguish them from the following, which are spelled like them—viz., *hable,* first and third persons singular, *present subjunctive; hablo, hablamos,* first person singular, and first person plural, *present indicative.*

Future.—Every person in this tense is accented; as, *hablaré, hablarás, hablará, hablarémos, hablaréis, hablarán,* to distinguish them from the following,—viz., *hablara, hablaras, hablaran,* first, second, and third persons singular, and third person plural, *imperfect subjunctive;* and *hablare, hablaremos, hablareis,* first or third persons singular, and first and second persons plural, *future subjunctive.*

Some writers employ the accent on the first and second persons plural of the *imperfect indicative,* and the *imperfect and future subjunctive,* but its employment there appears of no utility, and is consequently not generally practised. The *employment* of the accent is therefore now generally confined to the following :—viz., the first and third persons singular, and first person plural of the *perfect indicative,* and every person of the *future indicative.*

If one or more pronouns of the dative or accusative case be affixed to an unaccented person of a verb, the syllable on which the stress falls should be marked with the accent; as, from *pide, pídalo, pídaselo;* from *recverde, recuérdeme, recuérdemelo.*

LECTURE XXV.

CONJUGATION OF IRREGULAR VERBS.

1. The irregularity in these verbs is sometimes found to be in the root, at others in the termination, and occasionally in both. In the following conjugations, those moods, tenses, and persons only that have any irregularity in them are exhibited; the rest being omitted, that the learner may see at one view where the irregularity lies. Observe that all irregular compound and reflective verbs are conjugated like the simple ones from which they are formed.

IRREGULAR VERBS OF THE FIRST CONJUGATION.

ACERTAR, TO GUESS, TO HIT A MARK, TO ASCERTAIN.

The irregularity of this verb is in the root, and consists in its admitting an *i* before the *e,* in the three persons singular and the third person plural of the present indicative and present subjunctive, and the second and third persons singular and third person plural of the imperative: Ex.

Indicative Present.

| Aciérto, | aciértas, | aciérta, | —— | —— | aciértan. |

Subjunctive Present.

| Aciérte, | aciértes, | aciérte, | —— | —— | aciérten. |

Imperative.

| | aciérta, | aciérte, | —— | —— | aciérten. |

VERBS CONJUGATED LIKE *ACERTAR*.

Acrecentar, adestrar, alentar, apacentar, apretar, arrendar, asentar,
asestar, aterrar, atestar, atravesar, aventar, Bregar, Calentar, cegar,
cerrar, cimenar, comenzar, concertar, confesar, Decentar, derrengar,
desertar,* desmembrar, despertar, despernar, desterrar, dezmar, Empedrar, empezar, encomendar, encubertar, enmendar, ensangrentar,
enterrar, errar,† escarmentar, estregar, Fregar, Gobernar, Herrar,
helar, Infernar, invernar, Manifestar,* mentar, merendar, Negar,
nevar, Pensar, plegar, Quebrar, Regar, reventar, Segar, sembrar,
sentar, serrar, sosegar, Temblar, tentar, tropezar.

 · See the English translation of these and the following
verbs in the alphabetical list of all the Spanish irregular
verbs, at the end of these conjugations.

ACORDAR, TO AGREE.

This verb changes the *o* of the root into *ue*, in the
same moods, tenses, and persons as are irregular in the
verb *acertar :* Ex.

Indicative Present.

Acuérdo,   acuérdas,   acuérda,   ——   ——   acuérdan.

Subjunctive Present.

Acuérda,   acuérdes,   acuérde,   ——   ——   acuérden.

Imperative.

          acuérda,   acuérde,   ——   ——   acuérden.

VERBS CONJUGATED LIKE *ACORDAR*.

Acostar, agorar, almorzar, amolar, aporcar, aportar, apostar, apro-
bar, asolar, asoldar, avergonzar, Colar, colgar, consolar, contar,
costar, Descollar, degollar, demostrar, desfogar, desolar, desovar,
Emporcar, encontrar, encordar, enrodar, engrosar, Forzar, Holgar,
hollar, Mostrar, Poblar, probar, Regoldar, renovar, rescontrar,
resollar, rodar, rogar, Solar, soldar, soltar,‡ sonar, soñar, Tostar,
trocar, tronar, Volar, volcar.

---

* *Manifestar* and *desertar* have regular and irregular past participles: the latter are *desiérto* and *manifiésto.*

† In this verb a *y* is substituted for the *i* which precedes the *e*,
in the irregular tenses; thus, *yérro, yérre,* etc.

‡ *Soltar* has a regular and an irregular past participle; the
latter is *suélto.*

ANDAR, TO WALK, TO GO.

Indicative Perfect.

Andúve, anduviste, andúvo, anduvimos, anduvisteis, anduviéron.

Subjunctive Imperfect.

Anduviéra, —viéras, —viéra, —viéramos, —viérais, —viéran.
Anduviése, —viéses, —viése, —viésemos, —viéseis, —viésen.

Future.

Anduviére, —viéres, —viére, —viéremos, —viéreis, —viéren.

Note.—In almost all the irregular verbs, the terminations *ra* and *se* of the imperfect subjunctive, and the future of the same tense are formed from the perfect indicative.   See also note in page 175.

DAR, TO GIVE.

Indicative Present.

Doy,   ——   ——   ——   ——   ——

Perfect.

Dí,   diste,   dió,   dimos,   disteis,   diéron.

Subjunctive Imperfect.

Diéra,   diéras,   diéra,   diéramos,   diérais,   diéran.
Diése,   dieses,   diése,   diésemos,   diéseis,   diésen.

Future.

Diére,   diéres,   diére,   diéremos,   diéreis,   diéren.

ESTAR, TO BE.

See this verb conjugated, page 162.   With the exception of the first person singular present indicative, which admits of a final *y*, *estar* has the same irregularities as *andar*.

JUGAR, TO PLAY.

This verb admits an *e* after the radical *u*, in the following tenses and persons:—

Indicative Present.

Juégo,   juégas,   juéga,   ——   ——   juégan.

Subjunctive Present.

Juégue, juégues, juégue,   ——   ——   juéguen.

Imperative.

juéga, juégue,   ——   ——   juéguen.

IRREGULAR VERBS OF THE SECOND CONJUGATION.

ABORRECER, TO HATE.

The irregularity of this verb, and of those terminating in *acer*, *ecer*, and *ocer*, consists in admitting a *z* before the *c* in the root, whenever the *c* is followed by *a* or *o* : Ex.

Indicative Present.

Aborrézco, —— —— —— —— ——

Subjunctive Present.

Aborrézca, —rézcas, —rézca, —rezcámos, —rezcáis, —rézcan.

Imperative.

—— —rézca, —rezcámos, ——   —rézcan.

HACER, TO DO, TO MAKE.

This verb is an exception from the foregoing rule.

Indicative Present.

Hágo, —— —— —— —— ——

Perfect.

Híce, hicíste, hízo, hicímos, hicísteis, hiciéron.

Future.

Haré, harás, hará, harámos, haréis, harán.

Subjunctive Present.

Hága, hágas, hága, hagámos, hagáis, hágan.

Imperfect.

Hiciéra, hiciéras, hiciéra, hiciéramos, hiciérais, hiciéran.
Hiciése, hiciéses, hiciése, hiciésemos, hiciéseis, hiciésen.
Haría, harías, haría, haríamos, haríais, harían.

Future.

Hiciére, hiciéres,   hiciére,   hiciéremos, hiciéreis,   hiciéren.

Imperative.

has,   hága,   hagámos,   ——   hágan.

Participle past.   Hécho.

COCER, TO BAKE, TO BOIL, TO COOK.

Of those verbs ending in *ocer*, just mentioned, we must also except *cocer*, to bake, etc., *escocer*, to smart, and *recocer*, to reboil. These do not admit the *z* before *c*, but change the *o* of the root into *ue*, in the same moods, tenses, and persons as are irregular in *absorver*, the next in conjugation. They likewise change the *c* of the root into *z* before *o* and *a*, in order to preserve the soft sound which the *c* has in the infinitive : Ex.

Indicative Present.

Cuézo,   cuéces,   cuéce,   ——   ——   cuécen.

Subjunctive Present.

Cuéza,   cuézas,   cuéza,   cozámos,   cozáis,   cuézan.

Imperative.

cuéce,   cuéza,   cozámos,   ——   cuézan.

Cocer has a regular and an irregular past participle; the latter is *cócho.*

VERBS CONJUGATED LIKE *ABORRECER*.

Abastecer, acaecer, acontecer, adolecer, adormecer, agradecer, amanecer, anochecer, aparecer, apetecer, Canecer, carecer, conocer, convalecer, crecer, Embravecer, emplumecer, empobrecer, encallecer, encalvecer, encarecer, encrudecer, encruelecer, endentecer, endurecer, enflaquecer, engrandecer, enloquecer, enmohecer, enmudecer, ennoblecer, enrarecer, enriquecer, ensoberbecer, entallecer, enternecer, entorpecer, entullecer, entumecer, entristecer, envejecer, enverdecer, escarnecer, esclarecer, establecer, estremecer, Fallecer, favorecer,* fenecer, fortalecer, Guarnecer, Humedecer, Merecer, Nacer, negrecer, Obedecer, obscurecer, ofrecer, Pacer, padecer, parecer, perecer, pertenecer, placer, prevalecer, Remanecer, restablecer.

---

* *Favorecer* has a regular and an irregular past participle; the latter is *favorito.*

ABSORVER, TO ABSORB.

Indicative Present.

Absuérvo,　absuérves,　absuérve,　——　——　absuérven.

Subjunctive Present.

Absuérva,　absuérvas,　absuérva,　——　——　absuérvan.

Imperative.

absuérve,　absuérva,　——　——　absuérvan.

Absorver has a regular and an irregular past participle; the latter is *absórto.*

VERBS CONJUGATED LIKE *ABSORVER.*

Absolver,* Disolver,* doler, Llover, Moler, morder, mover, Oler,† Resolver,* Torcer,* Volver.*

ASCENDER, TO ASCEND.

This verb takes an *i* before the *e* of the root, in the same moods, tenses, and persons as are irregular in *acertar;* but its conjugation is here exhibited from its being of a different termination : Ex.

Indicative Present.

Asciéndo,　asciéndes,　asciénde,　——　——　asciénden.

Subjunctive Present.

Asciénda,　asciéndas,　asciénda,　——　——　asciéndan.

Imperative.

asciénde,　asciénda,　——　——　asciéndan.

VERBS CONJUGATED LIKE *ASCENDER.*

Atender,‡ Cerner, Defender, descender, Encender, entender, Heder, hender, Perder, Tender, Verter.

---

* The past participles of *absolver, disolver, resolver,* and *volver,* are *absuélto, disuélto, resuélto,* and *vuélto :* the rest of this list have regular past participles ; and *torcer,* in addition to its regular past participle, has an irregular one, namely, *tuérto.*

† The irregular persons of this verb must be written with an *h :* as, *huélo, huéla,* etc.

‡ *Atender* has a regular and an irregular past participle ; the latter is *aténto.*

CABER, TO BE CONTAINED, *or* TO BE CAPABLE OF
BEING CONTAINED.*

Indicative Present.

| Quépo, | —— | —— | —— | —— | —— |

Perfect.

| Cúpe, | cupíste, | cúpo, | cupímos, | cupísteis, | cupiéron. |

Future.

| Cabié, | cabrás, | cabrá, | cabrémos, | cabréis, | cabrán. |

Subjunctive Present.

| Quépa, | quépas, | quépa, | quepámos, | quepáis, | quépan. |

Imperfect.

Cupiéra,	cupiéras,	cupiéra,	cupiéramos,	cupiérais,	cupiéran.
Cupiése,	cupiéses,	cupiése,	cupiésemos,	cupiéseis,	cupiésen.
Cabría,	cabrías,	cabría,	cabríamos,	cabríais,	cabrían.

Future.

| Cupiére, | cupiéres, | cupiére, | cupiéremos, | cupiéreis, | cupiéren. |

Imperative.

| —— | quépa, | quepámos, | —— | quépan. |

CAER, TO FALL.

This verb admits *ig* after the *a* in the root, when the
termination begins with *a* or *o*: Ex.

Indicative Present.

| Cáigo, | —— | —— | —— | —— | —— |

Subjunctive Present.

| Cáiga, | cáigas, | cáiga, | caigámos, | caigáis, | cáigan. |

Imperative.

| —— | cáiga, | caigámos, | —— | cáigan. |

See also *Note*, PAR. 3, LECT. 24.

HABER, TO HAVE.

See this verb conjugated, page 157.

---

* See the different manners of employing this verb, LECT. 28,
PAR. 9.

PODER, TO BE ABLE.

Indicative Present.

Puédo, puédes, puéde, —— —— puéden.

Perfect.

Púde, pudíste, púdo, pudímos, pudísteis, pudiéron.

Future.

Podré, podrás, podrá, podrémos, podréis, podrán.

Subjunctive Present.

Puéda, puédas, puéda, —— —— puédan.

Imperfect.

Pudiéra, pudiéras, pudiéra, pudiéramos, pudiérais, pudiéran.
Pudiése, pudiéses, pudiése, pudiésemos, pudiéseis, pudiésen.
Podría, podrías, podría, podríamos, podríais, podrían.

Future.

Pudiére, pudiéres, pudiére, pudiéremos, pudiéreis, pudiéren.

(*No Imperative.*)

Participle Active. Pudiéndo.

PONER, TO PUT, TO PLACE.

Indicative Present.

Póngo, —— —— —— —— ——

Perfect.

Púse, pusíste, púso, pusímos, pusísteis, pusiéron.

Future.

Pondré, pondrás, pondrá, pondrémos, pondréis, pondrán.

Subjunctive Present.

Pónga, póngas, pónga, pongámos, pongáis, póngan.

Imperfect.

Pusiéra, pusiéras, pusiéra, pusiéramos, pusiérais, pusiéran.
Pusiése, pusiéses, pusiése, pusiésemos, pusiéseis, pusiésen.
Pondría, pondrías, pondría, pondríamos, pondríais, pondrían.

Future.

Pusiére, pusiéres, puisére, pusiéremos, pusiéreis, pusiéren.

Imperative.

pos, pónga, pongámos, ——— póngan.

Participle Past. Puésto.

QUERER, TO WISH, TO BE WILLING, TO LOVE.

Indicative Present.

Quiéro, quiéres, quiére, ——— ——— quiéren.

Perfect.

Quíse, quisíste, quíso, quisímos, quisísteis, quisiéron.

Future.

Querré, querrás, querrá, querrémos, querréis, querrán.

Subjunctive Present.

Quiéra, quiéras, quiéra, ——— ——— quiéran.

Imperfect.

Quisiéra, quisiéras, quisiéra, quisiéramos, quisiérais, quisiéran.
Quisiése, quisiéses, quisiése, quisiéscmos, quisiéseis, quisiésen.
Querría, querrías, querría, querríamos, querríais, querrían.

Future.

Quisiére, quisiéres, quisiére, quisiéremos, quisiéreis, quisiéren.

Imperative.

quiére, quiéra, ——— ——— quiéran.

SABER, TO KNOW.

Indicative Present.

Sé, ——— ——— ——— ——— ———

Perfect.

Súpe, supíste, súpo, supímos, supísteis, supiéron.

Future.

Sabré, sabrás, sabrá, sabrémos, sabréis, sabrán.

Subjunctive Present.

Sépa, sépas, sépa, sepámos, sepáis, sepán.

Imperfect.

Supiéra,	supiéras,	supiéra,	supiéramos,	supiérais,	supiéran.
Supiése,	supiéses,	supiése,	supiésemos,	supiéseis,	supiésen.
Sabría,	sabrías,	sabría,	sabríamos,	sabríais,	sabrían.

Future.

| Supiére, | supiéres, | supiére, | supiéremos, | supiéreis, | supiéren. |

Imperative.

| —— | sépa, | sepámos, | —— | sépan. |

SER, TO BE.

TENER, TO HAVE, TO HOLD.

See these two verbs conjugated, pages 160 and 158.

TRAER, TO BRING, TO FETCH.

Indicative Present.

| Tráigo, | —— | —— | —— | —— | —— |

Perfect.

| Tráje, | trajíste, | trájo, | trajímos, | trajísteis, | trajéron. |

Subjunctive Present.

| Tráiga, | tráigas, | tráiga, | traigámos, | traigáis, | tráigan. |

Imperfect.

| Trajéra, | trajéras, | trajéra, | trajéramos, | trajérais, | trajéran. |
| Trajése, | trajéses, | trajése, | trajésemos, | trajéseis, | trajésen. |

Future.

| Trajére, | trajéres, | trajére, | trajéremos, | trajéreis, | trajéren. |

Imperative.

| —— | tráiga, | traigámos, | —— | tráiga. |

Participle Active. Trayéndo.

VALER, TO BE WORTH.

Indicative Present.

| Válgo, | —— | —— | —— | —— | —— |

Future.

| Valdré, | valdrás, | valdrá, | valdrémos, | valdréis, | valdrán. |

Subjunctive Present.

Válga,   válgas,   válga,   valgámos,   valgáis,   válgan.

Imperfect.

Valdría,   valdrías,   valdría,   valdríamos,   valdríais,   valdrían.

Imperative.

——   válga,   valgámos,   ——   válgan.

VER, TO SEE.

Indicative Present.

Véo,   ——   ——   ——   ——   ——

Imperfect.

Veía,   veías,   veía,   veíamos,   veíais,   veían.

It has also a regular imperfect tense, as, *via, vias,* etc.

Subjunctive Present.

Véa,   véas,   véa,   veámos,   veáis,   véan.

Imperative.

——   véa,   veámos,   ——   véan.

Participle Past.   Visto.

IRREGULAR VERBS OF THE THIRD CONJUGATION.

ASIR, TO SEIZE.

Indicative Present.

Ásgo,   ——   ——   ——   ——   ——

Subjunctive Present.

Ásga,   ásgas,   ásga,   asgámos,   asgáis,   ásgan.

Imperative.

——   ásga,   asgámos,   ——   ásgan.

DECIR, TO SAY, TO TELL.

Indicative Present.

Dígo,   díces,   díce,   ——   ——   dícen.

Perfect.

Díje,   dijíste,   díjo,   dijímos,   dijísteis,   dijéron.

Future.

Diré,   dirás,   dirá,   dirémos,   diréis,   dirán.

Subjunctive Present.

Díga,   dígas,   díga,   digámos,   digáis,   dígan.

Imperfect.

Dijéra,   dijéras,   dijéra,   dijéramos, dijérais,   dijéran.
Dijése,   dijéses,   dijése,   dijésemos, dijéseis,   dijésen.
Diría,   dirías,   diría,   diríamos,   diríais,   dirían.

Future.

Dijére,   dijéres,   dijére,   dijéremos, dijéreis,   dijéren.

Imperative.

           dí,   díga,   digámos,   ——   dígan.

Participle Active.   Diciéndo.
Participle Past.   Dícho.

Contradecir, to contradict, and *predecir*, to predict, are
conjugated like *decir*, except that the second person
singular of the imperative is *contradíce* and *predíce*.

Bendecir, to bless, and *maldecir*, to curse, are also
conjugated like *decir*, except that the future of the indicative, and the imperfect subjunctive of the termination
ria, are regular, and that the second person singular of
the imperative is *bendíce, maldíce*. These two verbs
have each a regular and an irregular past participle;
the latter is *bendíto* and *maldíto*, and partake of the
nature of adjectives.

DORMIR, TO SLEEP.

Indicative Present.

Duérmo, duérmes, duérme, ——   ——   duérmen.

Perfect.

——   ——   durmió, ——   ——   durmiéron.

Subjunctive Present.

Duérma, duérmas, duérma, durmámos,   durmáis,   duérman.

Imperfect.

Durmiéra,—miéras, —miéra, —miéramos,—miérais, —miéran.
Durmiése,—miéses, —miése, —miésemos,—miéseis, —miésen.

Future.

Durmiére,—miéres, —miére, —miéremos,—miéreis, —miéren.

Imperative.

duérme, duérma, durmámos, ——   duérman.
Participle Active.   Durmiéndo.

Morir, to die, is conjugated like *dormir,* except that
its past participle is *muérto.*

INSTRUIR, TO INSTRUCT.

When the root of verbs of the third conjugation ends
in *u,* (as in *instruir,*) this vowel takes a *y* after it before
those terminations beginning with *e, a,* or *o :* Ex.

Indicative Present.

Instrúyo, instrúyes, instrúye, ——   ——   instrúyen.

Subjunctive Present.

Instrúya, instrúyas, instrúya, instruyámos, instruyáis, instrúyan.

Imperative.

instrúye, instrúya, instruyámos, ——   instrúyan.
See also *Note,* PAR. 3, LECT. 24.

VERBS CONJUGATED LIKE *INSTRUIR.*

Argüir, atribuir, Concluir,* constituir, construir, contribuir, Des-
truir, disminuir, distribuir, Excluir, Fluir, Huir, Imbuir, incluir,*
instituir, Luir, Obstruir, Prostituir, Recluir, restituir, retribuir,
Sustituir.*

IR, TO GO.

This verb is remarkable for having the perfect tense
of the indicative, and the termination *ra* and *se* of the

---

* *Concluir, incluir,* and *sustituir,* have regular and irregular
past participles ; the latter are *conclúso, inclúso,* and *sustitúto.*

imperfect subjunctive, and the future of this mood precisely like the same in the verb *Ser* : Ex.

Indicative Present.

| Vóy, | vas, | va, | vámos, | váis, | van. |

Imperfect.

| Íba, | íbas, | íba, | íbamos, | íbais, | íban. |

Perfect.

| Fuí, | fuíste, | fué, | fuímos, | fuísteis, | fuéron. |

Future.

| Iré, | irás, | irá, | irémos, | iréis, | irán. |

Subjunctive Present.

| Váya, | váyas, | váya, | vayámos, | vayáis, | váyan. |

Imperfect.

Fuéra,	fuéras,	fuéra,	fuéramos,	fuérais,	fuéran.
Fuése,	fuéses,	fuése,	fuésemos,	fuéseis,	fuésen.
Iría,	irías,	iría,	iríamos,	iríais,	irían.

Future.

| Fuére, | fuéres, | fuére, | fuéremos, | fuéreis, | fuéren. |

Imperative.

| | vé, | váya, | { vámos, or, vayámos, } | —— | váyan. |

| *Participle Active.* | Yéndo. |
| *Participle Past.* | Ído |

LUCIR, TO SHINE.

This verb has the same irregularities as *aborrecer*, but its conjugation is here exhibited, being of a different termination : Ex.

Indicative Present.

| Lúzco, | —— | —— | —— | —— | —— |

Subjunctive Present.

| Lúzca, | lúzcas, | lúzca, | luzcámos, | luzcáis, | lúzcan. |

Imperative.

———   lúzca,   luzcámos,   ———   lúzcan.

Verbs ending in *ducir*, as CONDUCIR, to conduct, in addition to the irregularities in *lucir*, have also the following:

Indicative Perfect.

Condúje,   —dujíste,   —dújo,   —dujímos,   —dujísteis, —dujéron.

Subjunctive Imperfect.

Condujéra, —dujéras, —dujéra,—dujéramos, —dujérais, —dujéran.
Condujése, —dujéses, —dujése,—dujésemos, —dujéseis, —dujésen.

Future.

Condujére, —dujéres, —dujére,—dujéremos, —dujéreis, —dujéren.

VERBS CONJUGATED LIKE *CONDUCIR*.

Deducir, Inducir, introducir, Producir,* Reducir, Traducir.

OIR, TO HEAR.

The irregularities in this verb are like those in *caer*; they are nevertheless exhibited from its being of a different conjugation: Ex.

Indicative Present.

Óigo,]   óyes,   óye,   ———   ———   óyen.

Subjunctive Present.

Óiga,   óigas,   óiga,   oigámos,   oigáis,   óigan.

Imperative.

         óye,   óiga,   oigámos,   ———   óigan.

See also *Note*, PAR. 3, LECT. 24.

PEDIR, TO ASK, TO BEG.

Indicative Present.

Pído,   pídes,   píde,   ———   ———   píden.

---

* *Producir* has a regular and an irregular past participle; the latter is *prodúcto*.

Perfect.

——   ——   pidió,   ——   ——   pidiéron.

Subjunctive Present.

Pída,   pídas,   pída,   pidámos,   pidáis,   pídan.

Imperfect.

Pidiéra,   pidiéras,   pidiéra,   pidiéramos,   pidiérais,   pidiéran.
Pidiése,   pidiéses,   pidiése,   pidiésemos,   pidiéseis,   pidiésen.

Future.

Pidiére,   pidiéres,   pidiére,   pidiéremos,   pidiéreis,   pidiéren.

Imperative.

pide,   pída,   pidámos,   ——   pídan.

Participle Active. Pidiéndo.

VERBS CONJUGATED LIKE *PEDIR*.

Apercibir, arrecir, Ceñir, colegir, competir, concebir, constreñir, Derretir, desleir, Elegir, embestir, engreir, Freir, *p.p.* frito, Gemir, Heñir, Medir, Regir, reir, rendir, reñir, repetir, Seguir, servir, Teñir,* Vestir.

PODRIR, TO ROT.

Indicative Present.

Púdro,   púdres,   púdre,   ——   ——   púdren.

Perfect.

Pudrí,   pudríste,   pudrío,   pudrímos,   pudrísteis,   pudriéron.

Subjunctive Present.

Púdra,   púdras,   púdra,   pudrámos,   pudráis,   púdran.

Imperfect.

Pudriéra, pudriéras, pudriéra, pudriéramos, pudriérais, pudriéran.
Pudriése, pudriéses, pudriése, pudriésemos, pudriéseis, pudriésen.

Future.

Pudriére, pudriéres, pudriére, pudriéremos, pudriéreis, pudriéren.

---

* *Teñir* has a regular and an irregular past participle; the latter is *tinto.*

Imperative.

púdre,　　púdra,　　pudrámos,　　——　　púdran.

Participle Active.　Pudriéndo.

SALIR, TO GO OUT.

This verb has the same irregularities as *valer*, except the second person singular of the imperative ; and it is here exhibited from its being of a different termination : Ex.

Indicative Present.

Sálgo,　　——　　——　　——　　——　　——

Future.

Saldré,　saldrás,　saldrá,　saldrémos,　saldréis,　saldrán.

Subjunctive Present.

Sálga,　sálgas,　sálga,　salgámos,　salgáis,　sálgan.

Imperfect.

Saldría,　saldrías,　saldría,　saldriamos,　saldríais,　saldrían.

Imperative.

sal,　　sálga,　　salgámos,　　——　　sálgan.

SENTIR, TO FEEL, TO REGRET, TO PERCEIVE.

Indicative Present.

Siénto,　siéntes,　siénte,　——　　——　siénten.

Perfect.

——　　——　sintió,　——　　——　sintiéron.

Subjunctive Present.

Siénta,　siéntas,　siénta,　sintámos,　sintáis,　siéntan.

Imperfect.

Sintiéra,　sintiéras,　sintiéra,　sintiéramos,　sintiérais,　sintiéran.
Sintiése,　sintiéses,　sintiése,　sintiésemos,　sintiéseis,　sintiésen.

Future.

Sintiére,　sintiéres,　sintiére,　sintiéremos,　sintiéreis,　sintiéren.

Imperative.

siénte,　siénta,　sintámos,　——　　siéntan.

Participle Active.　Sintiéndo.

VERBS CONJUGATED LIKE *SENTIR*.

Adherir, advertir, adquirir, arrepentir, asentir, Conferir, controvertir, convertir, Deferir, diferir, digerir, divertir, Erguir,* Herir, hervir, Inferir, ingerir,† invertir,† Mentir, Pervertir,† preferir, proferir, Referir, requerir, Sugerir, Zaherir.

VENIR, TO COME.

Indicative Present.

| Véngo, | viénes, | viéne, | —— | —— | viénen. |

Perfect.

| Víne, | viníste, | víno, | vinímos, | vinísteis, | viniéron. |

Future.

| Vendré, | vendrás, | vendrá, | vendrémos, | vendréis, | vendrán. |

Subjunctive Present.

| Vénga, | véngas, | vénga, | vengámos, | vengáis, | véngan. |

Imperfect.

Viniéra,	viniéras,	viniéra,	viniéramos,	viniérais,	viniéran.
Viniése,	viniéses,	viniése,	viniésemos,	viniéseis,	viniésen.
Vendría,	vendrías,	vendría,	vendríamos,	vendríais,	vendrían.

Future.

| Viniére, | viniéres, | viniére, | viniéremos, | viniéreis, | viniéren. |

Imperative.

| | ven, | vénga, | vengámos, | —— | véngan. |

Participle Active. Viniéndo.

VERBS IRREGULAR IN THE PAST PARTICIPLE ONLY.

Infinitive.		*Past Participle.*	
Abrir,	to open.	abierto,	opened.
cubrir,	to cover.	cubierto,	covered.
escribir,	to write.	escrito,	written.
freir,	to fry.	frito,	fried.
imprimir,	to print.	impreso,	printed.

And their compounds.—To these may be added all those in the following list marked with an asterisk.

---

* The irregular persons of *erguir* are written with an *h :* as, *hiérgo, hiérgas,* etc.

† *Invertir, ingerir,* and *pervertir,* have regular and irregular past participles ; the latter are *invérso, ingérto,* and *pervérso.*

2. The following is a list of regular and irregular verbs that have two participles past, the one regular, the other irregular: the former are employed with the auxiliaries, to form the compound tenses; the latter partake of the nature of adjectives, and are not always employed in the formation of compound tenses: however, *preso, prescrito, provisto,* and *roto,* are sometimes seen used with *haber,* instead of *prendido, prescribido, proveido,* and *rompido;* and those marked with the dagger may be employed with *estar.* Those marked with an asterisk are regular throughout their conjugations.

Infinitives.		*Reg. Past, Part.*	*Irr. P. Part., or Adj.*	
Absorver,	to absorb.	absorvido,	absorto,†	absorbed.
abstraer,	to abstract.	abstraido,	abstracto,	abstracted.
aguzar,*	to sharpen.	aguzado,	agudo,	sharpened.
alertarse,	to be alert.	alertado,	alerto,†	alert.
angostar,*	to narrow.	angostado,	angosto,	narrowed.
atender,	to attend.	atendido,	atento,†	attended.
ahitar,*	to surfeit.	ahitado,	ahito,	surfeited.
bendecir,	to bless.	bendecido,	bendito,	blessed.
bienquerer,	to esteem.	bienquerido,	bienquisto,†	esteemed.
cocer,	to boil.	cocido,	cocho,†	boiled.
compeler,*	to compel.	compelido,	compulso,	compelled.
completar,*	to complete.	completado,	completo,†	completed.
concluir,	to conclude.	concluido,	concluso,	concluded.
concretar,	to concrete.	concretado,	concreto,	concrete.
confundir,*	to confound.	confundido,	confuso,†	confounded.
contentar,	to content.	contentado,	contento,†	contented.
contraer,	to contract.	contraido,	contracto,	contracted.
convencer,*	to convince.	convencido,	convicto,	convinced.
convertir,	to convert.	convertido,	converso,	converted.
convulsar,*	to convulse.	convulsado,	convulso,	convulsed.
corregir,	to correct.	corregido,	correcto,†	corrected.
corromper,*	to corrupt.	corrompido,	corrupto,	corrupted.
corvar,*	to curve.	corvado,	corvo,†	curved.
cultivar,*	to cultivate.	cultivado,	culto,	cultivated.
densar,*	to condense.	condensado,	condenso,	condensed.
descalzar,*	to un-shoe.	descalzado,	descalzo,†	barefooted.
desertar,	to desert.	desertado,	desierto,	deserted.
desnudar,*	to undress.	desnudado,	desnudo,†	undressed.
despertar,	to awake.	despertado,	despierto,†	awaked.
difundir,*	to diffuse.	difundido,	difuso,	diffused.
dirigir,*	to direct.	dirigido,	directo,	directed.
dispersar,*	to disperse.	dispersado,	disperso,	dispersed.
distinguir,*	to distinguish.	distinguido,	distinto,†	distinguished
dividir,*	to divide.	dividido,	diviso,	divided.
elegir,	to elect.	elegido.	electo,	elected.

Infinitives.		Reg. Past Part.	Irr. P. Part., or Adj.	
enjugar,*	to dry.	enjugado,	enjuto,†	dried.
erigir,*	to erect.	erigido,	erecto,†	erected.
exceptuar,*	to except.	exceptuado,	excepto,	excepted.
excluir,*	to exclude.	excluido,	excluso,	excluded.
exentar,*	to exempt.	exentado,	exento,†	exempted.
expeler,*	to expel.	expelido,	expulso,	expelled.
expresar,*	to express.	expresado,	expreso,	expressed.
extender,	to extend.	extendido,	extenso,†	extended.
extinguir,*	to extinguish.	extinguido,	extinto,†	extinguished.
extraer,	to extract.	extraido,	extracto,	extracted.
eximir,*	to exempt.	eximido,	exento,†	exempted.
faltar,*	to fail.	faltado,	falto,†	failed.
favorecer,	to favour.	favorecido,	favorito,	favoured.
fechar,*	to date.	fechado,	fecho,†	dated.
fijar,*	to fix.	fijado,	fijo,†	fixed.
hartar,*	to satiate.	hartado,	harto,†	satiated.
imprimir,*	to print.	imprimido,	impreso,†	printed.
improvisar,*	to improvise.	improvisado,	improvisto,	improvised.
incluir,*	to include.	incluido,	incluso,†	included.
incurrir,*	to incur.	incurrido,	incurso,	incurred.
infectar, inficionar, }	to infect.	{ infectado, inficionado, }	infecto,	infected.
infundir,*	to infuse.	infundido,	infuso,	infused.
ingerir,	to ingraft.	ingerido,	ingerto,	ingrafted.
ingertar,*	to ingraft.	ingertado,	ingerto,	ingrafted.
insertar,	to insert.	insertado,	inserto,	inserted.
invertir,	to invert.	invertido,	inverso,	inverted.
juntar,*	to join.	juntado,	junto,†	joined.
limpiar,*	to clean.	limpiado,	limpio,	cleaned.
maldecir,	to curse.	maldecido,	maldito,	cursed.
manifestar,	to manifest.	manifestado,	manifiesto,†	manifested.
manumitir,*	to emancipate.	manumitido,	manumiso,	emancipated.
marchitar,*	to wither.	marchitado,	marchito,†	withered.
ocultar,*	to conceal.	ocultado,	oculto,†	concealed.
omitir,*	to omit.	omitido,	omiso,	omitted.
oprimir,*	to oppress.	oprimido,	opreso,	oppressed.
pervertir,	to pervert.	pervertido,	perverso,	perverted.
perfeccionar,*	to perfect.	perfeccionado,	perfecto,†	perfected.
prender,*	to seize.	prendido,	preso,†	seized.
prescribir,*	to prescribe.	prescribido,	prescrito,†	prescribed
producir,	to produce.	producido,	producto,	produced.
profesar,*	to profess.	profesado,	profeso,	professed.
propender,*	to incline.	propendido,	propenso,†	inclined.
proveer,*	to provide.	proveido,	provisto,†	provided.
raciocinar,*	to reason.	raciocinado,	raciocinio,	reasoned.
recluir,	to seclude.	recluido,	recluso,	secluded.
reflejar,	to reflect.	reflejado,	reflejo,	reflected.
refringir,*	to refract.	refringido,	refracto,	refracted.
remitir,*	to relax.	remitido,	remiso,†	relaxed.
repeler,*	to repel.	repelido,	repulso,	repelled.

Infinitives.		*Reg. Past Part.*	*Irr. P. Part., or Adj.*	
restringir,*	to restrict.	restringido,	restricto,	restricted.
romper,*	to break.	rompido,	roto,†	broken.
salvar,*	to save.	salvado,	salvo,†	saved.
secar,	to dry.	secado,	seco,†	dried.
sepultar,*	to bury.	sepultado,	sepulto,	buried.
soltar,	to loosen.	soltado,	suelto,†	loosened.
sujetar,*	to subject.	sujetado,	sujeto,†	subjected.
surgir,*	to anchor.	surgido,	surto,†	anchored.
suprimir,*	to suppress.	suprimido,	supreso,	suppressed.
suspender,*	to suspend.	suspendito,	suspenso,†	suspended.
sustituir,*	to substitute.	sustituido,	sustituto,	substituted.
teñir,	to dye.	teñido,	tinto,	dyed.
torcer,	to twist.	torcido,	tuerto,†	twisted.
zafar,*	to rid.	zafado,	zafo,†	rid.

ALPHABETICAL LIST OF ALL THE IRREGULAR VERBS
IN THE SPANISH LANGUAGE,

Arranged in three divisions according to their terminations, with references to the verbs which they are conjugated like in the Examples.

First Conjugation.

Acertar	to ascertain,		*conjugated* *page* 192
acordar	agree,		ib. 193
acordar	remember,	*like* acordar.	ib.
acostar	lie down,		ib.
acrecentar	increase,		acertar. 192
adestrar	guide, to instruct,		ib.
agorar	augur,		acordar. 193
alentar	encourage,		acertar. 192
almorzar	breakfast,		acordar. 193
amolar	grind,		ib.
andar	walk, to go,		*conjugated* 194
apacentar	graze,		acertar. 192
aporcar	dirt,		acordar. 193
aportar	arrive at port,		ib.
apostar	bet,		ib.
apretar	press,		acertar. 192
aprobar	approve,		acordar. 193
arrendar	rent,		acertar. 192
asentar	note down,		ib.
asestar	take aim,		ib.
asolar	destroy,		acordar. 193
asoldar	furnish money,		ib.
asonar	accord in sound,		ib.

aterrar	to terrify,	*like* acertar,	*page* 192
atentar	attempt,	ib.	
atestar	cram,	ib.	
atravesar	cross, to pierce,	ib.	
aventar	fan,	ib.	
avergonzar	be ashamed,	acordar.	193
bregar	contend,	acertar.	192
calentar	warm,	ib.	
cegar	blind,	ib.	
cerrar	to shut, to close,	ib.	
cimentar	found,	ib.	
colar	strain liquor,	acordar.	193
colgar	hang,	ib.	
comenzar	commence,	acertar.	192
comprobar	corroborate,	acordar.	193
concertar	concert,	acertar.	192
concordar	agree,	acordar.	193
confesar	confess,	acertar.	192
consolar	comfort,	acordar.	193
consonar	agree in tone, to rhyme,	ib.	
contar	count,	ib.	
costar	cost,	ib.	
dar	give,	*conjugated*	194
decentar	handsel,	acertar.	192
degollar	decapitate,	acordar.	193
demonstrar	demonstrate,	ib.	
denegar	refuse,	acertar.	192
denostrar	revile,	acordar.	193
derrengar	cripple,	acertar.	192
desacertar	mistake,	ib.	
desacordar	be discordant,	acordar.	193
desalentar	discourage,	acertar.	192
desapretar	loosen,	ib.	
desaprobar	disapprove,	acordar.	193
desasosegar	disturb,	acertar.	192
desatentar	perplex,	ib.	
descolgar	unhang,	acordar.	193
descollar	surpass,	ib.	
desconcertar	disarrange,	acertar.	192
desconsolar	afflict,	acordar.	193
descontar	discount,	ib.	
desencerrar	let out, *or* loose,	acertar.	192
desengrosar	diminish in thickness,	acordar.	193
desenterrar	disinter,	acertar.	192
desflocar	ravel out,	acordar.	193
desfogar	give vent to passion,	ib.	
deshelar	thaw,	acertar.	192
desherrar	unshoe horses,	ib.	
desmembrar	dismember,	ib.	
desolar	desolate,	acordar.	193
desollar	flay,	ib.	
desovar	spawn,	ib.	

despernar	to cut off legs, *or* break legs, *like* acertar,		*page* 192
despertar	awake,		ib.
desplegar	unfold,		ib.
despoblar	depopulate,	acordar.	193
desterrar	banish,	acertar.	192
desvergonzar	be impudent,	acordar.	193
dezmar	tithe,	acertar.	192
descordar	disagree,	acordar.	193
empedrar	pave,	acertar.	192
empezar	begin,		ib.
emporcar	soil,	acordar.	193
encensar	cense,	acertar.	192
encerrar	enclose,		ib.
encomendar	recommend,		ib.
encontrar	find, to meet,	acordar.	193
encordar	string,		ib.
encubertar	cover with clothes,	acertar.	192
engrosar	grow stout,	acordar.	193
enmendar	mend,	acertar.	192
enrodar	break on the wheel,	acordar.	193
ensangrentar	stain with blood,	acertar.	192
enterrar	bury,		ib.
errar	err,		ib.
escarmentar	learn by experience,		ib.
esforzarse	endeavour,	acordar.	193
estar	be,	*conjugated*	162
estregar	scour,	acertar.	192
forzar	force,	acordar.	193
fregar	rub, to scrub,	acertar.	192
gobernar	govern,		ib.
helar	freeze,		ib.
herrar	shoe horses,		ib.
holgar	rest,	acordar.	193
hollar	trample,		ib.
infernar	provoke, to damn,	acertar.	192
invernar	winter,		ib.
jugar	play,	*conjugated*	194
manifestar	manifest,	acertar.	192
mentar	mention,		ib.
merendar	take a collation,		ib.
mostrar	show,	acordar.	193
negar	deny,	acertar.	192
nevar	snow,		ib.
pensar	think,		ib.
perniquebrar	break legs,		ib.
plegar	plait, to fold,		ib.
poblar	people,	acordar.	193
probar	prove,		ib.
quebrar	break,	acertar.	192
recomendar	recommend,		ib.
recordar	remind,	acordar.	193
recostar	recline		ib.

reforzar	to reinforce,	*like* acordar,	*page* 193
regar	water,	acertar.	192
regoldar	belch,	acordar.	193
remendar	mend,	acertar.	192
renegar	abjure,	ib.	
renovar	renew,	acordar.	193
replegar	fall back from a position,	acertar.	192
reprobar	reprove,	acordar.	193
requebrar	cajole, to flatter,	acertar.	192
rescontrar	compensate,	acordar.	193
resollar	breathe,	ib.	
resonar	resound,	ib.	
retemblar	vibrate,	acertar.	192
retentar	threaten with a relapse,	ib.	
reventar	burst,	ib.	
revolar	fly again,	acordar.	193
revolcar	wallow,	ib.	
rodar	roll,	ib.	
rogar	pray,	ib.	
segar	reap corn,	acertar.	192
sembrar	sow,	ib.	
sentar	sit,	ib.	
serrar	saw,	ib.	
solar	sole,	acordar.	193
soldar	solder,	ib.	
soltar	let go, *or* loose,	ib.	
sonar	sound,	ib.	
soñar	dream,	ib.	
sosegar	tranquillize,	acertar.	192
soterrar	bury,	ib.	
temblar	tremble,	ib.	
tentar	tempt,	ib.	
tostar	toast,	acordar.	193
trascolar	strain, to percolate,	ib.	
trascordar	forget,	ib.	
trasegar	decant,	acertar.	192
trasoñar	dream, to fancy,	acordar.	193
trocar	barter,	ib.	
tronar	thunder,	ib.	
tropezar	stumble,	acertar.	192
volar	fly,	acordar.	193
volcar	overset,	ib.	

Second Conjugation.

Abastecer	provide	aborrecer.	195
aborrecer	hate,	*conjugated*	ib.
absolver	absolve,	absorver.	197
absorver	absorb,	*conjugated*	ib.
abstraer	abstract,	traer.	201
acaecer	happen,	aborrecer.	195

acontecer	to happen,	*like* aborrecer,	*page* 195
adolecer	be seized with illness,	ib.	
adormecer	fall asleep, to lull,	ib.	
agradecer	be thankful,	ib.	
amanecer	dawn,	ib.	
anochecer	grow dark,	ib.	
anteponer	prefer, to place before,	poner.	199
antever	foresee,	ver.	202
aparecer	appear,	aborrecer.	195
apetecer	long for,	ib.	
ascender	ascend,	*conjugated*	197
atender	attend,	ascender.	ib.
atenerse	stand to,	tener.	158
atraer	attract,	traer.	201
caber	contain, etc.,	*conjugated*	198
caer	fall,	ib.	ib.
canecer	become grey headed,	aborrecer.	195
carecer	be deficient,	ib.	
cerner	sift,	ascender.	197
cocer	boil,	*conjugated*	196
con:padecer	pity,	aborrecer.	195
comparecer	appear before,	ib.	
complacer	give pleasure,	ib.	
componer	compose,	poner.	199
condescender	condescend,	ascender.	197
condoler	condole,	absorver.	ib.
conmover	excite commotion,	ib.	
conocer	know,	aborrecer.	195
contender	contend,	ascender.	197
contener	contain,	tener.	158
contrahacer	counterfeit,	hacer.	195
contraer	contract,	traer.	201
convalecer	be convalescent,	aborrecer.	195
crecer	grow,	ib.	
decaer	decay,	caer.	198
defender	defend,	ascender.	197
demoler	demolish,	absorver.	ib.
deponer	depose,	poner.	199
desaparecer	disappear,	aborrecer.	195
desatender	neglect,	ascender.	197
descender	descend,	ib.	
descomponer	decompose,	poner.	199
desconocer	disown,	aborrecer.	195
desentender	feign ignorance, mistake,	ascender.	197
desentorpecer	recover from numbness, to reanimate,	aborrecer.	195
desenvolver	unroll,	absorver.	197
desfallecer	pine,	aborrecer.	195
desflaquecer	become emaciated,	ib.	
desguarnecer	ungarnish,	ib.	
deshacer	undo,	hacer.	ib.
aesobedecer	disobey,	aborrecer.	ib.

desplacer	to displease,	*like* aborrecer,	*page* 195
destorcer	untwist,	absorver,	197
desvanecer	vanish,	aborrecer.	195
detener	detain,	tener.	158
devolver	restore,	absorver.	197
disolver	dissolve,	ib.	
disponer	dispose,	poner.	199
distraer	distract, to amuse,	traer.	201.
doler	ache,	absorver.	197
dolerse	grieve,	ib.	
embravecer	become furious,	aborrecer.	195
embrutecer	become brutal,	ib.	
emplumecer	become fledged,	ib.	
empobrecer	impoverish,	ib.	
encalvecer	become bald,	ib.	
encallecer	render callous,	ib.	
encarecer	enhance the value,	ib.	
encender	light, to kindle,	ascender.	197
encrudecer	become raw,	aborrecer.	195
encruelecer	render, *or* become cruel,	ib.	
endentecer	cut the teeth,	ib.	
endurecer	harden,	ib.	
enflaquecer	grow lean, *or* weak,	ib.	
enfurecer	become furious,	ib.	
engrandecer	aggrandize, to enlarge,	ib.	
enloquecer	become *or* render mad,	ib.	
enmohecer	grow mouldy,	ib.	
enmudecer	become dumb,	ib.	
ennegrecer	blacken,	ib.	
ennoblecer	ennoble,	ib.	
enrarecer	rarefy,	ib.	
enriquecer	enrich,	ib.	
ensoberbecer	become haughty,	ib.	
entallecer	sprout,	ib.	
entender	understand,	ascender.	197
enternecer	soften,	aborrecer.	195
entorpecer	benumb, to stupify,	ib.	
entretener	entertain,	tener.	158
entristecer	sadden,	aborrecer.	195
entullecer	cripple,	ib.	
entumecer	swell	ib.	
envejecer	grow old,	ib.	
enverdecer	grow green,	ib.	
envolver	wrap,	absorver.	197
equivaler	be equivalent,	valer.	201
escarnecer	scoff,	aborrecer.	195
esclarecer	illuminate,	ib.	
escocer	smart,	absorver.	197
establecer	establish,	aborrecer.	195
estremecer	shudder,	ib.	
exponer	expose,	poner.	199
extender	extend	ascender.	197

extraer	to extract,	*like* traer,	*page* 201
fallecer	die,	aborrecer.	195
favorecer	favour,	ib.	
fenecer	terminate,	ib.	
fortalecer	fortify,	ib.	
guarnecer	garnish,	ib.	
haber	have,	*conjugated.*	157
hacer	make, to do,	ib.	195
heder	stink,	ascender.	197
hender	split,	ib.	
humedecer	moisten,	aborrecer.	195
imponer	impose,	poner.	199
indisponer	indispose,	ib.	
llover	rain,	absorver.	197
mantener	maintain,	tener.	158
merecer	deserve,	aborrecer.	195
moler	grind,	absorver.	197
morder	bite,	ib.	
mover	move,	ib.	
nacer	be born,	aborrecer.	19
negrecer	grow black,	ib.	
obedecer	obey,	ib.	
obscurecer	darken,	ib.	
obtener	obtain,	tener.	158
ofrecer	offer,	aborrecer.	195
oler	smell,	absorver.	197
oponer	oppose,	poner.	199
pacer	graze,	aborrecer.	195
padecer	suffer,	ib.	
parecer	seem,	ib.	
perder	lose,	ascender.	197
perecer	perish,	aborrecer.	195
pertenecer	belong,	ib.	
placer	please,	ib.	
poder	be able,	*conjugated.*	199
poner	put, to place,	*conjugated.*	ib.
preponer	place before,	poner.	ib.
presuponer	presuppose,	ib.	
prevalecer	prevail,	aborrecer.	195
prever	foresee,	ver.	202
promover	promote,	absorver.	197
proponer	propose,	poner.	199
querer	like, to be willing,	*conjugated.*	200
recaer	relapse,	caer.	198
recocer	re-boil,	cocer.	196
reconocer	acknowledge,	aborrecer.	195
recrecer	grow again,	ib.	
reflorecer	re-blossom,	ib.	
rehacer	do over again,	hacer.	ib.
remanecer	remain,	aborrecer.	ib.
remorder	bite repeatedly,	absorver.	197
remover	remove,	ib.	

Third Conjugation.

conducir	to conduct, to conduce,	*conjugated, page*	206
conferir	confer,	*like* sentir.	208
conseguir	obtain, to succeed,	pedir.	206
consentir	consent,	sentir.	208
constituir	constitute,	instruir.	204
constreñir	constrain,	pedir.	206
construir	construe,	instruir.	204
contradecir	contradict,	decir.	202
contravenir	oppose,	venir.	209
contribuir	contribute,	instruir.	204
controvertir	controvert,	sentir.	208
convenir	suit,	venir.	209
convertir	convert,	sentir.	208
correjir	correct,	pedir.	206
decir	say, to tell,	*conjugated.*	202
deducir	infer,	conducir.	206
deferir	defer,	sentir.	208
derritir	melt,	pedir.	206
desavenir	disagree,	venir.	209
desceñir	ungird,	pedir.	206
descomedir	grow rude, unruly,	ib.	
desconsentir	dissent,	sentir.	208
desdecir	retract,	decir.	202
desleir	dilute,	pedir.	206
deslucir	tarnish,	instruir.	204
desmentir	contradict,	sentir.	208
despedir	dismiss,	pedir.	206
despedirse	take leave,	ib.	
desteñir	discolour,	ib.	
destruir	destroy,	instruir.	204
diferir	differ, to defer,	sentir.	203
digerir	digest,	ib.	
disminuir	diminish,	instruir.	204
distribuir	distribute,	ib.	
divertir	divert,	sentir.	208
dormir	sleep,	*conjugated.*	203
elegir	elect,	pedir.	206
embestir	assail,	ib.	
engreirse	become vain,	ib.	
enlucir	whitewash, to scour plate,	lucir.	205
entreoir	hear indistinctly,	oir.	206
envestir	invest,	pedir.	ib.
erguir	hold up the head,	sentir.	208
estreñir	produce astringency,	pedir.	206
excluir	exclude,	instruir.	204
expedir	expedite,	pedir.	206
fluir	flow,	instruir.	204
freir	fry,	pedir.	206
gemir	moan,	ib.	
heñir	knead,	ib.	
herir	wound,	sentir.	208
hervir	boil,	ib.	

huir	to flee,	*like* instruir,	*page* 204
imbuir	imbue,	ib.	
impedir	impede,	pedir.	206
incluir	include,	instruir.	204
inducir	induce,	conducir.	206
inferir	infer,	sentir.	208
ingerir	ingraft,	ib.	
intervenir	intervene,	venir.	209
instituir	institute,	instruir.	204
instruir	instruct,	*conjugated.*	ib.
introducir	introduce,	conducir.	206
invertir	invert,	sentir.	208
investir	invest,	pedir.	206
ir	go,	*conjugated.*	204
lucir	shine,	ib.	205
luir	wear by friction,	instruir.	204
maldecir	curse,	decir.	202
medir	measure,	pedir.	206
mentir	lie,	sentir.	208
morir	die,	dormir.	203
obstruir	obstruct,	instruir.	204
oir	hear,	*conjugated.*	206
pedir	ask, to beg,	ib.	
perseguir	persecute,	pedir.	ib.
pervertir	pervert,	sentir.	208
podrir	rot,	*conjugated.*	207
predecir	predict,	decir.	202
preferir	prefer,	sentir.	208
presentir	have a presentiment,	ib.	
prevenir	prevent, to warn,	venir.	209
producir	produce,	conducir.	206
proferir	utter,	sentir.	208
proseguir	prosecute,	pedir.	206
prostituir	prostitute,	instruir.	204
provenir	proceed from,	venir.	209
recluir	cloister,	instruir.	204
reducir	reduce,	conducir.	206
referir	refer,	sentir.	208
regir	rule,	pedir.	206
reir	laugh,	ib.	
rendir	yield,	ib.	
reñir	quarrel, to scold,	ib.	
repetir	repeat,	ib.	
reproducir	reproduce,	conducir.	ib.
requerir	require,	sentir.	208
resentir	resent,	ib.	
restituir	restore,	instruir.	204
reteñir	dye again,	pedir.	206
retribuir.	compensate,	instruir.	204
revestir.	revest, to dress,	pedir.	206
salir.	to go out, to come out,	*conjugated.*	208
seducir	seduce,	conducir.	206

seguir	to follow,	*like* pedir,	*page* 206
sentir	feel,	*conjugated.*	208
servir	serve,	pedir.	206
sobresalir	surpass,	salir.	208
sobrevenir	happen,	venir.	209
sonreirse	smile,	pedir.	206
substituir	substitute,	instruir.	204
sugerir	suggest,	sentir.	208
teñir	dye,	pedir.	206
traducir	translate,	conducir.	ib.
venir	come,	*conjugated.*	209
vestir	dress,	pedir.	206
zaherir	censure,	sentir.	208

ANCIENT MANNER OF FORMING SOME OF THE TENSES OF IRREGULAR VERBS.

3. Formerly, irregular verbs in Spanish had the same difference in spelling from the modern style, in the second person plural, as regular verbs had, as noticed in LECT. 24, PAR. 4: thus, *Sódes, habédes, acertádes, ascendédes, sentídes,* instead of, *sóis, habéis, acertáis, ascendéis, sentís.*

Likewise those which now terminate in *i* or *y*, in the first person singular of the present indicative, were written without this final vowel; thus, *so, do, vo,* instead of, *soy, doy, voy.*

Many of those which now end in *go* and *ga* were written without the *g;* thus, *cáyo, cáya, óyo, óya, tráyo, tráya, válo, vála,* instead of, *cáigo, cáiga, óigo, óiga, tráigo, tráiga, válgo, válga,* etc.

Those which now have a *u* in their root had formerly *and o* instead; thus, *cobrió, cópo, óvo, morió, dormió, póso, sópo,* instead of, *cubrió, cúpo, húbo, murió, durmió, púso, súpo,* etc.

Likewise *verná* was used for *vendrá; diz,* for *dícen; pornía,* for *pondría; víde,* and *vído,* for *ví* and *vió; trúje, trujéra,* etc., for *tráje, trajéra,* etc.

LECTURE XXVI.

IMPERSONAL VERBS.

HABER, THERE TO BE.

1. The verb *haber*, used impersonally, is employed alike in both numbers; and, like most impersonal verbs, it is used only in the third person of the several tenses, as follows.

Infinitive.	Habér,	There to be.
Indic. Present.	Háy,	There is, *or* there are.
Imperfect.	Había,	There was, *or* there were.
Perfect.	Húbo,	There was, *or* there were.
Future.	Habrá,	There will be.
Subj. Present.	Háya,	There may be.
Imperfect.	{ Hubiéra, hubiése, habría, }	There should, might, *or* would be.
Future.	Hubiére,	If there should be.
Imperative.	Háya,	. Let there be.
Part. Active.	Habiéndo,	There being.
Comp. ditto.	Habiéndo habído,	There having been.

EXAMPLES.

Hay un hombre allí.	*There is* a man there.
Habia muchos.	*There were* many.
Habrá gran cantidad.	*There will be* a great quantity.
Jamas ha habido tantas quejas.	*There* never *have been* so many complaints.

2. AMANECER, to dawn, and ANOCHECER, to become night, are irregular in their conjugations like *aborrecer :* Ex.

Amanece muy temprano.	*Day breaks* very early.
Amaneció lloviendo.	It rained at *day break.*
Anochece muy tarde.	It *grows dark* very late.
Presto anochecerá.	It will soon *be night.*

The verbs AMANECER and ANOCHECER are sometimes used with the three persons singular and plural, and denote the situation or condition of the nominative at the time expressed by the verb: Ex.

Amanecímos en Cadiz y *anochecímos* en Sevilla. — We reached Cadiz at the *dawn of day*, and Seville at *dusk*.

Amaneció de mal humor. — He *awoke* in a bad humour.

3. GRANIZAR, to hail; LLOVIZNAR, to drizzle; and RELAMPAGUEAR, to lighten, are also regular in their conjugations.

HELAR, to freeze, and NEVAR, to snow, are irregular like *acertar*.

LLOVER, to rain, and TRONAR, to thunder, are irregular like *absorver*: Ex.

Graniza ahora, y quizá *helará* luego. — *It hails* now, and probably *it will freeze* presently.

Ha *lloviznado* un poco. — *It* has *drizzled* a little.

Ayer *tronó y relampagueó* repetidas veces. — *It thundered* and *lightened* repeatedly yesterday.

Habia *nevado* mucho. — *It* had *snowed* much.

No *llueve* tanto. — *It* does not *rain* so much.

4. The following impersonal verbs are employed in the third person singular and plural of every tense; viz. ACAECER, ACONTECER, and SUCEDER, all three signifying *to happen*. The first two are conjugated like *aborrecer*, and the third is regular. CONSTAR, *to consist, to be evident*, and ANTOJARSE, to fancy, are likewise regular: Ex.

Acaeció esta mañana. — *It happened* this morning.

Acontecieron esas desgracias sin esperarlas. — Those misfortunes *happened* without expecting them.

Puede que le *sucederán* iguales chascos. — Similar disappointments may, perhaps, *befall* him.

Constan esos papeles de varios asuntos importantes. — Those papers *consist* of various important subjects.

Consta por lo que él dice. — *It is evident* from what he says.

Me *consta* á mí saberlo. — I have reasons (*evidence*) for knowing it.

Se me *antojó* ir con ellos. — It *took* my *fancy* to go with them.

Se les *antojan* cosas muy raras. — They *fancy* very curious things.

5. There are also some verbs which do not belong to the class of impersonal verbs, but which are sometimes employed as such — namely, SER, HACER, BASTAR, CONVENIR, SUCEDER, PARECER, etc. : EA.

Es tarde, *será preciso* ir. — *It is* late, *it will be necessary* to go.

Es menester que se haga hoy. — *It must* be done to-day.

No *es necesario* quedarse. — *It is* not *necessary* to stay.

Hace un mes que vine. — *It is* a month since I came.

Hace buen tiempo, *hace* frio. — *It is* fine weather, *it is* cold.

Basta que Vmd. lo diga. — *It is sufficient* that you say so.

Conviene hacerlo. — *It ought* to be done.

Sucedió conforme lo pensaba. — *It happened* as I thought.

Parece que lo sabe. — *It appears* that he knows it.

DEFECTIVE VEBRS.

6. The defective verbs, commonly in use in Spanish, are PLACER, to please ; SOLER, to be wont ; ABOLIR, to abolish ; YACER, to lie ; SALVE, and VALE.

PLACER is used in the third person singular of the following tenses and persons : —

Indic. Present.	Pláce,	It pleases.
Imperfect.	Placía,	It pleased.
Perfect.	Plúgo,	It pleased.
Sub. Present.	Plégue, *or* plázga,	It may please.
Imperfect.	Pluguiéra, *or* pluguiése,	It should, might, *or* would please.
Future.	Pluguiére,	If it should please.
Imperative.	Plégue,	May it please.

EXAMPLES.

Mucho me *place.* — It *pleases* me much.

Plegue á Dios que se salve. — God *grant* that he may be saved.

Pluguiera á Dios que jamas le hubieras visto. — *Would* to God that thou hadst never seen him.

SOLER is used only in the two following tenses : —

Indicative Present.		*Imperfect.*	
Suélo,	I am wont.	Solía,	I was wont.
suéles,	thou art wont.	solías,	thou wast wont.
suéle,	he is wont.	solía,	he was wont.
solémos,	we are wont.	solíamos,	we were wont.
soléis,	you are wont.	solíais,	you were wont.
suélen,	they are wont.	solian,	they were wont.

ABOLIR, to abolish, is not employed in the present of the indicative, the present and future subjunctive, nor the imperative.

Of YACER, only the third person singular and plural of the present and imperfect of the indicative are now in use, and generally in epitaphs; as, *Aquí yace*, or *yacen* —Here lieth, *or* lie. *Aquí yacia*, or *yacian*—Here lay.

Formerly it was used in the sense of *to repose, to rest,* generally, and conjugated throughout the entire verb.

SALVE, and VALE, are only used in the second person singular of the imperative of the Latin verbs *salveo,* and *valeo;* the first denotes *I hail thee,* or *God preserve thee;* and the second means, *Farewell,* or *Adieu.* They are seldom used now-a-days.

LECTURE XXVII.

AGREEMENT OF THE VERB WITH ITS NOMINATIVE.

1. The verb agrees with its agent, or nominative case, in *number* and *person*; as, *Yo leo y ella canta* — I read and she sings. *El sol luce*—The sun shines. *Los árboles crecen*—The trees grow.

2. If the verb has a *collective* noun for its nominative, the following rule should be observed. Collective nouns *definite,* or those which denote a *distinctive* body of objects, require the verb in the *singular.* But collective nouns *indefinite,* or those which do not apply to any definite number, or organized body, may have the verb in the plural: Ex.

El *egército salió* al amane-	The *army sallied* out at day
cer.	break.
Un gran *número* de hombres *fueron* apresados.	A great *number* of men *were* taken prisoners.

3. When a verb has several nominatives connected by the copulative conjunctive *y*, it agrees in number and person with the pronoun understood, if it follows the subjects; but if it precedes the subjects it is generally made to agree in number and person with the nearest: Ex.

Mi hermana y él *han* salido.	My sister and he are gone out.
Tú y él *seréis* premiados.	Thou and he will be rewarded.
Nunca *fué* tan expuesto su *valor* y constancia.	Never was his valour and constancy so much exposed.
Me *ha* gustado mucho la *novela* y los poemas.	I was much pleased with the novel and poems.
Me *parecieron* muy bien *escritas* las *cartas* y el episodio.	The letters and episode appeared to me to be very well written.

4. If the nominatives be connected by any other conjunction than *y*, the verb is frequently made to agree with the last: Ex.

| No solamente él, *pero yo* tambien lo *sé*. | Not only does he, but I also know it. |
| No solamente yo, *mas ellos* tambien *perdieron*. | Not only did I lose, but they lost also. |

Or each nominative may have a separate verb; as, *No solamente él lo* sabe *sinó yo tambien lo* sé. *No solamente* perdí *yo, mas ellos tambien* perdieron.

5. When there are two or more nominatives in a sentence, of the same number and person, separated by a disjunctive conjunction, the verb may agree with either nominative; but if they differ in number or person, each nominative must have a separate verb: Ex.

Ni *él* ni *ella* me *conoce*.	Neither does he, nor she know me.
O *él va*, ó *voy yo*.	Either he goes, or I go.
Ni *llama ella*, ni *llaman ellos*.	Neither does she, nor do they call.

6. When two nouns are connected by the preposition *con* (with), the verb which they govern may be put in either number : Ex.

El Conde *con* su secretario   The Count with his secre-
　partió, or *partieron* ayer.　　　tary departed yesterday.

7. When the verb *ser* stands between two nominatives of different numbers, it should be made to agree with the one which is more properly its agent : Ex.

Los agradecimientos que   The thanks that they gave
　me dieron *fué censura.*　　　me was censure.
Los *libros eran* su diver-   Books were his amusement.
　sion.

8. When in English the pronoun *it*, connected with any part of the verb *to be*, refers to a noun or pronoun, the verb always remains in the third person singular, whatever may be the number or person of the noun or pronoun referred to ; as, *It is I who; It was we that; It was the men that.* Care must be taken, however, in the translation, to make the verb *to be* agree in number and person with the noun or pronoun referred to : Ex.

Soy yo que lo digo.　　　*It is I* who say so.
Somos nosotros que lo pedi-　*It is we* that ask for it.
　mos.
Eran ellos los que lo hicieron.　*It was they* that did it.
Fueron los *hombres* que vi-　*It was the men* that came.
　nieron.

9. A verb having a relative pronoun for its nominative, agrees with the word to which the relative refers : Ex.

Yo *que* lo *veo.*　　　I who see it.
Tú *que* los *tragiste.*　　Thou that broughtest them.
Aquellos *que* lo *creen se*　Those that believe it are
　engañan.　　　　　deceived.

EXERCISE ON THE AGREEMENT OF THE VERB WITH ITS
NOMINATIVE.

You and he consented to it.　We and they were
　　　　　consentir

appointed. The coach, gig, and horses belong to
nombrar　　　coche calesa　　　　　pertenecer

him. Her modesty and her virtues were much extolled.
                                        alabar

Herodotus was the first writer of profane history.
 Heródoto   escritor   profano

Plato was a disciple of Socrates. The meeting is
Platon   discípulo   Sócrates   junta

dissolved. The regiment was defeated. A quantity
disolverse   regimiento   derrotar

of prisoners fled. An infinity of birds died. I dislike
  prisionero huir.   infinidad   disgustarse

 slander and quarrels. Terrible were his threats and
calumnia   quimera   ———   amenaza

his vengeance. Never was his dignity and his pride
  venganza   dignidad   orgullo

so humbled. It is not we, but they that must yield.
 humiliado   deber ceder

It is not they, but we that must yield. He that comes

first shall be rewarded. Those who know it say so. It
        premiado   saber

was Constantine who commanded that all the heathen
   Constantino   mandar   gentil

temples should be destroyed. It was the Arabians that
templo   destruirse   Árabe

introduced the figures of arithmetic into Europe. It is
introducir   figura   aritmética

those two houses that [are to be sold].
          estan por vender

LECTURE XXVIII.

GOVERNMENT OF VERBS.

1. Active transitive verbs have the power of governing
other words. The regimen, or the word governed by
the verb, may be either a noun, a pronoun, or an
infinitive ; and it is sometimes preceded by a preposition,
and sometimes not ; and very frequently a different preposition is required in Spanish to the one used in
English, as we have seen is the case with prepositions
employed with adjectives. The choice of the preposition
depends chiefly on the meaning of the verb, and on the
direction of its action. No *fixed* rule can possibly be
given for a matter so mutable and unstable as this, and
what constant reading alone can render familiar to the
student. A few general rules, nevertheless, will here
be given, in order to point out such cases only wherein
the two languages frequently differ in the choice of the
preposition required, and which will be of much assistance to the learner. Previously to which, however, the
following examples, that have verbs accompanied by
prepositions different from those used in English with
the same verbs, have been extracted from the GRAMMAR
OF THE ACADEMY, and their translations in English
given as illustrations of the foregoing remarks.

Comprar *al,* or *del* vende- dor.	To purchase *of* the seller.
Contestar *á* la pregunta.	To answer the question
Pedir *á* alguno.	To solicit any one.
Parecerse *á* otro.	To resemble another.
Salvar *á* alguno del peligro.	To rescue any one from the danger.
Armarse *de* paciencia.	To arm oneself *with* pa- tience.
Mantenerse *de* yerbas.	To live *on* herbs.
Depender *de* alguno.	To depend *on* any one.
Descuidarse *de* su obliga- cion.	To neglect one's duty.

Prendarse *de* alguno.	To be taken *with* any one.
Proveer *de* víveres.	To provide *with* provisions.
Barar *en* tierra.	To run aground.
Cavar la imaginacion *en* alguno.	To fix the attention *on* any one.
Contenerse *en* su obligacion.	To hold *to* one's contract.
Estribar *en* alguna cosa.	To rest *on* anything.
Saltar *en* tierra.	To jump *on* shore.
Acertar *con* la casa.	To hit *upon* the house.
Desposarse *con* alguno.	To be betrothed *to* any one.
Encararse *con* alguno.	To face any one.
Salir *con* la pretension.	To succeed *in* one's pretension.
Asparse *por* alguna cosa.	To be vexed *at* anything.
Atufarse *por* poco.	To be affronted *at* trifles.
Salir *por* fiador.	To stand security.
Nacer *para* trabajos.	To be born *to* troubles.
Prestar la dieta *para* la salud.	The diet to contribute *to* health.

2. Active transitive verbs in Spanish govern the word
to which their meaning is directed in the accusative
case, with or without the preposition *á*, as the occasion
may require. See observations on the employment of the
preposition *á* in the accusative case, LECT. 8, PAR. 13:
Ex.

Amar *á* Dios.	To love God.
Hirió *al* hombre.	He wounded the man.
Despreciar la mentira.	To despise falsehood.
Ella le mandó.	She sent him.

Many neuter verbs have not the power of conveying
their meaning to another object, and have therefore no
government; such are *nacer*, to be born, *crecer*, to grow,
and all those in which there is no apparent action in
their meaning; the action being confined to the nominative. There are, however, some neuter verbs that
have an active signification, and convey their meaning
to another object by means of prepositions: Ex.

Ir *á* Madrid.	To go *to* Madrid.
Vengo *de* casa.	I come *from* home.
Siéntese *en* el sofá.	Be seated *on* the sofa.

Reflective verbs also govern their regimen in the accusative case; which regimen is the personal pronoun annexed to them : Ex.

Se aman.	They love one another.
Nos prometimos.	We promised ourselves.
Estan vistién*dose*.	They are dressing themselves.

If to the reflective verb, there follow a noun, a pronoun, or an infinitive, these are generally preceded by prepositions : Ex.

Se deshizo *en lágrimas*.	She melted into tears.
Me acordaré *de él*.	I will remember him.
Se acostumbran *á trabajar*.	They accustom themselves to work.

3. Verbs of *asking, thanking, buying, taking away, borrowing, opposing*, and *resembling*, generally require *á* before their indirect regimen : Ex.

Pregunte Vmd. *al* criado.	Ask the servant.
Agradezco *á* Vmd. el favor.	I thank you for the favour.
Compré la sortija *al* joyero.	I bought the ring of the jeweller.
Quitaron el libro *al* muchacho.	They took away the book from the boy.
Pedí prestado el dinero *á* Juan.	I borrowed the money of John.
Se opuso *á* las órdenes.	He opposed the orders.
El hijo se semeja *al* padre.	The son resembles the father.

The following require the same preposition before the *direct* regimen—namely, verbs of *answering, playing*, and *suiting :* Ex.

Responda Vmd. *á* mi pregunta.	Answer my question.
Jugámos *al* ajedrez.	We played at chess.
¿ Le conviene *á* Vmd. eso ?	Does that suit you ?

4. Verbs denoting *fulness* or *abundance, want,* and *dependence,* generally require *de* with their regimen : Ex.

Abundar *de* riquezas.	To abound in riches.
Estaba llenando el baul *de* vestidos y *de* libros.	He was filling the trunk with clothes and books.
Faltar *de* juicio.	To be wanting in judgment.
Dependa Vmd. *de* mí	Depend on me.

Passive verbs likewise require *de* before the noun by which they are followed: Ex.

Virginia fué amada *de* Pablo.	Virginia was beloved by Paul.
Son aborrecidos *de* todos.	They are hated by every body.

Sometimes, however, the preposition *de* may be substituted by *por;* but it must be observed that these two prepositions are not always indiscriminately used with passive verbs. If the verb denote an action of the body, *por* should be employed; as, *Fué muerto por un asesino* —He was murdered by an assassin; but if the action expressed by the verb denote a will, or an effect of the mind, then either *de* or *por* may be used; though the preference appears to be more generally given to the former; as, *La obra fué censurada* de *or* por *los críticos*— The work was censured by the critics. *Él es estimado* de *or* por *todos*—He is esteemed by everybody.

5. The noun or pronoun that denotes the person or thing in which the meaning of the verb is concentrated is preceded by *en:* Ex.

Piensa *en* tus propios asuntos.	Think on your own affairs.
Fijar la atencion *en* algo.	To fix the attention on anything.

If the regimen be an infinitive, the same preposition is required; as, *Esmerarse* en *hacer algo*—To delight in doing anything.

6. The noun denoting the instrument with which the action of the verb is effected, is governed by *con;* but the noun expressive of the injury inflicted by the instrument is preceded by either *de* or *con* in the singular, and by *á* in the plural: Ex.

La mató *con* un puñal.	He killed her with a dagger.
La mató *de,* or *con* una puñalada.	He killed her by the thrust of a dagger.
Le hirió *á* golpes.	He wounded him with blows

Verbs denoting *conduct* or *behaviour* also generally require *con* before the regimen: Ex.

Se porta bien *con* los suyos.	He behaves well with, or towards his relations.

Para con may be used in the same sense; as, *Se porta bien* para con *los suyos.*

The verb *meterse* governs the regimen with *con*, if it be a person, and with *en*, if it be an inanimate object: Ex.

Meterse con alguno.	To meddle with any one.
Meterse en negocios agenos.	To interfere with other people's business.

7. The regimen denoting the *cause* or *motive* that gives rise to the action of the governing verb, is preceded by *por:* Ex.

Trabajan *por* ganar.	They work in order to gain.
Lo hice *por* miedo.	I did it through fear.
Anhelar *por* saber.	To be eager to know.

Para may be used instead of *por*, when we wish to denote the *end* or *purpose* of the action expressed by the governing verb: Ex.

Lo hice *para* salvarla.	I did so in order to save her.
Vino *para* verle.	He came for the purpose of seeing him.

Sometimes the distinction between these two prepositions is so close that they may be indiscriminately used with nearly the same effect; thus, *Trabajan* por *ganar*, means, They work *for the sake of* gain; that is, they were induced by the idea of gain to work; and *Trabajan* para *ganar*, signifies, They work *for the purpose of* gaining, or *in order to* gain.

Another peculiarity in the use of these two prepositions is, that after the verb *estar*, or *quedar*, the infinitive governed by *por* signifies that the action expressed by it is not yet completed: as, *Ese edificio está todavía* por *acabar*—That edifice is not yet finished. *Nos queda aun una legua* por *andar*—We have yet a league to walk. The infinitive, preceded by *por*, also expresses an inclination on the part of the agent to do the act denoted by the infinitive; as, *Estoy* por *decírselo*—I have a mind to tell it to him. But, preceded by *para*, the infinitive denotes that the action is just about to take place; as, *El buque está* para *ponerse á la vela*—The vessel is about to set sail. It sometimes also expresses the inclination, or the capacity of the agent to do the act; as, *No estoy* para *chancear*—I am not inclined, or fit to joke.

To inquire after, or *for* any one, is translated *preguntar por*; as, *Pregunté* por *su hijo*—I inquired after his son.

Observe that when the preposition is suppressed in English, it must be expressed in Spanish; as, *Presté el libro á Henrique*—I lent (*to*) Henry the book. *Di un duro* al *hombre*—I gave (*to*) the man a dollar.

See also Employment and Government of Prepositions, LECT. 30.

GOVERNMENT OF VERBS AS RELATES TO MOODS AND TENSES.

8. A verb active transitive may govern another verb either in the infinitive, the indicative, or the subjunctive mood. But as the governed verb is not always put in the same mood and tense in Spanish and English, the student's attention is called to the following observations, which are intended to point out, in most cases, the difference that in this respect exists in the two languages. He will, however, observe that they do not apply in every case, this being likewise a matter that is in a great measure governed by taste. They will, nevertheless, assist him very materially.

1st. In Spanish the governed verb is frequently put in the infinitive when there is but one agent to both verbs; that is, when the verb governed expresses something relative to the nominative of the governing verb; or when the governed verb is not preceded by the conjunction *que*: Ex.

Él pretendia *fingir*.	He pretended to feign.
Querian *engañarle*.	They wanted to deceive him.
Yo no puedo *exponerle*.	I cannot expose him.

2nd. In these examples we see that both languages agree in the employment of the infinitive with the governed verb. But when the second verb is preceded by the conjunction *que*, or that each verb has a different agent, the governed verb in Spanish is generally put either in the indicative or the subjunctive mood, as the occasion may require: Ex.

Ellos se creen *que son va-* lientes.	They believe themselves *to be* brave.

Él queria *que* yo me *some-*   He wished me *to submit.*
tiese.

Mandó *que* (ellos) *tragesen*   He ordered them *to bring*
vino.   wine.

Me parece *que* (ella) *está*   She appears to me *to be* ill.
enferma.

Literally, *They think that they are brave. He wished that I should submit. He ordered that they might bring wine. It appears to me that she is ill.*

Here we see that the governed verb in Spanish is put in one of the tenses of the indicative or subjunctive mood, while in either case it may remain in the infinitive in English. The placing of the governed verb in Spanish in one or the other mood is not a matter of indifference, but one which mostly depends on the nature of the governing verb, and not unfrequently on choice, as will be noticed presently.

These rules extend also to intransitive verbs, the signification of which does not pass over to the governed verb without the assistance of a preposition : Ex.

Vendré *á arreglar* con   I will come and settle with
Vmd.   you.

Nacemos *para morir.*   We are born to die.

Me quedaré aquí *para que*   I shall remain here that
él me *vea.*   he may see me.

3rd. We have seen that the infinitive is sometimes preceded in Spanish by a preposition and sometimes not; this also depends on the nature of the governing verb. We will now see what verbs govern infinitives with prepositions, and what prepositions they govern with.

The following verbs generally govern infinitives with *á*; namely, *acostumbrarse*, to accustom oneself ; *aprender*, to learn ; *atreverse*, to venture, to dare ; *ayudar*, to help ; *convidar*, to invite ; *considerarse obligado*, to consider oneself obliged ; *disponerse*, to prepare oneself ; *empezar*, to begin ; *enseñar*, to teach ; *exortar*, to exhort; *ponerse*, to set about ; and also verbs of movement *to* any place : Ex.

Me acostumbro *á* andar.   I accustom myself to walk.
Aprenden *á* leer.   They learn to read.

No se atreve *á* exponerse.	He does not venture to expose himself.
Ayúdeme *á* vestir.	Assist me to dress myself.
Le convidé *á* comer.	I invited him to dine.
Me considero obligado *á* obedecer.	I consider myself obliged to obey.
Nos dispusímos *á* trabajar.	We set about to work.
Empiezo *á* entenderlo.	I begin to understand it.
Me enseñó *á* dibujar.	He taught me do draw.
Exortar á alguno *á* hacer su deber.	To exhort any one to do his duty.
Se pusieron *á* reñir.	They set about quarrelling.
Voy *á* encontrarlos.	I am going to meet them.
Vengo *á* informar á Vmd.	I come to inform you.

Several reflective verbs also govern infinitives with *á*, when the latter indicate what has produced the effect implied in the governing verb : Ex.

Matarse *á* estudiar.	To kill oneself with studying.
Cansarse *á* trabajar.	To tire oneself with working.

The same preposition is sometimes put between two infinitives, to mark the distinction in the respective meanings of their actions : Ex.

Va mucho de decir *á* hacer.	There is a great difference between saying and doing.

The verbs *acabar*, to finish, and *cesar*, to cease, govern infinitives with *de* : Ex.

¿Acabó Vmd. *de* escribir?	Have you finished writing?
Cesaron *de* perseguirle.	They ceased persecuting him.

Tener and *hacer* govern infinitives with *de*, when a noun intervenes between them : Ex.

Tuvo la bondad *de* venir.	He had the kindness to come.
Hágame Vmd. el favor *de* darme.	Do me the favour to give me.

Infinitives are governed by *con*, when they express the *manner how*, and the *means by which* anything is obtained : Ex.

El saber se logra *con* estudiar.	Knowledge is obtained by study.
Nada se gana *con* enfadarse.	We gain nothing by being angry.

Infinitives are governed by *en*, when they do not express any kind of motion: Ex.

Se ocupa *en* leer.	He occupies himself in reading.
Se esmera *en* hablar bien.	He delights in speaking well.

Sobre and *tras*, when used in the sense of *besides*, govern infinitives: Ex.

Sobre, or *tras* ser rico es muy avaro.	Besides being rich he is very parsimonious.

For infinitives governed by *para* and *por*, see PAR. 7.

Some Spanish reflective verbs govern infinitives in the *active* voice, when the passive would be used in English: Ex.

Me dejé *engañar* de él.	I allowed myself *to be deceived* by him.
Se hizo *oir* de ellos.	He caused himself *to be heard* by them.

4th. It hast just been noticed in Obs. 2nd, that when the governing verb has a different agent from the verb governed, the latter is placed either in the indicative or the subjunctive mood, as the occasion may require; this also sometimes occurs when both verbs have the same agent. Rules will now be given to direct the learner in what mood and tense to employ the governed verb.

5th. The following verbs generally govern their regimen in the subjunctive mood—namely, verbs of *commanding, requesting, fearing, wishing, wondering, doubting, permitting, requiring, preventing, persuading, suiting,* and sometimes those of *thinking, believing, rejoicing,* and *hoping;* likewise *impersonal* verbs, and those verbs preceded by conjunctions expressive of *doubt, wish, supposition,* or *uncertainty,* as noticed in LECT. 20, PAR. 22.

6th. Verbs in the *present,* or *future indicative,* or the *present subjunctive,* govern their regimen in the *present subjunctive,* simple or compound: Ex.

Manda que se *haga* luego.	He orders it to be done immediately.
Suplico que me *dispense* Vmd.	I beg you will excuse me.
Que yo *tema* que me *insulte*.	That I may fear he might insult me.
Me *alegro* que lo *haya vencido*.	I am glad that he has overcome it.
Dudo que *pueda* conseguir.	I doubt that he is able to succeed.
Conviene que *sepan*.	It is proper that they should know.
Desearé que Vmd. se *divierta*.	I hope you may be amused.
Para que yo *desee* que él me *obedezca*.	That I should wish him to obey me.
Me *maravillo* que lo *hayan* creido.	I wonder that they should have believed it.
Es preciso que *desaparezca*.	It is necessary that it should disappear.

The verb that follows the relative *que*, preceded by a superlative, is also sometimes put in the subjunctive in Spanish; as, *Es la idea mas sublime* que conozca—It is the most sublime idea that I know of.

7th. Verbs in any of the *past* tenses, *simple* or *compound*, of the *indicative* or *subjunctive*, or in the compound future of the indicative, have generally their regimen in the *imperfect* of the *subjunctive, simple* or *compound*, with the termination *ra* or *se :* Ex.

Dudaba, or *dudé* que le *convinciese*, or que le *hubiera convencido*.	I doubted that he would convince him, or that he would have convinced him.
Ha mandado que lo *llevara*, or *llevase* Vmd.	He has ordered that you should carry it.
Habia pedido que no lo *digeramos*, or *digesemos*.	He had requested that we might not tell it.
Me *alegrara* que lo *hubiera hecho*.	I would rejoice that he had done it.
Le *habria ordenado* que *volviera*, or *volviese*.	I would have ordered him to return.
Les *habrá permitido* que le *siguieran*, or *siguiesen*.	Perhaps he may have allowed them to follow him.

The *compound* of the *present*, and *compound* of the *future indicative*, however, may also govern their regimen in the *present* of the *subjunctive;* as, *Ha mandado que lo lleve Vmd. Les habrá permitido que le* sigan.

8th. Generally speaking, in any case where the verb governed expresses a *will* or *inclination*, it is used with the termination *ria :* Ex.

Prometió que me *contestaria.*	He promised that he would answer me.
Creí que no *vendria.*	I thought he would not come
Habia prometido que *cantaria.*	She had promised that she would sing.
Hubiera creido que *vivirian* felices.	I should have thought that they would live happily.

9th. Verbs, however, of *declaring* or *saying, thinking* or *believing,* in any of the tenses of the indicative or subjunctive, may govern their regimen with the conjunction *que,* in the same mood and tense in both languages : Ex.

Declaro que lo sé, lo supe, lo habia sabido, lo sabria, etc.	I declare that I know it, knew it, had known it, would know it, etc.
Si digere que no puede, no pudo, no pudiere, etc., pagar.	If he should say that he is not, was not, should not be, etc., able to pay.
Pensaba que Vmd. no tardaria; que no habia tardado, etc.	I thought that you would not be late ; that you had not been late, etc.
Creo que ni la ha visto, ni desea verla.	I believe that he neither has seen, nor wishes to see her.

Note.—The rules which have been given for verbs governing with certain prepositions, will, in many cases, extend to the same verbs when they govern the indicative or the subjunctive mood with a conjunction (see Observation 3rd) : Ex.

Tengo miedo *de que* no lo hayan sabido.	I fear that they may not have known it.
Se empeñó *en que* se lo prestara.	He insisted on my lending it to him.
Le enseñaron *á que* fingiese mil escusas.	They taught him to feign a thousand excuses.

PECULIAR MANNER OF EMPLOYING CERTAIN VERBS.

9. ACABAR DE.—The expressions, *to have just*, and *to be just*, employed in English before a past participle, are rendered in Spanish by *acabar de*, preceding an infinitive; as, *Acabo de oir de su llegada*—I have just heard of his arrival. *Acaba de entrar*—He is just come in.

ALEGRARSE.—The verbs *to be glad*, and *to be rejoiced at*, are translated by the reflective verb *alegrarse* ; as, *Me alegro de saberlo*—I am glad to know it. *Se alegró de la noticia*—He was rejoiced at the news.

SENTIR and PESAR.—*To be sorry*, and *to grieve*, are translated by these verbs ; as, *Lo siento mucho*—I am very sorry for it (*i.e.*, I *feel* it much). *Me pesa mucho saberlo.*—I am verry sorry to know it (*i.e.*, It *grieves me* much to know it).

CABER, *to be capable of containing*, etc. This verb is employed in different manners in Spanish ; as, *Cuántas personas caben en este salon ?*—How many persons does this saloon contain, or is it capable of containing ? *No cabiamos todos en la cámara*—The cabin could not contain us all. *¿Puede caber eso en tu imaginacion ?*—Can that enter thy imagination ? *Cabe mucho en este baul*—This trunk holds a great deal. *Caber de pies*—To have room to stand. *Cabe mucha malicia en él*—He harbours much malice. *Tal es lo que á mí me cupo en suerte*—Such has fallen to my lot. *No caber en sí*—To be well satisfied with oneself. *No caber de gozo*—To be overjoyed.

CAER, *to fall*, is sometimes employed in the sense of *to look into*, in the following manner : *Estas ventanas caen al corral*—These windows look into the court-yard.

When *to become* is employed with reference to any part of a person's dress, it is translated CAER, or SENTAR ; as, *Este vestido le cae*, or, *le sienta muy bien*—This dress becomes you very well.

CAER EN GRACIA, means *to take one's fancy ;* as, *Parece que esa señora le ha caido á Vmd. en gracia*—It seems that that lady has taken your fancy.

DAR, *to give*, is employed with different meanings ; as, *Dar en el blanco*—To hit the aim. *Dar el pésame*—To condole. *Dar que hacer*—To give trouble. *Darse á la vela*—To set sail.

DARSE DE, and DARSE CUIDADO, are used in the sense of *to care about*; as, *Qué se le da á Vmd. de eso?*—What do you care about that? *No se me da cuidado de nada*—I care about nothing.

DAR POR SUPUESTO, means *to take for granted*; as, *Di por supuesto que ya no volveria*—I took it for granted that he would not return.

DEJAR DE, before infinitives, means *to fail*, and *to leave off*; as, *No deje Vmd. de hacerlo*—Do not fail to do it. *Dejemos de hablar mas del asunto*—Let us leave off speaking on the subject.

ECHAR, *to throw*, is used with various meanings; as, *Echar á perder*—To spoil. *Echar á pique un navio*—To sink a ship. *Echar en olvido*—To forget.

ECHAR MÉNOS, means *to miss* (*i.e.*, to be sensible of the absence of); as, *Acá echo ménos mis acostumbradas diversiones*—Here I miss my accustomed amusements. *Le eché á Vmd. ménos en el baile*—I missed you at the ball.

ECHAR DE VER, means *to be evident*, or *visible*; as, *Se echa de ver en eso la prudencia de Vmd.*—Your prudence is evident, or visible, or shows itself in that.

ECHAR Á PERDER, means *to spoil*; as, *Todo lo echan á perder*—They spoil every thing. *Así se echará á perder*—It will get spoiled in that manner.

ESTAR EN QUE, signifies *to be inclined to think*; as, *Estoy en que no vendrá hoy*—I am inclined to think that she will not come to-day.

ESTAR Á PIQUE DE, means *to be within an ace of*; as, *Estuvimos á pique de perdernos*—We were within an ace of being lost.

FALTAR DE, before an infinitive, means *to fail*; as, *Faltó de venir dos veces*—He failed twice to come.

GUARDARSE DE, before an infinitive, signifies *to take care not to*; as, *Se guardará muy bien de venir*—He will take good care not to come. *Me guardaré de decirle nada*—I will take care not to say anything to him.

GUSTAR, *to like*, and FALTAR, *to want*, have a peculiar regimen in Spanish, inasmuch as the objective case of the corresponding verb in English becomes the nominative in Spanish, and the nominative of the English verb becomes the objective in Spanish; as, *Me gustan los libros*—I like books. *¿Le gusta á Vmd. este vino?* Do you like this wine? *¿Qué les falta?* What do they require? *Les faltan muchas cosas*—They require many things. *Hacer falta* may be used in the place of *faltar;* as, *Qué les hace falta? Les hacen falta muchas cosas.*

The verb *Gustar*, however, sometimes retains the same kind of regimen as in English, only that the object of the verb is preceded by *de;* as, *Los porfiados siempre gustan de quimeras*—Obstinate people are always fond of disputes.

HACER, *to do, to make*, is employed in various colloquial phrases; as, *Haré por verle*—I will try or endeavour to see him. *Hacer caso de lo que dicen otros*—To mind what other people say. *Hacerse á la vela*—To set sail. *Hacer castillos en el aire*, or *torres en el viento*—To build castles in the air. *Se hace muy soberbio*—He becomes very proud. *Quién hizo el papel de gracioso?*—Who acted the part of clown? *El hacia de cónsul*—He acted as consul.

IR, *to go*, is also employed in several familiar phrases; as, *Ir con alguno*—To agree with any one. *Ir*, or *quedar en zaga*—To remain behind hand. *Irse á pique*—To founder at sea. *Irsele de la memoria á alguno*—To escape one's memory.

LLEVAR, *to take, to carry*, has several idiomatical meanings; as, *Llevar á mal*—To take amiss. *Me llevó dos duros por la compostura*—He charged me two dollars for the repair. *Llevaba una casaca á la francesa*—He wore a coat in the French fashion. *Llevarse chasco*—To be disappointed. *Me llevé chasco en eso*—I was disappointed in that.

MANDAR and HACER, both signify *to order*, and *to cause to be done ;* as, *Mandé que me tragesen vino*—I ordered them to bring me wine. *Haré que sepa su deber*—I will make him know his duty. *Mandé* (or *ordené*) *que me hiciese un vestido*—I ordered him to make me a dress.

OLER Á, is *to smell of*, and SABER Á, *to taste of ;* as, *Esto huele á aceite y sabe á sebo*—This smells of oil, and tastes of tallow.

SALIR is employed in various ways; as, *Salir á luz*—To come to light; to be published. *Salir con algo*—To obtain one's end. *Salir de sí*—To be enraptured. *Salga lo que saliere*—Happen what may. *Esta casa me sale en mas de mil libras*—This house stands me in more than a thousand pounds.

SERVIRSE is used in the third person only in the sense of *to be pleased to ;* as, *Sírvase Vmd. hacerme este favor*—Be pleased to do me this favour. *Se sirvió enviarme este regalo*—He was pleased to send me this present.

TARDAR EN, before an infinitive, means *to be long in doing any thing ;* as, *tarda mucho en decidir*—He is long in deciding. *Cuánto tarda en venir !*—How long he is in coming.

TENER, *to have*, is variously employed; as, *Tener á menos hablar con uno*—Not to deign to speak to one. *No tiene que ver con lo que yo digo*—It has nothing to do with what I say. *Tiene Vmd. razon*—You are right. *El no tiene razon*—He is wrong.

VOLVER, *to return*, expresses the repetition of the action denoted by the governed infinitive, as, *Vuelva Vmd. á leerlo*—Read it over again. *Volveré á venir mañana*—I shall come again to-morrow.

TRATAR DE, means *to endeavour to ;* as, *Trate Vmd. de venir mas temprano*—Endeavour to come earlier. *Trataré de hallarlo*—I shall endeavour to find it.

[For further idioms in verbs, see the Author's " Guide to Spanish and English Conversation."]

EXERCISE ON THE GOVERNMENT OF VERBS.

Courage   often   overcomes those difficulties that
   brio [muchas veces] vencer   dificultad

cause the weak to [give way].   Ask counsel of thy
hacer   flojo   desmayar   pedir consejo

friend. I am very thankful for your attention. We
            reconocido   ————

purchased our goods of a very respectable merchant.
  comprar   género   ———— negociante

We should deprive no one of his own. Of whom did
        privar

you   borrow   the money ?   He resembles his
  [pedir prestado]   semejarse

sister.   It concerns you to know that you incur
      importar   incurrir

danger in opposing the laws of the state. I am going to
peligro   oponerse

 answer this letter whilst you play a game at billiards.
contestar   miéntras   jugar partida   billar, s.

Will this suit your brother?   The room is filled
       convenir   cuarto   lleno

with smoke.   Never depend   entirely on others.
   humo   jamas depender enteramente

I remember well the past.   We must not neglect our
 acordarse   pasado   descuidar

duty.   Knowledge is gained by study.   Adonis was
deber   saber   lograr   estudio Adónis

beloved by Venus and by Proserpina.   They were
       Vénus

impelled by necessity.   It is very difficult to possess
impeler   necesidad   dificultoso   tener

moderation in prosperity. Behave   kindly   towards
          prosperidad portarse benignamente

everybody.   I am going for him, that he may conclude
                                        concluir

the business, since there remains but little to finish. I
  asunto   quedar

have a mind to go and see if he is ready to leave. We
                                partir

ought to yield to circumstances.   I do not pretend
     ceder   circunstancia   pretender

to sacrifice your interests.   I wish you may obtain your
 sacrificar   interes   lograr

end.   They advise me to wait.   I repented of
     aconsejar   aguardar   arrepentirse

having taken such a step.   I began to understand
          paso   empezar comprender

French before I learned to read it.   I accustom
 ántes que aprender   acostumbrarse

myself to do now what I once did not dare to do.
            atreverse

Assist me to carry this. He went to see if he could
ayudar   llevar

teach him to sing. If he should invite me to dine
enseñar   convidar   comer

with him, I shall consider myself obliged to go.
     considerar   obligado

Preparing myself to submit, I sat down to weep
disponerse   someter ponerse *   llorar

bitterly. We have finished writing. At last he
amargamente   acabar

ceased tormenting me. Have the goodness to tell me.
 cesar atormentar   bondad

He did me the favour to accompany me. Little is
       acompañar

obtained by fretting. I amuse myself in looking at
 lograr afligirse divertirse   mirar

the pictures. He caused himself to be respected by his
 pintura   hacerse   respetar

acquaintances. I beseech you to remain. I hope
 conocido   suplicar   quedarse desear

you may soon recover your health. He must behave
    recobrar   salud   portarse

better in order that I may wish him to come back.

I feared he might have suspected me. I had wished
 temer   desear

that they had deserved it. I never would have permitted
    merecer   consentir

it to be known. Perhaps he may have told him to bring
  saber quizá

them. If he thinks that I want him. They declared

that they would not trust him. I would have believed
     fiar

it impossible that he could have acted in this manner.
        obrar   manera

LECTURE XXIX.

ETYMOLOGY AND SYNTAX OF ADVERBS.

1. Adverbs are either simple or compound. Those which constitute but one word are simple, and the compound are formed by the addition of one or more syllables to the adverb in its simple form, or they consist of more than one word. Thus, *mas*, more, *ménos*, less, are simple; and *ademas*, besides, *asímismo*, in the same manner, *para siempre*, for ever, are compound.

The following is a classified list of Spanish adverbs:—

ADVERBS OF PLACE.

Donde,	Where.	hacia adelante,	forwards.
adonde,	whither.	hacia arriba,	upwards.
de donde,	whence.	hacia abajo,	downwards.
aquí,	here.	arriba,	above.
acá,	hither.	abajo,	below.
ahí,	there.	debajo,	under.
allí,	thither.	por debajo,	underneath.
allá, acullá,	yonder.	delante,	before.
de aquí,	hence.	detras,	behind.
de allí,	thence.	alrededor,	around.
dentro,	within.	aparte,	aside.
fuera,	out.	cerca,	near.
por fuera,	without.	léjos,	far.
hasta,	till, even.	al lado de,	by the side of.
hacia,	towards.	junto,	{ next, adjoining.
hacia aquí,	towards here.		
hacia allí,	towards there.	enfrente,	facing.
hacia atras,	backwards.	encima,	upon.

ADVERBS OF TIME.

Ahora,	Now.	ahora mismo,	just now.
ántes,	before.	mucho ha,	long since.
despues,	{ after, afterwards.	poco ha,	lately.
		miéntras,	whilst.

entónces,	then.	anteriormente,	formerly.
hoy,	to-day.	recientemente,	recently.
manaña,	to-morrow.	frecuente-mente,	frequently.
ayer,	yesterday.		
anoche,	last night.	en breve,	shortly.
anteayer,	the day before yesterday.	desde,	since.
		desde cuando,	since when.
luego,	presently, soon, then.	desde entón-ces,	siuce then.
nunca, jamas,	never.	hasta aquí,	hitherto.
tarde,	late.	hasta ahora,	till now.
temprano,	early.	aun, todavía,	yet.
siempre,	always, ever.	entretanto,	meanwhile, whilst.
para siempre,	for ever.		
ya,	already, now.	casi siempre,	almost always.
amenudo,	often.	casi nunca,	never hardly.
presto,	quickly.	una vez,	once.
cuando,	when.	dos veces,	twice.
así que,	as soon as.	tres veces,	three times.
no bien, apénas,	hardly.	rara vez,	seldom.
		otra vez, de nuevo,	another time. again.
hasta,	till, until.		
hasta cuando,	until when.	algunas veces,	sometimes.
pronto,	soon.	aun no,	not yet.
antiguamente,	anciently.		

ADVERBS OF QUALITY AND MANNER.

Bien, buenamente,	Well.	como,	like, how, as.
		despacio,	slowly.
mal, malamente,	badly.	recio, fuertemente,	strongly.
admirable-mente,	admirably.	aprisa, aprie-sa, deprisa, de priesa,	hastily, swiftly.
mejor,	better.	presto,	quickly.
peor,	worse.	exactamente,	exactly.
cuan,	how.	alto, en alta voz,	loudly.
así,	thus, so.		
así así,	so, so.	bajo,	lowly.
asímismo,	in the same manner.	fácilmente,	easily.
conque,	so, therefore.	sabiamente,	wisely.

justamente,	justly.	negligente- mente,	negligently.
lindamente,	neatly.	directamente,	directly.
abiertamente,	openly.	mayormente, especial- mente,	} chiefly, especially.
injustamente,	wrongfully.		
temeraria- mente,	rashly.		
enteramente,	entirely.	quedo,	softly, quietly.
voluntaria- mente,	voluntarily.		

ADVERBS OF ORDER.

Primera- mente,	Firstly.	juntamente,	together.
segunda- mente,	secondly.	ordenada- mente,	orderly.
terceramente,	thirdly.	totalmente,	totally.
en seguida,	next.	al reves, al contrario,	{ topsy-turvy, on the con- trary.
finalmente,	finally.		
últimamente,	lastly.	ántes,	before.
al fin, al cabo,	at the end.	despues,	after.
por último,	at last.		

ADVERBS OF QUANTITY AND COMPARISON.

Poco,	Little.	en parte,	partly.
mucho,	much.	enteramente,	entirely.
bastante,	enough.	por mitades,	by halves.
harto,	sufficiently.	tan, así,	so.
mas,	more.	tanto,	so much.
ménos,	less.	muy,	very.
ademas,	{ besides, moreover.	cuanto,	{ as much, how much.
demas,	over and above.	tanto como,	as much as.
		cerca,	nearly, almost.
demasiado,	too, too much.	peor,	worse.
casi,	almost.	mejor,	better.
apénas,	scarcely.		

ADVERBS OF DOUBT.

Quizá, acaso,	Perhaps.	probable- mente,	probably.
por ventura,	perchance.		
ántes, ántes bien,	} rather.		

ADVERBS OF AFFIRMATION AND NEGATION.

Sí,	Yes.	tambien, asímismo,	{ too, also, likewise.
cierto,	truly.		
ciertamente,	certainly.	ademas,	{ moreover, besides.
aun,	even.		
verdadera-mente,	indeed, truly.	otrosí,	{ furthermore, besides.
sin duda,	without doubt.	no,	no.
realmente,	really.	nada,	nothing.
indubitable-mente,	undoubtedly.	tampoco,	neither.
en verdad,	in truth.	de ningun modo,	by no means.
de véras,	indeed.		

2. In addition to the foregoing adverbs, an indefinite number of adverbial expressions may be formed, of which the following are a few specimens :—

esta manaña,	This morning.
esta tarde,	this afternoon.
esta noche,	to-night.
ayer tarde,	yesterday afternoon.
pasado mañana,	after to-morrow.
mañana por la mañana,	to-morrow morning.
á la tarde,	in the evening.
de cuando en cuando,	now and then.
de aquí en adelante,	henceforth.
demasiado presto,	too soon.
poco á poco	little by little.
á manos llenas,	plentifully, by handfuls.
á toda prisa,	with all speed.
de buena gana,	willingly.
de mala gana,	unwillingly.
con intencion,	on purpose.
á la mano,	at hand.
á la española,	in the Spanish fashion.
á la inglesa,	in the English fashion.
á caballo,	on horseback.
cuanto ántes,	as soon as possible.
en cuanto á,	with regard to.
lo demas,	the rest (of it).
los demas,	the rest (of them).

Note.—Several adverbs of time require the conjunction *que* after them when followed by a verb either in the indicative or subjunctive mood; namely, *ántes, desde, despues, entretanto, hasta, luego, miéntras*: Ex.

Ántes *que* lo *supe,* or *supiera.*	Before I knew it.
Ántes *que* lo *sepan.*	Before they (may) know it.
Desde *que víne.*	Since I came.
Despues *que* lo *dige.*	After I said it.
Despues *que* lo *digan.*	After they (may) say it.
Entretanto *que leen ó lean.*	Whilst they read.
Hasta *que murió.*	Until he died.
Hasta *que muera.*	Until he die.
Luego *que* lo *hice.*	As soon as I did it.
Luego *que* lo *hicieran.*	As soon as they should do it
Miéntras *que* ellos *jugaban.*	Whilst they played.
Miéntras *que* él *venga.*	Whilst he comes.

The placing of the verb in the indicative or subjunctive mood in Spanish, when in the past tense, appears in many cases to be a matter of choice, since we may either say, *Fuí allá ántes que* supe *de su llegada,* or, *ántes que* supiera *de su llegada*—I went there before I knew of his arrival. *No lo supe hasta algun tiempo despues que me lo* digeron *or* digesen—I did not know it until some time after they told me of it.

Antes and *despues* require the preposition *de,* when followed by an infinitive; as, *Ántes de salir*—Before going out. *Despues de escribir*—After writing.

For adverbs governed by certain prepositions, see LECT. 30, PAR. 33 to 39.

OF ADVERBS ENDING IN *MENTE.*

3. Adverbs terminating in *mente* for the most part denote *manner*, though they sometimes denote *affirmation, order, time,* etc. : Ex.

Habla elegantemente.	He speaks elegantly.
Me recibió cortesmente.	She received me courteously.
Se cansará ciertamente.	He will certainly tire himself.
Anteriormente era así.	Formerly it was so.

This class of adverbs is generally formed from adjectives, by adding *mente* to the feminine termination of adjectives that have two terminations, and to the common termination of those that have but one; as from *sabio*, wise, is formed *sabiamente*, wisely; from *caro*, dear, *caramente*, dearly; from *fácil*, easy, *fácilmente*, easily.

Most of the English adverbs ending in *ly*, terminate in *mente* in Spanish. The greater part of these adverbs may be expressed with the preposition *con* and a substantive, instead of the adjective with the termination *mente*; thus, instead of *fácilmente*, we may say *con facilidad*; instead of *sabiamente*, *con sabiduría*; and so forth.

When several adverbs formed from adjectives follow each other in succession, the termination *mente* is retained only with the last: Ex.

Ciceron habló *sabia* y *elocuentemente.*	Cicero spoke wisely and eloquently.
César escribió *clara, concisa* y *elegantemente.*—(GRAMMAR OF THE ACADEMY.)	Cæsar wrote clearly, concisely, and elegantly.

4. As adverbs that end in *mente* sometimes denote *manner*, at others *order, time,* etc., in a like manner do many other adverbs belong to more than one class; for instance, *luego* and *despues* are adverbs of time, when we say, *Luego vendré*—I will soon come. *Iré despues*—I will go afterwards; but they are adverbs of *place* and *order* in the following phrase: *El padre iba primero, despues la madre, y luego los hijos*—The father went first, then the mother, and next the children.

5- Adverbs are subject to degrees of comparison like adjectives, and have the same irregularities as those adjectives have from which they are derived: thus, from *velozmente*, swiftly, are formed *mas*, or *ménos velozmente*, more or less swiftly; *muy velozmente*, or *velocísimamente*, very swiftly; from *amablemente*, amiably, *mas amablemente*, more amiably; *muy amablemente*, or *amabilísimamente*, very, or most amiably; from *bien*, or *buenamente*, well, *mas bien*, or *mejor*, better, *muy bien*, or *óptimamente*, very well, etc. See LECTURE 11, PAR. 16 to 28.

6. When *sí* and *no* are employed as objective cases to a verb, they are preceded by the conjunction *que*; but when

preceded by an article, the conjunction is dispensed with : Ex.

Yo digo *que sí*; él dice que no.	I say yes; he says no.
No le dí ni *un sí*, ni *un no*.	I made him no reply whatsoever.

7. Adverbs are sometimes used in the place of adjectives, and *vice versá*. When used as adjectives, they are made to agree with the noun to which they refer, but not otherwise : Ex.

Esta *agua* es muy *clara*.	This water is very clear.
Hable Vmd. mas *claro*.	Speak more clearly.

The following are some words of this double signification—viz., *bajo*, low, lowly ; *alto*, high, highly ; *recio*, strong, strongly ; *mal*, bad, badly.

8. There are also some adverbs that are occasionally employed as nouns ; in such cases they must be treated as nouns : Ex.

Es necesario precaver *el mal*.	It is necessary to guard against the evil.
Que se contente cada cual con su *poco* ó su *mucho*.	Let every one be contented with the little or the much that he has.

SITUATION OF THE ADVERB.

9. With regard to the situation of the adverb in a sentence, no rule can be given but what would be subject to many exceptions. It is a matter that depends much on taste : however, when no particular emphasis is intended to be laid on the adverb, it generally follows the verb, and precedes other parts of speech ; and for energy, or elegance, it frequently changes its situation. Nevertheless, the strength of the adverb depends very much on its position in a sentence ; and the perspicuity of the construction also demands care in the proper placing of the adverb ; thus we must be guided according to the stress we wish to lay on the adverb to give it a more or less conspicuous position, taking care, however, to place it where it shall not create ambiguity in the sentence.

OBSERVATIONS ON CERTAIN ADVERBS.

10. *Aquí* and *acá*. The first means *here*, and the second *hither;* as, *Aquí está*—Here it is. *Ven acá*—Come hither.

Hasta aquí means *hitherto*, and *de aquí*, *hence;* as, *Hasta aquí hemos vivido en paz*—Hitherto we have lived peaceably. *De aquí esos males*—Hence those evils.

He aquí, signifies *behold*, or *here is;* as, *He aquí mi bolsa*—Behold, or here is my purse.

Ahí, allí, allá. Ahí generally denotes a place not very distant from the speaker : it also alludes to the place where the person addressed is; as, *Ahí está mi casa*—There is my house. *Ahí donde esta Vmd.*—There where you are. *Allí* and *allá* generally refer to a more distant place than *ahí;* as, *Le dejé allí*—I left him there. *Allá en aquellos paises*—There, in those countries. *Allá* is also equivalent to *thither;* as, *Voy allá*—I am going thither.

Mas acá and *mas allá* are always accompanied by the preposition *de*, when followed by another word. *Mas acá* signifies *on this side;* and *mas allá*, *on that side*, or *beyond;* as, *Mas acá de Madrid*—On this side of Madrid. *Mas allá de los Alpes*—On that side, or beyond the Alps.

Ademas and *demas*. The first means *besides* and *moreover;* as, *Ademas de eso*—Besides that. *Ademas, ya es tarde*—Moreover, it is now too late. The second, as an adverb, means either *over and above*, or *useless;* as, *Cúantos hay demas?*—How many are there over and above? *Es por demas*—It is useless. As an adjective and a substantive *demas* means *the rest;* as, *Lo demas vendrá mañana*—The rest (of it) will come to-morrow. *Los demas de los escritos*—The rest of the writings. *Las demas cartas*—The rest of the letters.

Donde and *adonde*. The first signifies *where*, and the second *whither*, or *where to;* as, *Dónde está? Donde Vmd. le dejo*—Where is he? Where you left him. *Adónde ha ido? Adonde Vmd. le mando*—Whither is he gone? Where you sent him.

Jamas and *nunca* may be used indiscriminately; as,

Jamas or *nunca ví tal cosa*—I never saw such a thing.
Nunca joined to *jamas* adds greater energy to the nega-
tion; as, *Nunca jamas ví tal cosa*—Never did I see such
a thing.

Jamas is often used after the words *por siempre*, and
para siempre, for ever; then, instead of its negative
signification, it means *eternally;* as, *Me acordaré de él
para siempre jamas*—I will remember him all the days
of my life, or for ever. It is sometimes used alone
interrogatively, in the sense of *ever.;* as, *¿ Ha visto
Vmd. jamas tal proceder ?*—Did you ever see such
behaviour ?

No. This adverb does not always convey a negative
meaning; on the contrary, it strengthens the affirmation
when used with comparatives, and renders the contrast
more striking; as, *Mejor es el trabajo que no la
ociosidad*—Labour is better than idleness. *Mas vale
ayunar que no enfermar*—It is better to fast than to fall
ill.—(GRAMMAR OF THE ACADEMY.) The *no*, however,
in such sentences is not *absolutely* required, since their
grammatical construction would be perfect without it.—
(See also LECT. 24, PAR. 8.)

Ya. This adverb has a variety of significations, as
will be observed in the following examples :—

¿Ha venido Vmd. *ya ?*	Are you come *already ?*
Ya lo sé.	I *already* know it.
Ya vendré á verle.	I'll *soon* come and see you.
Vaya Vmd. que *ya* yo iré.	Go you, I will go *presently.*
¿Me entiende Vmd. *ya ?*	Do you understand me *now?*
Si, *ya* le entiendo.	Yes, *now* I understand you.
¿Ha acabado *ya* de escribir ?	Has he finished writing *yet?*
Ya no me quejo de mi suerte.	I *no longer* complain of my fate.
Ya lo sabrá Vmd.	You will know it *by and by.*
Ya quiere esto, *ya* aquello.	*Sometimes* he wants this, *sometimes* that.
Iré, *ya* que Vmd. lo manda.	I will go, *since* you desire it.
Ya sea por esto, *ya* por aquello.	*Whether* it be for this, *or* for that.
Ya no le veré mas.	I shall *never* see him again.
Ya se ve.	It is evident.　Of course.

EXERCISE ON ADVERBS.

He seldom comes but when it is too late. Carry this
        venir sinó   llevar

first, and then that. Come and see me now and then.
                                   á

We generally dine early. He was already at home.
        comer   en casa

Write to me soon. Have you breakfasted already ? Yes,
                          desayunar

I have quite finished. The horse runs swiftly. This is
        acabar   veloz

done easily. She dances elegantly, and plays wonderfully.
               bailar   marvilloso

He behaved nobly and generously. He spoke distinctly
    portarse   distinto

and wisely. Some say yes, and some say no. Mildness
                                     dulzura

governs better than anger. I would assist you
  regir   cólera

    willingly   if I could. Where is your brother ?
[de buena gana]

Here he is. Let him come hither. I am going there

with him. Put it there, where you are. I have never

seen him. I will love her for ever. I will go, since

there is no remedy. I did not do it on purpose. He

dresses in the French fashion, and rides on horseback
  vestir   montar á   caballo

every day. Hitherto we have never quarrelled. Hence
                                 reñir

those discords and dissensions. It is on this side of
    discordia   ——————

Valladolid, and on the other side of the river. Where is
  ——————   rio

he, and where is he going to ?

LECTURE XXX.

ETYMOLOGY AND SYNTAX OF PREPOSITIONS.

1. Prepositions are of two kinds—namely, such as only have meaning in composition with other words; as in-*mortal*, abs-*tracto*, su-*poner*, etc. (immortal, abstract, to suppose, etc.), and such as have meaning both by themselves and in composition with other words; as the following :—

A,	to, at.	*hacia,*	towards.
ante,	before.	*hasta,*	till, as far as, even.
bajo,	under.	*para,*	for, for the purpose
con,	with.		of, in order to.
contra,	against.	*por,*	by, for, through.
de,	of, from.	*segun,*	according to, *or as.*
desde,	since, from.	*sin,*	without.
en,	in.	*sobre,*	upon.
entre,	between.	*tras,*	behind.

EMPLOYMENT OF PREPOSITIONS.

2. As prepositions in Spanish have frequently other meanings than those attached to them in English in the foregoing list, it will be necessary to treat on the various significations and use of each separately.

3. *A.* This preposition generally indicates the *end*, *object*, or *tendency* of the action, and besides its general signification of *to* and *at*, is employed before certain adverbs and adverbial expressions; as, *Vamos á pasear*—Let us go and take a walk. *Me volví á casa*—I returned home. *Andar á pié, á caballo*—To go on foot, on horseback. *Vestirse á la moda*—To dress in the fashion. *A consecuencia de eso*—In consequence of that. *A la verdad*—In truth. It signifies *conformity*; as, *A ley de Castilla*—In conformity with the law of Castile. *A fé de caballero*—On the word of a gentleman. *Instrumentality;*

as, *Se hace á martillo*—It is done by the hammer. It is frequently seen between two numbers of the same value, and denotes *order;* as, *Dos á dos*—Two by two. It marks the *distance* between two objects ; as, *A tiro de pistola*—Within pistol shot. *A veinte pasos de aquí*—At twenty paces hence. It indicates the *time* when, and the *place* where a thing happens; as, *A la tarde*—In the afternoon. *Nos sentámos á la mesa*—We seated ourselves at table. *Motive;* as, *A causa de su venida*—On account of his coming. (See **Par.** 26, and also Government of Verbs, Lect. 28)

4. *Ante* means *before,* or *in the presence of;* as, *Compareció ante al juez*—He appeared before the judge. *Pasó ante mí*—He passed before me. It denotes *preference;* as, *Nuestro deber es ante todo*—Our duty is before every thing. In the composition of other words it denotes *priority of time* and *place;* as, *anteayer,* the day before yesterday ; *antecámara,* antechamber.

5. *Bajo* denotes *subordination, inferiority* of position, and *dependence;* as, *Bajo tal gobierno*—Under such a government. *La puerta está bajo la ventana*—The door is under the window. *Estoy bajo sus órdenes*—I am under his orders. *Bajo* also signifies *under some restriction;* as, *Que se guarde de venir bajo pretexto alguno*—Let him be careful not to come under any pretext whatever. The antiquated preposition *so*, which has nearly the same signification as *bajo,* is now scarcely used except before the words *capa,* cloak ; *color,* colour ; *pena,* pain, or penalty; *pretexto,* pretext, and a few others ; as, *So capa de santo*—Under the cloak of sanctity. *So pena de muerte*—Under pain of death.

6. *Con* denotes *conjunction;* as, *Está casada con la Marquesa*—He is married to the Marchioness. *Vino conmigo*—He came with me. When preceded by *para* it signifies *towards;* as, *Es muy cortes para con todos*—He is very courteous towards, or to every body. It denotes *manner;* as, *Habla con gracia*—She speaks gracefully. *Means* or *instrumentality;* as, *Le hirió con una espada*—He wounded him with a sword. United to an infinitive it gives the latter the value of a substantive ; as, *Con enseñar se aprende*—By teaching one learns. In composition it denotes *union;* as, *concurrencia,* an assem-

blage; *confederacion*, a confederation. (See PAR. 27, also Government of Verbs, LECT. 28.)

7. *Contra*, in its most general signification, *is against*; as, *Habla contra mí*—He speaks against me. *Es contra la ley*—It is against the law. *La casa está contra el oriente*—The house faces the east. In composition it implies an opposite meaning to the word to which it is prefixed; as, *contradecir*, to contradict; *contraórden*, a countermand.

8. *De*, besides its most general significations of *belonging to*, and *separation from*, has several other meanings. It is employed after adjectives that express the *moral* or *physical characteristics* of objects; as, *Duro de corazon*—Hard-hearted. *Largo de piernas*—Long-legged. It precedes nouns denoting the *employments*, or *offices* of persons; as, *Va de encargado de negocios*—He goes as chargé d'affaires. *Trabaja de platero*—He works as silversmith: when, however, the verb *ser* precedes such nouns, the *de* is omitted; as, *Es encargado de negocios; Es platero*. It is placed before nouns designating the manner or style of dress; as, *Estaba vestido de militar; de luto; de gala*—He was dressed as a military man; in mourning; in full dress. It indicates the *passive* voice instead of *por*; as, *Amado de sus amigos, y odiado de sus enemigos*—Beloved by his friends, and hated by his enemies. It is employed before nouns in a *partitive* sense. *Probé del Jerez*—I tasted some of the sherry. *Envíeme Vmd. de aquellos*—Send me some of those. It denotes the *materials* of which things are made, and the *use* for which things are designed; as, *casa de piedra*, a stone house; *caja de oro*, a gold box; *papel de escribir*, writing-paper; *caballo de coche*, coach-horse. It indicates different *divisions of time*; as, *de dia*, by day; *de noche*, by night. It sometimes denotes *cause*; as, *Lo hizo de miedo*—He did it through fear. *Manner*; as, *Lo hizo de buena gana*—He did it with a good will. It is used with *epithets*; as, *El pícaro del muchacho*—The rogue of a boy. Also after certain interjections expressive of *complaint*; as, ¡ *Infeliz de mí !*—Ah, poor me! ¡ *Desdichada de ella !*—Unhappy her! (See PAR. 28, and also Government of Verbs, LECT. 28.)

9. *Desde* denotes the *beginning* of time and place; as, *Desde la creacion*—*From* the creation. *Desde Cartagena*

á Barcelona—From Carthagena to Barcelona. *Desde entónces acá*—From that time to this.

10. *En* has various meanings besides its general one of *in* and *within*, such as *into, as, to;* as, *La hija de Tántalo se convirtió en estátua*—Tantalus' daughter was converted into a statue. *De puerta en puerta*—From door to door. *Sírvase admitir este anillo en señal de amistad*—Be pleased to accept of this ring as a token of friendship. *En* united to *cuanto* signifies *with regard to;* as, *En cuanto á mí*—With regard to myself. *En cuanto á lo que Vmd. dijo*—As to, *or* with regard to what you said. (See PAR. 29; also Government of Verbs, LECT. 29.)

11. *Entre.* The general meaning of this preposition is *between;* as, *Entre los dos*—Between the two. *Entre el padre y el hijo*—Between the father and son. It likewise signifies *amongst;* as, *Entre todos*—Amongst all.

12. *Hacia*, in its general signification, is *towards;* as, *Voy hacia casa*—I am going towards home. It forms an adverbial expression when preceded by *de;* as, *Venia de hacia allí*—He came from that direction.

13. *Hasta* signifies *till, until, even, to, as many as, as far as,* and denotes the *end* of time, place, or action; as, *Hasta Lúnes*—Till, or until Monday. *Hasta el año próximo*—Till next year. *Tenia hasta mil*—He had as many as a thousand. *Voy hasta Segovia*—I am going as far as Segovia. *No volveré hasta Mayo*—I shall not return till May. *Hasta la vista*—Until we meet again. *Hasta* in the sense of *till,* or *until,* is followed by *que* before a verb, except in the infinitive mood; but in the sense of *even* the *que* is not used; as, *Hasta que vengan*—Until they come. *Hasta ellos mismos lo saben*—Even themselves know it. *Hasta* sometimes governs infinitives, giving to the action a future, or conditional signification; as, *Probaré hasta conseguir*—I shall try till I succeed. *No descansaré hasta merecerlo*—I shall not rest till I deserve it. *Pelearé hasta vencer, ó morir*—I will fight till I conquer, or die.

14. *Para* and *por.* Each of these two prepositions has its peculiar meanings, and their application will be pointed out in the following observations.

Para denotes the *end* or *purpose* of an action, and is equivalent to *in order to,* or, *for the purpose of;* as, *Estudio para aprender*—I study in order to learn, or for the purpose of learning. It denotes the *use*, *intention*, *benefit*, and *injury* of a thing; as, *La tinta es para escribir* —Ink is to write with. *Esto es para Vmd.*—This is for you. *El perjuicio es para él*—The evil is for him. It expresses *capacity* or *incapacity*; as, *Es hombre para mucho*—He is able to do much. *No es hombre para nada*—He is fit for nothing. It points out the place *whither* a thing is *directed*; as *Va para Almería*—He is going towards Almeria. It sometimes specifies a particular *time*; as, *Estarémos de vuelta para las Pascuas*— We shall be on our return by the holidays. *Para que* means *what for*, and *in order that*; as, *¿Para qué es bueno esto?*—What is this good for? *Para que no fuese allí*-In order that he might not go there. (See PAR. 30; also LECT. 28, PAR. 7.)

15. *Por* denotes *motive*, *cause*, or *reason*, also the *means* by which a thing is done; as, *Lo hice por favorecerle*—I did it to favour him. *Lo hizo por malicia*—He did it through malice. *Agrada por su cortesía*— He pleases by his courteous manner. *Lo alcanzó por su erudicion*—He obtained it by his learning. It denotes *instrumentality*; as, *El libro fué escrito por él, é impreso por su hermano*—The book was written by him, and printed by his brother. It signifies, *for the sake of*; as, *Hágalo Vmd. por caridad*—Do it for charity's sake. It sometimes means *in the place of*; as, *Obro por él*—I act for him. It denotes *distribution*; as, *Tanto por docena, por ciento*—So much a dozen, per cent. Between two nouns or infinitives it denotes *preference*; as, *Casa por casa, mejor quiero esta que aquella*—Of the two houses, I prefer this. *Vivir por vivir, prefiero vivir en mi pais*— If it be for the sake of living only, I prefer to live in my own country. It sometimes indicates *time*; as, *Salí por una hora*—I went out for an hour. *Por el mes de Mayo* —About the month of May. It is employed in matters of *buying, selling, exchanging*, etc. *Vendió su caballo por dos mil reales*—He sold his horse for two thousand reals. *¿Por cuánto le habia comprado?*—How much did he buy it for? *Cámbieme Vmd. este baston por aquel*—Change me this stick for that. It sometimes has a *distributive* meaning; as, *Á un duro por docena, por libra*, etc. At one dollar a dozen, a pound, etc. *Un por uno; letra opr letra*—One by one; letter by letter. When it pre-

cedes a verb in the subjunctive mood it is equivalent to *however*, or *although*; as, *Por grande que sea*—However large it may be. It is generally used where *though* and *by* are in English; as, *Pasé por Toledo*—I passed through Toledo. *Por descuido*—Through inattention. *Por envidia*—Through envy. *Pasó por mi ventana*—He passed by my window. *Lo hice por yerro*—I did it by mistake. And in most instances it is equivalent to *for*, except where the latter means *for the purpose of* (which requires *para*); as, *Vengo por Vmd.*—I come for you. *Murió por la patria*—He died for his country. *Lo tomé por médico*—I took him for a doctor. (See Par. 31, also Lect. 28, Par. 7.)

16. *Segun* denotes *conformity*; as *Segun mi parecer*—According to my opinion. *Lo cuento segun me lo han contado*—I relate it as it was related to me. *Segun eso vamos bien*—If that be the case we are well off.

17. *Sin* denotes *privation* or *want*; as, *Estoy todavía sin comer*—I have not dined yet. *Voy sin Vmd.*—I am going without you. It also signifies *besides*; as, *Llevaba joyas de diamantes, sin otras alhajas de oro*—She wore diamonds, besides other jewels. There is, however, an ellipsis in this Spanish phrase, to express which fully we should say, *sin contar*, or *sin mencionar otras alhajas*, etc.

18. *Sobre* denotes *superiority*, both as regards locality and dignity; as, *El sombrero está sobre la mesa*—The hat is upon the table. *La caridad es sobre todas las virtudes*—Charity is above all virtues. It indicates the *subject* on which a work treats, or on which we are speaking; as *Tratado sobre la matemática*—A treatise on mathematics. *Habló sobre la educacion*—He spoke on education. It sometimes is used in the place of *hacia*, or *cerca*; as *Llegué sobre el anochecer*—I arrived towards nightfall. *Costó sobre mil ducados*—It cost about a thousand ducats.

19. *Tras* denotes *order* of things; as, *Tras el padre vino el hijo*—After the father came the son. *Tras la adversidad viene la fortuna*—Fortune succeeds adversity. (See Par. 32.)

20. Besides the foregoing prepositions, there are many adverbs and adverbial expressions employed as

substitutes for prepositions, and when so employed they are generally followed by *á* or *de*. The Spanish language admits of a great variety of these expressions; a few of these which are in constant use are here given as specimens.

The following require *á* after them :—

Con respecto á él.	With regard to him.
Conforme á la ley.	According to the law.
En cuanto á mí.	With regard to me.
Junto á la puerta.	Close to the door.
Tocante á lo que Vmd. dice.	Concerning what you say.

The following require *de* after them :—

A lo largo del rio.	Along the river.
Al derredor de la mesa.	Around the table.
Al lado de mi.	Next to me.
Acerca de eso.	Concerning that.
Antes del amanecer.	Before day-break.
Cerca de la ciudad.	Near the city.
Debajo de la ventana.	Under the window.
Delante de mi vista.	Before my sight.
Dentro del sombrero.	Within the hat.
Dentras de la casa.	Behind the house.
Encima del techo.	Upon the roof.
Enfrente de la iglesia.	Opposite the church.
Fuera de la ciudad.	Without the city.
Léjos de mi pais.	Far from my country.
Por encima del puente.	Over, *or* across the bridge.

21. The same word may sometimes be a preposition, and at others an adverb, according to the sense in which it is taken; for instance, *desde* is a preposition in *Desde Cádiz á Sevilla*—From Cadiz to Seville; and an adverb in *Desde ayer*—Since yesterday.

PECULIAR MEANINGS OF CERTAIN ENGLISH PREPOSITIONS, WITH THEIR CORRESPONDING TRANSLATIONS IN SPANISH.

22. When English prepositions have other meanings besides those which constitute their most general signifi-

cation, they must be translated by words corresponding with those which they stand in the place of: Ex.

ABOUT—To run *about* the streets—*Correr* por *las calles.* He spoke *about* that affair—*Habló* de, *or* sobre *ese negocio.* What are you *about?*—*Qué está Vmd.* haciendo? I was *about* to tell it to you—*Estaba para decírselo á Vmd.*

ABOVE—His liberality is *above* his means—*Su liberalidad* pasa *á sus medios.* It is *above* my comprehension—*No* alcanzo *á comprenderlo.*

AFTER—He does things *after* his own fancy—*Hace las cosas* á *su antojo.* I was looking *after* a friend—*Iba* en busca de *un amigo.*

AGAINST—I set my face *against* it—*Me* opuse á *ello.* I shall be back *against* the end of the month—*Estaré de vuelta* para *fines del mes.*

ALONG—*Along* the shore—*Á* lo largo de *la ribera.* Come *along* with me—*Venga Vmd. conmigo.*

AT.—Are they *at* home?—*¿Estan en casa?* I am at a loss how to act—*No sé como determinar.* Not *at* all—*Del todo.* He came in *at* the window—*Entró* por *la ventana.* I was *at* Salamanca—*Estuve* en *Salamanca.* He is *at* dinner—*Está comiendo.*

BEFORE—*Before* my window—Delante de *mi ventana. Before* the judge—Ante *el juez.*

BEHIND—He leaves him *behind—Le deja en* zaga. You are *behind* your time—*Viene Vmd.* tarde.

BENEATH—Such actions are *beneath* a gentleman—*Tales acciones son* indignos de *un caballero. Beneath* the mask of hypocrisy—Bajo *capa, or so capa de santo.*

BESIDE—He appeared *beside* himself—*Parecia* fuera de sí. *Beside* me—*Al* lado *mio.*

BEYOND—It is *beyond* all praise—Excede á *toda elabanza. Beyond* my reach—Fuera de *mi alcance. Beyond* doubt—Sin *duda alguna.*

BY—*By* day—De *día. By* accident—Por *accidente.* Impelled *by* necessity—*Impelido* de *la necesidad.* One *by* one—*Uno* á *uno.* How did you come *by* it?—Por *dónde le vino á Vmd.? By* and *by—Luego. By* sea—Por *mar.* Close *by*—A *la mano.*

DOWN—*Down* the hill—*Cuesta* abajo. Throw it *down—Echelo* en tierra.

FOR.—*For* my sake—*Por amor de mí.* *For* fear—*Por miedo.* I act *for* him—*Actuo por él.* I start to-morrow *for* Segovia—*Parto mañana para Segovia.* It will last *for* many years—*Durará por muchos años.* I bought it *for* a dollar—*Lo compré por un peso.* It is impossible *for* me—*Me es imposible á mí.* As *for* me—*En cuanto á mí.*

FROM.—He did it *from* fear—*Lo hizo de miedo.* Tell him *from* me—*Dígale Vmd. de mi parte.* I speak *from* what I hear—*Hablo por lo que oigo.*

IN, INTO.—*In* the morning, *in* the afternoon—*Por la mañana, por la tarde.* Deficient *in* intellect—*Falto de intelecto.* *In* consequence of that—*Á consecuencia de eso.* *In* accordance with—*De acuerdo con.* I was *in* hopes that it would do—*Tenia esperanzas que serviria.* To descend *into* the garden—*Bajar al jardin.* They entered *into* an alliance—*Entraron en alianza.*

NEAR.—*Near to* the Exchange—*Cerca de la Bolsa.* *Near* me—*Junto á mí.*

OF.—All *of* us—*Todos nosotros.* I beg *of* you—*Le pido á Vmd.* To be well spoken *of*—*Tener buena fama.* *Of* course—*Por supuesto.* To be ignorant *of* the fact—*Ignorar el hecho.*

OFF.—How far *off* is it?—*Cuánto dista?* *Off* the port—*Sobre el puerto.* *Off* hand—*De improviso.* Lift it *off* the ground—*Levántelo del suelo.* Take *off* your hat—*Quítese el sombrero.* He carried her *off*—*Se la llevó.* I let him *off*—*Le perdoné; le dejé ir.* I shall soon leave *off*—*Pronto acabaré.*

ON, UPON.—Keep *on* your cloak—*Quédese con la capa puesta.* He came *on* Monday last—*Vino Lúnes pasado.* I met them *on* the road—*Les encontré en el camino.* *On* that account—*Por ese motivo.* *On* this side and *on* that—*De este lado y de aquel.* *On* certain occasions—*En ciertas ocasiones.* *On* the contrary—*Al contrario.* *On* foot ; *on* horseback—*Á pié; á caballo.* Go *on*—*Adelante.* Rely *on* me—*Dependa Vmd. de mí.* *On*, or *upon* my word—*Sobre mi palabra.* They are not *on* terms—*No se tratan.* He imposed that duty *on*, or *upon* them—*Les impuso esa obligacion.* He was looked *upon* as a spy—*Le miraron como espía.* They heaped many favours *upon* them—*Les colmaron de favores.* To

feed *on*, or *upon* hopes—*Alimentarse* de *esperanzas.*
Seated *on* the sofa—*Sentado* en *el canapé.* Come *on* the
twelfth of May—*Venga Vmd. el doce de Mayo.*

OVER.—The coach ran *over* him—*El coche le pasó*
encima. All *over* the world—*Por todo el mundo.* *Over*
the way—*Al or* del *otro lado.* It is *all* over—*Se acabó.*
Read it *over*—*Vuelva Vmd. á leerlo; Repáselo Vmd.*
There was nothing *over*—*No* sobró *nada.* Give *over—*
Acabe Vmd.

OUT.—*Out* of fear—De *miedo. Out* of danger—*Fuera*
de *peligro. Out* of doors—*Fuera de casa.* He is *out* of
money—*Está* sin *dinero. Out* of order—*Descompuesto.*
Out of vengeance—*Por, or* de *venganza.* She is *out* of
her mind—*Perdió el juicio. Out* of curiosity—*Por curio-*
sidad. To be *out* of humour—*Estar de* mal *humor.*

ROUND.—All the year *round*—*Todo el año.* To sail
round the world—*Circunnavegar el mundo.* I will come
round to you—*Passaré á su casa de Vmd.* To go *round*
and *round*—*Ir dando* vueltas.

THROUGH.—We passed *through* France—*Pasámos* por
Francia. He ran him *through*—*Le atravesó* de parte á
parte. I passed *through* the mob—*Pasé* por entre *la*
caterva. Through (*i. e.* on account of) him—Por razon
de *él. Through* (*i. e.* by means of) him—Por medio *de*
él. Through envy—*Por or* de *envidia. Throughout* the
whole country—Por *todo el pais.*

To.—From day *to* day—*De dia* en *dia.* From door *to*
door—*De puerta* en *puerta.* According *to* appearances—
Segun las apariencias. That is yet *to* come—*Eso está*
aun por *venir.* This is new *to* me—*Esto es nuevo* para
mí. Secretary *to* the embassy—*Secretario* de *la embajada.*
A victim *to* his passions—*Víctima* de *sus pasiones.* Ten
to one—*Diez* contra *uno. To* this day—*Hasta el dia de*
hoy.

UNDER.—The ship is *under* sail—*El navío está á la*
vela. He is *under* age—*Es* menor *de edad. Under* oath
—*Bajo de juramento.* It is *under* its value—*Es* ménos
de su valor.

UP.—*Up* that way—*Hacia allá.* Are they *up?*—
¿ Estan levantados? *Up* two pairs of stairs—Al *segundo*
piso. Let them serve *up* the dinner—*Que* suban *la*
comida. He was taken *up*—*Le pusieron en custodia.* To

be puffed *up* with pride—*Hincharse de soberbia.* I cannot put *up* with her—*No la puedo aguantar.*

WITH.—They quarrelled *with* one another—*Riñeron entre sí.* The room is filled *with* people—*El cuarto está lleno* de *gente.* He was charged *with* the crime —*Le acusaron* del *delito.* Arm yourself *with* patience—*Ármese* Vmd. de *paciencia.* Fraught *with* danger—*Lleno* de *peligro.* I was struck *with* her beauty—*Me quedé sorprendido* de *su hermosura.* Endowed *with* virtues— *Dotado* de *virtudes.* I am not acquainted *with* her—*No la conozco.* I was pleased *with* his discourse—*Me agradó su discurso.*

WITHIN. — *Within* pistol-shot — *Á tiro de pistola. Within* my reach—*Á mi alcance. Within* a little way from here—*A poca distancia de aquí.* It is *within* a mile—*No llegá á una milla.* There is nobody *within*— *No hay nadie* en casa.

WITHOUT.—I came *without* her—*Vine sin ella. Without* exception—Sin *excepcion. Without* doors—Fuera de *casa. Without* his reach—Fuera de *su alcance.*

23. There are a vast number of verbs in English that have certain prepositions affixed to them, and become, as it were, inseparable from them; but the prepositions so used are seldom translated in Spanish, the verb and preposition together being construed by a verb alone, corresponding with the meaning contained in both: for example, to go down, *bajar;* to come in, *entrar;* to go out, *salir;* to go up, *subir;* to draw out, *sacar;* to set out, *partir;* to fall down, *caer;* to pull down, *derribar;* and many more.*

PLACE OF PREPOSITIONS.

24. Prepositions in Spanish always precede the word which they govern, wherever their situation be in English : Ex.

¿A quién escribió Vmd?	*Whom* did you write *to?* or, *to whom* did you write?
Este es el libro *de que* hablaba.	This is the book *which* I spoke of; or, *of which* I spoke.
¿Para qué lo hizo?	*What* did he do it *for?*

---

* See the Author's English Grammar for the use of Spaniards.

GOVERNMENT OF PREPOSITIONS.

25. Prepositions govern nouns, pronouns, verbs, and adverbs. The manner in which they govern nouns and pronouns has been treated on in the Government of the Cases, LECT. 8, PAR. 1 to 13. With respect to their power of governing verbs, we have to observe that *á, con, de, en, para, por, sobre,* and *tras* govern verbs in the infinitive in the same manner as they do nouns. The following rules (which are in accordance with the GRAMMAR OF THE ACADEMY) will explain their manner of governing.

26. *A* governs infinitives that denote the *end* to which the action of the governing verb is directed; as *Voy á salir*—I am going out. Between two infinitives it marks the distinction in the respective meanings of their actions; as, *Va mucho de decir á hacer*—There is a great difference between saying and doing. This preposition is sometimes elegantly employed before an infinitive instead of the conditional *si,* if; as, *A saber yo eso; á decir verdad;* which expressions are equivalent to, *Si yo supiera eso*—Had I known that; *Si se ha de decir la verdad*—If the truth is to be told.

27. *Con* governs infinitives that signify *means, manner,* and *instrumentality;* as, *Con estudiar se alcanza la sabiduría*—By study we gain wisdom.

28. Infinitives are governed by *de,* when the *time* or *season* proper for doing any thing is expressed by the preceding noun; as, *Es hora de comer*—It is dinner hour. It sometimes is equivalent to *para;* as, *Es fácil de digerir*—It is easy to digest.

All infinitives, preceded by *haber,* are governed by *de* where a necessity is implied; as, *Ha de venir*—He is to come. *Hubo de escaparse*—He was obliged to escape. There are also many other verbs that govern infinitives with *de* that cannot be reduced to rule; as, *Acabo de llegar*—I have just arrived. *Es digno de oir*—It is worth hearing. *Es de esperar*—It is to be hoped. *Debia de ir* —He ought to go.

29. *En* governs infinitives that do not denote motion; as, *Se ocupa en leer*—He occupies himself in reading. *No hay dificultad en decirlo*—There is no difficulty in saying it.

30. *Para.* Infinitives are preceded by *para*, that denote the *end*, or *purpose* of the action of the governing verb; as, *Trabajo ahora para descansar luego*—I work now in order to rest afterwards. *Para* also expresses the *relative capacity* of a person to perform an action; as, *Para ser principiante no dibuja mal*—For a beginner he does not draw badly.

31. *Por*, meaning the *end* or *motive* of an action, governs infinitives like *para*; as, *Estudio por saber*—I study in order to learn.

32. *Sobre* and *tras*, in the sense of *besides*, govern infinitives; as, *Sobre*, or *tras ser culpado, todavía es insolente*—Besides being guilty he is insolent.

33. With respect to adverbs, *de, desde, hacia, hasta, para*, and *por*, govern those of *place*; as, *De aquí á Toledo*—From here to Toledo. *Desde allí á Madrid*—Thence to Madrid. *Hacia allá*—Towards there. *Hasta acá*—As far as here. *Va para Cádiz*—He is going to Cadiz. *¿Por dónde salió?*—Which way did he go out? *Por aquí; por allí*—This way; that way.

34. *Por* and *para* may govern all those of *time*, except *ya*; as, *Por temprano que fuí*—However soon I went. *Lo dejarémos para mañana*—We will leave it for to-morrow. *Hoy, ayer*, and *mañana* are also governed by *con, de, desde*, and *entre*; as, *Con hoy hace ocho dias*—It makes eight days with to-day. *De hoy en quince dias*—This day fortnight. *Desde ayer*—Since yesterday. *Entre mañana y pasado*—Between to-morrow and the day following.

35. All those of *manner*, except *así*, may be governed by *por*; as, *Por recio que le llame*—However loud I called him. *Por mal que le suceda*—Whatever ill may happen to him. *Bien* and *mal* may be governed besides by *para* and *entre*; as, *Ni sirve para bien ni para mal*—He is fit for nothing. *Entre bien y mal*—Between well and bad. *Quedo* and *recio* may likewise be governed by *de*; as, *Dar de quedo, de recio*—To strike softly, hard. Those ending in *mente* are not governed by prepositions.

36. Those of *quantity* may be governed by *por* and *para*; as, *Se tiene por muy sabio*—He considers himself very wise. *Por poco que coma*—However little he may eat. *Poco* and *mucho* may likewise be governed by *á, de*,

and *en;* as, *Á poco que ande*—However little he may walk. *De poco se queja*—He complains of a very little. *Los excede á todos en mucho*—He exceeds them all by far.

37. Those of *comparison* by *á, entre, para,* and *por;* as, *Iba á mas andar*—He was going at the greatest speed. *Entre mas y ménos*—Between more and less. *No sirve para mas*—He is fit for nothing else. *Por mucho que hable*—However much he may talk. *Mas* and *ménos* may also be governed by *con, de, entre, sin,* and *sobre. Mejor* and *peor* by *á, de,* and *en;* as, *Con mas brillante efecto*—With a more brilliant effect. *Sobre mas ó ménos*—A little more or less. *De peor en peor*—worse and worse.

38. Of those of *order, ántes,* and *despues* are governed by *de, desde,* and *para;* as, *De ántes lo sabia*—I knew it formerly. *Desde ántes lo pensé*—I thought so before. *Queda para despues*—It remains for by and by. *Para ántes de comer*—For before dinner.

39. The affirmative adverb *sí,* the negative *no,* and the adverb of doubt *acaso,* are governed by *por;* as, *Por sí ó por no*—Whether it be so or not. *Si por acaso sucediere asi*—If perchance it should happen so.

EXERCISE ON PREPOSITIONS.

Hernan Cortes fought on horseback, assisting with his
         pelear   socorrer

troops the greatest emergencies, and carrying with his lance
  tropa   aprieto   llevar   lanza

terror and devastation into the enemy. True history
———   estrago   —— verdadera

leaves no virtue without its praise, nor vice without a
  dejar   loor

reprimand; to everything it gives its true value and
reprension   valor

place: it is a witness against the wicked, and the reward
lugar   testigo   malo   abono

of the good; a treasury and deposit of great virtues and
          tesoro   depósito

deeds.   Fame is of [such high] value amongst mortals,
hazaña   fama   tanto   aprecio
that we cannot with reason despise it, since it is a sure
                        aborrecer   seguro
means for undertaking great acts of virtue. Let us
medio   emprender   hecho
contemplate man issuing from the hands of nature, and
contemplar   salir
entering by successive degrees into the necessities which
  entrar   sucesivo   grado   necesidad
the weakness of his own existence exposes him to. She
    fragilidad   ser   exponer
does not sing badly for a beginner.   I shall remain
                        principiante   permanecer
here till the summer. After passing through Segovia, I
                        pasar
went towards Madrid.   He wrote on different subjects.
                                                asunto
He has been out of place since he was dismissed from
                    empleo   despedir
court.   After this time there will come a better. We
corte   tiempo
will fight till we conquer or die. Our duty is before every
    pelear   vencer   deber
thing. What do you inquire for? Whom do you
                        preguntar
inquire for? That is what I referred to. Did he speak

about that? I found him at home, at breakfast. Moved
                hallar   mover
by compassion. Leave off tormenting yourself. On your
  ————   atormentarse
account and his. Out of pity. Through envy. The
  motivo   piedad   envidia
   first rail-road established in Spain was that from Bar-
[camino de hierro] establecer
celona to Mataró, about the year 1848.

LECTURE XXXI.

ETYMOLOGY AND SYNTAX OF CONJUNCTIONS.

1. Conjunctions are either simple or compound. Simple conjunctions consist of one word, and sometimes of one letter only; as, *si, ni, y,* etc., if, nor, and, etc. The compound consist of two or more words; as, *así que, fuera de que,* etc., so that, besides that, etc. The following are the conjunctions employed in Spanish :—

Conjunctive.

Y *or* é,	And.
que,	that.

Disjunctive.

ó *or* ú,	or, either.
ni, tampoco,	nor, neither.
ora, ya, bien,	whether, or.
siquiera,	at least.

Adversative.

mas, pero,	moreover, but
cuando,	when.
aunque, bienque, mas que, si bien, dado que,	} though, although.
siendo que,	whereas.
no obstante, sinembargo, comoquiera, con todo, á pesar de,	} nevertheless, although, yet however, notwithstanding
aménos que,	unless.
empero,	{ but, yet, however.
no sea que,	lest.
sinó,	but.

Conditional.

si,	if, whether.
como, con tal que,	} provided.
sea que, bien,	whether.
cuando,	when, though.

Causative.

Porque,	{ because, why, for.
pues,	since, then.
pues que, ya que, puesto que,	} since.

Restrictive.

no mas que, sinó,	} only, except, but.

Continuative.

pues, por tanto,	} then, since, therefore.
con que,	so.
así que,	so that.
puesto que, supuesto que,	} since.
otrosí,	besides.

Comparative.		*Conclusive.*	
como,	as.	á fin de que,	that,
así,	thus, so.	para que,	in order that.
tal como,	such as.	por, que,	
segun,	according as.	de suerte que,	so that.
así como,	just as.		
que,	than.		

2. *Conjunctive* conjunctions are those which unite the several words or members of a sentence together : Ex.

Yo *y* él irémos,	I *and* he will go.
Es cierto, *y* él lo sabe.	It is certain, *and* he knows it.

Note.—The conjunction *y* changes into *é* before a word beginning with *i* or *hi :* Ex.

Es malo *é* ingrato.	He is wicked *and* ungrateful.
Padre *é* hijo.	Father *and* son.

Que serves to connect the sense of the *governing* verb with the verb *governed :* Ex.

Dijo *que* ellas vendrian.	He said *that* they would come.
Quiere *que* yo vaya.	He wishes *that* I should go.

3. The *disjunctive* conjunction *ó* denotes an alternative, or distinction between two things; *ni* marks the second or subsequent branch of a negative proposition : Ex.

Ó cállese, *ó* váyase.	*Either* be silent, *or* begone.
El libro *ó* la carta.	The book *or* the letter.
No es para mí *ni* para él.	It is neither for me *nor* for him.

Ni is also frequently used in the *first* member, in the sense of *neither :* Ex.

Yo *ni* me amo *ni* te amo.	I *neither* love myself *nor* thee.

Note.—*Either* or *neither*, preceded by a negative, is translated *tampoco :* Ex.

Yo no sé, ni Vmd. *tampoco.*	I do not know, nor do you *either.*
Ni él *tampoco.*	Nor he *neither.*

Note.—The conjunction *ó* is changed into *ú* when the

word following it begins with *o* or *ho;* as, *Uno* ú *otro*—
One or the other.　*Muger* ú *hombre*—Woman or man.

4. *Adversative* conjunctions denote some opposition
or contradiction in the second proposition as regards the
first: Ex.

Me dijo que lo sabia, *pero,* or *mas* parece que no es verdad.	He told me that he knew it, *but* it appears that it is not true.
Salió, *no obstante* que estaba indispuesto.	He went out, *although* he was ill.

5. *Conditional* conjunctions denote some condition or
supposition: Ex.

Yo iré, *como* él venga.	I will go *provided* he come.
Si yo te llamare, responderás?	*If* I should call thee, wilt thou answer?

6. *Causative* conjunctions express the cause or reason
of a thing: Ex.

Descanso *porque* estoy cansado.	I rest *because* I am tired.
Lo haré, *pues que* lo manda.	I will do it, *since* he desires it.

7. *Restrictive* conjunctions confine the proposition
within certain limits: Ex.

No traiga Vmd. *sinó* dos.	Bring *only,* or *but* two.

8. *Continuative* conjunctions indicate the continuation
of a sentence: Ex.

Ya podemos ir, *puesto* que nos dan licencia.	We may now go, *since* they permit us.

9. *Comparative* conjunctions denote a relation or
parity between two objects: Ex.

Así como el alma anima al cuerpo, *así* la imitacion da alma á la poesía.	Just as the soul animates the body, *so* imitation gives life to poetry.

10. *Conclusive* conjunctions denote the object, end,
or motive of an action: Ex.

Lo dijo *á fin de que* conociesen su determinacion.	He said it *in order that* they might know his determination.

Le he dado el libro *para*   I have given him the book
que aprenda su leccion.   *that* he may learn his
                  lesson.

11. Besides the foregoing conjunctions, there may be formed a variety of expressions that answer the same end as conjunctions; as *como quiera que*, however; *fuera de que*, besides; *por cuanto*, whereas; *por mas que*, however, etc.

12. The conjunction *si*, besides its general meaning of *if* and *whether*, has several other significations in familiar language, as will be seen by the following quotations from the comedies of MORATIN.

DON ROQUE.—¿ Si *será el lloro por esto ?*—I *wonder if* this is the reason of her weeping? (*El Veijo y la Niña.* Act 2, Scene 9.)

DON ROQUE.—*Es verdad.* Si *estoy loco !*—It is true. I *must* be mad! (IBID. Act 3, Scene 4.)

PASCUAL.—Si *la he visto á la ventana.*—*Why,* I have seen her at the window. (*El Baron.* Act 2, Scene 10.)

DON CLAUDIO.—Si *yo lo dije;* si *Perico me ha metido en esta danza*—I have *already* said it; *it is* Peter who has get me into this mess. (*La Mogigata.* Act 3, Scene 8.)

LUCIA.—Si *no me quereis oir:* si *es locura declarada la que teneis*—*It is that* you wont listen to me: *it is that* you are positively mad. (IBID.)

DON CLAUDIO.—*Digo bien:* si *no hay cosa que yo haga que no se tilde y se riña*—I am right: *for* (because) there is nothing that I do that is not censured and blamed. (IBID. Scene 14.)

13. It frequently happens with conjunctions, as with adverbs and prepositions, that the same word may belong to more than one part of speech; for instance, *que* is a conjunction in *Ordenó que se fuesen*—He ordered that they should go ; but it is a relative pronoun in, *El hombre que llama*—The man that calls.

14. The English conjunction *but*, preceded by a negative, is generally translated *sinó;* but if the verb be repeated in Spanish, it is preferable to use *pero* or *mas*, instead of *sinó;* as, *Nunca sale* sinó *cuando hace buen tiempo* — She *never* goes out *but* in fine weather. No

vino, hoy, pero *or* mas *vendrá mañana*—He did *not* come to-day, *but* he will come to-morrow.

But is also translated *pero,* or *mas,* when it is not preceded by a negative; as, *Iré,* pero, *or* mas, *no puedo quedarme mucho tiempo*—I will go, *but* I cannot stay long.

When *but* is used in the place of *yet,* it is also translated *pero,* or *mas ;* as, *No caminé muy deprisa pero,* or *mas llegué a tiempo*—I did not walk very fast, *but,* or *yet,* I arrived in time.

PECULIAR MEANINGS OF CERTAIN ENGLISH CONJUNCTIONS, WITH THEIR CORRESPONDING TRANSLATIONS IN SPANISH.

15. There are several conjunctions in English that are frequently used as substitutes for other words ; these conjunctions are generally rendered in Spanish by the words which they stand in the place of, as follows.

As, meaning *when,* is translated *cuando ;* as, We saw them *as* we were going in—*Los vimos* cuando *entrabamos.*

But, meaning *if it were not,* is translated *si no ;* as, *But* for me, they would have killed him—Sí no fuera *por mí, le habrian matado.* I would go, *but* that I think it useless—*Yo iria,* si no *creyera que fuese inútil.*

But, meaning *only,* is translated *solo,* or *no mas que ;* as, I have *but* two to finish—Solo *me quedan dos para acabar.* I went *but* once—No *fuí* mas que *una vez.*

But, meaning *except,* is translated *sinó,* or *mas que* after a negative and after an interrogative pronoun ; and *ménos* when not preceded by a negative ; as, He speaks *nothing but* nonsense—*No habla* sinó, *or* mas que *tonterías.* Who would think so *but* you ?—*Quién creyera tal* sinó *Vmd. ?* Everybody knows it *but* he—*Todos lo saben* ménos *él.*

Whether, meaning *if,* is translated *si ;* as, Say *whether* you will come or not—*Diga Vmd.* si *quiere venir ó no.*

Whether, meaning *be that,* is translated *que ;* as, *Whether* he come or not—Que *venga ó* que *no venga.*

Whether, meaning *that,* is also translated *que ;* as, I doubt *whether* she knows it—*Dudo* que *lo sepa.*

However, employed before an adjective, is translated in the following manner; as, *However attentive* they are, and *however kind* they may be—*Por atentos y bondadosos que sean;* or, *no obstante lo atentos que son, y por bondadosos que sean.*

Why and *because* are translated *porque*; as, I do not know *why*—*No sé* porque. *Because* I could not—Porque *no pude.*

For, meaning *because*, is translated *porque;* as, You must take care of yourself, *for* if you do not, you will be ill—*Es menester que se cuide Vmd.*, porque *si no, se enfermará.*

Whereas, meaning *it being so that*, is translated *siendo así que;* as, Whereas *certain individuals* appeared before me, etc.—Siendo así que *parecieron ante mí ciertos indivíduos.*

Whereas, meaning *on the contrary*, is translated *de lo contrario;* as, You must obey the orders; *whereas*, if you transgress them, you will suffer the consequences—*Es menester que obedezca Vmd. á las órdenes;* de lo contrario, *si las traspasare, sufrirá las consecuencias.*

Either and *or* are both translated *ó;* as, *Either* I am right, *or* he is—*Ó yo tengo razon, ó él la tiene.*

Neither and *nor* are both translated *ni;* as, *Neither* promise *nor* act without thinking—Ni *prometas*, ni *obres sin pensar.*

EXERCISE ON CONJUNCTIONS.

Gold and silver are precious metals.   Neither he nor
precioso ——

she can refuse.   She is virtuous and industrious.   The

translations or works of which you speak.   Why did
traduccion   obra

you not come?   Because it was raining.   Since there is

no remedy, I suppose that I must submit.   I did so
remedio   suponer   someter

because I could not help it.   However that may be,
remediar

he never remains but when he likes; but that matters
    quedarse   querer   importar

not. You may either take this or that. He never views
                                               mirar

things but [on the wrong side]. It is not only better but
          al reves

cheaper. You must attend, notwithstanding [all that]
 barato   atender   cuanto

you have said. I will go, provided you come with me.

Since we are men, let us act as such. What is to be
                     obrar

done then? He cannot, nor can you either; neither

can I. I cannot point out to thee thy soul, which is
           señalar *

neither visible, nor is it corporeal; but I shall
   ————   tiene   cuerpo

endeavour to make thy very body teach thee the
 procurer   enseñar

dignity of thy soul. However probable it may appear,
                                     parecer

I doubt whether it be true. Whether he know it or

not. It is wide enough, but too short. Morality
         ancho   corto

consists in the practice of virtue; thus, if we would be
            ejercicio

moral, we must be virtuous. As the vigour of a
                                vigor

   morbid   appetite increases, and as [it makes itself]
desordenado apetito   crecer   se va haciendo

master of man, so does the use of his reason, and its clear
señor   uso

and limpid light decrease and diminish. Nothing
   limpia   descrecer   amenguarse

but innocence can give us a pure conscience. Commerce
comercio

is the true regulator of the power and importance of
regulador

nations; whether [it be considered] in relation to
se le considere

their wealth   or with respect to their political
[las riquezas de estas]

influence.   Prosperity is a state full of danger; so that
estado   peligro

we should content ourselves with the middle state.
mediocre

LECTURE XXXII.

INTERJECTIONS.

1. Some grammarians have divided interjections into different classes, according to the various emotions which they express; but as the same interjection very frequently expresses different affections, they cannot, with any degree of precision, be arranged into classes. Some of them, however, are more limited in their meaning.

2. *Ah, ay,* and *O,* are employed indifferently, to denote emotions of *grief, joy, indignation, jest,* and *admiration;* as, *¡ Ay, qué pena !*—Alas, what grief! *¡ Ah, qué desgracia !*—Ah, what a misfortune ! *¡ O, qué desdicha !*—Oh, what wretchedness! *¡ Ay, qué gozo !*—Oh, how delightful! *¡ Ah, qué alegría !*—Oh, what joy! *¡ O, que felicidad !*—Oh, what happiness !

3. *Ce, ha, he,* and *ola* serve to call attention. *He* is also sometimes used to denote that one has not understood what has been said to him, and means, What did you say? *Ola* is sometimes an interjection of admiration. *Ha,* besides serving to call the attention, denotes that one has recollected what he had forgotten; as, *Ha ! ya* *me acuerdo*—Oh! now I recollect. *Chito !* and *chiton !* impose silence, and are equivalent to *hush !* *Ea* is used to excite courage ; as, *Ea ! vamos, ánimo !*—Come! cheer up, courage ?

4. When adjectives are employed as interjections, the preposition *de* is put between them and the noun or pronoun following ; as, *¡ Desdichada* de *mí !*—Unhappy me ! *¡ Infeliz* de *mi hijo !*—Oh my unhappy child !

The interjection *ay*, in the sense of *woe* or *alas,* is followed in a like manner by *de* before nouns or pronouns referring to persons ; as, *¡ Ay* de *tí !*—Woe is thee ! *¡ Ay* de *ellos !*—Alas for them ! *Ay* de *mi hijo !* Alas, my poor son !

5. There are a variety of other terms and expressions that may be used as interjections; such as, *Qué lastima !* —What a pity ! *¡ Dios mio !*—My God ! *¡ Bien !*— Well ! *¡ Hola, poco á poco !*—Hallo, gently ! *¡ Qué ver- güenza !*—For shame ! *¡ Ciudado !*—Take care ! *¡ Otra, Otra !* — Encore ! *¡ Quita ! —* Pshaw ! *¡ Hurra !—* Hurrah ! *¡ Viva !*—Huzza !

6. *Ete*, behold, is used with personal pronouns in the objective case ; as, *Éteme aquí !*—Behold me here ! *¡ Ételos allí que vienen !*—Behold! or lo! they are coming !

APPENDIX.

———

OF THE FIGURES OF SYNTAX.

(From the Grammar of the Academy.)

Figures of syntax are certain deviations from the natural construction, which are allowed for the sake of brevity, energy, or elegance of expression. They consist sometimes in altering the order and position of words; sometimes in omitting certain words, or adding others; and sometimes even in apparent infringements on the rules of syntax. These figures are called *hipérbaton* (hyperbaton), which signifies *inversion; elípsis* (ellipsis), which means *deficiency,* or *curtailing; pleonasmo* (pleonasm), which means *superfluity;* and *silépsis* (syllepsis), which means *false concord.*

HYPERBATON.

In the following examples, the figure *hypérbaton,* or the inversion of the syntactical order, is conspicuous:—

Dichosos los *padres* que tienen *buenos hijos.* — Happy the parents that have good children.

Feliz el *reino* donde *viven* los *hombres* en paz. — Happy the kingdom in which men live in peace.

Acertadamente gobierna el que sabe evitar los delitos. — He governs well who knows how to prevent crimes.

In the first example, the adjectives *dichosos* and *buenos* are placed before the nouns, contrary to the rule which generally requires them to be put after. [This figure of syntax has already been alluded to in LECT. 8, on the Construction of Nouns, and in LECT. 10, on the Situation of the Adjective.] In the second example, the adjective *feliz* is also put before the noun, and the verb *viven* before its nominative *hombres*. And in the third, the adverb *acertadamente* is put before the verb *gobierna*, by which it is governed.

The foregoing examples acquire by these inversions more elegance than they would have, were they constructed in the natural order; and greater energy, because the clauses begin with those words that it is intended should appear the most striking in the sentence, and call the attention first. And though the use of this and other figures of speech may sometimes appear arbitrary, it is generally founded on some reason.

ELLIPSIS.

Ellipsis is a figure that allows certain words to be omitted in a sentence (provided that obscurity do not arise from the omission), the insertion of which would in many cases deprive it not only of brevity but of energy also. This figure is of constant use, and may affect every part of speech; since as we aim at expressing our thoughts as concisely as possible, we omit those words which are not absolutely necessary to make ourselves understood. Almost every familiar expression is elliptical; take, for instance, *Buenos dias*—Good day. *Muchas gracias*—Many thanks. The first, to be complete, should be, *Buenos dias tenga Vmd.*; or, *Le deseo á V.md. los buenos dias*—I wish you a very good day; and the second, *Le doy á Vmd. muchas gracias*—I give you many thanks.

This figure is not less frequent in the grave style than it is in the familiar, for wherever we open a book we are almost sure to meet with it. The following sentence from a classic author may be given as an instance.

Un vasallo pródigo se destruye á sí mismo: un príncipe, á sí, y á sus vasallos.—(SAAVEDRA Y FAJARDO.)

A prodigal vassal ruins his own self: a prince, himself and his vassals.

In the second member of this clause the adjective *pródigo* and the pronoun *se* are omitted once each, and the verb *destruye* twice; and to be complete it should run thus : *Un príncipe* pródigo se destruye *á sí, y* destruye *á sus vasallos.*

PLEONASM.

This figure, which means redundancy, is vicious when words are superfluously added without necessity, and useful when employed to give greater strength and clearness to the expression, and leave our hearers no doubt whatever as to the precise meaning of what we wish to convey.

When we say, *Yo lo ví por mis ojos*—I saw it with my own eyes; *Yo lo escribí de mi propia mano*—I wrote it with my own hand, we make use of pleonasms, because, strictly speaking, the words *por mis ojos*—*con mi propia mano,* are not necessary in the construction of the sentence; but no one will doubt the degree of energy which these additional words give to the expressions.

With the same end are redundant pronouns employed in reference to the same person, as we have seen in LECT. 14, PAR. 18; as, *á* mí me *dicen*—they tell *me:* te *llama á* tí—he calls *thee: á* él le *digeron*—they told *him:* le *hablaron á* ella, *no á él*—they spoke to *her,* not to him.

SYLLEPSIS.

This figure is employed when we sometimes make words agree, not precisely with one another, as they stand in a clause, but with some other words or idea understood; as when in Spanish the adjective is made to agree, not with the attributes of the persons of distinction to which they refer, but with the persons themselves : Ex. *Vuestra Majestad es justo*—Your Majesty is just. *Su Alteza es muy bondadoso*—Your Highness is very kind. Here, though the nouns *majestad* and *alteza* are of the feminine gender, the adjectives *justo* and *bondadoso* are not made to agree with *them,* but with the nouns *rey,* and *príncipe,* understood. The same would occur with *excelencia,* excellency, *señoría,* lordship, etc.—See LECT. 9, PAR. 13.

AN EASY METHOD OF CONVERTING A GREAT NUMBER OF
ENGLISH AND LATIN WORDS INTO SPANISH BY A
SLIGHT ALTERATION IN THEIR ORTHOGRAPHY.

[Observe that in making these transpositions, no consonant, except *c, n, r,* is to be doubled in Spanish.]

Many nouns and adjectives ending in English in the
following syllables, are rendered Spanish by altering
their terminations, thus :—

act, into *acto ;* as, abstract,	abstracto,	compact,	compacto.
ant .. *ante* .. constant,	constante,	distant,	distante.
ery .. *ario* .. alimentary,	alimentario,	dictionary,	diccionario.
ate .. *ado* ... consulate,	consulado,	delicate,	delicado.
ent .. *ente* .. accident,	accidente,	negligent,	negligente.
ic ... *ico* ... laconic,	lacónico,	poetic,	poético.
ical .. *ico* ... dramatical,	dramático,	economical,	económico.
ict ... *icto* .. conflict,	conflicto,	convict,	convicto.
ious .. *ioso* .. ingenious,	ingenioso,	prodigious,	prodigioso.
ism .. *ismo* .. barbarism,	barbarismo,	laconism,	laconismo.
ist ... *ista* .. conformist,	conformista,	deist,	deista.
ive .. *ivo* ... conclusive,	conclusivo,	productive,	productivo.
ory .. *orio* .. declama-	declamato-	observatory,	observatorio.
	tory,	rio,	
our .. *or* ... ardour,	ardor,	honour,	honor.
y ... *ia* ... academy,	academia,	geology,	geología.
nce .. *ncia* .. constance,	constancia,	province,	provincia.
cy ... *cia* ... clemency,	clemencia,	efficacy,	eficacia.
tion .. *cion* .. attention,	atencion,	nation,	nacion.
ty ... *dad* ... humanity,	humanidad,	simplicity,	simplicidad.
tor .. *dor* ... administra-	administra-	senator,	senador.
	tor,	dor,	
ce .... *cia* ... justice,	justicia,	clemence,	clemencia.
thy .. *tia* ... apathy,	apatía,	antipathy,	antipatía.
my .. *mia* .. economy,	economía,	academy,	academia.

Nouns terminating in *sion* are spelled alike in both
languages ; as, *confusion, infusion, profusion.*
Words written in English with *ph,* change these
letters into *f,* in addition to the alterations above
named ; as, Philosophy, *filosofía :* phosphoric, *fosfórico.*
Several English nouns ending in *tude,* are made
Spanish by dropping the final *e ;* as, Amplitude, *ampli-
tud ;* multitude, *multitud.*
Nouns derived from the Latin or Greek ending in

sis, terminate in the same letters in Spanish; as, Metamorphosis, *metamorfósis;* paralysis, *paralisis.*

Several adjectives ending in *al*, are spelled alike in Spanish and English; as, *legal*, *nominal*, *proverbial.* Adjectives derived from the Latin ending in *bilis*, terminate alike in Spanish and English; as, *culpable*, *inviolable, probable.*

Several English verbs are turned into Spanish by altering their terminations as follows :—

ate,	into	*ar ;*	as, abrogate,	abrogar,	imitate,	imitar.
duce	..	*ducir*	.. conduce,	conducir,	produce,	producir.
fy	..	*ficar*	.. amplify,	amplificar,	justify,	justificar.
bute	..	*buir*	.. attribute,	atribuir,	contribute,	contribuir.
vert	..	*vertir*	.. controvert,	controvertir,	divert,	divertir.
est	..	*estar*	.. detest,	detestar,	manifest,	manifestar.
ist	..	*istir*	.. consist,	consistir,	desist,	desistir.
mit	..	*mitir*	.. admit,	admitir,	permit,	permitir.
end	..	*ender*	.. defend,	defender,	offend,	ofender.
are	..	*arar*	.. compare,	comparar,	declare,	declarar.
ize	..	*izar*	.. economize,	economizar,	moralize,	moralizar.
fer	..	*ferir*	.. confer,	conferir,	prefer,	preferir.
tract	..	*traer*	.. contract,	contraer,	retract,	retraer.
eive	..	*ibir*	.. conceive,	concibir,	perceive,	percibir.

Several English adverbs ending in *lly*, formed from adjectives, are made Spanish by changing these final letters into *mente;* as, Dramatically, *dramáticamente;* identically, *idénticamente.*

Some admit an *l* before the termination *mente;* as, Grammatically, *gramaticalmente ;* totally, *totalmente.*

Those formed in English from adjectives ending in *le*, changing the *e* into *y*, are formed in Spanish by adding *mente* to the adjective; as, *culpable*, culpably, *culpablemente ; probable*, probably, *probablemente.*

The following alterations will convert several Latin words into Spanish; namely, by changing—

au,	into	*o ;*	as, AURUM, *oro*, gold ; TAURUS, *toro*, bull.
	...	*e*	... INFIRMO, *enfermo*, infirm ; TIMOR, *temor*, fear.
o	...	*ue*	.. FORTE, *fuerte*, strong ; NOSTRO, *nuestro*, our.
u	...	*o*	... UNDA, *onda*, wave ; JUVENIS, *jóven*, youth.

as   mto   *dad*   ... PROBITAS, *probidad*, probity ; SIM-
PLICITAS, *simplicidad*, simplicity.

us and *um*, into *o ;* as, TACITUS, *tácito*, tacit; DOCTUS, *docto*,
learned ; MOMENTUM, *momento*,
moment.

ch, into *c,* or *qu ;* as, CHARUS, *caro*, dear ; CHORUS, *coro*,
chorus ; CHERUBIM, *querubin*,
cherubs ; CHIRURGICUS, *quirúr-
gico*, chirurgical.

f,   into   *h ;*   as, FUMUS, *humo*, smoke ; FACERE,
hacer, to do.

m ...   *n*   ... LYMPHA, *linfa*, lymph.

t ...   *c,* or *z,*... AVARITIA, *avaricia*, avarice ; MI-
LITIA, *milicia*, militia.

tor ...   *dor*   ... AMATOR, *amador*, lover ; SENATOR,
senador, senator.

x ...   *z*   ... AUDAX, *audaz*, audacious; FALLAX,
falaz, fallacious.

Many Latin words beginning with *s*, followed by
another consonant, have an *e* prefixed to the *s* in Spanish ;
as SPLENDOR, *esplendor*, splendour ; SCRIBO, *escribo*, I
write.

Many Latin infinitives are made Spanish by dropping
the final *e ;* as, AMARE, *amar*, to love ; ARDERE, *arder*, to
burn ; VENIRE, *venir*, to come.

Several adjectives ending in *ens* are formed into
Spanish by *ente ;* as, PRUDENS, *prudente*, prudent ;
SAPIENS, *sapiente*, sapient.

Others ending in *ilis*, drop the final *is ;* as AGILIS,
agil, nimble ; FACILIS, *fácil*, easy; UTILIS, *útil*, useful.

Many Spanish substantives and adjectives are formed
from Latin *ablative* cases in the *singular :* as, DOMINO,
Dómino, Lord ; GRADU, *grado*, degree ; TRISTI, *triste*, sad ;
FELICE, *feliz*, happy.

And from *accusative* cases *plural ;* as, DOMINOS,
dóminos ; GRADUS, *grados ;* TRISTES, *tristes ;* FELICES,
felices.

MANNER OF ADDRESSING PERSONS IN SPANISH, AND THE
TITLES COMMONLY USED WITH PERSONS OF RANK.

SEÑOR AND DON.—These titles, which are equivalent
to *Mr.* in English, are prefixed to the names of individuals
in the third person, and are employed as follows :—

Señor admits of a feminine and a plural termination,
with their diminutives, and is employed before baptismal
or surnames; as, *Señor Carlos, La Señora de Gómez,
Los Señoritos Pérez, La Señorita Pérez.*

Don has a feminine termination which is *Doña;* but
no plural termination. It is never used immediately
before surnames, but is employed either before baptismal
names alone, or before these together with the surname.
It is politely used either singly, or coupled with *Señor,*
in addressing, or in speaking of persons whom we
respect; sa, *Don Juan, Señor Don Andrés, El Señor Don
Francisco Álvarez, Doña María, La Señora Doña Fran-
cisca de Jiménes.*

In addressing young ladies, *Doña* is used with their
baptismal names, giving a diminutive termination to
them; as, *Doña Clarita, Doña Isabelita.*

In polite society, *Señor* is not used alone, either before
baptismal or surnames; but *Don* should be employed
before baptismal names as above described, or, *Señor
Don,* which is still more respectful; and with regard to
surnames, if we address, or speak of a gentleman, instead
of *Señor,* the word Caballero is prefixed; as, *Caballero
Hernández, El Caballero Ramírez.* Sometimes the possessive pronoun is employed before the words *Señor Don ;*
a style, however, only sanctioned by intimacy; as, *Mi
Señor Don Alejandro. Mi Señora Doña Teresa.*

Don and *Caballero* are titles of rank, equivalent to
Sir or *Knight:* nevertheless they are employed in polite
conversation with persons who have no rank.

TITLES OF RANK.

Vuestra Majestad.	Your Majesty.
Su Majestad.	His *or* Her Majesty.
Vuestra Alteza Real.	Your Royal Highness.

Su Alteza Real.	His *or* Her Royal Highness.
Vuestra Señoría, Vueseñoría, *or* Usia.	Your Lordship, *or* Your Ladyship.
Su Señoría.	His Lordship, *or* Her Ladyship.
Vuestra Santidad.	Your Holiness.
Su Santidad.	His Holiness.
Vuestra Ilustrísima.	Your Grace *or* Honour.
Su Ilustrísima.	His, *or* Her Grace *or* Honour.
Vuestra Excelencia, *or* Vuecencia.	Your Excellency.
Su Excelencia.	His *or* Her Excellency.

As a respectful way of speaking of a person of title, Spaniards sometimes form the title into an adjective in the superlative degree (except *Majestad, Alteza,* and *Señoría*). The adjective is then used in the first member of the sentence, and the title in a subsequent member; as, *El* Ilustrísimo *Señor Don Pedro de Aguilar llegó esta mañana, y su* Ilustrísimo *fué recibido por el Gobernador*—The *Most Illustrious* Lord Don Pedro de Aguilar arrived this morning, and *His Grace* was received by the Governor.   Also, *El* Excelentísimo *Señor General dio órden que no hiciesen salva á su* Excelencia—*His Excellency* the General gave orders that they should not salute *His Excellency.*

LIST OF ABBREVIATIONS MOST COMMONLY USED IN SPANISH.

AA.	Autores, ó Altezas,	Authors, or Highnesses.
A.C.	Año Cristiano. ó comun,	Anno Christi.
A.D.	Año Dómini,	Anno Domini.
Ag.to	Agosto,	August.
A.M.	Año Mundo,	Anno Mundi.
Art.	artículo,	article.
Arzbpo.	Arzobíspo.	Archbishop.

A^s *or* @^s	Arrobas,	Q^{rs}, *or* 25 lbs.
b. *or* v.	vuelta,	turn over.
B^{mo} P^e	Beatísimo Padre,	Most blessed Father.
B^r	Bachiller,	Bachelor of Arts.
Cap.	Capítulo,	Chapter.
Capⁿ	Capitan,	Captain.
Comp^a *or* C^a	Compañía,	Company.
Cor^{te}	Corriente,	Current.
C^{ta}	Cuenta,	Account.
DD.	Doctores,	Doctors.
dhŏ. dhă.	dicho, dicha,	ditto, *or* said.
Dic^{re} *or* 10re	Diciembre,	December.
Dn. *or* D.	Don,	Mr.
Dña.	Doña,	Mrs.
D^r	Doctor, *ó* deudor,	Doctor, *or* debtor.
En^o	Enero,	January.
Exmo, Exma	Excelentísimo, ma,	Most Excellent.
Feb^o	Febrero,	February.
fhŏ. fhă.	fecho, fecha,	dated.
fol.	folio,	folio.
Fr.	Fray, *ó* Frey,	Brother of a religious order.
Genl	General,	General.
H^r	Haber,	C^r *or* Creditor.
Ib.	Íbidem,	Ibid, ditto.
Il^{mo} Il^{ma}	Ilustrísimo, ma,	Most Illustrious.
J. C.	Jesu Cristo,	Jesus Christ.
Lib.	Libro,	Book.
lib^s *or* lbs.	libras,	pounds.
lin.	línea,	line.
M.P.S.	Muy Poderoso Señor,	Most Powerful Lord.
mrs.	maravedis,	the smallest Spanish coin.
m^s a^s	muchos años,	many years.
MS.	Manuscrito,	Manuscript.
MSS.	Manuscritos,	Manuscripts.
Nov^{re} *or* 9re	Noviembre,	November.
nrŏ. nră.	nuestro, ra,	our.
N.B.	Nota bene,	N.B.
N.S.	Nuestro Señor,	Our Lord.
N.S^{ra}	Nuestra Señora,	Our Lady.

n°, *or* núm.	número,	number.
Ob^po.	Obispo,	Bishop.
Oct^re *or* 8re	Octubre,	October.
on. on^s	onza, onzas,	ounce, ounces.
ōrn.	órden,	order.
P.D.	Posdata,	Postscript.
p^a	para,	for.
p^r, *or* ⅌	por,	per, *or* for.
pág.	página,	page.
par.§	párrafo,	paragraph.
Q.D.G	Que Dios guarde,	Whom God preserve.
q^e	que,	that, what.
q^n	quien,	who.
R^l, R^les	Real, Reales,	Royal.
rl. rs.	real, reales,	real, reals. (the 20th part of a dollar).
Rev^mo	Reverendísimo,	Most Reverend.
Rev^do	Reverendo,	Reverend.
S. *or* S^n	San, ó Santo,	St. *or* Saint.
S.M.	Su Majestad,	His, *or* Her Majesty.
S.A.R.	Su Alteza Real,	His, *or* Her Royal Highness.
S.S^a	Su Señoría,	His, *or* Her Ldshp.
S. S^d	Su Santidad,	His Holiness.
S. Il^ma	Su Illustrísima,	His Grace, *or* Lordship, Her Grace, etc.
Sr. *or* S^or	Señor,	Sir, *or* Mr.
S^res	Señores,	Sirs, Messrs., *or* Gentlemen.
S^ra	Señora,	Madam, Lady, *or* Mrs
S^ras	Señoras,	Mesdames, *or* Ladies.
Set^re *or* 7re	Setiembre,	September.
Ser^mo	Serenísimo,	Most Serene.
Serv^r	Servidor,	Servant.
sig^te	siguiente,	following, next.
SS^mo P^e	Santísimo Padre,	Most Holy Father.
Super^te	Superintendente,	Superintendent.
Ten^te	Teniente,	Lieutenant.
tom. *or* vol.	tomo, ó volúmen,	volume.
tpō.	tiempo,	time.
V̄., V^e, *or* Ven^e	Venerable,	Venerable.
V.M.	Vuestra Majestad,	Your Majesty.
V.A.	Vuestra Alteza,	Your Highness.

V.B^d	Vuestra Beatitud,	Your Blessedness.
V.E.	Vuecelencia, *ó* Vuecencia,	Your Excellency.
v.g.	verbi gracia,	for example.
V., Vm., *or* Vmd.	Vuesamerced *ó* Usted,	You, *or* Your Grace.
V.S.	Vueseñoría, *ó* Usía,	Your Lordship, *or* Ladyship.
V.S.	Vuestra Santidad,	Your Holiness.
V.S.I.	Vueseñoría, *ó* Usía Ilustrísima,	Your Grace, Lord- ship, *or* Ladyship.
vn.	vellon,	bullion.
vol.	volúmen,	volume.
vrô. vrã.	vuestro, ra,	your.
Xptiano.	Christiano,	Christian.
Xpto.	Cristo,	Christ.
Xptóbal.	Cristóbal,	Christopher.

Ordinal Numbers are abbreviated in the following manner 1ro 2do 3ro 4to 5to 6to 7mo 8vo 9no 10mo, and so on till 20mo, then 21mo 22do, and so on till 30mo, 40mo, etc. The final *o* is changed into *a* for the feminine gender, and an *s* is added to form the plural number; as, 1ra 2^{das} 5^{tos} etc. Sometimes they are abbreviated thus—1° 2° 3ª 4ª, etc.

Besides the foregoing abbreviations, there are several others employed in letter writing, as will be seen in the following

FORMS OF EPISTOLARY CORRESPONDENCE.

The peculiarities of the Spanish epistolary style consist principally in the manner of beginning and ending a letter ; for instance, in addressing persons of different classes of society, except those of title, the letter begins with, *Muy Señor mio*, or *Muy Señor nuestro*, which expressions are equivalent in their import to *Sir*, or *Dear Sir*. The first would be used by one gentleman addressing another; the second by a plural number addressing one person ; *Muy Señores mios*, by one person addressing a plural number; and *Muy Señores nuestros*, by more than one person addressing a plural number, each corresponding with *Gentlemen*, or *Dear Sirs*.

In addressing ladies, *Señora* would be substituted for *Señor*; *mia* for *mio*, and *nuestra* for *nuestro*. These expressions are most generally abbreviated thus: *Muy Sr. mio*; *Muy Sr. nrō*; *Muy Srēs. mios*; *Muy Srēs nrōs*; *Muy Srā. mia*; *Muy Srās. mias*; *Muy Srā. nrā*; *Muy Srās. nras.*

In the body of the letter, *su ap^{ble}* (su apreciable), or *su est^{da}* (su estimada), or *su favor^{da}* (su favorecida)—*carta* (letter) being understood—are equivalent to *your favour*, or *your esteemed letter*.

With reference to the date of a letter, *Yours of the 2^d Inst; 4th ult°; 8th of May*, etc., are translated, *Las de Vmd. del 2 Cort^e* (corriente); *4 del pp^{do}* (proximo pasado); *8 De Mayo*, etc.

At the conclusion of a letter, the following forms, or others equivalent, with one or other of the sets of initials appended to them, are generally employed: viz.

Nos repetimos á la disposicion de Vmd.
C. M. B.
(*Cuyas manos besamos.*)
PEREZ, HERMANOS.

We reiterate our services to you, *whose hands we kiss.*

PEREZ, BROTHERS.

Manden Vms. cuanto gusten á
S. S. S.
(*Sus seguros servidores.*)
Q, S. M. B.
(*Que sus manos besan.*)
VICENTE LOPEZ Y C^a

Command at pleasure your faithful servants, *who kiss your hands.*

VINCENT LOPEZ & C°

Siendo cuanto se me ocurre decirle por hoy, mándeme sin reserva; interin
B. L. M. de Vmd.
(*Beso las manos de Vmd.*)
J. M. MIRASOL.

This being all that occurs to me to say at present, I beg you will command me freely; meanwhile *I kiss your hands.*

J. M. MIRASOL.

Se repite á las órns de Vmd. su at^{to} y sg° serv^r (*atento y seguro servidor*) y
B. S. M.
(*Besa sus manos.*)
PEDRO OLIVARES.

Your humble and faithful servant again places himself at your orders, *and kisses your hands.*

PETER OLIVARES.

In a more friendly style, a letter may begin with *Muy Sr. y amigo mio*—My dear Sir and friend: *Ap^{ble} Sr. mio*—My valued Sir: *Muy ap^{ble} Srā*—My dear Lady: concluding with, *Mande Vmd. con toda franqueza á su invariable amigo y S. S.*—Command with freedom your unalterable friend and faithful servant. *Es cuanto se le ofrece á su af^{mo} amigo y S. S.*—This is all that occurs to your affectionate friend and faithful servant. *Dios guade su vida los m^a a^a (muchos años) que desea su muy reconocido amigo y servidor*—May God preserve you many years: your grateful friend and servant.

In a very familiar style, a letter is begun in the following manner: *Mi ap^{ble} amigo*—My esteemed friend. *Mi muy querido,* or *estimado amigo*—My very dear friend. *Querido Francisco*—Dear Francis: concluding with, *quedándome todo tuyo af^{mo}*—Remaining affectionately yours. *De tu constante amigo que te aprecia*—From your constant friend, who esteems you. *Soy como siempre su agradecido é inalterable amigo que devéras le estima*—I am your ever grateful and unalterable friend, who truly appreciates you.

Esquelas, notes, are also written in Spanish, as in English, in the third person; for instance, *El Sr. N. N. presenta,* or *ofrece sus respetos,* or *cumplimientos al Sr. Dn. M. M. y le hace saber que,* etc.—Mr. N. N. presents his respects, or his compliments, to Mr. M. M., and begs to acquaint him that, etc.

El Capitan B. B. tiene el honor de saludar al Exmo Sr. General D. D., y en contestacion á la esquela de su Ex^{cia} de hoy participa muy respetuosamente á su Ex^{cia} que, etc.—Cap^n B. B. has the honour of presenting his respects to his Excellency Genl D. D., and in reply to His Excellency's note of this day, begs most respectfully to acquaint His Excellency that, etc.

El Conde de L. besa las manos á la Duquesa de R., y tiene el honor de hacer saber á su Ilus^{ma} que, etc.—Count L. presents his profound respects to the Duchess of R., and has the honour to inform her Grace that, etc.

La Marquesa de B., saluda muy cariñosamente á la Condesa de Z., y suplica á su Señoría que, etc.—The Marchioness of B. presents her kind love to the Countess of Z , and requests her Ladyship, etc.

The date of a letter is done in the following manner :
Madrid y 3 de Mayo de 1848—*Lóndres Enero* 1º *de* 1853;
and of a note, *Lúnes* 5 *de Agosto*—*Juéves por la mañana*
24 *de Set^{re}* ; and the superscription as follows :

- Sr. Dn. Juan de Aguilares—Toledo.
  Sres. Dn. Fran^{co} Soares Hermanos y C^{a}—Málaga.
  Sr. Dña. Josefa de Peralta y Miranda, Calle nueva,
  No. 5.
  Al Caballero Fuente Mayor—Plaza Sn. Juan.
  Al Exmo Sr. General S. P.
  Al Il^{mo} Sr. Marques de L. L.
  Al la Il^{ma} Srã. Condesa de M.

OF SPANISH FAMILIAR AND COMPLIMENTARY PHRASES.

The first salutation among Spaniards is ordinarily
Tenga Vmd. muy buenos dias—Good day to you; which
expression is used from the earliest part of the morning
till two or three hours after meridian ; from which time
till dark, *Buenas tardes*—Good afternoon, is employed ;
and from candle-light until the following morning,
Buenas noches—Good night, both on entering a room
and on taking leave. Observe that these expressions
are always used in Spanish in the plural number.

In greeting a lady, the first expression most frequently made use of is, *Á los pies Vmd. Señora*, which
means literally, *Madam, at your feet.* The lady's reply
to which is generally, *Beso á Vmd. la mano, caballero* ;
literally, *I kiss your hand, Sir.* Both these expressions
imply a polite respect for the persons to whom they are
addressed.

To enquire after another's health, the expressions
mostly used are, *Cómo lo pasa Vmd. ?* or, *Cómo está Vmd.
Caballero, or Señora ?*—How do you do ? And the reply
would be, *Medianamente bien,* or *perfectamente bien, para
servir á Vmd.*—Middling well, or perfectly well, at your
service. *Así, así,* or *tal cual: y Vmd. cómo lo pasa ?*

—So, so; and how do you do? *Sin novedad á la disposicion de Vmd.* This expression, *sin novedad*, one of
the most polite, and most frequently employed, has no
equivalent in English. Literally translated it is, *without
novelty;* that is, *without any alteration or change;* and
means that the health of the person inquired after con-
tinues very well. Gentlemen in greeting each other frequently employ, as respectful salutations, the following
expressions: *Servidor de Vmd. caballero.*—Your servant,
Sir. *Á la órden de Vmd.*—Your most obedient. *Beso á
Vmd. la mano*—I kiss your hand. A more familiar salutation in passing each other is, *Agur, agur*—Good by.
Vaya Vmd. con Dios—Adieu, or, God be with you.

The usual phrase for introducing one person to the
acquaintance of another is, *Señor Don S. tengo el honor
de presentarle al Señor Don V.*—Mr. S., I have the
honour of introducing Mr. V. to you; to which the reply
is generally, *Caballero, celebro la ocasion de conocer á
Vmd.*—Sir, I am happy of the opportunity of making
your acquaintance; or *Reconózcame Vmd. por un servidor
suyo*—I am much at your service.

The most usual expressions for *asking* or *requesting*
are, *Tenga Vmd. la bondad de darme*—Have the goodness
to give me. *Hágame Vmd. el favor de decirme*—Do me
the favour to tell me. *Sírvase Vmd. de,* or *tenga Vmd. la
complacencia de*—Have the kindness to. *Quiére Vmd.
tener la bondad,* or *la complacencia de ?*— Will you have
the kindness to? And for returning thanks: *Mil gracias,*
or *muchísimas gracias*—Many thanks. *Se lo agradezco á
Vmd. infinito*—I am very much obliged to you. *Le
devuelvo infinitas gracias*—I return you many thanks. *Se
lo agradeceria devéras*—I would feel truly thankful to
you.

To describe the state of the weather, the verb *hacer*
with a noun, is employed in Spanish, instead of the impersonal verb *to be,* with an adjective, used in English;
as, *Hace frio*—It is cold. *Hacia calor*—It was warm.
Hará buen tiempo pronto—It will soon be fine weather.
Si acaso hiciere mal tiempo—In case the weather should
be bad. *Hace un tiempo variable*—The weather is un-
settled.

To express that one feels *cold, warm, afraid, ashamed,*

hungry, thirsty, etc., instead of the verb *to be*, used in English with an adjective, the verb *tener* must be employed in Spanish with a noun; as, *Tengo frio*—I am cold. *Tenia calor*—I was warm. *Tienen miedo*—They are afraid. *Tiene vergüenza*—She is ashamed. *No tengo hambre*—I am not hungry. The same verb is also employed in Spanish to denote a person's age; as, *Qué edad tiene?*—What age is he? *Tiene viente años*—He is twenty years old.

NOTICE.

Considering the insertion of Conversational Dialogues, Proverbs, etc., misplaced in an elementary work, the author has not appended them to this Grammar. The annexing a few lists of words and familiar dialogues would only serve to increase the size and price of the book, without being of much utility to the learner. Moreover, how many are there that apply themselves to the study of a foreign language for the sole purpose of reading and comprehending the works written in it? To this class of learners dialogues would be of little avail. To those who learn a foreign language with the view of applying it immediately to practice, lists of words in most common use, and conversational dialogues and familiar phrases on the most usual topics, judiciously compiled, and displaying the force and elegance of the idioms of the language in which they are written, may be of much utility after a course of application to the rules of Grammar. With this view the author has published, separately, a Manual, in Spanish and English, which contains abundant lists of words properly classed, and a copious variety of complimentary and conversational dialogues, an extensive collection of Proverbs and Idioms, and comparative Tables of Weights and Measures: the whole forming a pocket companion of much usefulness to the student of either language.

READING LESSON FOR PRACTISING SPANISH PRONUNCIATION.

CALIDADES DEL TALENTO ORATORIO.

EL que pretende á un tiempo enseñar, mover y deleitar, que es el oficio del orador, qué conocimiento no es menester que tenga del corazon humano, de su propio idioma y del espíritu del siglo en que vive? Qué gusto para presentar sus conceptos en un semblante agradable? Qué estudio para ordenarlos del modo que hagan la mas viva impresion en el ánimo de los oyentes? Qué discernimiento para distinguir las circunstancias que deben tratarse con alguna extension de las que, para ser sentidas, bástales solo ser manifestadas? Qué arte en fin para hermanar siempre la variedad con el órden y la claridad?

El hombre elocuente huye de la aridez del estilo didáctico, porque no basta que sea magnífico, alto y sólido un pensamiento si no es felizmente expresado. La hermosura del estilo solo consiste en la claridad y colorido de la frase, y en el arte de exponer las ideas. Así pues hay gran diferencia entre el escritor elocuente y el escritor elegante. El primero se anuncia con una elocucion animada y persuasiva formada de expresiones valientes, enérgicas y brillantes, sin dejar de ser ajustadas y naturales. El segundo declara su pensamiento con nobles y galanas frases, formadas de expresiones cultas, fluidas, y gratas al oido.

El escritor elocuente, como sea su fin mover y persuadir, se sirve en el discurso de lo vehemente y sublime, dedicándose sobre todo á la fuerza de los términos, á la grandeza de las imágenes y al órden de las ideas. Y el elegante, como aspira á deleitar, solo busca la gracia de la elocucion, esto es, la hermosura de las palabras y la armónica coordinacion de la sentencia.

Puede un escritor ser diserto, es decir, puede hacer un discurso fácil, puro, claro, elegante y aun espléndido, y con todo no ser elocuente, por faltarle el calor y la energía. El discurso elocuente es vivo, animado, vehemente y político; quiero decir, hiere, eleva, arrebata, domina y suspende el ánimo. Así que, suponiendo en un hombre facundo, nervio en la expresion, elevacion en los pensamientos y calor en los afectos, basta para hacer un escritor elocuente.

El arte oratoria, como observa un autor de mucho ingenio, consiste mas que en otra cosa, en un estudio reflexivo de los mejores modelos, y en un contínuo ejercicio de componer y de comparar sus débiles ensayos con la perfeccion de los originales; ejercicio que hace fructificar el trabajo, mas que una ostentacion de reglas la mayor parte arbitrarias.

Dos cosas parece que concurren para formar un orador, la *razon* y el *corazon;* aquella para convencer, y este para mover y persuadir. Sobre estas dos disposiciones naturales se afianza la verdadera elocuencia, como el árbol en sus raices.

Sin embargo, los buenos oradores son muy pocos, porque son tambien muy raros los hombres dotados de aquella penetracion, extension y esquisito juicio necesarios para discernir lo verdadero y hacerlo evidente; porque en fin son muy raras aquellas almas delicadas que sientan interiormente la impresion de los objetos de sus meditaciones, y que puedan traspasar al corazon del oyente las afecciones de que estan poseidos.

Del modo de ver las cosas depende en gran parte la fuerza ó debilidad en sentirlas, y por consiguiente en expresarlas. Las ideas adquiridas por una sosegada y tibia reflexion en el retiro de un estudio, son ménos vivas y acaloradas que las que nacen de la vista y contemplacion de este teatro del mundo. Seria pues un prodigio hallar á un ciego de nacimiento, elocuente.

Los objetos grandes prestan elocuencia á los ingenios sublimes; pues vemos que Descártes y Newton, que no fueron oradores, son elocuentes cuando hablan de Dios, del tiempo, del espacio y del universo. En efecto todo lo que nos eleva el espíritu, ó nos engrandece el ánimo, es materia propia para la elocuencia, por aquel placer que sentimos de vernos grandes. Tambien, y por la misma causa, todo lo que nos anonada ante los ojos de nuestra consideracion, es objeto digno de la gravedad oratoria ; pues, qué cosa mas capaz para levantar nuestro espíritu humillándole, que el contraste de nuestra pequeñez con la inmensidad de la naturaleza creada ?

La verdadera elocuencia necesita del auxilio de nuestras ciencias y artes liberales. Cuenta ante todas la gramática, que tiene mas obra que ostentacion, y es fundamento del arte de bien decir, pues sin ella seriamos siempre niños. De la lógica saca el método y fuerza del raciocinio ; de la geometría el órden y enlace de las verdades ; de la historia el ejemplo y autoridad de los insignes varones; de la jurisprudencia los oráculos de las leyes ; de la filosofía moral el conocimiento del corazon del hombre y de sus pasiones ; y de la poesía el colorido de las imágenes y el embeleso de la armonía.—(CAPMANY —*Filosofía de la Elocuencia.*)

THE END.

WERTHEIMER, LEA, AND CO., PRINTERS, FINSBURY CIRCUS.